AS A NEW WORLD OF SPLENDOR AND
SAVAGERY EMERGES FROM UNDER THE ICE,
THE FIRST AMERICANS FOLLOW THEIR
DESTINY ALONG A TRAIL OF UNKNOWN PERIL

CHA-KWENA—A young shaman at the threshold of
adulthood, he is determined to lead his people in the footsteps of the sacred white mammoth, even to a mysterious
valley where a dark secret may shatter Cha-kwena's
sanity . . . and a chilling fate may claim his life.

MAH-REE—Though little more than a girl, she possesses all the passion of a woman. She longs for
Cha-kwena to be her mate in the ways of magic. But he
sees her as a child, not the powerful female spirit who
can help him lead their people from danger and prevent
the raven of death from devouring his heart.

DAKAN-EH—Braggart, womanizer, and headman of
the tribe Cha-kwena fled, he believes that the young
shaman has stolen his luck. Now Dakan-eh cruelly trades
his own woman to another chieftain . . . all for a
chance to find Cha-kwena and destroy him.

SHEELA—Slave to the ruthless Dakan-eh and descendant of an evil high priestess, she escapes and returns to
her own tribe . . . to perform the ritual of blood that
seals the doom of Dakan-eh and Cha-kwena.

TA-MAYA—Courageous men have died to possess her,
but she still mourns the slain warrior she loved. Now she
walks with Cha-kwena's band, and brings with her a
ghost that is leading them all to destruction.

BANTAM BOOKS BY WILLIAM SARABANDE

THE FIRST AMERICANS:
BEYOND THE SEA OF ICE
(VOLUME I)

THE FIRST AMERICANS:
CORRIDOR OF STORMS
(VOLUME II)

THE FIRST AMERICANS:
FORBIDDEN LAND
(VOLUME III)

THE FIRST AMERICANS:
WALKERS OF THE WIND
(VOLUME IV)

THE FIRST AMERICANS:
THE SACRED STONES
(VOLUME V)

THE FIRST AMERICANS:
THUNDER IN THE SKY
(VOLUME VI)

WOLVES OF THE DAWN

THE
FIRST
AMERICANS

THUNDER
IN THE
SKY

WILLIAM
SARABANDE

 Producers of **The Frontier Trilogy,
The Holts,** and **Children of the Lion.**

Book Creations Inc., Canaan, NY • Lyle Kenyon Engel, Founder

BANTAM BOOKS
NEW YORK • TORONTO • LONDON • SYDNEY • AUCKLAND

To Ferdinand Metz

THUNDER IN THE SKY

*A Bantam Domain Book / published by arrangement with
Book Creations Inc.*

Bantam edition / November 1992

Grateful acknowledgment is made for permission to quote a selection
from the prayer of Black Elk, reprinted from The Sacred Pipe: Black
Elk's Account of the Seven Rites of the Oglala Sioux, *edited by Joseph
Epes Brown. Copyright © 1953 by the University of Oklahoma Press.*

*Produced by Book Creations Inc.
Lyle Kenyon Engel, Founder*

ISBN 0-553-29106-8

Published simultaneously in the United States and Canada

*Bantam Books are published by Bantam Books, a division of Bantam
Doubleday Dell Publishing Group, Inc. Its trademark, consisting of the
words "Bantam Books" and the portrayal of a rooster, is Registered
in U.S. Patent and Trademark Office and in other countries. Marca
Registrada. Bantam Books, 666 Fifth Avenue, New York, New York 10103.*

PRINTED IN THE UNITED STATES OF AMERICA

RAD   0 9 8 7 6 5 4 3 2

. . . Grandfather, Great Spirit, lean close to the earth that you may hear the voice I send. Give me the eyes to see and the strength to understand, that I may be like you. With your power only I can face the winds. . . .

from the prayer of Black Elk

LAKE OF WATERED BLOOD

LAND OF MANY WATER

MOUNTAINS THAT WALK

WANAWUT'S CAVE

THE WONDERFUL VALLEY

ENCAMP ABOVE

MOUNTAIN THAT SMOKES

VALLEY OF SONGS

JUNCTION OF TWO GREAT RIVERS

GREAT ICEFALL

PLACE OF ENDLESS MEAT

GREAT GATHERING

PLAIN OF MANY WATERS

CORRIDOR OF STORM

ALASKA

MOUNTAINS THAT WALK

BERINGIA

©BOOK CREATIONS INC. '92

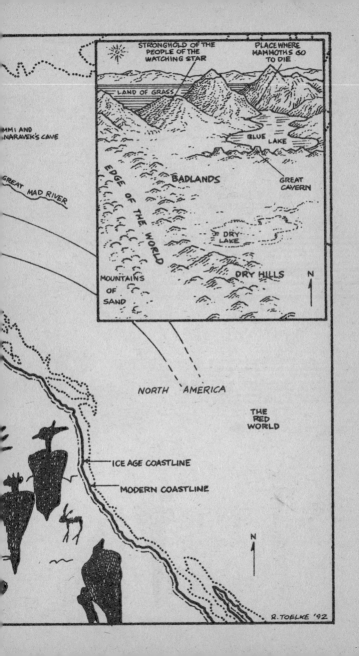

PART I

YELLOW SKY, YELLOW WOLF, YELLOW MAN

1

He was afraid. Deep within the marrow of his spirit, terror clawed like the talons of a hunting eagle. It savaged the back of his throat with words that he dared not speak: *Run! Flee across the Land of Grass! Save yourself! Spirit Sucker rides the Four Winds! Death is coming for you out of the yellow sky!*

In thong-laced, calf-high moccasins and loincloth cut from the spotted belly skin of a saber-toothed cat, Dakan-eh, Bold Man of the Red World, fought to keep himself from screaming as he stood with his fellow bison hunters and their dogs at the edge of a deep, mile-long ravine under the ominous shadow of an approaching storm.

Never—not even in the sun-scorched mesa country of his faraway homeland, where summer thunderstorms had once been a common occurrence—had Dakan-eh seen such a sky or such towering, tumultuous squall lines.

And never had he seen so many bison. The herd was about a mile away, directly between the ravine and the oncoming storm. The animals were no longer moving steadily forward across the wide, rolling, autumn-reddened plains; they were milling restlessly within strategically positioned ranks of spear-carrying men clad in robes of bison hide. With their summer-tanned skin lathered with bison dung and urine to mask their human scent, these drivers and callers had spent the last four days and nights skillfully manipulating the herd toward the bison jump, where Dakan-eh and his fellow hunters were now waiting for the final phase of the hunt to begin.

Squinting into the rising wind, Bold Man scanned the open grassland between him and the herd. It was a wide expanse. To close the distance, a man would need as much time as it took a woman to flay and butcher an antelope. If the bison broke and ran now, they would have the distance necessary to build a momentum that would make the speed and direction of their run completely uncontrollable.

Dakan-eh felt sick. It was the month of the Dry Grass Moon, and the bison were fat after a full season of summer grazing. The bulls were still with the cows and calves. The shaggy humps of the largest males crested some eight feet above their hooves, and their massive heads were weighted by a good six-foot spread of laterally aligned horns. If the herd stampeded, any man in its path would be trampled.

The ravine was in their path.

He was in their path.

And with the storm behind the beasts, the squall lines, not the hunters, were driving the herd now.

Again Dakan-eh fought back the need to scream. He did not know what terrified him more—the threat of an imminent stampede or the configuration of the approaching storm. Amazing things were happening to the clouds. From horizon to horizon, the flat bellies of the squall lines were churning, thickening, turning as dark as smoke rising from a greasewood fire. One moment the midmorning sun was there; the next it was gone, swallowed, and the world went dark and cold.

Yet, as the herd circled and snorted and pawed at the earth, Dakan-eh found himself transfixed. He barely felt the sudden chill or noticed the onset of darkness. Somehow the clouds were giving off a light of their own . . . a strange, grayish, threatening illumination that bathed both earth and sky in the livid, purulent colors of an old, yellowing bruise.

"Aiee ay! Under the yellow sky, the bison will run! The whirling wind will come!"

The exclamation came rasping from the inverted seam that was all that remained of the dry, withered lips of Nachumalena, one of several holy men among the People of the Land of Grass who had assembled for the annual autumn bison drive. Standing directly in front of Dakan-eh, the old man threw back his scrawny shoulders. He stood with head held high, hip-length hair streaming in the wind, and camellike nostrils splayed wide to scent the mood of the herd and of the approaching storm. Using his long-shafted, stone-tipped, feather-festooned spear as a staff, he took one bold step forward. Then he took another, noticeably less bold. It was obvious that he was afraid to take a third when, without warning, the southwest wind shifted hard to the northwest, and the air was filled with the strong, bitter smell of ice.

Ordinarily Dakan-eh would have been contemptuous of the old man's cowardice. But caught in the unenviable position of sharing the fear, the young headman from the Red World assured himself that on this day, under this sky, with a herd of long-horned bison about to stampede toward him, even he, the boldest and best of all men, might taste the bitter bile of fear and remain unashamed.

He shivered. *The whirling wind . . .* What, he wondered, had the old shaman meant by that? Although Dakan-eh had no idea, he sensed an unimaginable horror lurking in the meaning of the words. A mammoth began to trumpet nervously in the distant, storm-shrouded mountains to the west, and a pack of dire wolves bayed a high, restive answer. Their communication seemed to express Dakan-eh's own unvoiced terror as the howls echoed back and forth among the folds of the rolling land.

Death is coming! If the bison stampede and catch you on this side of the ravine, you will tumble into it and be crushed. They will try to leap across but, failing, will fall on top of you! Bison have died in this place for generations, since the children of First Man and First Woman first came walking over the mountains into the Land of Grass. Driven by hunters, the beasts never see the ravine in time to avoid it. But you see it! You know the danger! You are a man, not a bison born to be driven and butchered and turned into meat! Run! Death is coming! Why do you stand rooted like a mindless tree to the earth?

He answered his terror without speaking. *I will run when the others run! Not before! I am Dakan-eh, Bold Man of the Red World! I am not afraid!*

In that moment a flash of lightning named him Liar. Thunder cracked and rolled, while long, eddying fingers of cloud began to poke downward out of the churning black underside of the nearest squall line. Dakan-eh winced. He had never seen anything remotely like them. He stared, gape jawed, fighting against panic lest it prod him to break and run for the protection of the village.

The village! Yearning caused him to cast a quick look over his shoulder across the wide, twenty-foot-deep maw of the ravine. The bones of many a bison littered the bottom. Old bones . . . sun-bleached, time-whitened bones—and bones still fresh enough to be scabbed with the desiccated remnants of connective tissue. Stripped of hide, meat, and tendon, the skeletons lay where they had fallen, one on top of another—cows, bulls, and calves tangled in the pitiless embrace of death. Some had been dismembered; all had been picked clean by the butchering tools of men and by the fangs, beaks, and talons of the carrion eaters of earth and sky. Bold Man imagined his own body lying dead and broken amid the remains of past carnage.

Dakan-eh's long, angular black eyes narrowed, and he clenched his teeth and scanned the top of the ravine. On the far side, three miles of open grassland stood between him and the many tall, brightly painted hide lodges that had been raised close to the steep, cottonwood-shaded embankments of the river. His woman, Ban-ya, was there, with Piku-neh, their nearly two-year-old son. His mother, Pah-la, was with them, as was Sheela, his slave. His heart quickened with longing to be safe with them.

Again thunder growled. Dakan-eh flinched, suddenly aware of a palpable tension among the ranks of men and youths who stood to his right and left. Their spears were at ready and their faces set, but the hunters were afraid. He could sense it, smell it! And yet shame burned him as he realized that not even the dogs were looking back toward the security of the village. He forced himself to face the herd and oncoming squalls. As he did, he caught the eyes of the man standing closest to his right.

Scalded by his father's open glare of rebuke, Bold Man instantly broke eye contact. He knew that Owa-neh had no wish to be there; had it been up to his father, they would still be snaring lizards and eating grubs and ant eggs in the drought-stricken Red World. But it had not been up to Owa-neh. Dakan-eh was headman of their ancestral village by the Lake of Many Singing Birds! For the third autumn in a row, he had chosen to hunt with the Bison People in the Land of Grass; and this year, at the invitation of the great war chief Shateh, he had brought his entire band north with him to stay. Until this moment Bold Man had found no cause to regret his decision.

His gut tightened. Drawing a deep, steadying breath, Dakan-eh consoled himself with the reminder that he was a great warrior. He had proved himself in battle against the seasoned fighters of the marauding People of the Watching Star. The bison hunters of the Land of Grass had been his allies in that bloody war. They had shown him a better way to live, and he had chosen to make a new life among them. But he was still considered a guest and a foreigner in this land. He had a reputation to uphold and status to win if he and his people were going to be allowed to remain permanently in this game- and water-rich country of bison and mammoth hunters. For as long as they stood bravely before the oncoming storm and the threat of stampede, he could not allow himself to do less.

Raising his head and slitting his eyes against the wind, he continued to glare defiantly ahead. Surely Shateh knew what he was doing. Besides, the odd, fingerlike whorls of cloud had disappeared into the squalls. Dakan-eh was relieved; he had not liked the look of them any more than he appreciated the sharp, imperative nudge that now came from a young man of his own band.

Bold Man looked down and to his left. Na-sei's dark eyes were full of troubled questions for which Dakan-eh had no answers. Na-sei's loyalty and open adoration usually caused Dakan-eh to smirk with pride; now they annoyed and compromised him. With a warning snarl, he prevented the youth from speaking. Na-sei had yet to accept that in the Land of Grass, Dakan-eh was only one of many subordinate headmen. Shateh was chief above all chiefs. For now, at least, even Bold Man of the Red World must hold his tongue until Shateh told him what to do.

Dakan-eh looked back to the herd and the storm. Lightning veined the sky. The young headman held his breath. One moment passed, then another. Thunder growled before he counted the passage of a seventh second. *Close!* he thought. *Much too close. And coming closer. Why does Shateh keep silent? What is he waiting for?*

Fear rippled through the herd. A few bison skittered and bucked. Cows bawled, bulls bellowed, and calves bleated; but somehow the mass of animals held together.

But for how long? wondered Dakan-eh, chafing against his need to take control of the situation. He looked down the line of men to where Shateh stood immobile, slightly forward of his two sons, Kalawak and Atonashkeh. Like most hunters born to the People of the Land of Grass, the sons of Shateh were tall, broad-faced, good-looking men—yet compared to the chieftain, they seemed insignificant. Envy made Dakan-eh scowl. Compared to Shateh, who was past his prime and dressed like every other hunter in loincloth and lightweight moccasins, everyone looked insignificant—especially the smaller, stockily built hunters of the Red World. Shateh's tall, battle- and hunt-scarred body seemed clad in an invisible cloak of power and authority that set him apart.

To be a man like Shateh . . . to be the one to whom all turn in times of danger . . . ah, yes! Someday it will be so. It was Dakan-eh's lifelong dream. He had led his band north with the unspoken hope that among the aggressive big-game hunters of the Land of Grass, he would become what he never had hope of becoming in the country of his grub-eating, lizard-stalking ancestors—a war chief, a hunter of bison and mammoth, and even a killer of men when they proved to be his enemies.

Suddenly Na-sei exhaled a moan of pure, disbelieving terror, causing Dakan-eh to look back to the herd and the storm. Bold Man knew at that instant that the dream was about to die. His life was over. Death was coming toward him out of the yellow sky. And Shateh was not doing anything to stop it.

From out of the black and bilious belly of the nearest squall line, a series of mammular extensions were shaping themselves into a single long, roiling, spiraling cloud of monstrous proportions that reached toward the earth like the trunk of a questing mammoth.

"Aiyee!" cried Nachumalena. "The whirling wind! It comes!" He invoked the storm spirits in a high, terrified wail and jabbed his spear skyward as though attempting to pierce the underside of the onsweeping clouds.

At last the chieftain gave a command. "Everyone into the ravine! Now! It is our only chance."

Dakan-eh could not believe what he had just heard. To his right and left, men were hurrying into the ravine and pulling their dogs with them. Wide-eyed with incredulity, he stared at them, then at the tornado. The bison had seen it, and on the flanks of the herd, so had the hunters. They were casting off their heavy camouflage cloaks and were running now, but their race for safety came too late. The bison surged forward and spread wide across the plain and, with the whirling wind cutting a massive, zigzagging path behind them, overran the men. Appalled, Dakan-eh watched them die and felt his will to be obedient to Shateh crack as though struck by a hammerstone.

Suddenly he was a headman again, in command again. Screaming to be heard above thundering hooves and the roar of the oncoming tornado, he held his ground and called down into the ravine. "Hunters of the Land of Grass, if you hide in the earth the whirling wind will find you. If it does not kill you, you will die in a rain of bison! Come out of the ravine, hunters of the Land of Grass and men of the Red World! Run with Bold Man before the whirling wind! Do not be afraid!"

Shateh, in a rain-drenched fury, came stalking up to him. The heel of a broad hand rammed Dakan-eh's shoulder and attempted to shove him back. "Into the ravine, Lizard Eater."

Fury met fury as Dakan-eh, Bold Man of the Red World, was stung by the unexpected blow and insult to his origins. By what right did Shateh shame him? He would not

be humiliated or forced to obey the senseless command of
one who had apparently lost his ability to reason.

Glaring defiantly at the chieftain, he shouted through
wind and rain and the sound of the approaching herd,
"There is still time to get to the other side of the ravine, to
run before the storm and to find safety within the village. Or
does Shateh command his hunters to face death because he
is too old to race the whirling wind?"

Shateh's expression was lost to view under the long,
graying hair whipping before his face. "You cannot run
away from Thunder in the Sky, Lizard Eater!" he shouted
back. "When the whirling wind comes, you must hide
within the skin of Mother Below and hope that the fury of
the Great Mammoth Spirit's twisting trunk will not find you
and throw you away into the sky forever."

Shateh turned, suddenly distracted by a shrill, wind-
torn shriek of a wail. He squinted back to where the old
shaman stood, his spear still pointing skyward. The war
chief uttered a sharp curse before shouting, "Come back,
Nachumalena! Neither the bison nor the whirling wind will
stop for you! And lower your spear before it brings
lightning down upon you!"

The warning came too late. Dakan-eh would never
know whether Nachumalena even heard or saw the lightning bolt that killed him. But Bold Man saw it. And then he
saw no more, for in that instant the world exploded with
light and sound and the electrifying stink of ozone. In the
next instant the force field of the lightning blast hurled him
backward into the ravine.

"Dakan-eh!"

He awoke. The earth was shaking. The sky was
roaring. With his ears ringing and his skin and mind
strangely numb, he was aware of men screaming on both
sides of him. Had it been Owa-neh, Shateh, or young Na-sei
who called him from the edge of oblivion? Bold Man could
not tell. He lay splayed, flat on his back, at the bottom of the
ravine atop the rubble heap of bison bones, and gaped
through the pouring rain and pounding pellets of hail at a
horror so profound that he could not move.

The whirling wind had leaped ahead of the stampeding bison and now hovered some thirty feet directly above the ravine. Transfixed, Dakan-eh stared straight up into a gyrating hollow vortex that appeared to be over a mile high and sixty feet across. Stunned and awed, he raised an aching arm to protect his face from icy rain and hail. Squinting through his fingers, he could see that the spinning cloud walls of the tornado were giving birth to small, crackling bolts of lightning and to many lesser cyclones, which hissed and whirled within the greater core as though trying to break free of it . . . or to devour the hapless men and dogs who lay below.

Panic ran wild within him, and he tried to rise; but weakness and dizziness kept him where he lay. A dog went berserk with terror close to his right within the ravine. He heard its frenzied yaps and the equally desperate shouts of Kalawak. Turning his head slightly, Dakan-eh saw the animal leap and scramble to the rim of the defile and into the grasp of the whirling wind. Kalawak made the fatal error of lunging out to save his dog. Dakan-eh watched in horror as the dog and Shateh's eldest son were sucked up into the spinning walls of the storm. The dog yelped and the man screamed for an instant as they whirled, pawing and grasping for life, above Dakan-eh. Then, impaled by lightning and chewed by the whirling wind, both were consumed by the clouds, and Bold Man tasted the fleeting sweetness of blood and urine in the rain that fell upon his face.

Nauseated, he pressed his lips shut. Sickened less by the foul rain than by his meager prospects for survival, he knew that even if he were able to rise, he dared not run from the ravine. But where were the bison? he wondered.

The answer came quickly enough: The storm had scattered the main body of the herd, but the stampede continued. The bison were still running, still headed toward the ravine. He could feel the pounding of uncountable hooves vibrating through his body from the sides and bottom of the chasm.

"No!" he cried out, thinking of certain death beneath a bellowing avalanche of horn and hide.

"Dakan-eh!"

Someone pressed close to his left side and shook him imperatively.

"Dakan-eh!" shrieked Na-sei. He had been blasted into the ravine by the same lightning bolt that had felled Bold Man. "What should we do? Why have the spirits turned against us?"

Dakan-eh attempted to sit, but his body would not serve his will. He shivered violently. Under other circumstances he would have been gratified that even in the face of imminent demise Na-sei respected him enough to await his command. But now he had no idea what to do. A strange, humming befuddlement was expanding within his brain. A gift of the lightning strike? He did not know. In the land of his ancestors he had always been known as a man upon whom the spirits smiled. But he was no longer in the land of his ancestors, and the spirits were not smiling—not upon him, not upon any man. *Why?*

As thunder clapped overhead, and the shrieking of the wind combined with the cries of men and the barks of dogs to create a great, deafening stew of sound, the question roared within Dakan-eh's head. He had no answer. His only certainty was that on this day in the Land of Grass his luck had abandoned him as completely as had Cha-kwena, the sullen, stubborn, hot-tempered young shaman who had once walked with his band in the Red World.

Dakan-eh's head was suddenly full of clear memories. Cha-kwena's threats against him had been many before the young shaman had chosen to betray him and flee beyond the Mountains of Sand. Dakan-eh had hunted him to the edge of the world and beyond, but Cha-kwena had vanished without a trace into the snowstorms of winter. Nearly two years had passed since that day. Whether the magic man was alive or dead was anyone's guess. But either way the sacred stone talisman Cha-kwena had stolen from Bold Man's band was with him, as were Dakan-eh's favorite female and a treacherous handful of followers. They had all chosen to flee with the powerful magic man, driving before them the old, scarred, broken-tusked white mammoth that had once been totem to Dakan-eh's people.

A long-forgotten warning of the Ancient Ones

pounded in Dakan-eh's head: *The life of the People lies in the sacred stones, in the wisdom of the shamans, and in the heart of the totem. For a band deprived of these things, there can be no luck, no life.*

Bold Man's lips tightened over his teeth. Cha-kwena had deprived him of all three. "Trickster! Yellow Wolf! Coyote! Brother of Animals! *Thief!*" He shouted the many names by which he had known the young mystic. "If I have lost my luck, Cha-kwena, it is you who have stolen it!"

As though in response to the accusation, the walls of the tornado flexed, boiled, darkened, then took on the color of Coyote, the little yellow wolf whom Cha-kwena had recognized as one of his many helping animal spirits. Dakan-eh's mouth went dry. Disconcerted, he imagined that he saw Cha-kwena's face leering down at him from out of the clouds.

For one brief, stupefying moment he wondered if the shaman had found a way to command the storm to devour his enemies. Then the moment passed. The imagined face in the clouds disappeared.

Lightning stung horizontally across the rotating center of the whirling wind. Again and again multiarmed, white-hot veins of pure light and power arced and danced to the accompaniment of rolling roars of thunder. Na-sei began to sob. Within the long, deep confines of the ravine, men cried in the tone of those who know that they are about to die.

"Ai ee ay! Behold! Spirit Sucker comes!"

"Hay yah, it is finished for us!"

"Thunder in the Sky, turn away! Do not eat the People!"

"Great Spirit, let my death be a good death."

Dakan-eh could not imagine such a thing as a "good" death. With clenched jaws, he felt a sudden contempt for his fellow hunters . . . and for himself. Why was he lying there like a man already dead? He had been hurled to the brink of death, but he had not been killed; how many men were lucky enough to say that?

His right hand flexed. With a start, he realized that he still held his spear. He raised it, stared at it. It was intact; the very look of it inspired him. He snarled with newfound hope. Brave men made their own luck in the face of adversity. And he was the bravest man of all.

"The bravest!" His loud affirmation rivaled the thunder, and to his amazement, even the tornado seemed to hear him. Impressed by Dakan-eh's self-confidence, the funnel rose and shifted slightly to the east until it was no longer centered over the ravine! The headman actually laughed. The storm was moving away! The icy rain was refreshing, invigorating to him now. He had not lost his luck after all! His mind was clear; his weakness, confusion, and despair were passing—as were the seconds, *vital* seconds, seconds in which a man's decisions would determine whether he lived or died.

Prompted by a sense of purpose, Dakan-eh shouted to the departing storm. "I! I am Dakan-eh, Fearless Hunter of the Red World in this Land of Grass! I do not tremble before the wrath of Thunder in the Sky! The whirling wind has eaten the meat of man and dog this day! But perhaps it eats only of those who scream and piss in terror. Come, Na-sei! Come, all who have courage! Follow me! Raise your spears and shake them at this storm! Climb out of the ravine before the bison come!"

Dakan-eh was on his knees now, straining for balance on the uneven layers of bison bones. His head swam, and his heart was pounding; but he was no longer down and helpless. Somewhere above the cacophony of wind and rain, of hail and thunder, and of wailing men and barking dogs, Shateh countermanded Bold Man by ordering the hunters to take their animals and move as fast as they could southward along the bottom of the ravine.

Bold Man glared at the chieftain, who had not only survived the lightning blast but seemed strengthened by it. The older man was moving steadfastly along the line of dogs and cowering men. He snapped orders, angrily pulled his surviving son, Atonashkeh, to his feet, and then prodded others into action. If Shateh was mourning Kalawak, he gave no sign of it. Dakan-eh envied the man his control, then wondered if the lightning bolt had robbed Shateh of his logic. Already the sides of the ravine were trembling and beginning to crumble as the stampeding herd approached.

The men and dogs would never be able to put themselves out of harm's way before the first of the bison tumbled into the ravine.

"Obey the command of Shateh!" The chieftain was pointing and shouting at Dakan-eh. "Rise, Lizard Eater! Do not be afraid! Move! *Now!*"

Bold Man gritted his teeth. He did not move, but it was not fear that kept him from obeying the chieftain. Twice this day he had openly challenged Shateh. Now he took a deep breath and committed himself to another rebellion. Never again would he subordinate his superior judgment to Shateh or to any man! Using his spear for added leverage, Dakan-eh rose and glared at the chieftain. "The storm is passing! I will climb from the ravine while there is still time! Come, I say, to all who have courage! Follow this man who is not afraid to challenge Shateh, an old man who would see us all dead this day!"

They might have followed, but he would never know for sure. Shateh's answering roar of righteous indignation startled Na-sei, who was attempting to stand. The youth lost his balance, banged into Bold Man, and caused the smooth rawhide soles of Dakan-eh's moccasins to slip on the ice-and-rain-slick bones. He fell hard on his back.

Rain invaded Dakan-eh's lungs. He choked, fought for air, lost the fight, and, with his larynx momentarily paralyzed, blinked up to see that the storm had circled back over the ravine. Whirling more intensely than before, it was lowering, settling, threatening to touch the earth at the top of the chasm twenty feet above Dakan-eh's head and enter the ravine itself. He gasped and regained his breath in a terrible wave of pain.

Beside him, Na-sei lay in a sobbing, stinking clump; he had lost control of his bowels. Dakan-eh could not fault him. All along the bottom of the ravine older, braver men than Na-sei had stained their limbs and loin covers as they crouched and cowered.

Shateh—incredibly still standing, arms raised, face upturned to the yellow-black womb of the whirling wind—shouted to the forces of Creation. "Turn away!" he implored. "Overlook the rashness of Lizard Eater, whose arrogance has angered Thunder in the Sky and sent the whirling wind back to feed upon the People. Be content with the meat you have eaten this day! And if you cannot be content, let my flesh nourish the whirling wind! In the Land of Grass there is no man who is my equal! I am chief! I am shaman! Proudly will I give myself to Thunder in the Sky if Great Ghost Spirit will browse no more upon my people!''

Bravely spoken! conceded Dakan-eh. Irked by the man's brash display of selflessness, he hoped that the tornado *would* take the chieftain. For a moment he was certain that his death wish for Shateh was about to be fulfilled. The storm was different, more ominous, darker, heavier, as the whirling wind came closer to the ground. Dry-mouthed, he waited for the wrath of the storm god to strike Shateh where he stood; but suddenly, the sound of wind and rain and thunder fell away to a sigh.

All was quiet—so quiet that Bold Man wondered if he had gone deaf. Then, somehow he heard the spirit of the whirling wind whisper to him out of his own soul: *Dakan-eh . . . I will not eat of Shateh when I may have the meat of one who declares himself to be a younger, bolder, better man. Now I will see just how bold you are. Now I will see how bravely you will die.*

An appalling pressure was pushing him down, driving the air from his chest. Never had Dakan-eh felt anything to equal it. His eyes bulged. Blood surged and stressed his veins. His innards felt as though they were about to extrude through his body openings. The pain in his ears was excruciating. Somewhere close to him a man squealed like a gut-stuck peccary. It was a moment before he realized that the sound had ripped from his own throat. He did not care; the other hunters were squealing, too.

He screamed again. The storm was still poised above the ravine, but its terrible pressure was abating. He could breathe again. The stink of fear was as rank as the taste of vomit at the back of his mouth and nostrils. His eyes widened as something other than rain and hail fell from the sky.

''Nachumalena?'' The name of the old shaman came shrieking from Dakan-eh's lips as he saw the holy man's corpse emerge from the spinning wall of cloud a good one hundred feet above his head. The old man hung limply suspended in the updrafts of the vortex amid the debris of the tornado's rampage: stones and clumps of soil, blades of torn grass, uprooted and fragmented scrub brush, and the bodies of birds, rodents, and other hapless animals. There was no sign of Kalawak, but Nachumalena's spear floated in the eddying updraft, as did the dead dog.

And then, in an instant, the spinning cloud walls released their captives. The sky rained rocks and grass and animal corpses. A man screamed as the body of the old holy man landed on him. The stone point of Nachumalena's spear grazed Dakan-eh's cheek before the weapon imbedded itself in bison bones.

Bold Man was too stunned to scream, but Na-sei and the others were doing that for him. He squinted up to see that the whirling wind was rising and heading eastward now across the open grassland toward the village.

Something broke wide within him. Shrieking, with his spear still in hand, Dakan-eh was on his feet and scrambling for the top of the ravine. When someone grabbed his ankle and tried to pull him down, he kicked back viciously. His heel made contact with flesh and bone. His father's voice cried out in pain, but Dakan-eh did not care. Free of Owa-neh's grasp, he kept climbing. Using his spear as a brace, he pulled himself out of the ravine and ran for his life just as the first of the bison reached the opposite edge of the chasm and tumbled in.

"Bold Man! Wait!"

Dakan-eh heard Na-sei cry out, but he forced himself not to listen. The wind was at his back, driving the sounds of the storm, the stampede, and dying men before it. He refused to think of what was happening behind him. Those who had placed their loyalty with Shateh had chosen to die. He had chosen to make a run for life. He would not turn back.

Again Na-sei called. Dakan-eh cast a quick glance over his shoulder and saw that the young hunter had followed him from the ravine and was racing after him. Bold Man's heart leaped in terror, but not at the sight of the youth. Something infinitely more impressive than Na-sei was gaining on him: Above and beyond the enormous dust cloud raised by the bison as they pounded toward the ravine, squall lines were still massing. Marching across the rolling plain in dark, towering ranks, dozens of cyclones were forming.

Thunder in the Sky was no longer alone! That ancient and vindictive cannibal god of Shateh's world had loosed its malevolent, murderous children to wreak havoc upon the Land of Grass. The cyclones were swarming over the ravine and moving forward in a compassionless onslaught.

Lengthening his stride, Dakan-eh fled from the advancing squall lines by following in the tornado's wide, erratically laid track. Panic drove him. In this moment he was no longer Bold Man. In this moment he was even less than Lizard Eater. In this moment he was Man Who Runs Away, and he knew it. He ran as the bison ran—in pure, mindless hysteria.

He did not know that he had dishonored himself until he felt urine running hot upon the flesh of his inner thighs. Shame choked him. His heart was leaping like a captive hare within his chest; when it felt as if it had lodged in his throat, he nearly puked it up as he tripped and went to one knee. Then he stood and ran on. The earth had turned to mud under a slush of melting hail and wind-pulverized grass. Two miles ahead, the tornado was moving quickly away, sucking up everything in its path as it cut a twisting swath through the rolling grassland and headed for the river.

The river! Hope flared bright within Dakan-eh. If he could reach the river, he would throw himself into the water and be carried downstream, away from the storms. He was not much of a swimmer, but he would rather risk drowning than confront another tornado.

He urged himself on. *Run, Dakan-eh! Spirit Sucker rides on the backs of the children of the whirling wind! Death has feasted on the meat of men this day, but your bones need not lie amid the refuse of his feeding.*

The sheer bravado of his thoughts drove back the beast of panic. Squall lines were closing on him, but he had once outraced antelope across the sage flats of his homeland. He had survived the strike of a lightning bolt and looked up into the belly of the whirling wind! If any man could outrun the children of the angry sky, it was Bold Man.

"Hay yah hay!" he cried. Yipping and shrieking inflamed his courage. He saw no danger to himself in the tornado that whirled ahead of him; indeed, he thanked it for clearing his way, even though he knew that if it kept on its present course it would cut straight through the village where his mother, his woman, and his slave were waiting for him with his little son.

His heart leaped again—not in fear for his family but in resentment of them. Just thinking of their predicament caused a weakness in his knees. He would *not* think of them again! he vowed. What were women and children to him now? Pah-la, Ban-ya, Sheela, and Piku-neh would live or die according to the whim of the whirling wind. The tornado would reach them before he would, and for that he was glad; when he reached the river he would not have to lose time concerning himself with the well-being of others. His life was most important; he must save himself at all cost.

Panicked birds and animals were fleeing ahead of him up and over the crests of the vast, undulating, high-breasted land. With a start, he saw that a coyote was loping along beside him. Dakan-eh met the wary yellow eyes, and as the animal showed its teeth, Bold Man was reminded of Cha-kwena. Was it possible that he *had* seen the face of the young shaman leering at him out of the whirling wind?

In a sudden temper he shouted, "Cha-kwena! Yellow Wolf! Coyote! Betrayer of men and Brother of Animals! You have stolen my totem, the beautiful Ta-maya, and the sacred talisman of my band. But you will not steal my courage this day!"

Dakan-eh hurled his spear with all of his power at the coyote just as the animal veered and disappeared into deep, unbroken grass. Had his weapon struck true? He cursed because he could not be sure.

Na-sei called his name again. He looked back in the direction of the call, and his right foot came up under a root snag. He went sprawling, landed hard, then rolled sideways over and over until, at last, he came to rest at the bottom of a deep trough between two wind-blasted hills. Breathless, he shook his head to clear it. A moment later, Na-sei was at his side and hunkered low.

"The whirling wind must not eat the village!" Na-sei was more breathless than Dakan-eh as he gripped Bold Man's arm and shouted to be heard. Three small tornadoes danced across the depression in which Dakan-eh and the youth now cowered.

"The whirling wind will eat as it will, but not of us!" Dakan-eh shouted back. "We must thank whatever it was that tripped me, or we would both now be meat in the jaws of the children of Thunder in the Sky!"

There was a ferocity in Na-sei's eyes and voice as he asked, "What good is my life if my new woman and baby-to-be are dead in the village? I have faced Spirit Sucker in the ravine. I have shamed myself once. I will not do so again!"

When the young man started to rise, Dakan-eh jerked him down. "Let the storms pass!"

"There is no time! Come! Together we will run before the whirling wind! Together we will call upon Thunder in the Sky to feed upon us instead of upon our women and children in the village!"

Dakan-eh stared, amazed. Could this be the same youth whom he had left sobbing and pissing with terror in the ravine?

Na-sei seemed to know Dakan-eh's thoughts. "Bold Man has shamed me in my fear!" he blurted. "I have seen the hunters of the Land of Grass cower in the ravine while Dakan-eh dared to challenge the forces of Creation and run alone before the whirling wind to save the village!"

Dakan-eh blinked. Is *that* what the youth thought he had been doing?

There was fire in Na-sei's eyes now, and on his tongue. "Together we will run before the whirling wind! Together we will risk all to save the women and little ones. Na-sei is not afraid!"

Dakan-eh's face contorted with resentment. The realization that he had inspired the young man to bravery was unsettling. Any man willing to throw his life away for women and children was unworthy of Bold Man's respect!

He found himself hating Na-sei, wishing him dead; the very sight of the youth demeaned him. "You are too eager to die, Na-sei. In the Land of Grass there are many villages, many women!"

Na-sei's features tightened into shocked bewilderment. Then his nostrils quivered; he had picked up the stench of Dakan-eh's shaming. When he looked down at Bold Man's stained loins, his face reflected keen disappointment. "I think Bold Man is not so bold. I think Fearless Hunter *is* afraid in this Land of Grass!"

"Not even Dakan-eh can stop the will of Thunder in the Sky!"

Na-sei shook his head slowly, with infinite sadness. "Shateh was right. Dakan-eh is still Lizard Eater!"

Dakan-eh would have struck him down, but Na-sei, anticipating the blow, leaped to his feet and broke for the crest of the hill. In a moment he was gone, a lithe brown figure racing to do battle with the whirling wind and the children of the angry sky on behalf of his young pregnant wife and the rest of the villagers.

Dakan-eh turned his face upward and raged into the wind and clouds, "Take him! Eat him! Make him pay for challenging his headman!"

A sudden downpour silenced him. Another series of cyclones was swarming across the land, probing the furrows of the hills, searching for Dakan-eh. Bold Man looked up and knew that they had found him. Lightning struck directly above. Thunder followed almost simultaneously. Then lightning struck again and again. Aghast, Bold Man squealed in fear as he threw himself down and sprawled on his belly. "No, no! Eat *him,* not *me! Not me, not me, not me!"*

His plea was cut short, pounded into the earth by hailstones the size of antelope brains; they pummeled his body with the strength of war clubs. Gasping and convulsing in pain and terror, he tried to protect his head with his hands. The effort came too late. A hailstone struck his skull, and for the second time in one day, as the world exploded with light and sound, Dakan-eh lost control of his bladder as he plummeted into oblivion.

*   *   *

"Lizard Eater! Lizard Eater!"

Dakan-eh was awakened by Shateh's distant call and by the pulsing beat of drums. The hailstorm had stopped. The rain had ceased. The wind, still blowing hard from the northwest, carried the sounds of men and dogs on the move. He lay still, listening, amazed that not all of his fellow hunters had perished in the ravine under the crushing bison. Shateh *had* managed to lead some of them to safety along the bottom of the chasm!

A second shout came from so far away that Dakan-eh could not identify who had made it; but somehow he was certain that whoever had called was asking if he was alive or dead. He knew the answer to the question. It surprised him. He hurt too much to be a corpse; besides, he doubted if the dead could smell the stink of their own shaming.

He was wet and cold, and so shaken and weak that he could not move.

He was also acutely aware of the stench of the dung and urine in which he lay. Panic seized him. If the hunters found him like this, they would send him back to the Red World in disgrace, and his life's ambitions would be smashed as completely as marrowbones at a hunt feast. The women and children of his band would snicker and point and call him Man Who Shames Himself. The men whom he had enticed north with promises of a glorious new life as warriors and hunters of big game would turn away from him in disgust. Never again would he hope to be a war chief, a man among men, a hunt leader the equal of Shateh. He would be doomed to spend the rest of his days and nights in the Red World of his ancestors, among passive, insect-grubbing, lizard-eating people whom he despised.

No! I will not be one of them again! Better to have been killed by lightning or to have been meat for the whirling wind!

Dakan-eh wanted to rise, but when he tried to lever his weight up on his elbows, his arms went out from under him. He collapsed onto his chest with his face in an ooze of half-melted hailstones, saturated earth, broken grass stalks, and human waste. Tears of frustration smarted beneath his lids. He spat the unspeakable from his mouth and managed to pull himself to his knees. The back of his head was throbbing mercilessly. He reached up with exploratory fingertips to find a hot, gaping, vertical gash in his scalp. He cursed the injury and his weakness. Ban-ya, with her small, strong, steady hands, would suture the gash properly.

Ban-ya! For the first time since awakening, he thought of his woman, and then his mother, his slave, and his child. He looked up; the sky above was clear, blue, devoid of storm. Had the whirling wind reached the village before going on its way? He had to know.

He rose, rocked on his feet, and nearly fainted. Supreme concentration was required for him to remain upright, and more than that was necessary for him to stagger to the crest of the hill; but he did get there, casting off his soiled loin cover as he went. Panting, shaking from a rising gale of weakness, he scanned the grassland. Only then did he drop to his knees.

The retreating storm was a gray wall on the horizon. The whirling wind and the children of Thunder in the Sky had gone their way across the plain . . . straight through the village and cottonwood groves that greened the river-bank. The devastation was appalling. Not a single lodge remained standing. It was as though the encampment had never existed. The squalls had chewed through the groves, cutting a broad swath through the ancient trees, breaking and casting and smashing them about as though they had been of no more substance than blades of grass.

There was no sign of Na-sei. Had the young man reached the village? Had he died with the others, or had he been caught up into the death-dealing maw of the whirling wind before he reached them? Either way, he had failed to save his woman's life. Bold Man was glad. Na-sei had borne witness to his shaming and had openly questioned his courage. Na-sei had shown himself to be a treacherous dog who had been all too ready to nip at his master's pride. If he had survived the passage of the storms he would be a threat to Bold Man's reputation.

"May you be dead!" hissed Dakan-eh, finding momentary pleasure in a vision of the young man being blown across the world, held high in the vortex of the whirling wind, spinning away forever, with the corpses of Nachumalena and Kalawak and the many women, children, elders, and dogs who had died in the village this day.

His lips twitched with gratification until he remembered that the women, elders, and children of his own band had also been in the village. His smile disappeared. A hot lump that tasted of remorse formed at the back of his throat. No one who had been within the encampment could have survived.

Dakan-eh consoled himself with the assurance that across the most distant reaches of the Land of Grass, other villages, other tribes, and many women had not been eaten by the whirling wind. He trembled from the heady implications of this realization. A brave and fearless headman such as he could make new alliances, take new women, and soon have many new sons! The premise was as bold as the man who thought it, until a memory of Pah-la's plump face withered it. Even the most fearless man could not make himself a new mother.

The lump in Dakan-eh's throat went down hard; it left a residue of bitter regret. His father would certainly blame him for Pah-la's death. He could almost see Owa-neh standing before him now, fixing him with stern, reproving eyes and accusing: *If the only son of Owa-neh and Pah-la had been content to remain in the land of the ancestors, the whirling wind of Shateh's land would not have fed upon Dakan-eh's band—upon his women, his son, and his mother!*

"No!" Dakan-eh spoke aloud. Owa-neh and Pah-la had been man-and-woman-together ever since puberty had allowed their joining; neither had ever desired another mate. Widowerhood would not set easily upon Owa-neh's shoulders. But Dakan-eh would not hold himself accountable for Pah-la's death. It was *not* his fault! Any of it! Indeed, Pah-la had taken great pride in her bold, ambitious son. She had overcome Owa-neh's misgivings and convinced him to come north to the Land of Grass.

Of course, Dakan-eh had to admit, she had done so

only after he had vowed to go his way with or without his parents. He would never forget the stricken look on Pah-la's face, or the satisfaction that he had found in her pained reaction to his threat.

His head went higher. He was feeling stronger, better. What a clever and insightful man he was! He had known all along that a mother's loyalty to an only son was without bound. Once he had managed to put into Pah-la's mind the fear of being left behind to lament the loss of her son and grandchild, the woman had no alternative but to side with him. Nevertheless, no one could ever accuse him of physically forcing his mother to yield to his will. Pah-la had chosen the life she would live, and Owa-neh, like a disgruntled, tooth-worn old wolf, had chosen to stay at the side of his lifetime mate.

Bold Man's brows arched with speculation. Perhaps when all was said and done, his father would be thankful that Pah-la had become meat for the whirling wind. Her death would free him to take another mate—a younger woman, who could give him many sons.

Dakan-eh shrugged; he had never found it difficult to justify his self-serving behavior. He did not find it so now. No one in the Red World or in the Land of Grass could hope to contain the spirit of life forever. Besides, as the wind shifted and brought with it the sound of approaching men and dogs, Dakan-eh suddenly realized that there might be someone infinitely more important to mourn than one old woman, even if she was his mother. And that was himself!

He could accept the death of Pah-la and the women and children; but if his band's hunters had perished, then he would have lost his *entire* band and, with it, all status. In the Red World and in the Land of Grass, a headman who brought calamity to his people was cast out, shunned as one upon whom the forces of Creation no longer smiled.

He turned and squinted westward. Three broken lines of men and dogs were approaching from about a mile away. A moment later they were lost to view between the high shoulders of the rolling grassland. His heart sank. The number of men who had begun the hunt had been halved.

Whether any of his own hunters were among them remained to be seen.

He moaned in abject misery as the words of Shateh's impassioned imploration to the storm came back to haunt him: *Turn away! Overlook the rashness of Lizard Eater, whose arrogance has angered Thunder in the Sky and sent the whirling wind back to feed upon the People!*

Dakan-eh felt nauseated. Thunder in the Sky had not overlooked his rashness. The whirling wind had punished the People for his arrogance. Every hunter in the Land of Grass would blame Dakan-eh for the devastation. Every man in the ravine had witnessed his disobedience to Shateh. He dropped to his knees and retched until he could retch no more. The hunters would drive him off. They might even kill him. He had seen them kill others for much less. The deaths had been slow, terrible.

"Aiyee eh!" Dakan-eh's cry was the exhalation of a desperately frightened man. It occurred to him that he should run fast and far and never look back. But he was too weak. His eyes were tearing, and his nose was running. There was a vile taste in his mouth.

There was no escape. Shateh and Atonashkeh led the others over the crest of the opposite hill. They descended into the trough and came up the other side to stand before him, and suddenly, to his infinite shame, he was weeping with relief. Walking with Shateh's men were Ma-nuk and K-wok, Ela-nay and Atl, Xet and Tleea-neh and all the others. His heart soared. They were haggard, wet and muddied and bloodied by minor wounds, but they were his hunters from the Red World, and they were alive! He was still a headman!

But for how long? he wondered. What would these men say when they saw what was left of the village? They might kill him where he stood.

No one spoke. They stared past him toward the decimated village. Long, heavy moments passed. Then the men sighed as one, murmured restlessly as their eyes took in what their hearts could not believe.

Dakan-eh found it difficult to breathe. The air was as suffocating and full of threat as the whirling wind had been when it had lowered itself over the ravine. Somewhere, far away, a raven cawed. No omen could have been worse.

At last, Shateh broke the silence. "Rise, Man Who Chases the Whirling Wind!"

The chieftain's mockery was not unexpected. Dakan-eh was still too weak and sick to move. He remained as he was, waiting for further insult.

"Rise, I say! Rise and stand beside Shateh, Fearless Hunter. Truly this Dakan-eh *is* a bold man."

Stung by what he took to be sarcasm, Dakan-eh looked up warily. The chieftain's face was tight with fatigue; the wide, handsome features betrayed no emotion. Dark, wind-dried blood had congealed in the lines of his face and his long hair and was smeared across his forearms and thighs. It spattered in little clots that stuck to the tanned skin of his massive chest. It had to be the blood of other men, Dakan-eh thought, for aside from minor scratches on the chieftain's arms and legs, Shateh had no major wounds . . . except in his eyes. The grief there was great. So Shateh did mourn for his son Kalawak. And for how many others?

Dakan-eh had no wish to pursue the question, for in this moment he himself was struck by the burning hatred that came from Atonashkeh's glare.

Standing proudly beside the chieftain, Shateh's surviving son sneered down at Dakan-eh with unconcealed contempt. "Yes! Dakan-eh *is* bold! We have all seen how he sits boldly in his own puke! Smell now the bold stink of his piss and arrogance! Who has not seen how boldly this lizard eater spoke against the will of Shateh, then insulted the power of the whirling wind, and finally called down upon the People the wrath of Thunder in the Sky with his boasts and—"

"He has shamed us all this day!" Shateh interrupted, his voice as deep with resonant power as the growl of a riled lion.

Dakan-eh's intestines constricted defensively; if he had not already vomited up everything in his gut, he would have retched again. Instead he blanched like a frightened woman and tried not to faint as he saw Shateh's right hand tighten around the bone shaft of his spear. He stared with grim fascination at the chieftain's knuckles; he watched them flex, saw the tendons working, straining, stressing the skin that covered them until it whitened beneath its uneven wash of blood. In a moment the mighty hand would heft the spear. The long, muscular arm would lift it, and the man would reposition himself to make the killing thrust.

With a gasp, Dakan-eh found his tongue. It was stiff with fear. Nevertheless he made it move. "This Dakan-eh of the Red World . . . has not meant to shame any man."

"Yet Shateh *is* shamed!" The chieftain rammed the butt end of his spear into the ground for emphasis.

Dakan-eh cringed and prepared to die.

Shateh snarled and rammed his spear into the ground again. "Many a man has heaved up the contents of his belly and cast off his loin cover this day lest its stink betray his fear!"

Humbled, the hunters lowered their eyes, and Atonashkeh flinched. Obviously, Dakan-eh realized, Atonashkeh was among those who had shamed themselves.

Shateh nodded. "All saw Nachumalena's fate! All cowered in fear of sharing it! But only Dakan-eh dared to run before the children of the angry sky, wave his spear and shout his defiance of the whirling wind, and risk himself in an effort to turn Spirit Sucker away from the women and elders and little ones in the village. In the eyes of Shateh what this Bold Man has done was a good thing! A brave thing! A thing not expected of a lizard eater!"

Dakan-eh was overcome, not only by the enormity of the chieftain's misperception but by Shateh's willingness to castigate himself and his fellow hunters for not matching the courage of a lizard eater. The man had viewed Dakan-eh's mad race across the plain in the same false light in which Na-sei had seen it—not to save his own skin but as a valiant and potentially suicidal attempt to rescue others!

Relief flooded him. He was not to be killed! He was not to be banished! He was not going to be blamed for bringing the wrath of the cannibal sky god down upon the villagers! He was to be congratulated for his unprecedented bravery! The onus of shame lifted from his spirit; but it was a momentary reprieve. He did not like the look of jealous loathing that the chieftain's son was sending his way.

"No man of the Land of Grass would think to challenge the will of Shateh!" Atonashkeh said. "And no man would attempt to drive the whirling wind away from the encampment. The women, children, and elders would not stay in the village to face the onslaught of the whirling wind."

Dakan-eh frowned. *Where would they have gone?* he wondered.

Nakantahkeh, a sharp-eyed warrior with a face as hard and angular as a well-cut spearhead, saw confusion on Dakan-eh's face. "Atonashkeh speaks words of wisdom!" The man was often an echo of the chieftain's son; the two were as brothers. "At the first sign of the whirling wind, Lahontay, eldest man of the many assembled bands, would have taken the women, elders, and little ones to the cave that lies deep within the cliffs above the river. Lahontay is wise. He would not have hesitated."

"True," affirmed the chieftain impatiently, "but Bold Man could not have known this."

Dakan-eh's eyes widened. No! He could not have known! No one had thought to tell him! Not that it would have made any difference. He would still have run to save himself! He gaped, stunned. The village had never been in any danger! His mother was alive! And his woman, Ban-ya, and his slave, Sheela, and his little son, Piku-neh! Lehana, the woman of Na-sei, would live to have her baby. But her man had needlessly risked and lost his life for her. Dakan-eh almost laughed as he thanked the whirling wind for taking Na-sei's life and, with it, any chance of the young man's ever contradicting Shateh's opinion of Dakan-eh . . . Man Who Chases the Whirling Wind!

Shateh extended his hand. "Rise now, Fearless Hunter, Bold Man, band brother of Shateh!"

There was not a man or youth among the assembled hunters who did not suck in his breath at the honor that had just been extended to an outlander.

Dakan-eh took the chieftain's hand and accepted Shateh's assistance in getting to his feet. Ignoring Atonashkeh's grimace of loathing, he stood naked and brazen in the wind. He felt strong, steady, courageous. What need had he of the sacred stones of his ancestors, or of the totems of the Red World, or of the powers of a youthful shaman who had abandoned him and his people? He needed no one now! Truly, he *was* a man who made his own luck! He was certain of it!

Hah-ri, a short, thick-legged youth of the Red World, stepped unsteadily through the ranks of assembled hunters. His face had the pale, blank look of a man in shock. He was dragging a dead coyote. Dakan-eh's spear was in Hah-ri's hand, its stone projectile point shattered beyond repair.

"My headman's spear strikes true even when he runs before the wind," said Hah-ri, his voice so tightly controlled that it sounded as though about to break. "I have brought Bold Man these things that I have found while following Shateh from the ravine. This kill, this pelt, this meat, belong to Dakan-eh."

Bold Man smiled, elated. Being the astounding hunter that he was, he had killed the coyote even while running in a blind panic!

Dakan-eh had never paid much attention to Hah-ri before, but now he found himself liking the adoring youth immensely, finding him inordinately good to look upon and insightful beyond measure. The sudden quivering of the young man's chin went unnoticed as Bold Man accepted the coyote carcass without hesitation and nodded energetically. He felt better than he had in hours. He hefted the dead coyote by its hind paws, lifted it high, and found its body surprisingly light. Then, observing more closely, he saw that this was a young beast, small and sinewy, without much fat or muscle. Later in the year its pelt would have been prime. Now it was molting, patchy, a summer's end skin—as worthless as the meat it covered. Suddenly embarrassed, he lowered the carcass. This kill was nothing to brag about.

The other men were observing it with curiosity, no doubt wondering why any man would risk ruining a perfectly good projectile point in order to end such useless life. Dakan-eh fought the urge to cast the dead coyote away.

But that would be unthinkable. Once prey was taken on the hunt, its life spirit must be eaten. Anything less would dishonor the forces of Creation. His smile became a scowl. What would Ban-ya think when he handed such a scraggly, shedding sack of meat to her? And what must these men of the Land of Grass think of him for spearing it in the first place?

He felt the need to explain himself. "This little yellow wolf crossed and recrossed the path of Fearless Hunter as he ran to save the women and children and elders in the village. So Bold Man killed this coyote! Dakan-eh was thus able to chase the whirling wind away from the People! Because Bold Man gave death to this little yellow wolf, Thunder in the Sky and his children have gone their way, and the forces of Creation smile once more upon the Land of Grass!"

Shateh stiffened. Something watchful, wary, and dangerous ignited within his half-closed eyes as they fixed Dakan-eh with displeasure. Bold Man suddenly felt dismayed. He wondered what he had said to make Shateh hostile toward him. He dared to confront the chieftain's censorial gaze. "Why do the eyes of Shateh look with disfavor upon one whom he has just named Brother?"

"How can a brother of Shateh say that the forces of Creation are smiling upon the Land of Grass when Nachumalena and Kalawak and Na-sei have become meat for Thunder in the Sky?" the chieftain responded.

Dakan-eh's mood swung from darkness into light. *Of course!* In his joy at being honored by the chieftain, he had forgotten that it was a time for mourning. Bold Man was forced to concede that it had been rude to behave as though the death of Kalawak and Nachumalena had meant nothing to him. Feigning sadness, he said, "The heart of Dakan-eh is heavy if he has caused pain to one who has named him Brother. But the spirit of this man cannot help but sing in gladness because the forces of Creation have smiled upon the women and children and elders in the village. This man has not forgotten those who have been taken by the whirling wind this day."

The chieftain nodded, mollified. "Many have died in

the ravine this day, Bold Man of the Red World. *Many*. The blood you see upon me is their blood . . . and yours.''

"Mine?"

"It is so!" Young Hah-ri's chin was still quivering. "You must be bold indeed, Dakan-eh, to hear the words, for Owa-neh had no wish to leave the Red World. He came to the Land of Grass only because you came, and here his life spirit left his body."

Dakan-eh felt as though someone had punched him. He scanned the ranks of his hunters. His father was not with them.

"It is so," Shateh confirmed. "The horn of a bison caught him, opening him here, like this." He indicated his midsection just below the ribs, then stroked downward to his groin, indicating a massive gut wound. "Owa-neh was down and on his back when the bison fell. Because of the blood on his face, he could not see to move away in time." He paused, then shook his head as though to clear it of a bad dream.

A hunter came forward from behind the other men. He held Owa-neh's broken body in his arms. He set the corpse gently on the ground by Dakan-eh's feet.

After a respectful silence, Shateh continued, "We will go to the river now." His voice was low. Weariness weighted it, as did grief, which was infinitely heavier. "We will join our women and little ones and the elders who have survived the wrath of Thunder in the Sky. We will bring the women to tend the wounded and dying. Tonight when the fires and smokes and chants of mourning are raised, Shateh must ask the forces of Creation why they have turned upon my people this day."

Atonashkeh pinioned Dakan-eh with eyes as piercing as the talons of a hawk. "Perhaps the lingering stink of lizard eaters has tainted the Four Winds and offended the forces of Creation."

Dakan-eh, though sorely shaken, would not stomach the insult. "You were not offended by the 'lingering' of the men of the Red World when you had need of our spears and brave hearts to join with you in war against our mutual enemy, Atonashkeh!"

"The war is long done. The enemy is finished," Atonashkeh responded. Then he addressed his father. "Perhaps it is not a good thing for lizard eaters to remain in the Land of Grass. It is one thing to take pity on them for their desolate land and lack of game. But they are not and never will be our people."

Shateh closed his eyes. "In time beyond beginning the People were one. All tribes were the children of First Man and First Woman. All were brothers and sisters together. Has Atonashkeh forgotten the teachings of the Ancient Ones?"

Atonashkeh's face tightened. "The son of Shateh has not forgotten! Nor will he forget that on the day the whirling wind came to feed upon my brother, my father saw fit to name a lizard eater Brother in his place." He turned then, and was off at a lope toward the river. He did not look back.

Dakan-eh watched him go and knew that there would never be peace between them.

Shateh's eyes were open again. "Come," he said, sighing with sorrow. "The women, elders, and children must not hear our news from the lips of so harsh and impatient a man as Atonashkeh."

As the others obeyed the chieftain, Bold Man stood unmoving. His mind was numb, abraded by Shateh's revelation about Owa-neh. *Blood on his face? Down and on his back? He could not see to move away in time?*

Dakan-eh choked on his memories as he looked at his father's maimed body: the mad scramble from the ravine; his father's hard, desperate tug at his ankle, trying to drag him down; and then the force of his backward kick, the feel of flesh and bone and cartilage yielding to the brutal smash of his heel. He could still hear the cry of pain. He had known then—as he knew now—that the cry had come from his father. But Bold Man had kept on climbing. He had not looked back. He had left his father flat on his back, stunned by the blow, blinded by his own blood, unable to rise and save himself as the bison came charging into the ravine from the far side of the chasm.

No! That is too much blame to accept! Dakan-eh would not fault himself! Owa-neh should not have tried to stop him! His father would be alive now if he had not interfered with his son's valiant race to save the People.

Guilt pricked him with the truth; he would not accept that, either. This day he had chased the whirling wind, and a chieftain had named him Brother. Nothing could change that. *Nothing!* His hand curled into a fist, and startled, he realized that he still held the coyote. He lifted his arm, stared at the dead animal, and growled at it.

"The blame is yours, all of it yours! Coyote, Yellow Wolf, Thief, Trickster! Cha-kwena! Yes! Are you still inside the skin of the beast that is your helping animal spirit? Or have you fled upon the wind because you know that a bold man who is your enemy is on to your tricks? Where is your life spirit now, Shaman?"

Dakan-eh curled his fist as tightly as he could around the paws of the coyote, then squeezed until he felt the veins burst and the bones crack and the muscles turn to jellied rubble.

"If I ever find you, Cha-kwena, I will break you, kill you. You will regret the day you ever thought yourself shaman enough to steal the luck of Dakan-eh!"

2

Far to the south, a coyote howled on a craggy mountaintop beneath a sun that burned like an incandescent eye in the vast, cloudless sweep of the heat-bleached sky. The cry of the little yellow wolf was a high, threnodic wail usually not heard in the light of day. Halfway up the flank of the mountain, a ground sloth the size of a grizzly bear raised its massive, blunt-snouted head from the scrub growth upon which it had been feeding and listened in dull-witted confusion, its nostrils sucking air, sieving it for the telltale scent of predator.

High above, close to the summit of the peak, mice awoke, and rabbits shivered while pack rats stirred inside their mounded lodges of sticks. A startled bighorned ram broke from the meager shade of a weather-stunted grove of junipers and was off at a run across the open scree, its hooves displacing loose stones and causing a rock slide to cascade onto the ridge below.

Cha-kwena looked up just in time to see the rocks hurtling toward him. The cry of the coyote had invaded his meditations, but it was the dry, clinking sound of the bighorn's hooves striking and sliding on rock that jerked the young shaman from his trance. He was perched cross-legged on a sun-warmed boulder at the height of the ridge. Dawn's first light had called him there in search of solitude. Now, suddenly alert to danger, he snatched his short stabbing spear and the oiled antelope bladder that served as his water bag from beside him and in less time than it took to draw breath was up and vaulting from the boulder. He spread his arms wide, leaped, and landed lightly. Then, outrunning the rocks that could kill him, he was racing agilely downslope along the ridge, his sandaled feet kicking up dust and creating small rock slides of their own. Only when he was certain that he was safe did Cha-kwena, breathless, turn and look back. The coyote was gone.

Relieved, the young shaman attached the nearly flaccid waterskin to the woven fiber waistband of his rabbit-skin loin cover. With his spear gripped in his right hand, he reached up with his left to make certain that his medicine bag was still around his neck. It was. Just knowing that the sacred stone was in his possession calmed the beat of his heart. He touched the knotted length of sinew to which the precious little leather sack was attached, then pressed the medicine bag against his upper chest so that he could feel the hard substance of the fang-shaped, thumb-sized talisman it contained. As long as he possessed the sacred stone of the ancestors, no harm could come to him or to his totem, the great white mammoth, or to those who had chosen to walk at his side when he had followed the ancient tusker beyond the Mountains of Sand into this bleak and forbidding country beyond the edge of the world.

It should have been a soothing thought, but as Cha-kwena watched the last of the falling rocks bounce off the boulder and shatter in a deadly rain of dusty debris, he was not consoled. Death had just come close to him—so close he could smell its presence in the hot, heavy air of the windless noon.

He looked up at the sun. Never had he felt such heat. In his distant village to the north, by the Lake of Many Singing Birds, it would be the Moon of Ducks Coming Home. The air would be softened by the breath of a cooler, gentler season; rice grass would be ripe, the tule breaks would be rusty gold and bending close to the shrinking shores of his homeland's many shallow lakes. With a hiss of impatience, he loosed his water bag from his waist, popped out the bone stopper with his thumb, raised the vessel to his lips, and drained it dry.

There had not been enough water to ease his thirst. He growled, doubting that he would find a spring on this slag heap of a mountain from which to refill it. The walk was long to the stream and the miserable, algae-thick pool beside which his little band was encamped.

His fingers closed again around his medicine bag. Was it possible that the power of the sacred stone was connected with the Red World of the ancestors? Could it be that the farther he traveled away from his homeland, the weaker the magic of the stone became? The disconcerting premise had been troubling Cha-kwena for many moons. His grandfather would have been able to confirm the worry or put his mind at ease about it; but old Hoyeh-tay—shaman, guardian of the totem, keeper of the traditions of the People, and protector of the sacred stone—was long dead.

Cha-kwena's throat constricted painfully with grief. How intensely he missed the old man! Cha-kwena had never wanted to be shaman. He had not been *ready* to be shaman on that firelit night when Death, in the form of an enemy from a far land, had found his grandfather and teacher. The old man had been slain in their village, his talisman stolen, and his body pitched from his cave as though it had been of no more value than a haunch of time-ruined meat.

The memory caused anguish. Cha-kwena closed his eyes. Hoyeh-tay had foreseen his own death, but no one had believed him—not even the grandson who was destined to regain the sacred stone from the enemy of the People and travel the shaman's path.

Cha-kwena exhaled in a vain attempt to expel his memories along with his guilt. Had he heeded the warnings of his grandfather and recognized the enemy in time, Hoyeh-tay would not have been killed, war would not have come to his people, and he would not be standing here now, alone upon this desolate ridge with the smell of Death in his nostrils and the sacred stone in his hand.

"Cha-kwena!"

Startled by the sharply spoken sound of his own name, the young shaman opened his eyes. As sometimes happened when he was alone, troubled, and in need of his grandfather's counsel, he could have sworn that Hoyeh-tay stood before him. Perched on the old man's shoulder was Owl, the perpetually molting old raptor that had been Hoyeh-tay's constant companion in life and had disappeared on the night of his death.

Cha-kwena blinked. Was he seeing a shaman's vision or a madman's hallucination, or was he merely succumbing to the wishful thinking of one who lamented the death of a loved one? He could not be sure. He knew only that now, whether real or imagined, he saw his grandfather—straight backed in his short cape of twisted rabbit fur, skinny legged below his loin cover of antelope hide, and looking as irascible as he had been in life, with his black eyes flashing brightly. His thin, breathy voice rasped the oft-repeated admonition: "Remember all that I have taught you, Cha-kwena! Never forget! Never doubt! *Never!* You are shaman now, guardian of the totem and of the traditions of the People and of the sacred stone! And in all of this world and the world beyond, there are no stones like the ones that have been entrusted to the holy men of the Red World. Those stones were once the bones of First Man and First Woman, who gave life to the ancestors in time beyond beginning, when the People were one and the twin gods of war and divisiveness had not yet been born.''

"Grandfather?" Cha-kwena reached out, but the old man stepped quickly back. Owl, extending its broad wings, chortled a warning to stay away.

"Listen and remember, Cha-kwena!" demanded Hoyeh-tay sharply. "From out of the far north came First Man and First Woman. Following Life Giver, the great white spirit mammoth, they came across a Sea of Ice, through the vast, endless Corridor of Storms, and into the Forbidden Land. Walking always into the face of the rising sun, they came with their many children into the Red World. When First Man and First Woman gave up their life spirits to the Four Winds, the forces of Creation would not let them die forever. Their bones were turned into stones—*sacred* stones—and divided among the People. The spirits of First Man and First Woman speak to the shamans through the sacred stones so that the People would always remember and keep the ways of the Ancient Ones.''

It seemed to Cha-kwena that his grandfather shook his head and sighed with infinite regret before continuing. "Now the twin gods of war have divided the People into many tribes. Those who were once one family are now many, and each names the other Stranger and Enemy. Now men hunt and consume the flesh and blood of the mammoth children of Life Giver, for they have forgotten that the mammoth kind are totem, forbidden meat to the People. Only the People of the Red World remember the way it was in time beyond beginning . . . and only one band among them keeps and honors the ways of the ancestors. *Your* band, Cha-kwena.''

"My band is small, and my people are hungry. The land in which we walk is strange and hostile.''

"Yes, it is so. But the power of the sacred stone is in your keeping, and the totem walks before you. The great white mammoth will give life to your people as he gave life to First Man and First Woman as he led and protected them on their journey to the Red World. You must never doubt that as long as a single sacred stone remains in the keeping of a true and believing shaman of the Red World, the great mammoth cannot die. And as long as Life Giver survives as totem, the People will live forever."

Suddenly Hoyeh-tay's image dissolved, and a soft slur of cooling air brushed across Cha-kwena's cheek. Was it a random gust of wind or the invisible wake raised by the passage of an aged ghost and the beat of a phantom owl's wings? The young man was not sure. He tightened his grip on the talisman within the leather sack. The stone was so deceptively small and light! Yet he felt the full burden of it—the pressure of responsibility, the largeness of magic. It was a staggering weight for a youth of sixteen. It made him feel tired, unsure, and afraid.

The mass of the talisman's weight equaled three times ten thousand millennia and stretched so far back into the mists of time that only a shaman could fully visualize the enormity of distance that linked it to the past. In Cha-kwena's hand, that link was made. He could feel the power of the talisman emanating like the inner heat of a live ember drawn from a fire pit. The man who possesses a hot coal holds the life spirit of fire captive in his hand. He can release the flame to live again, or he can kill it; the power to do either is his.

It was the same with the sacred stone. With Hoyeh-tay dead, Cha-kwena, as shaman, had chosen to abandon his tribe and follow the great white mammoth into this far land. It was the only way to keep the power of the talisman alive and undefiled by those who had turned their backs on the traditions of the ancestors.

Eleven members of Dakan-eh's band had chosen to make a new life with Cha-kwena when Bold Man had embraced the warrior ways of mammoth-hunting strangers. Eleven people—one man, four women, one girl, and five children—had named Cha-kwena their headman and shaman and secretly fled their village on a snowy winter day. Dakan-eh, disregarding traditions in favor of feeding his ambitions, had left Cha-kwena no alternative but to turn his back forever upon the land of the ancestors. Had he stayed, it would only have been a matter of time before Dakan-eh would have claimed the sacred stone as his own and named himself Shaman as arrogantly as he had named himself Headman. He had not earned the name Bold Man for nothing!

Cha-kwena shook his head. It seemed so long ago. During the nearly two years of wandering from one unsatisfactory hunting camp to another, two female babies had been born to the women of his little band. At first the births had seemed to bode well for the travelers. But now, after two long, bitter winters and yet another summer of savage heat and virtually no rain, the babies were gaunt toddlers. And no one was pleased that Siwi-ni, aged and sickly, was about to give birth again. Soon snow would be upon the land once more. Even if Siwi-ni survived the ordeal of childbirth, it was doubtful that she would have milk for the infant; if she did not, the newborn would be one more mouth to feed in this brutally arid country. His people were barely surviving now. How much longer could they stay alive if things did not improve?

He frowned. If the sacred stone was safe in his care, why was life so difficult for his band? And where was the great white mammoth? Life Giver had not been seen in many days.

And so Cha-kwena stood alone on this sunstruck ridge, raised his face to the sun, and begged for an omen that would give him hope of a brighter future. "A sign is all I ask, so that when my people wonder where the great white mammoth walks, I may ease their fears and assure them that all is well with Life Giver!"

The sun did not answer.

"Father Above, I beg that I may find and follow Life Giver into country that will give life to my band. I beg that the women and children will be free at last of hunger and thirst!"

The sun did not reply.

"Behold me! I am the grandson of Hoyeh-tay! I have been true to the ways of the ancestors! I have abandoned all that displeases the forces of Creation and have dared to follow the great white mammoth across unknown country! I *am* shaman! And you *will* answer me!"

The sun, which would not answer the begging of a

youth, responded now to the audacious command of the shaman. The coyote reappeared on the mountaintop and stood silhouetted against the tremulous heat haze of noon. Little Yellow Wolf howled as though mourning the death of a brother.

Cha-kwena was perplexed. What kind of omen was this? Of all of the animals whom he named Brother, the coyote had always been closest to him in spirit. Only moments before, the howl of this coyote had startled a ram into causing a rock slide that had nearly killed him. Now the animal was back, keening in such a deep, melancholy way that Cha-kwena felt bruised by the sound. He watched as the coyote lowered its tawny, wolflike head and, with ears laid flat and tail tucked, stared silently at the young shaman. Its eyes were half-closed as though in pain.

Cha-kwena stared back. Something was unnatural about the animal's presence at this time of day. But, Cha-kwena reminded himself, Coyote's being there was a gift of the sun! Therefore he dared not question that it seemed ominous.

Now the coyote pointed its nose at the sun, uttered a single ear-piercing yip, then circled thrice. It trotted off a few paces in the direction of the rising sun and finally circled back to pause again.

Cha-kwena gasped, heartened, certain that Coyote had just beckoned him to ascend the peak and follow. This *was* the sign that he had come in search of! He would not question whether it was good or bad; he would find out soon enough. "I will come!" he cried and, daring to hope that the little yellow wolf might be leading him to his totem, followed without looking back.

It was not a difficult climb. He picked his way over boulders that lay in jumbled disarray just below the broad, treeless summit of the peak itself. Soon the ridge was below him. And all the while the shaman climbed, Coyote continued to urge him on.

"Cha-kwena!"

"Yes! I am following!"

"Cha-kwena!"

"I hear your call, brother of my spirit!"

A sense of rising excitement strengthened him, defined his purpose as he climbed faster, higher, certain for the first time in many moons that the power of the sacred stone was with him still. Truly, he *was* shaman, still fully capable of communicating with the spirits of animals.

"Wait for me, Little Yellow Wolf, brother of my spirit!" he called to Coyote. "I am coming as fast as the two legs of a man can carry me!" He hefted himself onto and over the last boulder. In just a few more steps upward and across the bare skull of the mountain, he would be at the summit and able to overlook the world and see whatever it was that Coyote was calling him toward.

"Cha-kwena!" This time Coyote called his name in a high, feminine shriek of impatience. "Cha-kwena! *Stop!*"

With a start, he obeyed, then realized that the call had come neither from the far side of the summit nor from the throat of an animal. It had come from behind and below him, and it had come from the mouth of a girl. He turned and stared down. "Mah-ree!"

He felt annoyed as he watched her small, suntanned figure hurrying after him along the ridge. Her favorite dogs—Friend and Scar Nose, One Ear and Will Not Listen—were with her. One of the dogs carried a two-sided pack slung across its mottled gray back. Cha-kwena scowled at the sight of the big, shaggy, high-eared animals. The dogs reminded him of violent, tragic events that he preferred to forget. The dogs had been puppies when Masau, shaman and emissary of the People of the Watching Star, had given them as a gift to Mah-ree. That had occurred well before Masau's murderous duplicity was discovered and the devastating war between the peoples of the north and south had erupted. Cha-kwena's lips thinned into an angry white line. He had trusted Masau. Everyone in the village by the Lake of Many Singing Birds had trusted him. As reward for the band's gullibility, Masau had slain Hoyeh-tay and brought Death to the Red World.

"Cha-kwena! Wait!" Mah-ree shouted. "I bring food. I bring fresh water! I bring good talk!"

Good talk? Cha-kwena rolled his eyes. *Endless chatter*

is more like it! Would Mah-ree always shadow his steps and buzz around him as irritatingly as a mosquito? He shook his head, knowing the answer. She would no doubt scold him for sneaking from the encampment and insist, as she always did, that she was also a shaman and, therefore, entitled to be at his side when he sought the mystic visions of his calling.

What gave the girl such ideas? He sighed begrudgingly. Mah-ree might not be completely mistaken. Even when she was a child his people had called her Medicine Girl because of her intuitive healing skills and the fearless way in which she walked with their totem among the mammoth kind. Nevertheless, in the Red World the shaman's path and power was for males only.

Yet how had Mah-ree known where to find him? How had she known that his water bag would be dry? He was thirsty and would be grateful for a drink. So he waited—not for the girl but for the water she was bringing.

She scooped up the dog's side pack, slung it over her shoulder, ordered the dogs to stay; then she was scrambling over the last of the boulders to stand red faced and panting before him—a small, bare-chested girl clad in a knee-length skirt of woven milkweed fibers and sandals of pounded, tightly woven sagebrush. She held a spear in one hand, and her stone skinning dagger was sheathed at her side.

"I did not think that you would ever slow down!" she exclaimed breathily. "Did you not hear me calling your name?"

He eyed her reproachfully. She was growing up, resembling her older sister more and more every day. But Mah-ree was still a child in Cha-kwena's eyes, and he doubted if she would ever be as good to look upon as Ta-maya. The comparison was unfair, and he knew it. No female in this world or the world beyond could compare to Ta-maya. Her beauty was such that many men had wanted to possess her. In the end, only the magnificent Masau from the People of the Watching Star had succeeded in winning her heart, and Ta-maya had become a widow before that union was consummated. Now she wanted no man at all and was content to live with Cha-kwena's band. But Ta-maya did not look upon him in the way a woman looks upon a man . . . in the way he would desire above all else. Little Mah-ree did, and that annoyed him.

"Why have you come after me?" he snapped. "Now Coyote is silent on the far side of the mountain to which he has summoned me. My solitude is broken, and my visions are no more."

Anyone else would have shrunk from his rebuke. Not Mah-ree. Having caught up with him at last, she was in a mood as sunny as the day. "I will always come after you, Cha-kwena! Surely you know that!" She beamed at him. "This woman has brought food and water to her man. But if you are fasting in the way of vision calling, then I will keep these things until you are ready."

"I am *not* your man. And you have yet to become a woman!"

"Soon!" she boasted, puffing out her chest. The first bloom of impending maturity was evident in the form of two tiny breasts that were as round and hard and pointed as freshwater shells.

He was not impressed. Indeed, her appearance concerned him. Mah-ree was nearly fourteen. She should have sprouted a woman's breasts long before now. Only yesterday he had overheard her mother, Ha-xa, confide her fears to his mother, U-wa. Ha-xa was worried that the hardships of the long overland trek may have caused "the woman-to-be spirits to wither within my younger daughter. Perhaps my poor little one will never shed moon blood! Perhaps my Mah-ree will become old and dry and die before the woman inside her is ever born!"

The recollection disturbed Cha-kwena. When Mah-ree took a flask from the side pack and offered it to him, he was glad for the distraction. He drank deeply, then returned the bladder with all of the disdainful authority expected of his gender and rank. "You should not have come, Mah-ree. Kosar-eh and the women will worry. And what are you doing with a spear? This is a man's weapon!"

"It is *my* spear! I have made it with my own hands!" Her eyes shone with pride. "I have been watching Kosar-eh teach his boys to make and use the hunting weapons of a man—the spear and the spear hurler. Soon I will be more than just a snarer of rabbits and lizards, of snakes and grubs and birds! I will be a bold hunter, like First Woman! I will hunt antelope, deer, and horse! I will protect my people from bears and cougars, from lions and leaping cats and wolves! Already I am good enough with this spear to come alone and unafraid into unknown country. Kosar-eh knows this. When he sees that I have gone, he will not let the others worry. He will tell them that Mah-ree has come to be with Cha-kwena! What harm can come to me when I am with my shaman?"

Cha-kwena was shocked by her audaciousness. "No woman can be like First Woman! She is Mother to all of the generations of the People. How can a half-formed little thing like you presume to walk in the shadow of First woman's memory?"

The words found their mark. "I will not be half-formed *forever*, Cha-kwena," she whispered.

Immediately he regretted his insult. What was it about her trembling chin and the tears in her large, soft brown eyes that made him feel so contrite? He had said nothing that was not the truth!

Perhaps she did have a bit more of the hunter in her than was present in an ordinary female. During the war between the peoples of the north and south, she had tricked one of the most powerful warriors of the People of the Watching Star into plunging over a cliff and to his death.

But, Cha-kwena decided, such tendencies should not be encouraged. In the Land of Grass, there had once been a female hunter and shaman of immense power. All men who came before Ysuna, Daughter of the Sun, were bent and twisted and broken to serve her will. "No!" he told Mah-ree. "Before we left the Red World it was determined that those who walk in this new land must be strong in the ways of the ancestors! Kosar-eh may teach his boys to hunt, and he may use a spear to protect himself and others. But he may not hunt with a spear nor teach a girl to use one!"

"But—"

"The forces of Creation chose Kosar-eh to carry the burden of a crippled arm and to wear scars upon his face so that he might be a clown, not a hunter. It is his path to make our people laugh and to lighten our hearts in times of hardship. He is—''

''A man who would be offended to hear you speak so of him!''

''No. I speak in the way of the ancestors, Mah-ree. I speak as Shaman! I have sworn by the power of the sacred stones to keep the old ways. And you know as well as I that the old ways teach that a man who has been disabled on the hunt is forever set apart from other men. He cannot take or keep the woman of his choice but must content himself with aged widows whose lives will not be considered a loss to the band if he fails to provide for them. From the moment of his disabling he may not hunt with a spear again! If he does, his prey will see his scars and ruined bones and be so offended that they will run away and refuse to die upon the spears of the other hunters. If this happens, the women and children of this band will go hungry.''

Mah-ree sulked. ''In this new land of little rain to which Cha-kwena has led us, the women and children of this band are already hungry. Can the spear of one man— even if he is shaman—bring down enough meat for all?''

There were times when Cha-kwena disliked Mah-ree intensely; this was one of them. ''Soon we will come into better country.''

Her chin ceased to quiver. Her hair, cropped straight across her brow and cut to just below her ears in the mandatory fashion of a girl child, shone as blue as a blackbird's wings where the sun's rays played on the thick dark strands. The tears were gone from her eyes. ''I believe this, Cha-kwena. I believe this because you say it.''

He held out his hand. Their eyes met. She knew what he wanted of her. She gave him her spear.

He nodded, satisfied. He liked her better now. ''I will talk to Kosar-eh. I will remind him that he has five sons . . . and that Mah-ree is not one of them.''

Her head went high. ''Do not be angry with him, Cha-kwena. Remember Kosar-eh went with my father to rescue Ta-maya from those who intended her to be meat for their storm god. No one spoke to him then of the ways of the ancestors or thought to deny him the use of a spear. Even after my father was killed, Kosar-eh bravely won the name Spits in the Face of Enemies. He fought for Ta-maya's life when even Bold Man was afraid!''

Cha-kwena winced at the reference to Dakan-eh. There was a time when the young shaman would have given anything to be like Dakan-eh—to stand tall and arrogant beneath the sun, to be fleet of foot and fine of face and form, with a body as tawny and well-made as a cougar's. He had wished to possess that same look of ever-present hunger in the arrangement of his eyes and mouth so that even when he slept he appeared to be stalking prey in his dreams, ready to spring to action, to prove himself to be the greatest hunter in the land of the ancestors.

But a day had come when the People of the Red World had discovered that beyond their land were other lands, other people. And from the moment Dakan-eh set eyes upon the big-game hunters of the north, he had known that he was a cougar among lions. That was not good enough for Dakan-eh. In the way of a serpent, he had forced himself to accommodate a larger skin, one that marked him as a man of another tribe. He wantonly abandoned the culture of the Ancient Ones in order to win his place among man-hunting, mammoth-killing strangers. During the war this had proved to be a good thing. In order to survive against their enemy, even Cha-kwena, barely fourteen, had been forced to become a warrior. But in the end he had set aside the warlike ways and returned to the traditions of the ancestors. Dakan-eh, on the other hand, had chosen to remain a lion and had led many of his people to believe that they might be lions, too.

A strong sense of guilt washed over Cha-kwena now, and his free hand went up to his medicine bag. He knew he had done the right thing by taking the sacred stone out of Dakan-eh's reach. Bold Man might have commanded his shaman to put the power of the stones to terrible use. Many people in the Land of Grass believed that if the great white mammoth, Life Giver, were hunted and killed, those who ate its flesh and drank its blood would become immortal and as powerful as the totem. To that end, Masau had made spearheads of chalcedony—''magic'' white-crystal spearheads reputedly the only weapons capable of killing the totem. Cha-kwena feared that Dakan-eh's ambition would impel him to join forces with such believers.

When the forces of Creation had conspired to place the spearheads into Cha-kwena's protection and the Four Winds had whispered warnings to him in his dreams, the young shaman had taken action: He had packed the spearheads and the sacred stone and, following his totem, put all potential enemies behind him. Even if Dakan-eh had tried to follow him, the storms of winter would have obliterated the trail of his little band. There, beyond the Mountains of Sand, at the edge of the world, Cha-kwena and his people were safe, and the great white mammoth, protected by the shaman, would live forever.

Cha-kwena sighed. It had been a terrible decision for a young man to make. No matter how just his cause, he had left Dakan-eh's band with no sacred relic and no shaman. Without a liaison to the spirits, Bold Man's people may well have been robbed of all success in life. He told himself that he should not care, but he *did* care.

"Cha-kwena! Listen!" Mah-ree's command drew the young man from his reverie.

Coyote was howling again on the far side of the mountain. Somewhere to the east a mammoth was trumpeting. The sound of the giant tusker filled Cha-kwena's heart with gladness. "I'm going to see where—"

"I'm coming, too," interrupted the girl.

Cha-kwena was not offended; he was already moving forward and had put her from his mind.

They reached the summit just in time to see Coyote disappear down a wide, gravelly draw that dropped steeply away into a shadowed canyon thick with broken stands of stunted evergreens. A soft, hot wind was rising from below, carrying the pungent smell of sage and artemisia, the rich, resinous aromas of ancient conifers and junipers, and the peculiarly sweet, dank, mildewy smell of decomposing leaves and acorn mast lying thick over moist loam.

Mah-ree leaned forward slightly, drew in the scent of the wind, then looked up hopefully at Cha-kwena.

He nodded in affirmation of her unspoken query. *Yes. I can smell it, too. Moisture!* Somewhere down there Coyote was steadily leading his human spirit brother to water! Hope flared briefly, then was gone. A cold, sweet creek of any size at all would, he knew, welcome moisture-seeking trees to grow along its banks: willows, alders, wide-leaved sycamores, and cottonwoods. He saw none of these. His mouth went dry. He knew what he would find: seeps of moisture from some dying spring deep within the mountain—just enough to sustain life but not enough to allow it to flourish.

Cha-kwena's brow furrowed. In his village by the shrinking shores of the Lake of Many Singing Birds, the land was drying up like an old woman when her last passage of moon blood has ceased. The Red World, which had been a cool, verdant grassland surrounding a vast inland sea in the days of the ancestors, was almost a desert by the time of Cha-kwena's birth. No one, not even old Hoyeh-tay, knew why.

Was I wrong, he wondered, *to think that I could find a better land than that into which I was born?* He had rightfully castigated Mah-ree for emulating the legendary ways of First Woman; but by daring to imagine that he might lead his people into unknown country and to a better life, had he not put himself into the sandals of First Man?

Mah-ree saw his self-doubt. "When the totem left the Red World, my shaman could not stay behind. As long as Life Giver walks before us, the spirits of the ancestors will smile upon the People. You will see!"

Cha-kwena appreciated her optimism. Now, drawing in a steadying breath, he stared into the green depths of the canyon. He was hopeful that the mammoth would trumpet again, but the only sounds on the mountain were the whispering of the wind and, well below, the occasional raucous scolding of crested jays and red-capped woodpeckers.

"Does Little Yellow Wolf wish us to follow him?" Mah-ree asked.

"No, it is too dry a canyon. Coyote may live in it with Cougar and Lynx, but it will be a hard, thirsty life as they compete for the meager meat of Rat and Hare, of Bird and Mouse, of Snake and Lizard."

"We have been living on less than that, Cha-kwena. If

my shaman wishes to follow Coyote and hunt, Mah-ree will not be afraid!''

At that very moment a white-headed eagle broke through the canopy of the trees below. As it flew upward out of the canyon, Cha-kwena was certain that the bird was coming directly at them. He was right. The eagle came so close that both Mah-ree and he were forced to dodge it. A moment later it was soaring high, its broad, dark wings spreading wide, its tail and head showing white in the light of the sun. It shrilled and *kleek*ed and soared, drawing Cha-kwena's eyes across the terrain. It was a world of such vast dimensions that the young shaman was spellbound.

With his attention drawn to the beauty of the world stretching wide before him, he was finding it difficult not to spread his arms and fly away after the eagle. Away toward the shimmering curve of the horizon! Away over the very edge of the world to only the eagle and the Four Winds knew where! Away over immense, broken spans of ochre badlands, over purple cinder cones, over black and rust-red lava flows, over an astoundingly huge white expanse of an enormous dry lake, which, save for a few stagnant sink-holes, was all that remained of an ancient inland sea.

As Cha-kwena looked at it, his mouth felt parched, and his spirit withered. The land was similar to but more desolate than the one he had left behind. He shook his head, despondent.

Then, his gaze still following the flight of the eagle, he turned north, blinked, and stared. There, on the horizon, through a haze of distance and heat, he saw a distinct mass of blue and purple rising under a pale gray wash of clouds. *Mountains!* Long, broad, high-shouldered mountains! Taller and more massive than the wondrous Blue Mesas of his homeland! And of a color that spoke of highland forests and foothills thickly furred and watered!

Cha-kwena salivated. There would be game in those mountains! Squinting across the distances, he saw the glistening, fingerlike, downward extensions that betrayed deep accumulations of snow in the folds of the upper reaches of the peaks. Excitement stirred him because where

cloud and snow spirits dwelled, rain spirits and melting
water spirits dwelled also. There would be cold springs in
those distant hills and canyons, and freshets and streams—
perhaps even tumbling, rushing rivers and shining lakes.
Clear and sweet, they would welcome wintering waterfowl,
fishing eagles, and bone-weary travelers who had journeyed
long and far across a parched and hostile land in which
Cha-kwena had seen no sign of other human beings or
found any hope of respite . . . until now.

Once again a mammoth trumpeted. Its high, ear-
piercing cry cracked the stillness of the day. No other
creature in all of this world or the world beyond could make
such a sound. Mah-ree pointed to its source, a pale,
lumbering form emerging from the scrub growth at the base
of the canyon. It walked toward the east and to distant
mountains.

"At last I see you again, Life Giver, Great Ghost
Spirit, Grandfather of All, Guardian of First Man and First
Woman and of all the Ancestors, Totem!" He sighed the
names, shivering as he spoke. No matter how many times he
set eyes upon the great white mammoth, he was awed by its
appearance and immensity. The tusker was the color of
snow at winter's end, after the wind has grayed it with
blown dust. Scarred from many a successful battle for
mating supremacy over lesser bulls, it stood some eighteen
feet tall at the shoulders, and its inwardly curling tusks were
nearly as long as the beast was tall.

The giant might have been a shaman's vision or a
mammoth hunter's nightmare. But as Cha-kwena stared
down at it, the young shaman knew that it was real enough.
Since time beyond beginning Life Giver had walked the
world of men—flesh and blood and bone—the physical
manifestation of spirit. And as long as Cha-kwena possessed
the sacred stone and kept the magic spearheads from his
enemies, the totem would be immortal. Cha-kwena felt
stronger just looking at it.

"I knew you would find him, Cha-kwena!" exalted
Mah-ree.

The young shaman turned his face to the sun and
thanked Father Above for having answered his prayers.

Then he looked down into the canyon again, searching for Coyote. He wanted to praise his spirit brother for having drawn him there, but Little Yellow Wolf had vanished in the green depths. There was only Life Giver. For Cha-kwena, that was enough.

Then, out of nowhere, a single cloud formed and drifted across the autumn sun, causing a shadow to fall upon the world. From far below, Coyote yapped once, then was still. Not for the first time this day, the sound communicated warning to Cha-kwena. But of what?

His hand grasped his medicine bag. Contact with the talisman within caused an instant flaring of vision: He saw a bold, young lion roaring in defiance at the sun. And then the lion was transformed into Dakan-eh, clothed in a coyote's skin. Cha-kwena saw Bold Man roaring in defiance, grief, and furious anger as he waved a bloodied spear and raged, *Cha-kwena! I will find you! I will take back the sacred stone! I will have Ta-maya, the woman who should have been mine! You follow a dying totem! And with my own hand I will haft the magic spearheads and slay the mammoth! Then I will be shaman! You will be dead! And no man will be able to turn my luck against me!*

Cha-kwena gasped. The vision stabbed him, hurt him. And then, suddenly it was gone.

Beside him, Mah-ree was smiling radiantly. "We must go back and tell the others to prepare for the journey to the far mountains into which our totem is leading us."

Cha-kwena nodded. It would be a long trek around the peak and across the dry lake to get to their destination. His eyes narrowed and fixed on the great white mammoth. How old Life Giver was—as old as the peak upon which Cha-kwena stood, as old as the land upon which he trod, as old as the mountains toward which he was heading.

You follow a dying totem!

Cha-kwena flinched at the words Dakan-eh had shouted out of his vision.

"No!" he shouted back. "I will not believe it!"

But as Mah-ree eyed him curiously, worriedly, he knew he did believe it. The enormity of the number of years that the mammoth had lived weighted Cha-kwena and frightened him. He found himself asking a question that no shaman who claimed the mammoth as totem should ask: Was it possible for any beast to live forever?

"Yes!" he replied defensively, for he had not forgotten his grandfather's warning that if the great white mammoth died, the People would also perish. "Life Giver *will* live as long as Cha-kwena is shaman and Bold Man of the Red World is content to remain a lion in the far country beneath the Watching Star!"

"Why do you speak so, Cha-kwena?" Mah-ree demanded. "Surely you do not think that Dakan-eh is following us?"

He did not answer. Once again he turned his face to the now clouded sun and spoke aloud to Father Above. "Whatever I have seen with the inner eye that lights a shaman's vision, the forces of Creation know what is in my heart: I wish Dakan-eh no more bad luck than he may already have brought upon himself!"

Mah-ree's eyes went round with fear. "What are you saying, Cha-kwena? Have you forgotten what the ancestors have counseled? Speak aloud against no man, lest his helping spirits turn your words against you instead!"

He had not forgotten; but she had not seen his vision, nor would he tell her of it. "I have not spoken against him," he replied tersely.

"Your words held more curse than blessing, Cha-kwena."

"I do not curse lions, nor do I bless them. They are what the forces of Creation have made them. They will live and hunt as they must."

Her brow furrowed. She thought for a moment, then whispered with obvious dread, "Are they hunting *us*, Cha-kwena?"

He did not reply.

"Dakan-eh is not a lion," she declared emphatically. "He has chosen the way he would walk and the animal he would name as totem."

"As have I," responded Cha-kwena evenly.

"Yes, but if vision has shown my shaman that lions are hunting us, then we must not linger here. Life Giver walks toward distant mountains. We must follow."

The single cloud that had drifted before the sun evaporated, allowing intense light to pour across the world. Because the return of the sun could be construed only as a good omen, he felt better. Perhaps his vision had been nothing more than a resurfacing of old fears. Mah-ree was right. Why would Dakan-eh be following now when, after so many moons, there had been no sign of him? The vision made no sense.

He sucked in deep, nourishing breaths. He held the hot air captive, allowing it to warm his blood and send pure, bright energy into his brain. Coyote was silent now, but now Spirit Brother had led Cha-kwena to his totem, the little yellow wolf was free to go his own way within the green woodland at the base of the canyon.

Cha-kwena exhaled with explosive relief. He felt rejuvenated, righteous in his chosen course. Life Giver plodded toward mountains that promised water and to be rich with game. Surely the great white mammoth was leading his people to a new homeland!

"Come," he said to Mah-ree, setting his hand upon her bare shoulder and turning her in the direction of the encampment. "By tomorrow's dawn we will be on our way to the new and better land where our enemies and the lions of the Red World will never find us!"

3

"Aiyee!"

There was heartrending wailing on the riverbank beside the village that had been consumed by the whirling wind. Great gouges in the earth marked the place where, only hours before, over a hundred lodges had stood. Lahontay, eldest hunter among the many bands that had assembled for the huge bison hunt, had saved the women, children, and other elders from the passage of the storms; but there was no cause for celebration as the survivors of the wrath of Thunder in the Sky emerged from the cave to greet those who came to them from across the ravaged grassland.

"Aiyee!" was the moan that issued from the women and old men as they searched in vain for loved ones and walked like ghosts through their ruined village. The cherished belongings of a lifetime had been destroyed and strewn across the plain, along with the bodies of dead men and bison.

Now, before the full madness of grief descended upon his people, Shateh commanded them to bring the corpses and the wounded into the area of the storm-blasted cottonwoods that lined the river's edge. Already Raven and his clan were gathering.

Never had Dakan-eh seen so many ravens—not even in the days immediately following the war between the tribes when slain women, children, and warriors had made plentiful food for carrion eaters. He paused. Pah-la and Ban-ya were hurrying toward him. He was in no hurry to receive their greeting; he knew that he was about to be abraded with tearful embraces and scalded by his mother's tears. His slave, Sheela, lagged behind, not so happy he was alive.

Bold Man's eyes narrowed as he scanned the sky. Shifting the weight of the coyote carcass upon his shoulder and hefting his father's cruelly maimed and broken body into a more manageable position within his arms, he scowled up at the dark-winged, black, shrieking harbingers and affirmers of death. He had lived among the bison hunters long enough to know that Raven and his kind always gathered after every major hunt. Raven led his clan to follow the great herds even as men and wolves and lions followed them, for when the hunt was done, there were always leftovers for Raven to feast upon.

What sort of flesh would bloody the long, black beaks and talons of Raven today, Dakan-eh wondered—the flesh of men or beasts, predator or prey? *Both*, he realized, if the dead hunters were not carried into the protection of their families quickly enough.

Beside him, young Hah-ri, ashen faced and shaking, was still in shock. "So many," he whispered, looking up at the birds. "Do they follow the storm spirits in the same way that they follow the herds?"

"I am your headman, not your shaman!" Dakan-eh snapped as his women reached him. With a cry that cut him deeply despite his resolve not to be moved, Pah-la rushed to him and embraced the body of his father. Though not tall, she was well fed; she nearly knocked him down.

"Owa-neh! Owa-neh!" Pah-la shrieked the name of her beloved. "Man of my heart! This cannot be! This cannot be! This—"

"*Is!*" Dakan-eh cut off his mother's lamentations. "Come. We will take my father to the shade of the grove below the village as Shateh has commanded." He broke into a long stride, hoping that Pah-la would fall behind. But she kept up, plucking at her man, mewling over him now, repeating that his death could not be.

Ban-ya, with little Piku-neh hefted on her hip, looked with love and relief at Dakan-eh. "It is good to see that my man has returned from the hunt this day," she said, walking beside Pah-la. Ban-ya stroked the older woman's buckskin-clad back in a vain attempt to offer comfort. The fat-cheeked little boy reached out to Dakan-eh, but Bold Man's heart was cold to the child; Piku-neh still drew nourishment from Ban-ya's breasts—and as long as the child nursed, its father was, by the laws of the bison hunters, prevented from taking pleasure on his woman.

That left only Sheela.

Bold Man's scowl sent the toddler shrinking away. Although he took pride that Piku-neh was a male, he had no patience with babies. They stank of urine, were generally disruptive, and, if left without a loin wrap, dropped turds about the lodge. He was impatient for his son to reach an age of acceptability—in his opinion children became human at about four years of age—because he preferred a clean, orderly lodge in which his own needs were the center of all concern.

But Piku-neh—if the boy's father was ever honored by the elders with full acceptance into this new tribe—was considered the future of the People. The importance of Ban-ya's attendance upon her male child therefore superseded all other obligations, even those to her man.

Dakan-eh grimaced as he walked on. He should have brought more than one wife with him from the Red World, and he should have taken more female war captives . . . or at least been gentler in his handling of the three he had taken. Until Piku-neh was weaned, Bold Man had only one slave left to serve him—and a man with only one slave and one wife was pitied in this land where a hunter's worth was measured in the number of women for whom he could hunt and upon whom he could make sons. Sheela, in the manner of a well-trained, albeit perpetually surly slave, walked close at Ban-ya's side so that she might readily respond to the whims of her master's wife.

Dakan-eh was painfully aware of his origins and of the minimal size of his own family. Around him the many wives and female slaves of the hunters and warriors of the Land of Grass joined their men and offered solace to those who brought the dead and wounded to the shade of the cottonwoods. As these women of the broad plains keened in high, ferocious lamentation, Pah-la's pathetic whimpering offended Dakan-eh's ears. How could she moan like an eviscerated animal that had lost the strength to scream? If he had not been burdened with Owa-neh's body, he would have struck her down.

"You are no longer in the Red World, woman!" He growled his rebuke, refusing to call her Mother. "You are now of the Land of Grass! Stand tall! Make the proper sounds of mourning for Owa-neh, father of this brave hunter!"

Pah-la gave no sign of having heard her son's command. She kept touching the body in Dakan-eh's arms, assuring Owa-neh's corpse that he was alive and that when he woke she would tend his wounds and bring him oil of willow to ease his pain. Sunlight played on the tiny gold nuggets of her nose ring, but not even the reflection of the sun lent color to her pale face or lips.

Dakan-eh was not surprised when his mother swooned. Nor did he feel pity for her. He was mortified and would have left her where she lay. But Ban-ya, anticipating Pah-la's fainting spell, quickly handed Piku-neh to Sheela, then slipped a strong young arm beneath the older woman's fleshy armpit.

"Walk proudly, Mother!" insisted Ban-ya sternly, pinching Pah-la's cheeks as she forced the older woman to keep moving. "How will our Dakan-eh ever become a chief in this far country if his women appear weak in the eyes of others?" This said, she obliged Dakan-eh by beginning to wail and trill in the way of the women of the Land of Grass.

Bold Man appreciated what he heard and saw. All things considered, he was glad that Ban-ya had survived the wrath of the whirling wind. A woman of such strength, insight, and loyalty would not be easily replaced. Even though she had not been his first choice for an all-the-time woman, he had to concede that since agreeing to walk with him out of the land of the ancestors, she had not displeased him. Ban-ya had adapted to the traditions of her new homeland without hesitation or complaint, even casting away most of the many fine garments that she had brought from the Red World so that she might take on the simpler dress of the women of the northern tribes.

Today she wore the loose-fitting garment of a nursing mother—a summer tunic open seamed from her neck to her waist, then laced across her breasts so that she might yield ready access to the questing hands and mouth of her suckling. In Ban-ya's haste to assist Pah-la, she had neglected to retie the lacings after passing Piku-neh to Sheela. Dakan-eh saw Ban-ya's breasts swinging free as she strained to support Pah-la. Dakan-eh's loins went hot and hard at the sight of them—heavy, moist, with a thin veneer of sweat that caught the light of the sun.

He looked away quickly. What was the matter with him? This was no time to think of coupling! What would Shateh say if he were to see Bold Man's sexual arousal after he had already castigated Dakan-eh once this day for his failure to show grief? His father lay dead in his arms! His mother was in shock. His body was bruised and aching from his ordeal in the ravine! But his penis was up and ready. He was not certain whether he should curse or congratulate himself.

Dakan-eh lowered his arms and allowed Owa-neh's corpse to slump downward until the dead man's flanks and buttocks covered Bold Man's own loins. No one must see him like this! But it was too late. He felt someone staring at him. Dakan-eh looked to see that his slave, Sheela, was smirking at him.

Glaring past Ban-ya and Pah-la, Bold Man's face twisted with open irritation. "What do you stare at, slave?"

The tall young woman's expression did not change. "At nothing of value."

Dakan-eh flushed; he was grateful that Ban-ya was too busy ministering to Pah-la to have heard the insult. His eyes narrowed dangerously. "You will say nothing of what you have seen."

Her smirk became a leer. "I assure you, this woman has seen nothing worth speaking of in the bared bone of your manhood."

Had she been within striking range and had his arms been free, he would have knocked her down, even though this would have unseated Piku-neh. The child sat astride Sheela's shoulders, with his hands gripping the two shoulder-length braided forelocks on either side of her comely face. The style identified her as a slave, for the People of the Land of Grass believed that a portion of the life force of each man, woman, and child lived within their hair. Cut the hair and kill the spirit, they said. Cut only half the hair, and kill only half the spirit—the half in which lived the will to resist enslavement.

"Take that smile from your mouth," he commanded savagely, "or I will cut off the remainder of your hair and set your life spirit free to join your sister, Rikiree, in the world beyond this world!"

Sheela did not flinch at his warning or at the mention of her dead sister's name. She did not break stride. Her eyes half-closed and her smile faded as she turned her face away—although not in time to prevent him from glimpsing

sadness and hatred pool beneath her lids like water drawn
up from the depths of a bitter spring.

He snorted with satisfaction. *Good!* It gave him pleasure to hurt Sheela. She was a rare beauty, but he did not
like her—he had never liked her. There was something
about this woman of his enemies, the People of the
Watching Star, that set her apart from other females—she
possessed a quiet, measuring watchfulness and proud,
contemptuous bearing that often motivated him to take her
down and humble her through rape.

His mouth tightened as he observed her profile. Now,
as on the day she had been taken into captivity along with
her younger sister, something about Sheela's face reminded
him of someone else. . . . Ta-maya, beautiful Ta-maya,
who had twice spurned him . . . who had run away with a
boy shaman and a crippled clown rather than accept
Dakan-eh as her man!

Somehow, Sheela's resemblance to Ta-maya lightened
the terrible burden of his humiliation. He found himself
sneering, glad that Ban-ya often beat Sheela about the head
and shoulders with stirring bones and sage-stalk brooms. He
felt paid back in some measure because other men eyed this
slave with lust and because the customs of this land allowed
him to share her with them. He did so often, to shame and
degrade her as he would shame and humiliate Ta-maya for
her unwarranted rejection of him.

His jaws clenched. How could she have refused him?
How? He was the best man among all men! No woman
except Ta-maya had turned her back upon him. *No!* He
would not think of her! Thoughts of her always unmanned
him. Perhaps, at this moment, however, this was just as
well; his organ was down and cool again.

He reached the cottonwoods at last, and as the weight
of his father's corpse brought his aching, fatigued body to
his knees, he looked up to see Shateh walking toward him.

"To see the whirling wind in the time of the Dry Grass
Moon is a rare thing." The chieftain's tone and expression
were grim as he scanned the ravaged grassland. His women
searched for the missing corpse of Kalawak. The pathetic

women of Na-sei, meanwhile, looked for their lost son and husband, and Nakantahkeh, father of Na-sei's woman, stood by. Shateh scowled and turned away from their tragic quest. "Never has this man seen anything as devastating as this. Men have died on hunts and in war, but always the injured have had a village to return to, in which to heal and grow strong again. What have my people done to call down the wrath of the storm spirits or to rouse the anger of Thunder in the Sky?"

Shateh was not the only chief standing in the shade of the tree. The leaders of all the assembled bands were present. But no one presumed to answer. They were too appalled by his admission of doubts. Shateh was chief above all chiefs, the heart of the entire tribe. If his strength faltered, how could the People be strong enough to look with hope upon tomorrow?

No one dared to shame Shateh by replying to his runaway words . . . no one except the ravens that circled and cawed overhead and Atonashkeh.

The chieftain's son stood tall, imperious, fixing his sharp and dangerous gaze upon the still-kneeling Dakan-eh. "Shateh has brought lizard eaters into the Land of Grass! What else is there to understand? Their presence is an affront to the spirits of the ancestors, my father! Now the spirits have spoken. Now my brother, Kalawak, is dead. Now the village of the many bands is no more. Now—"

"Enough!" Shateh brought his son to instant silence and, for the second time in one day, openly chastised Atonashkeh in front of the others. "Would a son of Shateh impugn his father's wisdom? Would one who is neither chief nor shaman presume to speak as both?"

To the amazement of all who had gathered in the shade of the trees, it was Sheela who spoke out in bold reply. "Shateh is a great chief, and Shateh is also a shaman. Shateh must know that it is what his people have *failed* to do that has offended Thunder in the Sky. Since the war between the tribes, no human meat has been offered to Thunder in the Sky. Why then is Shateh mystified because Great Spirit Father hungers for flesh? This day Thunder in the Sky has loosed his anger upon those who wantonly feed upon his offspring—the great mammoth and the long-horned bison—but refuse to reciprocate by offering that which is most precious to them, the flesh and blood of their virgin daughters of childbearing years.''

A stunned silence settled at the edge of the grove. No one had ever heard a woman, much less a slave, speak so; Sheela stood proudly before them as she continued her reckless tirade.

''You have killed the People of the Watching Star because we stole your daughters and sacrificed them to the Great Spirit Father. You had neither the courage nor the stomach for it, so you let us do it for you. You enjoyed the benefits as you turned away in self-righteousness. The People of the Watching Star, led by our high priestess Ysuna and our mystic warrior Masau, made life good through war and sacrifice! Now Ysuna and Masau are dead. You have killed them! Now the bad times come again! Behold! The truth is all around!''

The blow that sent Sheela reeling did not come from Shateh, Dakan-eh, or any man of the Red World or the Land of Grass. It was Ban-ya who rose from where she had been crouching beside the still whimpering Pah-la. Ban-ya swung her son from Sheela's shoulders, placed him on his feet beside her, then, without warning, struck the slave a hard right uppercut to the jaw. Sheela went down.

''Never again will the bloodthirsty ways of your tribe be the ways of the people of this land or any other,'' Ban-ya vowed. ''And if you ever again open your arrogant mouth to speak without the permission of our man, I will beg his permission to use my skinning dagger and sacrifice you myself!''

A girl on the brink of womanhood hurried forward to kick Sheela hard on the flank. ''My dagger will leap to work with yours, woman of Bold Man!'' she cried, then danced back from the stunned slave. The girl's eyes flashed with satisfaction as many a voice was raised and many a hand clapped in approval. The affirmations emboldened the child even further. She was Wila, younger daughter of Nakan-tahkeh. ''If poor, brave Na-sei is not found alive, then my sister, Lehana, will be a widow, and everyone will know that the bad luck of the People of the Land of Grass will be *her* fault—Sheela's fault, hers and her murdering people's!''

Sheela sat up, one hand tentatively testing her jaw. Blood seeped between her long fingers as she took hateful measure of the girl.

Atonashkeh's face displayed similar animosity toward Wila for having taken the tribe's focus away from the man he had come to view as his rival. ''The younger daughter of Nakantahkeh has big opinions for one so small and unfit to speak before the chieftain! Nakantahkeh will hear of this, and he will wonder why Wila has not joined him and her sister in this time of sadness.''

''I stay behind at Nakantahkeh's command, to be with my mother, who fell and turned her ankle when Lahontay rushed us all to the cave!'' Wila's mouth puckered. ''And *I* do not speak against the wisdom of Shateh!'' she added defensively.

With an upraised hand, the chieftain silenced the bickerers, then spoke a solemn reminder to the battered slave. ''Had Thunder in the Sky been pleased by the offerings of the People of the Watching Star, he would have kept your tribe safe from its enemies. The thanksgiving ceremonies of my people's ancestors have always been satisfying to Great Spirit Father. He has kept peace with us. Behold! See the truth. It is all around. My people *have* suffered this day, but my tribe still lives. You are enslaved to them, and your tribe is no more.''

Shateh's eyes then rested speculatively on the tight, defensive expression on his son's face. Finally the chieftain's troubled gaze moved to settle upon Dakan-eh.

''You were brave today,'' Shateh allowed, ''but you were also defiant. Because of your refusal to heed my command, your father and a youth of your band are dead. Atonashkeh is right. Though I have named you Brother and honor you as Bold Man Who Chases the Whirling Wind, perhaps it *was* the defiance of a lizard-eating stranger that has offended Great Spirit Father and brought Raven and his clan to feed upon the dead.''

Dakan-eh flinched. He felt trapped, helpless. He had

not expected this reversal. A moment ago Shateh had been speaking for him; now he was siding with Atonashkeh—blood to blood.

He rose, stark naked, his hair still wet and streaming down his back, his body bloodied from his own scratches and abrasions and from the mortal wounds of his father. He did not seem to care; if anything, he stood taller, proud of his ravaged look—it made him feel like a survivor.

"I do not fear Raven or his kind!" he blurted hotly. "Let them come! As I have come! It was by Shateh's invitation that I have brought my band here! I have been obedient. I have been proud and eager to learn the ways of the People of the Land of Grass. I have hunted the long-horned bison, many times! I have hunted mammoth, many times! How then can I be the one upon whom the Great Spirit Father no longer smiles? On this day a man of *your* tribe was struck dead by lightning before I encouraged others to flee from the stampeding bison!"

Ban-ya, sidling close to him, whispered, "Dakan-eh, beware of what you say!"

"Let them hear! Let Shateh know that Dakan-eh runs before no man or animal and that when the time comes for me to die, I will meet Raven on my own terms, unafraid!" He was so taken with his rhetoric that he actually believed it. "Such a bold man makes the spirits smile and Great Spirit Father rejoice! If Na-sei had stayed within the ravine, who is to say that he would have survived? Many women here mourn those who have died *because* they obeyed Shateh's command."

Anger flashed in the chieftain's eyes.

Atonashkeh's head went up as though a wasp had stung him beneath his loin cover.

Sheela's hand moved away from her mouth, allowing everyone to see that she was smirking despite her pain.

The chiefs and shamans of the People of the Land of Grass exhaled in resentment and anger.

Seeing the hostile expressions of every man, woman, and child, Dakan-eh had to know that this time he had been too brave and bold for his own good. He had gone too far. Looking uncomfortable in his nakedness, he shifted the weight of the coyote carcass that still lay over his shoulder. Suddenly his face brightened, as if an idea had come to him. Afire with righteous indignation, he cried out, "If anyone has caused the tragedies of this day, it is one who is far away! If I possessed the sacred stone of my band and if the totem of my people still walked in the land of the ancestors, no one would have died this day, and the many lodges of Shateh would still be standing!"

"Is it so?" the chieftain pressed. "Yet was it not a mere youth who stole the sacred stone and totem from you?"

Dakan-eh flushed. "Not a boy—a spiteful, malicious shaman! Cha-kwena is to blame for this!" The accusation sounded so fine that he found himself embellishing it, growing strong upon it, believing it. He nodded, satisfied. "Yes, it must be so. Because I have left the Red World, Cha-kwena has turned against me as surely as he has turned against any man who hunts mammoth. He is jealous of our brave hearts. He was afraid to test his own spears against bison and mammoth, the only game worthy of the People of the Land of Grass! It is because of Cha-kwena that my father is dead and that the women of the many bands have cause to mourn!"

Before Shateh could reply, a terrible keening drew all eyes toward the decimated village. Ree-la, the widowed mother of Na-sei, threw herself to the ground just as Lehana, the wife of the young hunter, dropped to her knees. Nakantahkeh knelt beside his pregnant daughter as she raised her arms, uttered one high, plaintive wail of excruciating anguish, then fell across the mounded form before which Ree-la had just collapsed.

There was no doubt that they had found Na-sei's body—in whatever condition the angry sky had seen fit to return it to earth. Shateh thought of his own missing son, and lest grief smash him where he stood, he raised his arms, held them straight out, then lifted them to the sun. "May the forces of Creation grant that Lehana, woman of Na-sei and older daughter of Nakantahkeh, bring forth from her belly a male child, who may be named for one who has been taken by the whirling wind, so that the life spirit of Na-sei, man of the Red World, may come back to live again among the People through his son."

The other chieftains and shamans rose, assumed the posture of invocation, and echoed Shateh's words.

Someone spoke, but Shateh did not reply. His sorrow had silenced him. After all, how many sons could a man lose in one lifetime and still maintain the heart to endure? And if Spirit Sucker were to come to Shateh now, without newborn sons or grandsons to assume his name, the chieftain would die *forever*. His spirit would be denied all hope of access to walk ever again in the realm of the living.

Shateh looked suddenly old, weakened. If he were asked to mark the number of winters that he had seen since birth, he would have to hold up the fingers of both hands four times, and then raise the fingers of one hand yet again. It was a staggering number of years for any man to have lived.

"Where are the many sons who will mourn for me? All dead save one. All dead save Atonashkeh, maker of girl children—not of a single son!"

"Two of my women are big with babies!" protested Atonashkeh. "The old women say that both carry low and wide—a sure sign of sons! Come forward, women of Atonashkeh! Show Shateh that this is so!"

The women obeyed, but Shateh did not look at them. He stared unheeding at his son. The chieftain's eyes were focused inward. He saw his many sons—strong sons, to make a father proud. He ached at the recollection of all the sons that his many women had borne to him. All, save Atonashkeh, were dead, killed in war or on the hunt. Regret spread deep and wide, for despite his strength and virility, despite his secret invocations and best medicine, his women failed to give birth to male children.

Why? The question roused Shateh from his somber reverie. He looked up and stared fixedly at Dakan-eh. Had the alliance with the southern tribes caused his problems? This day he had seen disturbing qualities in Dakan-eh. The young headman was arrogant, quick to speak in anger, and harsh and unfeeling toward his women and slave. Na-sei lay dead; Owa-neh lay gutted and lifeless at his feet; his mother mourned. Yet Bold Man of the Red World stood unmoved. Shateh could find nothing worthy in the man's apparent lack of concern for anyone except himself.

"Perhaps it was a mistake for you to come to the Land of Grass," he surmised. "I will have to think about this. When the time of mourning is over, I will call a council. The shamans and chiefs and elders of the many tribes of the People of the Land of Grass will decide."

"Ay yah!" affirmed Atonashkeh, nostrils flaring in vindication.

Dakan-eh's eyes went so round that they stressed his lids. "This day I have looked into the belly of the whirling wind, and I have seen Cha-kwena in it!" Panic had taken his voice so high that it cracked and fell like a youth's. "Cha-kwena is the enemy of every man who has ever slain a mammoth! We must seek him out and kill him for what he has brought to us this day!"

"If the shaman Cha-kwena still lives, he is far from the Land of Grass," Shateh reminded quietly.

"He sends his spirit to us," Dakan-eh insisted. "He *lives!*"

"Perhaps," conceded Shateh, "but there are those in the Land of Grass who do not. Is Bold Man of the Red World such a brave hunter that his heart does not bleed for his dead?"

"My blood is hot for vengeance against one who has brought pain to the People of the Land of Grass!" Dakan-eh replied.

"His blood is cold!" refuted Atonashkeh with contempt and pleasure. "As cold as the blood of the lizards eaten by the woman from whose breast he sucked the milk of life!"

Had Ban-ya not grabbed his arm, Dakan-eh would have flown at the man. "No!" she cried. "It is not the time for this!"

Shateh appraised the woman expressionlessly. "You speak the words of truth, woman of the Red World. The dead are many. Their spirits must be honored. We must prepare to mourn them. Now."

4

Moon, Mother of Stars, was rising over the edge of the world. There was no rejoicing in the Land of Grass or in the heart of Dakan-eh. His mood was as dark as the night; and he knew it would not brighten even when the moon was fully risen.

For hours his band and he had been forced to stand apart and watch as the women and elders of the People of the Land of Grass moved over the dank earth, searching for dry wood within the wind-blasted groves; with their men and children and dogs to help them, they had dragged all that they could find to the place of Shateh's choosing—the center of what had once been the great hunting camp of the assembled bands.

The mourning fire burned high, nourished by oil salvaged from the ruined camp and by the downed lodgepoles of the devastated village. No man, woman, or child would ever dare to dwell beneath them again; the sky god had felled the poles, and so, along with the bison and mammoth hides that had covered them, they were given in the form of smoke to Thunder in the Sky, the Great Father.

Now Shateh's people circled and wailed and keened. The shamans of the various bands gathered to begin the solemn rites that would send the spirits of the dead to the world beyond this world. The beat of drums throbbed across the plains and in Dakan-eh's blood. Although he was bathed in the light of the great, smoking fire, Shateh had forbidden the band from the Red World to take part in the ceremonies.

"I would mourn in the way of Shateh's people!" Dakan-eh insisted not for the first time.

The chieftain, standing before him, would not be swayed. "I would ask this of no man or woman not born to our ways. There are pain, blood, much suffering."

"What Shateh endures, this man will endure! I am not afraid!" declared Dakan-eh.

The chieftain, with Atonashkeh and old Lahontay standing on either side of him, shook his head. "You, Bold Man, are not afraid of anything, it seems."

Dakan-eh winced. Once again he had been too bold, and he knew it; but what else was he to do? He had seen these men in mourning after the great war, witnessed their howling dances and shrieking self-mutilations and had secretly longed for and feared—the moment when he might dare to join them and prove his courage to them and to himself. Now the moment had come, and Dakan-eh was afraid of only one thing in this life: being condemned to live it as a lizard eater!

Shateh's expression hardened. His eyes strayed past the assembled hunters of the Red World, to the embankment above the river where their women and children clustered around the bodies of Owa-neh and Na-sei.

Dakan-eh flushed with shame. He cursed himself for having yielded to Pah-la's desire to lay out the bodies in the way of the Red World—not like the corpses of the men of the Land of Grass, upon hides of freshly skinned bison, but upon sleeping mats of woven reeds. His mother had managed to roll most of her family's belongings within the mats before fleeing the village.

Pah-la and Ree-la rubbed the cold, stiffening skin of their dead, meticulously salving and tending wounds that had been stitched and bandaged as though that savaged flesh might heal and spring to life again. Bold Man shook his head with humiliation as he observed the quiet, loving, gentle ministrations of the women of his band. Why could his women not behave in a manner similar to the grieving, shrieking women of the Land of Grass? Had they no passion in their blood?

"You may have no fear of our ways," said Shateh,

"but what of your own people? They have their own old and honored rituals at such a time as this."

"Our ways will become Shateh's ways!" informed Dakan-eh eagerly.

"Hmmph!" Atonashkeh's snort of contempt expressed his disbelief.

Close to Dakan-eh's left, Ma-nuk, eldest and strongest of the hunters who had come with him out of the Red World, glared at Shateh's son. "This man stands with Dakan-eh!" he said defensively. "The hunters of the Red World are not afraid to show their grief in the way of the People of the Land of Grass, whatever those ways may ask of us."

"Dakan-eh and his people cannot join us!" Old Lahontay was adamant. "Dakan-eh has no shaman to act on his behalf with the spirits of the dead in the world beyond this world. His ignorance of our ways will be an offense to the spirits of our ancestors and an insult to their own!"

Dakan-eh's last hope faded with the eldest hunter's words. Again he found cause to hate Cha-kwena.

Shateh nodded somberly. "Yes, it is so. The People of the Red World will stay here by the river, apart from the People of the Land of Grass. They will mourn their dead according to the customs of their ancestors. This is fitting. North Wind blows to the south this night; it will carry their grief to the spirits of the land from which they have come."

"I have made this land my land, this people *my* people!" Dakan-eh protested.

The ire in Shateh's eyes was intense. "You have made *nothing!* When the sun has risen and set four times, the time of mourning will be over. Then the elders will decide whether you will stay or go from this land. The *elders!* Not *you,* Lizard Eater!"

Dakan-eh stood shaking with helpless frustration while Shateh stalked away with Atonashkeh and Lahontay. They had shamed and insulted him before his own people. It did not matter that he had hunted and nearly died with them this day! He would always be a lizard eater, and unworthy to be one of them.

"Look at their shamans, Dakan-eh." The awestruck

exhalation came sighing from Ela-nay. "Perhaps it is just as well that we stand apart. Their ways are *not* our ways."

Dakan-eh did not speak; his contempt for the short, burly-armed Ela-nay was too great. On either side of him, the other hunters of the Red World were murmuring like trees shaken by a rising wind. He could not blame them. The scene before him took his own breath away.

The shamans were dancing in and out of the circling people. The flames sparked, exploded, leaped so high that the savage splendor of the moment set fire to Bold Man's blood and caused his memories of his own tribe's holy men to shrivel and pale in comparison. Never had he seen anything like this. *Never.*

Each naked shaman moved to the rhythm of his own spirit; each had painted his flesh with the ashes of the fire and with the blood of the dead. Shateh, the tallest and easily the most powerful, danced with the holy men. His body carried so many scars that not even the swirling, sacred patterns of blood and ash symbolizing life and death, could hide them. The scars added to his overwhelming physical presence by stating unmistakably that this was a man who had survived many hunts, many battles, many wars.

Dakan-eh's mouth pressed inward against his teeth as he experienced a malevolent surge of jealousy. How could a man of so many years appear so transcendently young and magnificent? It was almost as though the chieftain's slain son, the infamous mystic warrior Masau, was dancing before him. Bold Man growled with envy; before the great war, Ta-maya had shamed him by turning her back upon her promise to be his woman and giving herself to Masau instead. All women had wanted Masau. And now, as Dakan-eh glared at Shateh, he saw the way the women touched him as he passed through the circle, brushed against him as though his power might imbue them with the strength to bear them up for the intensity of the rites to come.

The families of the slain were coming forward to throw the salvaged belongings of their loved ones into the fire.

"For my brother Manatiba," cried a young warrior, "I

send his spears to the world beyond this world so that he may hunt proudly with his favorite weapons!''

"For Joteh, I send this winter robe, that my man may be warm in the snows of the country of the ancestors!'' wept a disconsolate woman.

"For Tekel, I send these moccasins, that he may walk the straight path back to me from the land of the dead and be born again in the child I carry!'' sobbed a young mother-to-be.

"For Nral, I send this dog, that my son may walk safely from serpents upon the sky trails and know always when predators are stalking him!''

Dakan-eh winced as the woman who had just spoken hefted a marrow joint and brained the dog that she had been leading by a tether; the animal had barely gone limp before she hurled it into the flames.

"For Tchanak, this woman comes . . . to be with him always in the world beyond this world, as she has been with him in this good life that we have shared since childhood!''

"No!'' someone screamed. "Mother, no!''

Dakan-eh's eyes went wide as a middle-aged woman pushed a younger woman back, then leaped without hesitation into the pyre. For a terrifying moment, he thought of Pah-la and looked around. He was relieved to find her still bending over Owa-neh's body. He turned back to the fire just in time to see the woman who had consigned herself to the flames appear as a dark silhouette, hair flying, arms upraised, before she was transformed into a human torch of white-heat and screaming light. And then she disappeared.

Her daughter collapsed, weeping, but the ceremony continued. Others simply stepped over and around her.

Dakan-eh could not move. The smell of meat was strong in the air—rank with burned fat and hair, and incinerated skin and nails—dog and human. The smoke from the fire had thickened and turned blue. Men came forward, dragging more wood for the flames. Women approached, too, to toss additional oil onto the pyre.

And now the shamans, led by Shateh, danced a new dance and sang a new song while the warriors beat upon

painted drums and chanted words and songs of encouragement and praise of what would happen next. Armed with
stone knives, the beaks and talons of raptorial birds, the
stabbing teeth of lions, and the claws of bears, the shamans
mutilated themselves as they waved their arms and limbs.

"Behold . . . true power . . . true beauty. . . ."

Dakan-eh was startled to hear the low, sibilant voice of
Sheela. He turned and met her narrowed, hate-filled eyes.
She had left the other women and must have forced her way
through his fellow hunters in order to stand shoulder to
shoulder with him. Even now Ma-nuk attempted to elbow
her back, but she would not budge.

Her voice was low, throaty, just loud enough for the
others to hear, and designed to sting as she leaned close to
Dakan-eh. "Behold the shamans of the Land of Grass.
Behold their blood. Behold their wounds. Behold their pain.
Behold their love! *They* take the pain of their people into
themselves. They will carry the scars of grief for their tribe.
Beside them, Bold Man . . . *Brave* Hunter . . . you and
your lizard-eating bandsmen are nothing!"

Had Dakan-eh not just suffered the indignity of
Shateh's repudiation, Sheela's provocation might have
passed with nothing more than a slap or a warning. But he
could not be shamed again in the eyes of his followers—not
if he intended to maintain their respect and his own dignity.
He felt them staring at him, waiting for him to react.

He entertained the notion of throwing her into the
flames as a "gift" to the departed life spirit of his father, but
the urge passed. Even if the mourning rituals had not been
forbidden to him, he would not have wished such a
truculent, vindictive, grudge-bearing female upon Owa-neh
in the world beyond this world. The dead deserved the best
of memorial gifts, not the worst. Besides, Dakan-eh knew a
better way to punish a woman . . . and to please himself
while doing it.

He had her by the wrist and jerked her through the
ranks of hunters, out of the firelight, beyond the sight of the
other women, into the deep darkness of the grove, and
down, down into the cool blackness of the trees that grew to

the river's edge. She did not resist; nothing she could say or do would turn him from his purpose.

With a brutal kick to her ankles, he tripped her and took her down upon the cold, rough stones of the shore. She gasped as she fell but did not fight him as he forced her onto her back and straddled her. Instead she glared up at him in the darkness and, as he pinned her wrists hurtfully to the ground, she showed her fine, white teeth and hissed at him in the manner of a trapped feline.

"How bold you are! How strong against this slave and enemy."

"Enemy?" Amused, he mocked her. "Hah! Yes! You *are* my enemy, Sheela, daughter of a dead tribe! And I fear you, woman, as I fear nothing else!"

"You should fear me, Bold Man. If you are wise you will kill me, as you have killed my sister—or someday I will find a way to give you cause to mourn the day you ever took her and—"

He lowered his head so quickly that she could not turn away. His forehead came down hard on her face, and light flared inside his head as his brow smashed into her nose and mouth. He felt her go limp beneath him. Dakan-eh cursed, realizing that he had opened a gash in his face on the sharp edge of her lower teeth. Yet, strangely, his pain pleased as much as it rankled him, for as he raised his head and looked down at his captive in the moon's light, he saw that he had broken her nose and split her lips much more severely than she had pierced his thin, tanned skin.

He smiled as he knelt back, raised his left hand, and explored the gash. Finding it minor, he wiped away the blood, then smeared it across Sheela's face, touched and pressed the smashed cartilage of her high-bridged nose, felt the warm ooze of blood welling from her torn mouth. When she moaned with pain, he was glad. Sheela had always hated him, but never as much as since the death of her much younger sister.

Why did she continue to blame him for Rikiree's death? The girl had become pregnant, then had refused his command to rid herself of the contents of her womb. A puking, whining burden, she had refused to spread herself for his pleasure or for the enjoyment of those men with whom he wished to share her. Irritated and perhaps more than a little jealous of the girl, Ban-ya had complained ceaselessly of Rikiree's insubordination and uselessness.

Dakan-eh frowned. Rikiree had been a pretty, childlike little thing. Even after she had become useless and sickly, he had enjoyed taunting her and forcing her to accept his man bone. But once his people had reached the Land of Grass, the taboos of the big-game hunters forbade intercourse with a pregnant female, and Dakan-eh had found his young slave to be of no value. Again he had insisted that she scour her womb so that he could take his rightful pleasure of a man's release into her. But by then her belly had been big, and the old women had warned that it was too late to abort the baby safely.

They had comforted him with reminders of his right to kill the unwanted infant after it was born or to kill the mother before she gave birth, if this was his desire. Bold Man could have killed Rikiree merely as punishment for her outrageous behavior. Indeed, he might well have done so had Sheela not begged for her sister's life and vowed to amend her own sullen ways if Rikiree was spared.

So, instead of killing the girl, Dakan-eh had taken up a skinning dagger and sawed off her remaining hair very close to her scalp to sap all strength and insolence out of her. Then, to please Ban-ya, he had given her away to old Nachumalena, the only man who had wanted her. Sheela had never forgiven him for that.

Alone with Rikiree within his lodge, the old man had conjured some ancient, mysterious shaman's magic to expel the fetus from her womb. It had been his right; no one would speak openly against him . . . but the old women had exchanged meaningful glances and whispered of dangers and pain associated with "the claw of taking."

Rikiree, deprived of the life spirit that lived within her hair, had somehow found enough strength to scream and scream against the invasion of her body by what Dakan-eh later learned was the curved, eight-inch digging claw of a giant ground sloth. He had been forced to bind Sheela's arms and legs in order to keep her from running to her sister's side.

Now, frowning, Dakan-eh touched Sheela's torn mouth. Still moaning, she was gradually coming out of her stupor and once again focusing her eyes upon his face. How dark they were. How full of loathing.

He could not understand her rancor toward him. Out of kindness, when Rikiree had nearly bled to death and fever spirits had come to feed upon her body, Dakan-eh had allowed Sheela to tend her young sister. Of course, as part of the bargain, she had been expected to yield service to Nachumalena. To the surprise of everyone in the village, Rikiree survived the old man's medicine. Sheela was sent back to Dakan-eh's lodge.

Afterwards Nachumalena had kept Rikiree confined to his lodge for many days and nights, allowing her to do no physical labor and feeding her chewed food out of his own mouth. All that he had required of Rikiree was that she spread herself and endlessly lead his "woman pleaser" to heights of gratification.

Dakan-eh would never understand what had motivated the girl to run howling into the night of the last full moon, or why bad spirits had driven her to leap into the river from the high, north-facing bluffs below which he now knelt upon her sister. As far as he was concerned, he had dealt more than fairly with the youngest of his slaves.

Now Rikiree and Nachumalena were both dead, and Sheela blamed him for the girl's death. But at this moment, with the sound of the river racing close by, with drumbeat throbbing in his veins, and with the ceremonial blaze lightening the night beyond the shadowed groves, firing his blood and temper, Dakan-eh did not care.

His organ was up and high and pulsating. He touched himself. How big he was! How quick to rise! Leering with pride, he removed his loin cover, raised Sheela's buckskin dress, repositioned himself, and, grateful that the woman was still stunned, opened her thighs and rammed deep.

He laughed when she sucked in her breath against the pain of his forced entry. Although she attempted to unseat him, she had no defense against his strength. He moved, probed, and pumped violently toward culmination.

Her only recourse was to insult him; the words came painfully, slowly through her battered mouth and loosened teeth. "How brave you are, Dakan-eh, to be able to take a man's pleasure on a slave while your people mourn and your mother weeps over the body of your father."

He would not be turned from his purpose. "Say no more. Move beneath me! Now!"

But she lay as motionless as a corpse. "Move? And give you cause to think that what you do pleases me?"

He did not care that she was trying to unman him. In fact, he barely heard her. His senses were focused within his loins, driving him toward that well-known peak over which he would soon plummet into a black, shivering ecstasy.

"What a slavering, rutting dog you are, Dakan-eh! In the past when I moved for you, I was thinking of *other* men . . . of Tsana of the Watching Star, and sometimes of Shateh. How small and wormlike is your man bone compared to theirs . . . or to that of the one called Mystic Warrior . . . Masau . . . the one who took Ta-maya from you."

These words Dakan-eh heard. They shattered his concentration. Even now, even *dead,* Mystic Warrior came to taunt him with his loss of Ta-maya and to stand between him and his pleasures with other women. Enraged, Dakan-eh fell short of completion and, without thinking, silenced Sheela with yet another brutal downward smash of his forehead. She went limp beneath him as his head whirled from the impact. The pain seemed a further insult. Still joined to her, Dakan-eh slapped her back from the edge of unconsciousness.

"Hold your tongue, or I will see you as dead as your sister and your tribe. You live only as long as it pleases me to let you live."

It was dark in the cottonwood grove, but the moon and stars and firelight combined to grant Dakan-eh a good view of Sheela's swollen, bloodied face. Still incoherent, she nevertheless attempted to spit her disdain at him. Despite his anger, he was impressed by her valor.

Although vain and arrogant, Dakan-eh was not always a brute with women. Since even before puberty his good looks had consistently attracted females, and he had never suffered a lack of sexual partners willing to oblige his every whim. With the exceptions of Ta-maya and Sheela, he had never known a woman who had not thrilled to his touch or longed for a liaison with him. Rape had been unnecessary—indeed, unheard of—until war, raiding, and the taking of captives introduced him to the violent, uniquely sensuous thrill of it.

Now, having overpowered and punished Sheela, he savored this moment of physical mastery and basked in the knowledge that in a moment he would come to completion inside her, whether she liked it or not. Beginning to move on her again, he allowed himself to feel sorry for her. She was so weak; he was so strong! He touched her mouth and nose, gently this time, and hoped that he had not ruined her beauty. Other men admired her as much as he, and he knew that he gained favor with the hunters of the Land of Grass every time he allowed them to ease themselves on her. Even though Sheela's appearance could not compare to Ta-maya's extraordinary beauty, the similarity in their features stirred him now, as it always did. His loins were hot again, his man bone engorged and seeking . . . until she bit him hard.

He snatched his hand away and stared at it. Her teeth had cut through to the bone of his right thumb. Furious, he struck her, mauled her with brutal poundings and twistings of her breasts and arms and belly. With every deep, uncompromising thrust, he inflicted more punishment. He drove to savage completion, and Sheela cried out in agony just as Ela-nay burst into the grove.

"Silence her!" Ela-nay's voice was strong with warning and concern. "Neither this man nor anyone else of the Red World knows the laws of the bison and mammoth eaters regarding the mating of man to woman on a night of mourning!"

Dakan-eh knelt back and, still joined to the ravaged Sheela, stared at the intruder. Proud that another man had observed the culmination of her well-deserved rape—even if the man was Ela-nay, for whom he held little respect—he said, "This is no woman. This is a *slave.*"

Anger twisted Ela-nay's wide, flat, unremarkable face. "In the Red World, it is forbidden to join with a woman on a night such as this!"

"I am headman. I will say what we will or will not do! And since when have you found the courage to speak against my will?"

The comment did not sit well with Ela-nay. His features tightened. He looked around the grove and toward the river, then spoke in a hushed and fearful voice. "Spirit Sucker walks the wind this night, waiting for the souls of those who have died and hungering for those among the seriously wounded who may not survive. To couple with a woman now, and like this, cannot be a good thing."

With a sneer of annoyance, Dakan-eh moved to work the last tremors of passion from his loins. "I have told you, this is Dakan-eh's *slave,* not his woman," he reminded.

Ela-nay came closer and stared down at Sheela. He caught his breath, dismayed by what he saw. "Her face . . . her beautiful face!"

"On the day we raided her village, you willingly traded her to me, Ela-nay. Now she is mine to do with as I will."

The man's eyes narrowed. "As you have said, you are headman. On that day you wanted my captive. On that day I yielded Sheela to you, but the choice was not mine to make . . . by the laws of the ancestors I was bound to make it."

Bold Man snorted, surprised. Ela-nay's behavior was puzzling; he was not usually a man to speak back to his woman or fellow hunters, let alone his headman.

Now Ela-nay's hands curled into fists. Staring at Sheela, his expression revealed his concern for her. "By treating even a slave like this," he said, "you shame her, Dakan-eh, and yourself."

"*She* has shamed *me.* I have brought her into this grove to punish her, not to reward her!" He withdrew from the woman, snatched up his loin cover, which Ban-ya had rescued from the village before the storm, and got to his feet. "If you want her, use her. Sate your man need. But do not forget to whom she belongs and do not speak in her defense again."

Ela-nay would not be swayed. "It is not good. It is not the way of the Red World. If our shaman were with us, he—"

"Cha-kwena is not with us! The Red World is far away! And since the time beyond beginning, the ancestral spirits for our people have taught that in changing times men must learn new ways or die! This I have done! This I will do!"

"The Creation stories are clear and true," Ela-nay said quietly. "First Man and First Woman kept no slaves. They did not raid the villages of other tribes. Their shaman and their totem did not abandon them. They mourned when their loved ones died. How can you take pleasure on a woman when this day has brought death to the People, Dakan-eh? What greater misfortune could there be for us?"

Dakan-eh snapped back hotly, "I will tell you what greater misfortune could befall us: We could still be eating lizards in the Red World!"

"I would gladly return there tomorrow!"

"Then go! I will not miss such a poor excuse for a man as you!" Securing his loin cover, Dakan-eh looked Ela-nay up and down with open contempt, shoved him out of the way, and began to stalk away.

"What of the slave? You cannot just leave her."

Dakan-eh stopped. "She will follow me when she is ready."

"You would leave her alone? Do you imagine that Raven and his clan were the only carnivores to have followed the whirling wind this day? There may be lions lurking near, or wolves or—"

Bold Man's mouth flexed with derision. "Protect her then. You have your spear and your skinning dagger with you. But your concern for this woman is wasted. She is nothing! Lie on her now if that is what you want. Then escort her safely back to me. But I warn you, speak to Shateh of what you have seen here this night, and you will not live to see the dawn!"

*   *   *

For a long while Ela-nay stood as he was, staring after Dakan-eh and regretting the day that he had allowed his woman to talk him into following Bold Man into this distant land.

"You are a bolder, braver man than he," Sheela told Ela-nay.

She reached out to him, and he tenderly took her arm and helped her as slowly, unsteadily, she climbed to her feet. Ela-nay was startled to see that the woman was half a head taller than he. He looked up at her. With the full light of the moon shining erratically through the wind-combed trees, her face was in shadow, then in light. He grimaced at what he saw—blood, black in the moonlight, and swollen, distorted features. Tomorrow's dawn would see her beauty gone. Who could say if it would ever be fully restored?

His heart swelled with pity and then with rage as, suddenly, he hung his head, ashamed to look at her. Another man . . . a braver man . . . a *better* man would have protected her from Dakan-eh's outrages. "Forgive me, woman. Forgive my yielding you to him. I would do anything to undo that day, anything!"

Her breathing was pained, shallow, as slowly she rested her hand upon his forearm. "Then flee with me across the Land of Grass. Take me away from him, away from all who have made war upon my tribe!"

Her words and her touch were almost more than he could bear; he wanted her so, loved her so, and despised himself for his weakness. "You cannot flee, Sheela. Wherever you go, your hair marks you as a slave. It would be the same life for you in any band."

"But you would be with me. Your strong spear arm will protect me from the slavers of other bands and from predators."

He was incredulous. "You would flee with *me*? With Ela-nay? A *lizard eater?*"

She nestled close, bent one knee so that she would not be so tall against him, and, sighing, rested her head upon his shoulder. "I would go with you, Ela-nay."

He had not expected this. "But where would we go?

How would we live without the protection of a band or tribe, with all of our enemies searching for us?''

"This land is not strange to me, Ela-nay. I know this place . . . these groves . . . these bluffs. To the south the river forks and bends toward the country of my ancestors and my people.''

"Your people are dead, Sheela," he reminded her gently.

"No." Swaying a little, she stepped back so that she could look at him as she spoke. "Shateh and Dakan-eh and their warriors have not killed them all. Before I was captured, plans were set for retreat and survival. Some bands still live—and I know where they gather. Run with me now, Ela-nay, before the wrath of Thunder in the Sky descends once more upon those who have degraded his favorite children—the People of the Watching Star. What have you to lose? A woman who nags and belittles you? Children who show you no respect? A band that will always be looked down upon by Shateh and his people?''

He was thrilled and terrified; his heart was thudding like that of a youth who has gone hunting in hope of winning a hare but has found himself capturing a lion instead. "Sheela, I . . . I am . . . uh, I have . . . I cannot do this.''

"How can you *not* do this? Dakan-eh is jealous of you, Ela-nay. He knows you are the better man, and stronger and more pleasing to the eyes of women, and more bold than he has ever dared to be!''

"I am?''

"Yes. And because you are wise and strong and bold, my people will embrace you as one of their own.''

"But I have opposed them in war.''

"It will not matter. The brothers and sisters of my tribe will not turn you away if you bring me safely to them.''

He frowned, suspicious, on edge. "I have lived among the warriors of the Land of Grass long enough to know that no man among them would put aside his enmity for the sake of a woman.''

Her face tightened from her injuries. Yet she went on urgently. "Not for the sake of a woman, true. But they would for me. I will tell you a secret that I have shared with no living spirit since I was made a captive: The daughter of my father's eldest brother was the one they called Ysuna, high priestess of the Watching Star. The blood that flowed in her flows in me—*only* in me. She had no children, and all of her father's and mother's line were slain in the great war. Those of my people who have survived the many raids of Shateh and Dakan-eh have no way of knowing that I am still alive. They will reward you greatly for my safe return."

Ela-nay drew back from Sheela as though she had slapped him. Her revelation was appalling. "Ysuna? Her blood cannot flow in you! She was the one who turned the tribes against one another and caused the plains to run with the blood of war and human sacrifices!"

"Lies. All lies."

Ela-nay shivered, recalling the violent past, then whispered tremulously, "Sheela, if Shateh knew of this, he would command your death."

"Yes, and Dakan-eh, in his desire to win favor in the eyes of the northern tribes, would not hesitate to obey!" Tears welled within her eyes. "You must help me, Ela-nay! Let me be your woman! Surely you are not afraid?"

Ela-nay was not afraid; he was horrified. But he wanted Sheela. From the first moment that he had set eyes upon her he had wanted her. He thought about his wife and two children, his slave, and his aging mother. He was responsible for their food and shelter. How could he possibly run away with Sheela now?

The question snagged. How could he *not*? He was not happy in this land, far from the country of his birth. He had too many responsibilities, and fulfilling them provided no satisfaction to him. His wife was fat; his slave was homely; his children did not like him; his mother was overbearing; and his headman took perverse pleasure in humiliating him.

"Come away with me, Ela-nay," implored Sheela, her long, tender fingers stroking his face. "Has not Dakan-eh *told* you to go?"

"Back to the Red World, yes—not in search of the People of the Watching Star, and certainly not with you."

Her battered face contorted. "Dakan-eh is headman of a band with no totem. He is leader of a people whose shaman has abandoned them. The spirits of your ancestors and mine look with disfavor upon him. Atonashkeh hates him, and Thunder in the Sky has begun to feed upon those who are loyal to him. Why should you continue to obey him? Has he not said that in changing times, men must learn new ways or die? Are you not a man, Ela-nay? The best and the boldest man of all?"

"I . . ."

"No, do not speak. Listen: The beat of drums quickens. The chanting of the shamans grows louder. A long while will pass before either of us is missed. Decide. Come with me, or go back to your lizard-eating headman. Whatever you do, I will not stay among my enemies. I will go alone into the night. I will live or I will die by the will of the forces of Creation; but with or without you at my side, I will be a slave no longer!"

5

Cha-kwena was troubled but could not say exactly why. Moon, Mother of Stars, had long since climbed out of the east and now sat high above, a perfectly round, shining adornment in the star-speckled black robe of the night. As the young shaman looked up, he felt her watching him out of gray, unblinking eyes.

How serious Moon looked tonight! Her crooked mouth scowled in a face that glowed white around the many scars that cratered her cheeks. He had seen her in various phases and in a multitude of moods, but usually *he* looked at her;

tonight *she* was looking at him, and her gaze was as penetrating as it was commanding.

He sat at his place near the smoldering greasewood fire around which his people were gathered. The day-end meal of roasted rabbit, spitted snake, and lizard stew was finished, but there were bones to be sucked. The fire continued to emanate light and warmth; the band would sleep here tonight, close to the embers, bundled in winter cloaks and bedding of twisted rabbit skins, protected against the north wind, already dressed for traveling, and prepared to pick up their belongings and walk on to a new land.

The younger children were fast asleep beside or in the laps of their mothers. The last of the clown's songs had dwindled to mere whispered hummings in the darkness. Had it not been for the restlessness of the dogs and the intermittent chorus of several coyotes, everyone might have succumbed to sleep long before now.

Still gazing skyward, Cha-kwena cocked his head. Once before he had felt Moon watching him like this. That had been long before, in the Red World, on the night he had climbed from the sacred juniper to follow old Hoyeh-tay and Owl through thick, black, mysterious woodlands. They had stopped at the very edge of an appalling abyss into which Moon had shed her light so that he might look down, down—into the very womb of the world, it had seemed— and glimpse his totem for the first time.

The memory made him shiver. Massive, invulnerable, as pale as the face of Moon, Life Giver had browsed with his herd, with his cows, adolescent offspring, and a calf as white as its sire—and as young and untested by the forces of Creation as the great bull was old and scarred by them.

Again Cha-kwena shivered. The herd had been slaughtered by mammoth-hunting enemies, the People of the Watching Star. Now the great mammoth walked alone, leading those who still named him Totem north, across unknown lands where there were no mammoth at all.

Why north? Not for the first time this day, the idea disturbed Cha-kwena more than he could say. Since First Man and First Woman, the ancestors had walked into the face of the rising sun. Why should it be different now?

Once again he squinted up at Moon. If she was not happy with him, he could not blame her—he had not behaved well since returning to camp. His people had rejoiced when he had told them that he had discovered the whereabouts of their totem and that tomorrow the great white mammoth would lead them to good hunting grounds at last. But then Ha-xa, mother of Ta-maya and Mah-ree, had chastised the girl for going off alone and without permission. If she had held her tongue against her mother's tirade, perhaps everything might have gone smoothly; but Mah-ree had spoken in her own defense, prompting Kosar-eh to offer an additional rebuke.

The cripple had actually shouted. "Did you think that I would not look for you? Did you think I would allow your mother and sister to worry? No! I left my band and walked all the way to the base of the ridge before discovering that your tracks were following close on Cha-kwena's. This was not a good thing! With Cha-kwena and Kosar-eh both gone from this camp, only Gah-ti was left to protect the women and children!"

Gah-ti, thirteen and Kosar-eh's eldest son, had not taken kindly to this. He had leaped from among his pack of younger brothers to stand boldly beside his father. He gazed adoringly at Mah-ree and proclaimed, "I would have gone with you! My strong arm and spear would have protected you! Mah-ree should not walk alone when Gah-ti is here!"

The girl had appraised the youth with a look that withered him on the spot. "I was in no danger. My dogs were with me, and my spear. I could defend myself."

Cha-kwena's lips compressed; he still regretted castigating Kosar-eh in that moment. True, Mah-ree should never have been taught to make or use weapons. But he could easily have taken Kosar-eh aside and discussed it privately. Instead, in the presence of Kosar-eh's woman and sons and the entire band, he had said with thoughtless cruelty, "You are a cripple! You are forbidden the use of a spear except for self-defense or for the protection of the band! You may work stone into spearheads. You may shape the shafts and haft the projectile points. You may instruct your sons in the making and use of these weapons. But you may not teach females, and you may not hunt with the weapons."

Cha-kwena's reprimand angered everyone but Kosar-eh. He was a large man for one born to the People of the Red World—big and heavily muscled across the upper back and neck. When he lowered his head in deference to Cha-kwena's repudiation, there had been something of the look of a weary elk to his stance. "Shaman is right. It *was* wrong of me to teach Mah-ree. It will not happen again."

How, he wondered now, could he have spoken so cruelly to Kosar-eh? Kosar-eh was his friend! A man did not shame his friends! Cha-kwena shook his head. He knew the answer to his question. He would never have addressed Kosar-eh so hurtfully if Ta-maya had not been watching.

Beautiful Ta-maya.

Cha-kwena looked across the fire to where she sat across from him, one among the other females, yet apart . . . always apart—for just as Moon shone forth among the stars and made their light seem as nothing when compared to her own, so it was with Ta-maya.

Cha-kwena's heart gave a thunk. His mouth went dry with longing. He had known her all of his life, but still this happened whenever he saw her. Now she looked back at him and smiled. It was that sad, rare, and tender smile of hers. Relief soared within him. She had forgiven him! He was transfixed by love and gratitude until she looked away, closed her eyes, and, still smiling, listened to the song Kosar-eh had raised to lighten the hearts of the band.

Jealousy flared within Cha-kwena as he realized that her smile had been intended for Kosar-eh all along. His resentment was without foundation. Even if she had not sworn after the death of Masau that she would never take another man, Cha-kwena was certain that she would not look with a woman's eyes at Kosar-eh. She called the clown Dear Friend and Brother of My Heart. She treated his woman, Siwi-ni, as her sister. Nevertheless, Cha-kwena *was* jealous.

He leaned forward to get a better view of Kosar-eh. The man lounged against his woven willow-wood backrest. His long legs were stretched out and crossed at the ankles as

he stared drowsily into the dying glow of the fire. In the
erratic light of glimmering flames, Cha-kwena saw a
mature, powerful man. Although Kosar-eh was swathed in a
full-length robe of rabbit and fox skins, Cha-kwena could
visualize the form beneath the robe: the right arm bent
upward and shriveled like the featherless wing of a
wounded hawk, the musculature of the left arm as pro-
nounced and impressive as the span of his thick shoulders,
broad back, and chest.

The broad stripes of black-and-white face paint, traditional for a clown, gleamed in the firelight. Kosar-eh
applied this paint every morning, even when he was not
entertaining the band; it was, Cha-kwena assumed, an
attempt, albeit futile, to mask the crooked, flattened bridge
of the man's broken nose and the scars that ran vertically
along one side of his mouth, cheek, and brow. Nevertheless,
despite paint and scars, Kosar-eh's once well-formed face
possessed strength, dignity, and intelligence.

Cha-kwena was suddenly painfully aware of his own
youth, of his boyish body and face. Kosar-eh had been
cursed by injury and paralysis, but sometimes the sixteen-
year-old shaman felt like a powerless boy in comparison.
Realizing this, Cha-kwena understood why he had yielded
to his perverse need to lessen the man in Ta-maya's eyes.
Although the motivation became clear, he could not justify
himself. What he had done was not worthy of a shaman.

He looked up. Moon had every right to be scowling at
him. He was scowling at himself.

"You should sleep, Shaman," said Kosar-eh.

"Yes, soon," he replied, surprised to find the cripple
eyeing him from beneath heavy lids. "But now I must think
of all of the omens that I have seen this day and—and you
know that I regret my words to you, Kosar-eh?"

"It is useless to regret the truth, Shaman."

"Some things should not be said."

"Some reminders should not have to be given."

The coyotes began to yap again. They were farther
away than before. Their cries came from the north. Their
barking was not an unusual sound; it did not rouse the
sleeping children or cause concern among the women. The

band had been in this camp long enough to know that often in the deep of night a small pack of coyotes came out of the darkness to drink at the pools before padding off along their own game trails in search of food—trails that Cha-kwena had followed and led his people to exploit. Now, however, after nearly a moon spent in this camp, little food was to be found upon them, for men or coyotes.

"It will be good to go from this place," said Kosar-eh.

"Yes," agreed Cha-kwena. "It will be good!" And though he believed his affirmation, he wished that Moon would stop scowling and that his troubling restlessness would go away.

6

In the Land of Grass the night was red and black, awash in blood and firelight, in smoke and darkness. The earth stank and steamed as it gave up mists that were the lingering ghosts of rain and hail, which had punished the plains. Now and then a lion roared—a deep, reverberant bellowing of warning to other carnivores, which had been drawn both by Raven and the stench of death.

Dakan-eh emerged from the grove to stand in the firelight with his fellow hunters. He was sexually drained, yet inexplicably unsatisfied and edgy.

Ma-nuk leaned close and, in a lowered voice, whispered worriedly, "Where are the others?"

"Others?"

"Ela-nay and the slave. I hear lions. I hear—"

Dakan-eh gestured Ma-nuk to silence. It was unlikely that Sheela and Ela-nay were in any danger; they would come from the grove when they would. In the meantime, he did not want to think about them.

Bold Man stared straight ahead. The shamans of the Bison People were still dancing. Their frenzied bloodletting rituals held him transfixed. They were dancing with their dead, Dakan-eh realized with a start. Led by Shateh, they had taken the bodies from the bison hides upon which they had been laid, held the corpses in their arms or hefted them across their shoulders; then they whirled and wept and wailed as they danced. They shouted the names of their lost beloved ones to the spirits of the wind until, at last, one by one, the shamans cast the bodies into the fire, then danced on.

Dakan-eh's eyes went wide. The fire became more smoke than flame until the scorched flesh yielded hot, bubbling fat. Suddenly the flames exploded, blowing high and hot. Of the holy men, only Shateh continued to dance with a corpse. Dakan-eh grimaced, for he knew that the body of the chieftain's son was still missing.

Not that there was any hope of finding Kalawak alive; hours before, a dog had brought one of the man's hunting moccasins, still laced to Kalawak's right foot at the end of a severely mangled limb, into the gathering of mourners. Even if Kalawak had survived his dismemberment, he would surely have bled to death or been easy prey for scavenging birds and animals. Atonashkeh had snatched his brother's severed leg from the dog and brained the animal to death with it.

Kalawak's woman had gathered her husband's salvaged winter tunic, buckskin trousers, and knee-high moccasins, stitched the garments together, and stuffed them full of leaves and grass—with the exception of the right trouser leg, into which she had placed the dismembered leg—thus creating a grotesque effigy of Kalawak with which Shateh now danced.

Something deep within Dakan-eh's gut tightened as he listened to the sorrow of the chieftain's song and observed the tumultuous, agonized power of his dance. When Shateh at last consigned Kalawak's effigy to the flames, Bold Man trembled—not with the empathy that one father should feel for another in such a moment, but with awe and envy.

Ah, to be a man like Shateh! To be a chieftain of such magnitude, I would do *anything, give* anything!

The fire burned higher, hotter. The dancing and drumbeat grew more frenzied. Bold Man watched, appalled and aching to join in.

If only Shateh would allow it, I would make them look at me and show them that I am Bold Man who—

"Dakan-eh! Please, my son, make her stop!"

He turned. Pah-la, sobbing, came through his assembled hunters. Ban-ya was at her heels and the other women of his band were right behind her.

"What is this?" Dakan-eh asked, glowering, as she fell at her son's feet.

Backlit by the fire, Pah-la's face was haggard from grief, her hair disheveled. "Ban-ya has forgotten that she is a woman of the Red World! Ban-ya would have us all forget! I do not want to forget, Dakan-eh! I cannot forget!"

He met Ban-ya's gaze and was startled by what he saw in her eyes: a strength of purpose that was more suited to a man than a woman. She stood naked before him, in the manner of the grieving women of the Land of Grass. Her sleepy boy was hefted on her hip. Her left hand was raised, and in its grip was a thin fleshing dagger. "It must be done," she said with grim purposefulness. "You can wait no longer, Bold Man. I, for one, am not afraid."

"Afraid of what?"

"Of this." Head high, she unflinchingly drew the blade across her upper chest. The cut was long, shallow enough to heal without stitching, but deep enough to cause blood to flow downward across her breasts.

Dakan-eh caught his breath. So did every man and woman of the Red World who observed her action. "What are you doing?" he demanded. "Shateh has forbidden this!"

"No," she disagreed, touching her fingertips to her wound, then raising her hand to mark her cheeks and brow with blood as the women and men of the Land of Grass had done. "Shateh has forbidden Dakan-eh to join his people at their fire in their rituals of mourning. Shateh has refused to command those not born to the ways of his tribe to endure what he and his people endure now, and he has allowed Dakan-eh and his band to mourn our dead in the way of *lizard eaters*."

Dakan-eh was stung by the unexpected contempt with which she had turned the last two words. His jaw clenched. He debated striking her. "We have proved ourselves warriors in this land," he snapped defensively.

"Yes!" Ban-ya agreed with quick fire. "This woman is proud to say that she is the woman of Bold Man of the Red World, who has become Brave Hunter in the Land of Grass."

He eyed her warily. What was she up to? One moment she was prodding him with insults, the next greasing his pride. It was not like Ban-ya to challenge him before others, for she was as ambitious for him to become a chieftain in this land of warriors as he was. "Why have you brought my mother to tears and slashed your skin in the way of the People of the Land of Grass?"

"Because Dakan-eh has made me one of them! My words would sting the others of my band into seeing the importance of the moment! My actions seek to shame them, as they shame my man!"

Ma-nuk growled with resentment. "How so?"

Ban-ya looked the hunter up and down and, from her snort of reproof, made it clear that she found little of merit in him. "The father of our headman and a youth of this band lie dead. How do you mourn them, Ma-nuk? With little moans and mutterings? Ah, what a brave man you are, standing and watching in silence as the shamans and warriors of Shateh's tribe dance and send their blood, pain, and lamentations to the spirits of the Four Winds!"

It was obvious to all that had Ban-ya belonged to any other man, Ma-nuk would have strangled her on the spot. "Dakan-eh obeys Shateh's command to stand apart! And I obey Dakan-eh!" He squinted at his headman. "Why do you let a female speak so to me? If she were mine, I would tame her wild tongue!"

"She is *not* yours." Dakan-eh lowered his head and menaced Ma-nuk, then Ban-ya, with his eyes.

Before he could reprimand her, something in her stance changed. "We must all obey Dakan-eh," she told Ma-nuk. "He has led us out of a starving land to a new and better life. My Bold Man is as great and benevolent a chief as Shateh! Now he risks banishment because, in his concern for his band, he will not ask any of you to do what must be done if we are to be allowed to remain in the Land of Grass! He waits for you to come forth to him, to tell him that you are not afraid to turn your back upon the old ways or to do as I have done—slash your skin and show your grief in the way of your adopted tribe."

"How many times must you be told that Shateh has forbidden us to join with his people at their fire!" Ma-nuk hurled the words as though they were spears aimed at her audacious heart.

"But Shateh has not forbidden us to raise a fire of our *own!*" she shot back. "He has not forbidden us to sing of our sadness! Nor has he said that we may not cast into the flames the belongings of those who have died. He has not commanded us to cut open our flesh as a sign of grief for our dead, but neither has he said that we may *not* do this! *Has* he, Bold Man?"

Dakan-eh's mouth sagged open. Ban-ya had always been a woman of insight and many surprises. Suddenly he knew where she had been leading him all along. The final statement toward which she had been building her argument was his to make. "Let Shateh see that our ways are no longer the ways of lizard eaters. Let the People of the Land of Grass see that our ways are their ways! Let them know that we *are* unafraid and worthy of remaining in this country!"

Ban-ya exhaled. It was a sound of explosive relief. "Yes!" she agreed, and had anyone but Dakan-eh been looking into her eyes, they would have seen her gladness and her repudiation: *Thickheaded man, it took you long enough to see the way in which you must lead them!*

They raised a small, smoky fire. It was no easy task, for Shateh's people had already collected the best of the dry wood. Dakan-eh instructed his hunters in their placement of wood and brush and of precious oil that his women had managed to carry away from the destroyed village.

"Have you seen my man?" Ela-nay's woman asked Bold Man. Her tone revealed annoyance rather than concern. "Nothing has gone well for us this day and—"

"Enough!" He eyed her with dislike. She was a nagger, unfailing in her ability to put a man on the defensive. He was glad that he had led his people downriver in the search for firewood, well away from where he had left Ela-nay to take his pleasure on Sheela. He had little respect for the man, but with such a badger of a woman awaiting his return, Dakan-eh could well understand why Ela-nay was taking his time getting back to his band. "Go away."

"But Ela-nay is—"

"Go, I say!" he demanded sharply. "Prepare yourself for the mourning rituals that will now begin! Your man will show himself when he sees fit! I will not tolerate the disobedience of another female this night!"

"My father, look at them! Listen to them!" Atonashkeh was incensed.

Shateh, drained of emotion and numb with grief, paused beside his son. The chieftain stared toward the groves. The lizard eaters had built a pitiful fire and were dancing around it. In the manner of the People of the Land of Grass, all of them save the mother of Bold Man had cast off their garments and darkened their faces and arms with their own blood.

Atonashkeh's face was dark with emotion. "You have forbidden this!"

"No," disagreed Shateh. "I have forbidden them to join us. I have not commanded the manner in which they were to mourn their dead."

"They have no shaman to intercede with the spirits on behalf of their dead, and yet they sing!"

Shateh listened. Above the drums and wails and shrieking songs of his own tribe, he heard the songs of Dakan-eh and the band from the Red World. After a moment he nodded. "I hear cries of grief—no sacred songs . . . nothing that would offend the spirits."

"They seek to mock us by imitating our ways."

Shateh's eyes narrowed thoughtfully. "No. They seek to honor us and to gain honor for themselves in our eyes."

"Lizard eaters can have no honor in this man's eyes!"

But Shateh was listening only to his own thoughts. "It takes courage to see through the smoke of Shateh's words, to raise the fire of mourning, to open the flesh in the way of our tribe. Perhaps this Bold Man is a lizard eater no longer?"

Atonashkeh's face twisted with jealousy. "Your thoughts toward the lizard eater are as fluctuating as the wind, my father! I say that Sits in His Own Puke did not run to save the People! He ran to save himself!"

"We will see," Shateh decided. "Come. Bring Lahontay and the shamans. We will see how badly this Bold Man wishes to be a brother of Shateh's."

The drums fell silent. Dakan-eh stopped dancing and looked toward the great fire of the People of the Land of Grass. They, too, had stopped dancing. The chieftain and the other shamans were coming toward him, with Atonashkeh and the warriors of the tribe following. Unsure of what was about to happen, Dakan-eh stood his ground; this was not the time to show fear, even though he was certain that when Shateh stopped before him, the stink of it would betray him.

"This is not the mourning ritual of lizard eaters," the chieftain began. "I have seen your quiet ways and have heard your gentle songs."

Dakan-eh's mouth was dry. He spoke out anyway— carefully, judiciously, for a change. He was arrogant and hot tempered but not always a fool. He would not risk angering Shateh again; he might not have another opportunity to win his favor. "Long has it been since this band has eaten lizards. Long has it been since this band first looked to the tribes of the north and knew that the forces of Creation favored them over all others. This man has turned his back on small fires, gentle songs, and quiet ways. This is the mourning fire of the band of Bold Man Who Chases the Whirling Wind to Save the People.''

"Whose people?'' sneered Atonashkeh, trying to goad Dakan-eh into an ill-advised reaction.

Earlier in the day it had been easy to ignite Dakan-eh's temper. It was not so easy now. He had seen the risks inherent in allowing his emotions to be prodded into flame. "The people of *Shateh* and the people of *Dakan-eh*,'' he replied coolly. "Shateh has said that the People are one. Has this not been taught to the tribes of the Red World and of the Land of Grass since time beyond beginning? Would you dispute your chief and father, Atonashkeh?''

Atonashkeh glared.

The women of Shateh's tribe had come forward. Slowly, Wehakna, the chieftain's eldest woman and mother of Kalawak, came to stand beside her man. She was worn and grief ravaged as she fixed her eyes upon Pah-la. "That one still wears adornments and garments as though sadness does not live within her heart. And behold Lehana, daughter of Nakantahkeh. She has become a stranger to my eyes. It is shameful to see her lack of despair, lack of pain, lack of blood.'' She shivered against revulsion. "Lizard eaters!''

Pah-la, red eyed and dazed, was kneeling over the body of her husband, well to one side of the little fire. The family of Na-sei knelt close by, around the hide-covered mound of their mutilated son.

The enormously pregnant Lehana rose shakily. She had already cast off her garments and all adornment in the way of her people, but her flesh was marked only by streaks of mud, which she had applied as a substitute for blood. She sought the eyes of her father, Nakantahkeh, among the repudiating stares of the warriors of her tribe. When she saw him, she spoke in a choked and agonized voice. "Wehakna is wrong if she believes that I do not grieve for the lost spirit of my poor, broken Na-sei. I am of his band now. The women of the Red World would not let me cut my skin. These women speak of the welfare of my child-to-be. But what does the child matter? Even before it is born it is dishonored by a mother who is not allowed to grieve in the way of—''

"Then grieve!" Dakan-eh was panic-stricken. "Grieve as you see fit! Ban-ya, bring the girl a blade so that she may open her flesh! And you, Mother, rise! Show the people of Shateh that you honor their ways."

Firelight was shining on Pah-la's tear-streaked cheeks and on the golden nuggets of her nose ring. She seemed befuddled.

For all his self-serving nature, Dakan-eh pitied her. She looked like a stunned, wounded old doe that has seen its mate slain and now, cornered by hunters, cannot comprehend its loss or predicament. Nevertheless he pressed her again. "Pah-la! You *will* obey!"

Ban-ya, still holding Piku-neh, came quietly up to Pah-la and, instead of giving her skinning dagger to Lehana, offered it to the older woman.

Pah-la stared at the curving, fluted edge of the stone blade, then at Ban-ya. She shook her head. "I am a daughter of the Red World. I will honor the spirit of my beloved in the way of the ancestors, with my tears, not my blood. It is the only thing that Owa-neh would want me to shed for him."

"She fears the pain. She fears blood—a true lizard eater!" said Atonashkeh.

Old Lahontay grunted and nodded in agreement with the younger man.

A deep calm swept through Dakan-eh. He knew what he must do, and he did it without hesitation. "You are no longer a woman of the Red World," he informed his mother. "You will grieve as the women of this ruined village grieve."

Pah-la did not move.

Dakan-eh fought back the urge to kick his mother. "You will take the blade."

Still Pah-la did not move.

Shateh looked down at the woman and said compassionately, "If you would be one among the women of this tribe, you must let the blood of your sadness wash the flesh of your man. He must know the taste of your grief before his body is given to the flames that will release his life spirit to the Four Winds. It is the way of your new sisters who mourn their own dead.''

Wehakna made a sour face, obviously insulted by having been named sister of a lizard eater.

Dakan-eh nearly shouted for joy. There *was* still a chance that his people and he would be accepted as brothers and sisters of the northern tribes. His heart soared . . . then plummeted as Pah-la smashed his hopes.

''This woman respects the ways of the People of the Land of Grass,'' she said with quiet dignity to the chieftain, ''but my Owa-neh was not happy in this land. He had no heart for making war or for hunting bison or mammoth and longed to return to the country of the ancestors. I cannot allow his body to be burned in this far land from which his spirit may never be able to find its way back to the Red World. This woman must take her man home. The Red World is where Pah-la and Owa-neh, their son, Dakan-eh, and his band belong. It was a mistake for us to come here.''

Dakan-eh's resolve to maintain control was consumed in a sudden fury. He went to his mother, jerked her to her feet, and, after taking the dagger from Ban-ya, cruelly slashed Pah-la's brow, upper arms, and the thongs that secured her skirt of woven cording. The garment fell away from her hips to tangle about her ankles. She was sobbing and shaking in his grasp. Dakan-eh did not care. He felt no regret.

Shateh was watching him. Lahontay and the shamans were watching him. Atonashkeh and Nakantahkeh and the hunters of the Land of Grass were watching him. Dakan-eh knew that whatever he did or said now would forever determine his destiny—either as a warrior and big-game hunter of the northern tribes or as a grub-gathering lizard eater of the Red World. Pah-la looked up at him and twisted her chunky arm in a pitiable attempt to be free of him. He found himself staring at the tiny golden nuggets of her nose ring. They sparked bright in the firelight, and they sparked inspiration into his soul. ''Take it off,'' he commanded. ''Throw it in the fire! The women of this tribe have given their adornments to the flames so that the life spirits of their dead will have some token of them in the world beyond this world!''

Pah-la's eyes widened as she wailed in absolute despair, ''No, Dakan-eh! You cannot ask this of me!''

''I am headman. I do not *ask*! I command!'' His face was set, hard. He knew how precious the nose ring was to Pah-la. It was more than casual adornment. It had been a gift from his father many years before, and she had never removed it from that day. Now that Owa-neh was dead, a part of Pah-la's own spirit would perish if she were forced to give it up. Nevertheless, circumstances gave Dakan-eh no recourse. And so, although he felt regret, he showed no emotion when he ripped it from her face.

Pah-la screamed as Dakan-eh turned and cast the bloodied trinket into the fire. ''Now has the mother of Dakan-eh cast off her old life,'' he declared sternly. ''Now does the mother of this headman mourn in the way of the People of the Land of Grass.''

Sobbing, with her hands tented before her face and blood oozing between her fingers, Pah-la hung her head.

Dakan-eh looked to Shateh for approval, but the man's blood-darkened face was unreadable. Bold Man observed the gashes on the chieftain's arms and face and chest. His own slashes were mere surface wounds compared to these. Head held high, he raised the stone blade to his already blooded brow and cut deep, to the bone, from temple to temple and then, unflinching, lowered his hand and raised a line of blood laterally across his chest from one armpit to the other, and then downward to his navel. The pain of his self-inflicted wounds was actually pleasing to him, for in this moment, as blood ran into his eyes and across his belly and genitals and thighs, he heard a murmur of approval rise from all who watched.

''For Owa-neh does Bold Man mark his flesh so that he may forever carry the scars of grief for his father!'' The words, he thought, sounded right.

Lahontay grunted in appreciation. The other shamans and lesser chieftains did the same. The women sighed, and Wehakna nodded with grudging admiration.

Atonashkeh's glower twisted with venomous resentment; the gashes of Shateh's son were not so deep as the cuts that Dakan-eh had made, and the resultant scars of the grief that he would carry for his lost brother, Kalawak, would be minimal compared to those that a lizard eater would carry for his father.

Standing close beside Dakan-eh, Ban-ya soothed little Piku-neh, who was whimpering as he eyed his grandmother. To silence the boy, Ban-ya offered him a great and bloodied breast.

Shateh's face remained expressionless as he eyed the woman and boy and noted her open wounds. "It was not necessary for the woman of Dakan-eh to scar herself. Owa-neh's blood was not your blood."

Ban-ya seemed unperturbed. "This woman will proudly carry the mark of her grief. Dakan-eh and Ban-ya are one. I willingly share his pain."

Once again a murmuring of approval rose from the watchers. This time even Atonashkeh eyed Ban-ya with interest.

It was all that Dakan-eh could do to keep from smirking. What a woman his Ban-ya was! True, she was no rare beauty like Ta-maya—or even Sheela—but she was better to look upon than most females, and he was proud to have as second choice such a brave, boy-bearing, wondrously bosomed woman at his side when he longed for Shateh's approval. And it was apparent that the chieftain was approving of Ban-ya. For the first time in all too many moons Dakan-eh was giddy with feelings of success. Bold Man yielded to his need to smile. It was a broad, white smile of triumph.

But then the roaring of lions sounded again from beyond the bonfire, and the woman of Ela-nay came forward to wipe the smile from Dakan-eh's face.

"Has Shateh seen my man?" she asked.

A knot tightened in Dakan-eh's gut. He had forgotten all about Ela-nay and Sheela! He looked around. They were not among his people. Was it possible that they were still within the grove? How long did it take the stubborn little hunter to come to release within a slave? Too long. *Much* too long!

Sweat pricked Dakan-eh's brow as he recalled Ela-nay's warning that the mating of man to woman on a night of ritual mourning might be forbidden by the People of the Land of Grass, as it was among the People of the Red World. What if Ela-nay had been right? If the man came traipsing out of the groves now with Sheela, Shateh would know immediately what had transpired between them. And given Sheela's feelings of hatred toward Dakan-eh, it would only be a matter of time before the chieftain was informed that Ela-nay had not been the only man to lie with her this night.

The ground seemed to shift beneath Bold Man's feet. Once again his hope of being accepted by the northern tribes was jeopardized, this time by his own actions. *No!* All was not lost yet, not if he acted and spoke quickly. And so he did, with a hastily formed lie. "The hunter Ela-nay was deeply distraught by the happenings of this day. I consented to allow him to mourn alone. This is sometimes the way of the men of the Red World." The last few words, at least, were true.

But Ela-nay's woman was not satisfied. "You made no mention of this when I came to you earlier, Headman."

"I did not wish to worry you," Dakan-eh answered, looking down at her with a concerned deference that masked his wish that the wretched, probing female would drop dead on the spot. And he wished that lions would make their way downriver to attack and consume her stupid, self-serving man and the recalcitrant slave.

He looked up, his attention drawn by the stares of Ma-nuk and the other hunters from the Red World. They were frowning, trying to discover the purpose of his lie. He glared them to silence. Their faces registered understanding, and when Ma-nuk nodded, Bold Man was confident that the older man would not betray him. Ma-nuk's desire to remain in the Land of Grass was as great as Dakan-eh's own.

"One man alone, with lions feeding all around?" Shateh asked. "This Ela-nay must own a brave heart."

"As brave as the lions with whom he walks the night!" responded Dakan-eh.

"My man?" The face of Ela-nay's woman puckered with incredulity.

"Yes! *Your* man!" Dakan-eh wished her dead again. Drawing in a deep breath that was not as steadying as intended, he made a silent plea to the forces of Creation that Ela-nay and Sheela remain in the grove until Shateh and the others were distracted. "Ela-nay will soon return. Until he does, his absence should not deter the tribe from continuing the customary rituals for the dead." *The tribe.* Dakan-eh's mouth went dry from his deliberate presumption; he had spoken as though the two peoples were one.

Shateh did not miss the inference. The chieftain measured Bold Man from beneath half-closed lids. "You will burn your dead. In the way of the People of the Land of Grass. *Now.*"

Pah-la's hands flew from her face. She looked at the chieftain, then at her son: "Dakan-eh, please! If you honor your father's life spirit, you will remember who you are and how far we are from the country of our—"

"I am Brave Hunter in this Land of Grass!" he interrupted sharply. "I will honor the dead of this band in the way of Shateh. The Red World is far away. Put it from your mind and dreams! You will not see it again, woman!"

The chieftain's head went up. He fixed his eyes on the face of the moon as it swam red within the smoke-stained sky. Wolves had begun to howl, and lions were roaring again. The chieftain listened, then said, "The omens are not good. For this night and three nights thereafter we will mourn. For four days we will fast. On the dawn of the fifth day, we will leave this place. We will follow the old game trails south. The bison will have gone there, beyond the place where the river forks. We will follow."

We.

The word sang in Dakan-eh's spirit. Shateh had said "we"! Dakan-eh was satisfied. Surely in four days he would find a way to impress Shateh and win back his confidence!

"It will not be good for your man Ela-nay to be alone," Shateh said. "There are many lions."

Dakan-eh, suddenly disconcerted, wondered if the

chieftain had seen through to the heart of his lies. "He has his spear. The lions make no secret of their presence. Ela-nay will avoid them."

Shateh nodded, apparently satisfied. "Burn your dead at your own fire. Mourn. Fast. Then we will see what dawn of the fifth day will bring to one who may—or may not—be a brother." This said, he turned away and walked back to the great fire, his son and his shamans and his people following.

Shaken, Dakan-eh stood immobile. Ban-ya came close to whisper softly, "Before those two who lie together by the river return to name this Bold Man a liar, a two-legged lion might stalk them and assure that they will not speak of what has transpired between them—and *you*—this night."

And so, in stealth, when he was certain that no one watched, Dakan-eh took up one of his spears. He did not thank Ban-ya for having rescued his weapons and his other belongings from the onslaught of the storm; it was a woman's obligation to think first of the needs of her man. Unafraid he went into the darkness while his people danced and mourned and the bodies of Na-sei and Owa-neh were given to the flames. Half expecting to encounter Sheela and Ela-nay on their way back to their people, Dakan-eh was prepared to stalk and kill them both. Afterwards he would give them to the river. But there was no sign of Sheela or Ela-nay within the groves or along the river's edge. Only after staring at the fast-flowing river for what seemed to be a very long time did Dakan-eh admit to himself that they must have fled together into the night.

His face contorted. He felt anger and then contempt. "Go! Both of you! Go fast and far!" he snarled, with only the moon and the river and the whispering presence of the north wind to hear him. "May you end your lives in the bellies of lions. You mean nothing to me! *Nothing!*"

Despite the injuries she had suffered at Dakan-eh's hand, Sheela led Ela-nay southward beneath the waning light of the moon. Soon the shining orb would slip behind the western hills and the world would be near darkness.

They would miss the moonlight, but they would also be glad to have it gone. For hours they had been looking back in fear, certain that they were being followed. At first they had taken great care to cover their tracks, sloshing along knee-deep at the river's edge, slipping and often falling over smooth stones that would not betray their passage.

Now, wet and shivering, they reached a wide fork in the river. Before Ela-nay could protest, Sheela was plunging in, then swimming away in black, racing, roaring turbulence. He could not believe his eyes as he watched her being carried downstream. He saw her head raised above dark, foam-spattered waves. He saw her long arms reach and pull, then reach again and again until, at last, she emerged onto a broad, pebbly sandbar. After kneeling with her head down for a few moments, catching her breath, she climbed to her feet, raised an arm, and beckoned to him.

Ela-nay hesitated. He had done some swimming—lake swimming—in the Red World. Bobbing among the late summer reed beds to set out his duck decoys of woven grass and wood, his head camouflaged in a bonnet of tule reeds and willows, he had found it as natural as breathing. But committing his body to this dark, cold river was something else, something frightening. He did not want to do it. But the woman for whom he had abandoned everyone and everything was beckoning. Ela-nay took a deep breath and, trying hard not to think about what he was doing, followed.

Soon, still clutching his spear, he was beside her on the bar, flat on his belly and puking up the river.

Sheela stood above him. "You have done well. We will live through this night, you will see. And someday soon, a foolish man who thinks himself bold will pay for the way he has shamed us both. Come, we will cross the second channel now. Once we are on the other side we can move more quickly without fear of our tracks being seen. No one will think to follow us there."

"No? Why?" The words burbled out of him.

"They would not dare to swim the river as we have just done!" she said proudly.

Ela-nay looked up. She was gone. He had not heard the splash that her tall, lithe body made when she sent herself forcefully into the flow of the current; the sound of the river was too loud. He rose, hunkered on his heels a moment, then shook his head and wondered what had possessed him to follow Sheela from the ruined village, much less across the river. But the answer was clear enough: He wanted her and badly.

He sighed, rose, and went after her. He had chosen this path and this woman, and although she was proving a difficult companion to follow, at least he could not accuse her of nagging him.

Finally he was beside her again on dry land. He shook himself like a wet dog. A cold wind was gusting from the north. Ahead and to the southeast, an occasional flash of lightning illuminated distant thunderclouds.

"Thunder in the Sky has gone there," said Sheela.

Ela-nay remembered the terror of the whirling wind as he crossed his arms over his chest and shivered. "We should not follow him, Sheela."

"Our way lies there!"

To his relief, he followed the line of her extended right arm northward. Glacier-capped mountains gleamed white on the horizon, under the light of the one star in the heavens around which all of the others turned—the Watching Star. He shivered again, longing for warm, dry clothes. He cursed himself for allowing Dakan-eh to talk him into leaving the Red World and for allowing Sheela to seduce him into helping her. Despite himself, Ela-nay turned and looked southward with longing. The beloved land of his ancestors seemed so far away. Life had been so simple there, without threat.

Wolves howled nearby. Ela-nay winced. In the distant mountains to the north, other wolves howled back. Something was odd, almost human about the sound. Sheela stiffened, listening. Shivers went up Ela-nay's skin.

"Do not be afraid," he told Sheela, and tried unsuccessfully to take his own advice.

"Your strong spear arm will protect me, Ela-nay."

"Y-yes. My strong arm will protect you . . . us." He wished that he sounded more sure of himself. Lovesick, he watched in misery as Sheela strode ahead of him. He did not understand his emotions. He wanted to be at her side, and yet he wanted to be away from her, back among the other mourners—no, back amid the canyons and buttes and many scattered, peaceful bands of the Red World, where a man did not feel vulnerable before the forces of Creation.

"Come, Ela-nay. We will be warm and safe as long as we walk and stay close together!"

He hefted his spear and hurried after Sheela. She was right. Movement warmed his bones. When he caught up and fell into stride beside her, she linked her arm through his and looked at him with approval and—dared he imagine it?—affection. Her face was swollen so badly that she was barely recognizable; it was impossible to discern the true meaning of her expression, but her touch was obviously the touch of encouragement. It warmed his heart.

Suddenly he was glad to be heading north, away from the flashing clouds that bulked high on the southern horizon. If Thunder in the Sky was moving south, he was grateful to be walking in the opposite direction. He hoped that the forces of Creation would look to the welfare of whatever men or beasts would soon lie under the storm shadows of the angry sky.

PART II

BLACK MOON

1

Far beyond the Land of Grass, Cha-kwena followed Life Giver toward the foothills of a mountain range that stood like a huge shimmering island in the late afternoon heat of the lowlands. The young shaman sang as he walked. He knew no fear—the sacred stone was safe in its medicine bag around his neck, and he carried the magic spearheads in a specially made parfleche that was looped to the woven fiber waistband of his loin cover. Their weight was comforting to him as he walked.

The wind was still out of the north. Cool, constant, it had raised a blue haze over the distant mountains and was now lifting eddying whorls of dust from the surface of the dry lake across which the shaman had been plodding. He leaned into the wind, using the butt end of his long spear as a staff. He pushed himself against the load of his pack frame of thong-braced elk antlers.

For hours Cha-kwena had been following the tracks of a lone coyote and of the great white mammoth as they stretched ahead, floating within the heat haze, and then disappearing into the distant foothills. He paused and looked back. He was well ahead of his band, even Mah-ree. He felt glad; solitude was sweet.

"By dusk we will be in the foothills," he said to the little yellow wolf and to his unseen totem. "My people will camp and rest, then go on into the mountains."

The wind, gusting sharply, blew from four different directions at once. It moved like a living thing around Cha-kwena, embracing him with cool, invisible arms. Then it came on strongly from the north again, combing the young man's shoulder-length hair from his face. His eyes stung and watered from wind-borne grit; it took a few moments for his tears to wash away the abrading, alkaline dust.

"What is this, North Wind? Would you turn me from the way I would go? You cannot. As long as the great white mammoth walks ahead of Cha-kwena's band, this shaman will follow."

Cha-kwena braced himself. He raised his arms to wave the wind away. It gusted angrily, then blew on, leaving him in still, hot air. He stared after it, his mouth agape, for in this moment, Cha-kwena could see the wind! Its contours defined with dust, it was a long, diaphanous, serpentine river of air rushing southward. It snaked through his little band, then raised a cloud of dust into which it plunged and hid itself from view—but not before turning back and looking at him as it roared, *Follow me!*

Never had Cha-kwena seen anything like this. The wind was gone now and, with it, his confidence. He watched his people trudging toward him, their footprints stretching behind them for miles. Fear chewed at his resolve; he was determined to ignore it. "I do not follow the north wind! I follow the totem of my people!" The proclamation made, he felt better. He turned and walked north again, following the footsteps of the great white mammoth.

It was day's end when Shateh awoke with a start. He had slept fitfully and felt exhausted. Leaping cats and wolves had come in the predawn hours to feed on what the lions had left behind of the bison. Throughout the night there had been the growls and yaps of canines—dire wolves and wild dogs and coyotes. Foxes had followed in their wake. Badgers and short-tailed lynx and meat-eating rodents had come close, waiting to take advantage of any opportunity to share in the feast. Toward dawn a skunk had tainted the air with its presence.

Later, in the pallid, smoky light of morning, Shateh had been roused by the huff of a great bear. The chieftain had arisen and made certain that Atonashkeh and his family were safe, that the watchmen were alert, and that all of the children of the tribe were within the protective circle of their families. Only after making sure all was secure had he returned to his own family and gone back to sleep.

Now the sun, hot and malevolent looking, was setting. He sat up and glared at it, allowing it to sear his vision. Soon he saw nothing but gold and white spots of livid, pulsing heat. Seated beside him upon a salvaged mammoth hide, his youngest woman, Cheelapat, put down the swan-bone medicine tube through which she had been blowing sage pollen onto the chieftain's wounds. Senohnim, his pregnant middle wife, looked at him out of worried eyes, then turned to the chieftain's three little girls and raised a finger to her mouth as a warning to be silent.

Wehakna, who had been sleeping against the chieftain's side, placed her hand upon his forearm. "Shateh will burn his spirit if he looks too long at the sun!"

"Shateh's spirit is beyond burning," he told her, and, wanting nothing to do with his women, stood up and stalked away.

Head high, he moved past the remains of the main fire. It was smoldering now, stinking in the ebbing heat of the afternoon. As his vision cleared, he became aware of his people watching him. They were both weary from the previous day's ordeal and rituals and hungry after their first day of fasting. No one spoke as he passed, but he felt the questions—and perhaps repudiation?—in their eyes.

His jaw clenched. What did they want of him? He could not relieve their sadness nor undo yesterday's tragedies. A terrible wave of inadequacy washed through him. What had happened to his powers to protect his people? How had he failed to anticipate the intensity of yesterday's storms? What had he done—or not done—that had brought the wrath of Thunder in the Sky down upon his people? He could not believe that the lizard eater's slave had been right about the sky god's hungering for the flesh of human sacrifices.

Shateh stopped after he had put the last of his people's family groups behind him. He scanned the open plain and saw what lions had left of the bison. Most had been consumed on the spot, bellies and throats opened and hollowed, intestines pulled free and devoured, limbs and haunches dismembered and dragged off in pieces to be cached for later eating by the pride. All that remained were bloodied brown mounds of bone and cartilage, grotesque islands in the golden, storm-ravaged grassland. Aside from an occasional glint of sunlight on horn or savaged skull, or the movement of wind in a flap of dark, thickly haired hump hide, all detail of remaining flesh and skin was lost to view beneath black, feathered convocations of beaked feasters. Raven and his clan had fed well this day.

Shateh looked up as he walked. The large black birds were circling idly in the pale, cloudless blue sweep of the sky. Their wings set long shadows upon the earth. Beyond the decimated village, other members of their raucous clan competed with vultures and various species of small carrion-eating mammals to feed at will upon the carcasses of bison and to harry the orphaned calves.

The chieftain's deeply incised brow furrowed, and blood seeped into his eyes from the long, self-inflicted cut. He wiped it away, uncaring of pain.

"Why such waste?" The query was bitter in his mouth and spirit. These bison had died for no purpose. Their hides and meat could not be consumed by the People. No meat or sinew or precious fat would be taken; Thunder in the Sky had claimed these things for himself and for the carrion eaters of the earth and sky. Only the skins of the bison that had fallen into the ravine—and crushed to death members of the hunting band—could be used, and only to cover the heaped, burned bodies of the dead.

Despair filled him. Soon winter would come down upon the land. Would his people have raised new lodges by then? Would the hunters find the bison again? Would they kill successfully and in time to assure survival?

Behind him, from where the lizard eaters gathered by the river's edge, Dakan-eh's mother raised a high, plaintive ululation, and from within the gathering of his own tribe, a newborn cried. A young man from one of the western bands keened. Again bitterness soured Shateh's mouth. He pitied Pah-la. He pitied whatever woman had brought forth new life during a time of mourning. He pitied the young hunter. And he pitied himself for the loss of Kalawak.

"Lizard Eater has brought this upon us."

Shateh was startled to see that Atonashkeh had come to walk at his side. His son's features were drawn, and the laceration across his brow was as long and livid as any the chieftain had ever seen. He frowned, knowing that Atonashkeh had reopened the shallow wound so that it would make a scar to shame any scar of Dakan-eh's.

"A brother should scar himself to show grief for a brother, not to prove himself to one whom he holds in contempt."

Atonashkeh's face twisted. "His presence offends the forces of Creation."

"Perhaps. In three days' time the council will—"

"Life has come forth from my first woman!" With a breaking voice Atonashkeh sobbed the shameful revelation.

The chieftain felt as though he had been struck. "The child cannot be allowed to live lest it offend the spirits of the dead! Not during a time of mourning!"

Atonashkeh could not bring himself to look at his father. "The life is finished . . . with my own hand."

Shateh was suddenly breathless. "Atli has borne other children. She is young. You will put other babies into her belly. And Nani, your new woman, will soon bear new life."

Atonashkeh nodded. "May it be so."

Shateh set a broad, strong hand upon his son's shoulder. "The forces of Creation could not be so unkind that they would allow otherwise."

Atonashkeh looked up. His face was set, his eyes were sharp. "No? My brother has been consumed by the whirling wind. My village is destroyed. My hunting brothers and my best dog are ashes upon the mourning pyre. My favorite woman has given birth at a forbidden time, and that which could not be allowed to live was a *son,* a firstborn son for Atonashkeh, a grandson for Shateh!"

Shateh stared. The long hoped-for male-child, dead before it could draw a second breath? "Ahhh . . ." The sigh bled out of him. He felt old and weak again. And then, suddenly, a cold fury shook him as he looked across his assembled tribe to where the lizard eaters gathered above the river. Perhaps Atonashkeh was right. Perhaps the strangers *were* an offense to the forces of Creation.

He could see the lizard eater now, crouching with his fellow hunters before the remains of his pathetic fire upon which the charred but not completely burned bodies of his dead lay smoldering. Had the man not, with his own mouth, claimed that a shaman had put a curse upon him and upon all mammoth hunters and sent it across the world on the back of the north wind?

As he stared off, he saw Ban-ya, bold and big breasted, emerge from the broken shade of the cottonwoods. She stopped and, aware that he was watching her, stared back at him.

How impressive she was. With her strong, well-made little boy straddling her shapely hip, she cupped a breast and offered it to the child . . . or to the man who watched her from afar?

Atonashkeh stiffened. "A mammoth could draw life from such teats! And look how she baits us with them. Does she imagine that we will look more kindly on her man if she entices us?"

"She is a maker of strong sons," Shateh observed thoughtfully.

"I tell you, she and the rest of her band should be driven from this land before it is too late!"

"Banishing them now will not bring back the dead, Atonashkeh."

"No, but it will prevent other deaths!"

"Will it?" Shateh's narrowed eyes remained fixed on the body of the bold woman whose loyalty to her man he had come to admire. "In three days' time the council will decide whether or not the lizard eaters remain in the Land of Grass."

"It is too long! If another son is born to me before—"

"Then you will kill it, as you killed the first!" Shateh had had enough of his son's self-pitying. "You are a man of the People, Atonashkeh, bound to obey the ways of the ancestors as tightly as any man."

"I am Shateh's son!"

"Yes," conceded the chieftain, not even attempting to hide his lack of enthusiasm. "The only son that is left to me." His weariness was suddenly absolute. "Remember your place, Atonashkeh, and do not speak to me of this again."

Ela-nay and Sheela watched the sun slip beyond the edge of the world. Ela-nay's hand tightened around his spear shaft. Fear of the approach of night slowed his steps. He longed for the confidence and well-being of a hunter who travels in the company of other armed men.

"Come!" Sheela urged. "We can walk far before the dark comes down!" Her words were slurred, thickened, as they came through her swollen, tightly clamped jaw, loosened teeth, and lacerated lips.

Ela-nay did not reply. His gaze was fixed on the mountains toward which they had been traveling since crossing the river the night before. *They are still so far away!* he thought, remembering how, in the light of this morning's dawn, he had been so certain that Sheela and he would be in the foothills before dusk. She had assured him that this would be so; but endless hours of walking had proved her wrong.

He scowled. The farther north he trekked across the wide, rolling, virtually treeless country, the less he liked it. All day Sheela and he had crossed old war-ravaged village and butchering sites. They had found much sign of antelope and horse and camel. But they had also found sign of wolves and lions, and of a bear with paws so huge that the animal must have been half the size of a mammoth. It did not soothe Ela-nay that the bear tracks were at least a day old.

"Ela-nay, come." Sheela spoke softly, and her right arm encircled his waist to draw him on.

Ela-nay gave her a wan smile. Her touch was magic to him. But he was tired and hungry, and his terror of lurking carnivores diluted her magic. "Would you not rather stop and rest awhile?" he asked. "I will raise a fire and set snares for whatever little animals the forces of Creation might see fit to send our way. Are you not hungry, Sheela?"

She was appalled by his suggestion. "We will rest and eat soon enough—but not here in the open! Now that I am no longer a slave, I will never again eat of the meat of rabbits or squirrels." Then, contrite, she lowered her head and leaned against him. "I know where there are deep, streamside woods ahead, in which deer will be browsing. You will find good water and much stone for the making of new spearheads."

Ela-nay salivated at the prospect of setting himself to a feast of roasted deer meat, and he was delighted by the possibility of finding workable stone. He had often lamented his poor judgment in leaving his band so precipitously, without his tool bag or extra spearheads. "How far is this place?"

"Just ahead."

He scanned across mile after mile of shadowless, dry-grassed hills. "I see nothing," he told her.

She looked at him with pity, then turned her eyes to the country ahead. "I see *everything,*" she whispered, and intense love for the land of her forebears was evident in her tone. "If only you knew this land as I know it . . . Trust me, Ela-nay. Soon we will rest. After the moon rises, you will hunt, and we will eat of meat that is not forbidden to the People of the Watching Star. Until then, the need to find my people is nourishment enough for me! Come. We will go on! I cannot rest knowing that they are near!"

The woman's resiliency amazed him. Since crossing the river they had not rested for any length of time or eaten anything except a few seeds and pulverized roots. But not once had Sheela complained of weariness or hunger. Her only concession to exhaustion was her use of a walking staff, a long, thin, fork-tipped branch that she had picked from a tangle of deadwood.

Now, hours later, with his sandals nearly worn through and the muscles behind his knees going soft with fatigue, he watched her striding ahead. If she could go on without food or rest, he would do the same. What choice did he have? It was too late to go back to his people; by now Sheela and he would have been missed, and Bold Man would kill him if they ever met again.

Sighing with grim resignation, Ela-nay hefted his spear across his shoulder and followed Sheela through knee-high grasses and tall, dried flowers. The screech of a leaping cat tore the evening air and ripped deeply into any self-confidence Ela-nay had managed to gather. An image of the cat flared behind his eyes. It was as big as a small lion, low hipped, lynx faced, with curving fangs the size of a man's upper arm. Ela-nay's mouth went dry. He felt small and vulnerable. *I try to be brave,* he thought, then added in misery, *but my spirit trembles at the sound of leaping cats. And my feet hurt, and my belly aches with hunger.*

The fang-toothed leaping cat screeched again. It was far away to the west and no threat to them; nevertheless Ela-nay was nervous. It was not a good thing for one man and one woman, with one spear and dagger between them, to be alone in the Land of Grass. "After we reach the foothills of the far mountains, how many sleeps will we share before we reach the country of your people?"

"Another night, or perhaps one more after that, depending on how quickly we travel. No more than three days."

"Three days . . ." It seemed an interminable length of time. "What then, Sheela? What if your people do not accept me as one of them?"

She saw his fear and rested her hand upon his arm. "We can only go forward, Ela-nay. Soon we will reach my people. The world will change for us on that day, as it will change for all those foolish enough to allow this daughter of the Watching Star to escape. They will pay for what they have done to me, my sister, and my tribe. By the blood of Ysuna, I swear to you that I will make them pay!"

2

Cha-kwena brought his people and dogs into the foothills long before dusk. The star-speckled wings of a clear night nestled upon the hills and mountain to which his totem and the little yellow wolf had led him as he and his band gathered around a high, hot fire of pinyon wood within a sparse but sheltering grove. The mixed pines and juniper reminded him of home.

"Our totem has led us well!" he declared.

The women had roasted twelve fat-thighed black-tailed hares that Kosar-eh's sons and Cha-kwena had flushed from the scrub growth and snared in throwing nets of woven milkweed fibers. The hares, skinned, with their heads, entrails, and feet tossed to the dogs, made fine eating. After the women had finished their portion, they happily set themselves to supervising the scorching of precious pinyon cones, which the boys knocked from the trees. Set to flame at the edges of the fire, the still-green cone bracts opened wide, then sap bubbled out and ran clear gold to fill the air with the pungent sweetness of resin.

"Hurry now." Ha-xa commanded Kosar-eh's boys to come to her assistance. She and her daughters Mah-ree and Ta-maya used long sticks to knock the many smoldering cones from the fire. Proudly wearing the rare, albeit tattered jaguar skin that had once been the pride of her deceased husband, Ha-xa looked like a big spotted cat as she bent to the work at hand. "Take up your own sticks, boys, and beat the cones until the nuts fall away!"

Considering himself much too mature for such work,

Gah-ti, the eldest of Kosar-eh's five boys, stood haughtily aside. His brothers—eleven-year-old Ka-neh, eight-year-old Kiu-neh, and five-year-old Kho-neh—leaped eagerly to the task. Klah-neh, their nearly three-year-old sibling, was not old enough to be included. The boys had been named in order of their birth, with the exception of Gah-ti, who had been given the name of his deceased paternal grandfather. They banged away at the blackened cones until they fell to pieces and hot, hard-shelled little pine seeds were flying everywhere.

"Now gather your harvest and share it!" Ha-xa told them. As a widow of the band's last chief, command came easily to her.

Again the children obeyed without hesitation. They popped nuts into their mouths as they did so, cracking them with their teeth and spitting shells. Then the boys passed palmfuls of the warm, mealy treasure into the eager hands of the assembled people.

The women reseated themselves at the opposite side of the fire, and the boys settled together close to the flames. Cha-kwena, having accepted his portion, appraised his happily munching little band and felt wonderfully proud and vindicated. They were still together, all alive, all in reasonably good health.

Old pregnant Siwi-ni had released petulant little Klah-neh into the care of her nut-chomping sons, who were now picking remnant seeds from the ground, cracking them for their little brother, and handing him the hulled nuts. Leaning against the backrest of woven chokecherry twigs that Kosar-eh had made for her, Siwi-ni nodded in satisfaction at the children's behavior and sucked marrow from a rabbit bone.

Cha-kwena's eyes moved from the frail, aged woman. U-wa was smiling at him across the flames in that special way that mothers smile when they are immensely pleased with the performance of a child. Twice widowed, U-wa was still a handsome woman and looked more content than Cha-kwena had ever seen her. His nearly two-year-old half sister, Joh-nee, dozed in her lap. The child's greasy little face shone in the firelight. Tla-nee, Ha-xa's girl of Joh-nee's same age, slept in her mother's embrace.

Ha-xa and U-wa were as sisters. During the last year spent in the Red World, both had been wives of the chieftain, Tlana-quah. So it was that their youngest daughters shared the same father.

Cha-kwena looked slightly to the left. Mah-ree was beaming unashamedly at him. Ta-maya sat beside her sister, with her arms crossed around her folded knees. Her hair was parted in the center, pulled back from her face, and secured above each temple by two well-twisted bone hairpins that were each adorned with a single lustrous magpie feather; the main body of her hair fell loose down her back and over her shoulders and arms. Ta-maya smiled slowly, tenderly, when their eyes met and held, and it stopped Cha-kwena's heart.

Ah! How lovely she was! He wanted to sit right there and drink in Ta-maya's smile forever.

She looked away from him, her attention drawn by an exhalation from Siwi-ni. In an instant Ta-maya was at the older woman's side. Cha-kwena found cause to admire more than her beauty; her compassion touched him deeply. In this advanced stage of Siwi-ni's pregnancy, Ta-maya had made Kosar-eh's woman her special concern. Now, as he watched Ta-maya attend to the swollen little woman, he pulled in a deep breath in a vain effort to steady his heartbeat. He sighed, hopelessly in love, wanting the woman of his heart to find him as wonderful as he found her. He cleared his throat and said boldly to Ta-maya, "Tomorrow your shaman, walking ahead of the band, will find the good country to which Life Giver is leading us."

"I will go with you, Shaman!" Gah-ti offered enthusiastically as he beamed across the fire at Mah-ree. "Gah-ti is not afraid! My spear will protect our shaman!"

Mah-ree turned up her nose. "My shaman walks in the favor of the Four Winds. The spear of a half-grown boy is not needed to protect him!"

Gah-ti's smile became a glower. "I have lived to see only one less summer than you!"

Her nose remained aloft. "Hmmph!"

The youth turned to Kosar-eh. "Tell her that Gah-ti's spear arm is strong! Tell her that Gah-ti is a *man*!"

"Yes, yes, Gah-ti," Kosar-eh answered with a father's tone of tolerance and dismissal. He obviously had more important concerns than his son's need to impress Mah-ree. When the clown spoke, it was to Cha-kwena. The words came in the manner of a man who does not wish to give offense. "Perhaps you need not go, Shaman. We could easily winter here. It seems a good place. If we set to work tomorrow, setting snares, raising brushwood shelters, and scouting for a dependable water supply and for berries and roots, we should have enough food set by to last until spring. But if we go on, Shaman, the children and Siwi-ni will be at risk. To winter in unknown high country presents great danger to us all."

Cha-kwena felt ashamed. Kosar-eh was right: He had not been thinking of the effects of a prolonged journey on the members of the band. Looking at Siwi-ni now, he chastised himself for having failed to take her pregnancy into consideration. Only a fool would ask her to leave this camp and walk anywhere until he was certain that she was up to the trek ahead. How frail she was, bundled in furs, a tiny, withered woman with a face as lined as a walnut. Her skin seemed gray even in the fire's glow. Her hands appeared as thin and horny as a bird's feet as they lay protectively over the huge mound of her belly. But Ta-maya was watching him again, so he felt impelled to justify himself.

"I have forgotten nothing, Kosar-eh! I will go into the mountains." He felt better, holding to one part of his position while conceding the other to the clown. "I *must* see where our totem leads us. If the way proves difficult, we will stay in this camp until Siwi-ni is parted from her new life and ready to travel."

Disagreement came from an unexpected source.

"Bah!" snapped Siwi-ni. "You would think that this is a first-time baby that I carry! I am Siwi-ni, Mother of Five Sons! I would not bring new life into a land in which the totem of my people has not seen fit to linger!"

Cha-kwena was thankful for the woman's display of

pride, but he could not ignore the weariness in her sunken eyes. Her continuing fertility was a never-ending source of amazement to everyone, and Cha-kwena did not need the gift of a shaman's Sight to know that this latest pregnancy was the most draining. He and the others would be relieved when her unborn child came forth, without, it was hoped, undue cost to her or to itself.

"No," he said. "In keeping with the traditions of the ancestors, Siwi-ni must obey the wishes of her man. Shaman will not stand in the way of this."

Kosar-eh's brows arched. "This man is grateful."

Siwi-ni, frowning, harrumphed.

Cha-kwena looked at her. She was sensing compromise on his part and objected to exceptions being made on her behalf lest she be made to feel old and unworthy in the eyes of her man and sons. He did not know what to say.

"Do as you must, Shaman, but not for my sake. If the others need to rest awhile, I would not mind, of course. I know that the little ones are tired. But you must walk in the shadow of the totem and see where Life Giver is leading us! If the way is not difficult, this woman would follow. The life in this belly has not yet settled into the birth position. Perhaps it knows that better country lies ahead, so it waits to be born there."

"Let it be so, then," the young man said. "The band will rest here—for the sake of the little ones. Tomorrow I will go on in the footsteps of the totem."

"I will go with you!" insisted Gah-ti, grasping yet again at an opportunity to impress Mah-ree.

"At dawn," agreed Cha-kwena after he saw that Kosar-eh was not going to object. He knew that he would be long gone and far away by the time the youth roused himself from his sleeping furs. He needed no spearman to protect him. He was Shaman. The sacred stone would be around his neck, and Moon, Mother of Stars, would light his way.

And it was so. Only the dogs saw him go. Gah-ti, dressed and ready for travel, had been awake much of the night but had at last succumbed to sleep—as had Mah-ree, who had been watching Cha-kwena from the corner of her eye for hours. The shaman felt no remorse in leaving the two would-be travelers behind; it was not their place to follow the totem. It was his.

With Moon rising nearly full, Cha-kwena followed the great white mammoth in the cool silver light that was Moon's gift to him. Now and then he came across coyote sign: the occasional paw prints, the unmistakable long, dark, granular fecal matter of summer's end. The scat was drier than usual, and impregnated with fewer berries, pine nuts, and mouse bones than he would have expected at this time of year. Mammoth spoor was not difficult to find in the moonlight—not for one trained in the ways of tracking.

Life Giver moved through scrub growth and trees, parting its way with trunk and tusks, breaking many a branch at a height that testified to a giant's passing. The sap of bleeding pines and junipers scented the night air, as did the pungent herbaceous aroma of crushed foliage and, occasionally, the high, acrid smell that was unique to the urine and feces of a mammoth.

Soon Cha-kwena was out of the pinyon groves and climbing wide, stony hills. The young shaman smiled with satisfaction. The way presented no difficulty to a man, nor would it cause hardship to his band or to a well-rested pregnant woman if she took her time.

Soon he was on the flank of the mountain itself, heading gradually upward to what seemed to be a broad pass that opened into the heart of the range. He was not sure just when he realized that he was no longer alone. But there was no one behind him, nor could he hear the footfall of man or beast. He looked right and left, then felt a sudden, sickening constriction of his gut. Dark inferences of form stood poised within the trees on either side of him and watched him with fixed eyes shining silver in the moonlight.

Bear? Puma? Wolf? Leaping cat? Lion? He dared not speak the names lest their utterance by a shaman assure their reality. Fear rose at the back of his throat. He forced himself to swallow it down as he called for courage and reason to rise in him instead.

He positioned his spear. But the shadows did not move. They made no sound. They gave off no scent. He stood tall, emboldened, knowing that if these shadow predators had wanted to make meat of him, they would have done so long before now. If these natural enemies and competitors on the hunt walked together in the night—if they gave off no scent and roused no sound—then they could not be real animals; they must be spirit creatures sent by the forces of Creation to protect a young, inexperienced shaman as he came alone into unknown country.

Protect me from what? he wondered. As long as he possessed the sacred stone and walked in the way of his totem, no harm could come to him.

Cha-kwena's left hand rose to curl tightly around his medicine bag. With his right holding his spear, he walked on. The shadow animals walked with him. He felt resolute but was discomfited by the realization that only predators kept pace with him this night.

On and on Cha-kwena walked along the high, gentle slope. It was such a broad, welcoming mountain that he was no longer afraid as the shadow carnivores plodded on beside him. When a great horned owl flushed from a snag-topped pine and flew ahead on silent wings, Cha-kwena's heart leaped with relief and gladness.

"Owl! Old friend! Does the spirit of my grandfather fly upon your back, as he once flew with you across the far land of the ancestors?"

The bird flew on in the way of an ordinary owl, silent and silken winged, soon lost in the moonlit unknown. Disappointed, Cha-kwena paused and looked up. The world was plunged into darkness. The stars were gone. Moon was gone in long, thin bands of cloud. Disoriented, his fears came to life despite his earlier determination to be unafraid. He imagined animals merging from all sides, claws and fangs and slavering jaws preparing to pierce his flesh and rake his bones.

Terrified, he bolted forward blindly until something caught him about the ankle and sent him sprawling.

Pain flared as he landed with an *"uch!"* of surprise. Stunned, Cha-kwena sat up and, spear positioned, faced whatever it was that had felled him.

"I am Cha-kwena! I am Shaman! And I am *not*

afraid!'' If he shouted loudly enough, he thought, perhaps whatever had attacked him would believe the lie.

His heart was pounding. His instep hurt badly, but he ignored the pain; he hoped he would live long enough to tend to it later. Now he stared into utter blackness at imagined lions, wolves, and great, lumbering bears. What he saw was not carnivores or phantoms but a giant serpent emerging from the bony skin of the mountain.

Cha-kwena gasped, horrified. The creature's head and tail tip were buried in the ground. Its long, curving body was extended, arched slightly upward in the middle. He felt sick with dread. When this reptile emerged from the flesh of the mountain, it would be longer than Cha-kwena was tall! How could he stand against such a predator?

An eternity of moments passed, but the great snake remained as it was, arched upward in the middle, head and tail buried in the slag. Cha-kwena's face puckered with perplexity. Why did the thing not move? Unable to fight his curiosity, Cha-kwena extended his spear and gave a quick, wary poke at the snake. Expecting it to be roused by the prick and come twisting into quick and dangerous animation, he was ready to flee for his life. But still the snake did not move.

Cha-kwena poked at it again. This time apprehension washed out of him as he heard the dull scrape of his stone projectile point making contact with bare, hard, weathereroded bone. A brief laugh at his own expense went out of him. He lowered his spear and felt foolish for ever having feared the mammoth rib over which he had tripped in the dark.

"Some shaman you are," Cha-kwena admonished himself. He rested his spear against his shoulder and, after rubbing his aching instep and finding only the most minor of bruises, moved forward to lay his hand upon that which had brought him to his knees.

Cha-kwena ran his hand over the arching span of bone. It was proof that he had at last followed his totem into a land where other mammoth had once dwelled and might dwell still.

He closed his eyes and allowed the bone to speak to

him of what must have transpired many a long year before at the crest of the pass: a big mammoth had succumbed to the infirmities of old age. Once it was down and dying, other mammoth would have stayed with the old one until the end, then eventually gone their way. In time, after carnivores and the sun and weather had done their work, only the largest bones would have remained where they had fallen. Storms would have washed them downslope and covered them with debris carried from the height of the pass. Finally all that remained visible was one portion of a great rib.

Excitement was rising in Cha-kwena. Life Giver had turned toward the north because somehow it knew that other mammoth were there. Hope sang in the young shaman's heart. "The omens are *good* this night!" he declared. "When Life Giver walks once more among the mammoth kind, then will my band find that good land toward which the totem has been leading us!"

Cha-kwena became suddenly aware of the faint stirring of the cold north wind. Restless, it ruffled his hair, chilled his scalp, and pushed against his body like the palms of invisible hands. He looked around uncomfortably, for the wind carried a vaguely familiar scent that held the threat of danger.

The last traces of cloud cover had vanished from the sky. Moon was beginning to settle over the western hills. Her face seemed smaller, weary, as coyotes began to howl on the other side of the pass.

Cha-kwena listened. The little yellow wolves were summoning one another to the hunt in high howls and yaps; he knew the sound well. He did not fear it. They were not stalking him. But something *was* coming toward him from the far side of the pass. He heard the thud of enormous footfall, the suck and wheeze of heavy breathing, and heard loose stones clink and clatter and skitter downslope. Cha-kwena rose, stared ahead to the height of the pass, and caught his breath.

The great white mammoth stood before him, with Coyote, the little yellow wolf, at his side.

Cha-kwena did not know how long he stood in silence. Slowly, so slowly that its movement was not perceptible at first, his totem came toward him and the mammoth stared down out of sunken, rheumy eyes. The young shaman saw his own image reflected as though in a film of opaque ice.

Fighting down instinctive terror of a creature that was the size of a walking mountain, the shaman raised his spear arm in salute and tried to sound bold and steady as he proclaimed, "Life Giver . . . Great Ghost Spirit . . . Grandfather of All Mammoth . . . the guardian of First Man and First Woman and of all the ancestors since time beyond beginning . . . totem of the People . . . Cha-kwena, grandson of Hoyeh-tay, offers greeting!"

The winglike, tatter-edged ears of the tusker twitched and pivoted forward as though waiting to hear more from the puny being. The long strands of sparse white hair, which grew from the massive twin domes of its skull, spine, shoulders, and trunk, shone like wisps of silver grass in the ebbing moonlight. Life Giver took a backward step, swung its head slowly from side to side, then came forward at a trot that brought it to a dead stop in front of Cha-kwena. Its trunk reached to envelop the stone tip of the young shaman's spear.

Cha-kwena nearly fainted. Transfixed, he could not have run away even if he had wanted to; he was trapped between the massive, inwardly curling extensions of the mammoth's tusks. If Life Giver wanted his spear, he would surrender it without argument; but the great mammoth released the weapon and with its trunk came scenting the young man.

"Ah!" Cha-kwena's exhalation expressed more fear and revulsion than awe. The moist, hot breath of his totem bathed him—not in the scent of clouds and mists upon which spirit animals were said to feed, but in the stench of old, plaque-rimed molars, fetid gums, and well-masticated, half-digested browse. It was putrid enough to overwhelm even a shaman on the spot. Cha-kwena held his breath until he feared he would either throw up or pass out.

The mammoth huffed, swayed, then released Cha-kwena and moved back.

As the tusker turned away, Cha-kwena sagged with relief. The great one was walking off now, to the crest of the pass where Coyote waited, head down, tail tucked, one forepaw raised. The mammoth paused beside the little yellow wolf, looked back at Cha-kwena, then continued on with Coyote.

Spellbound, Cha-kwena followed. The north wind was strong in his face as he paused at the height of the pass and looked down into the broad, lake-filled valley that lay far below. Once again Cha-kwena caught his breath. *This is the place to which the white-headed eagles flew!*

He could see it all: tall stands of forest to the west; grassland to the east; a river, hills, a lake sparkling silver in the moonlight—a land that was everything he had been dreaming of and yearning for across all of the long miles since leaving the land of his ancestors. In all of this world or the next he would never find a more beautiful or welcoming land than this valley into which he would soon lead his people to live forever.

When North Wind continued to blow cold against his face and body, he paid it no heed. When he saw the flash of lightning over distant ranges that lay far to the north beyond the range in which the valley lay, he saw no portent in it.

When the sound of trumpeting mammoth came up the mountain slope and Life Giver trumpeted back, Cha-kwena held up his arms and praised the forces of Creation for having reunited his totem with creatures of its own kind.

Coyotes were still howling in the beautiful valley. Cha-kwena listened and then loosed a howl of his own. It was a high, yapping ululation of pure delight. "I have brought my people home at last!" he cried.

As often happened in special moments of his life, Cha-kwena found himself thinking briefly of Dakan-eh. He wondered how the headman was faring without his totem, the sacred stone, and shaman. "Oh, Bold Man, if only you could have walked with me this night and set eyes upon the valley to which our totem has led our band! You would surely regret the day you chose to turn your back upon the ways of the ancestors!"

Intensely happy, Cha-kwena started back toward the encampment in the pinyon grove. He told himself that he should not care about Bold Man. Dakan-eh had chosen his own fate, as surely as Cha-kwena had chosen his own.

3

"Soon it will be dawn."

Dakan-eh winced, startled from his dark reverie by Ban-ya's throaty whisper. She had come alone to where he sat at the river's edge, glaring across the darkness. A day and most of a night had passed since Sheela and Ela-nay had run off together. Dakan-eh's pride was bruised by the slave's disloyalty, and he could not understand how slow-witted, less-than-courageous Ela-nay had been so bold for the sake of a woman. Now, as Ban-ya knelt beside him, he did not acknowledge her presence.

"You cannot sleep?" She waited for a reply; when he chose not to give her one, she said softly, "It is good that they are dead."

He looked at her. " 'They'?"

"The fool Ela-nay and the slave. She was bad luck for us. And as long as the rituals of mourning continue, concern for them will not build. It is good that you have finished with them." She nodded with grim satisfaction.

He did not correct her assumption that he had long since killed them and given their bodies to the river.

"When others ask," she continued, "you will say that the deaths of Owa-neh and Na-sei, of Shateh's son and hunters, so saddened your spirit that you took no notice of the absence of a slave. You have already told them that the fool Ela-nay has gone off to mourn alone. We will pretend to look for them. When we do not find them, we will grieve."

"They no longer concern me."

"They must concern you, Dakan-eh, lest Atonashkeh find in them another excuse to lay upon your back the blame for Shateh's turn of luck!"

"I do not fear Atonashkeh. His tongue runs loose like the bowel of a dog that has eaten only meat and no—"

"You would be the meat that Atonashkeh would eat, Dakan-eh! You *must* fear him! If he can convince Shateh to send you from this land in disgrace—"

"Your tongue is as loose as Atonashkeh's, woman!"

"Perhaps, but there is no venom for you in my heart. The only meat that this woman will ever eat is that which she would share with you forever."

His brows arched toward his hairline. Her loyalty pleased him, but it also annoyed him. He needed no one, especially a female, to tell him that the son of Shateh was his enemy. He eyed Ban-ya reproachfully. She was wearing her favorite garment—a full-length cloak of many prime, vertically aligned coyote tails that were attached to one complete skin, the upper portion of which formed a hood. The desiccated head of this pelt lay atop her own head. The forepaws draped downward around her face and were knotted below her chin.

The hooded cloak was a striking piece of apparel, and the sight of it usually pleased him; tonight it did not. With starlight granting just enough illumination to highlight her features in a soft, blue glow, Ban-ya's face resembled that of a slant-eyed little weasel hiding within the skin of a larger animal.

He knew that the garment was the only thing of her own that Ban-ya had taken to safety from the village. It was special to her for reasons that touched them both deeply. Long ago in a far land he had killed the coyote, as part of his bride gift for Ta-maya. He had snared it, slain it, prepared the skin until it was as soft as the hide of a newborn fawn, then combed and oiled the fur until it shone and slipped through his fingers like sun-warmed water.

The memories shamed and angered him. Ta-maya had spurned his gift, and him along with it. Cha-kwena had admonished him for killing an animal that the young shaman named Spirit Brother.

Dakan-eh snorted bitterly as he remembered how Ban-ya had taken up the coyote skin and followed him out of the village by the Lake of Singing Birds, a place he vowed to abandon after Ta-maya's treatment of him. Bold Man had taken Ban-ya as his woman; he had put life in her and knew that she would make him many bold sons. Ta-maya had been too foolish to see the error of her ways. Seduced by an enemy and widowed soon after, she had sworn that she would take no man ever again.

Ban-ya had given him no cause to regret his decision to take her as his woman, yet he still found himself longing for Ta-maya . . . still wondering *where* she was, and *how* she was, and what it would be like to possess and penetrate the body of the one woman who had ever refused him.

Thinking of her now, he felt his penis, heated, move and swell. He stared at the face of the long-dead coyote, which seemed to be staring back at him from atop Ban-ya's head. Dakan-eh's mouth tightened into a grimace of loathing. To get even with Cha-kwena, Bold Man had been spitefully killing coyotes ever since, adding the tails of the best slain animals to Ban-ya's robe until it had become a garment of such transcending warmth and beauty that all of the women of the Land of Grass envied her possession of it.

The corners of Dakan-eh's mouth curled into a smile of pure vindictiveness. Every time that he speared a little yellow wolf and added its tail to the cloak, Dakan-eh felt strong in the certainty that wherever Cha-kwena walked, Brother of Animals was bleeding a little, hurting a little, suffering the loss of some portion of his shaman's magic.

But would his powers ever die as long as Cha-kwena walked in the shadow of the great white mammoth and remained in possession of the sacred stone? *Could* they ever die? Or were they growing, maturing even as Cha-kwena must be maturing? Somewhere far away the grandson of Hoyeh-tay would be a man now, perhaps with Ta-maya as his woman.

"Dakan-eh, are you listening to me? Here, the air is cold. Put this on."

He was relieved to have been drawn from his troubled reverie and grateful for the warmth of his cloak of cougar skins that Ban-ya had brought to place around his shoulders. From beyond the grove, a long, distinctive ululation of grief came to him. He shuddered at the sound of his mother's voice and at the memory of how his father had died.

Your fault.

The words stabbed him; he would not hear them. "No! It is Cha-kwena's doing! All of it!"

Ban-ya nodded. "Yes. If such words are needed, it will be good if you speak so." She extended the flayed hide of the coyote that he had killed on the day of the stampede. "Carry this with pride. All who see it will remember that chasing the wind to save the People!"

Still thinking of Cha-kwena, he took the pelt and wished that the young shaman were lying flayed across his arm. He rose, slung the skin over his shoulder, and drew in a deep, steadying breath of the dying night. "Come, Ban-ya. We will go back to the others. From this sunrise on, we will make our own luck!"

"Listen!" Sheela whispered.

Eyes narrowed, Ela-nay obeyed. The song of wolves was coming from the bare, stony range of high hills just to the north. The sound of hunting predators raised prickles across the base of his neck.

Sheela gave no sign of being afraid. She stood with her back to the dawn, her battered face rapt. "They *are* there, and coming toward us." She sighed happily, as though listening to the greetings of beloved, long-lost friends.

He did not like the situation. "The wolves sound as though they are running in a pack. Perhaps we should turn our steps toward the Red World. It is far, I know, but I will keep you safe from—"

"Do not speak like a fool, Ela-nay! The land of your lizard-eating ancestors is the first place that Dakan-eh and Shateh would search for us!"

He frowned, disconcerted by the contempt that had curdled her reply. "You said that they would not dare to cross the river, that they would not care about us enough to follow," he reminded. The words sounded good to him. His tone was strong and deep, huskier than any that his woman, children, or mother had heard in years; it was the voice he used among females outside his own family when he hoped to impress and seduce them, and among other hunters when he was attempting to appear bold in their eyes—and his own.

Sheela shook her head at him as she might at a thick-brained child. "When they have finished mourning, Ela-nay, who can say what they will do? They may follow us. In the meantime, what are a few wolves to such a bold and reckless man as you, eh? Have you not stood between me and a pride of lions?"

He nodded. Late the night before, Sheela had quickly placed herself behind him when they had inadvertently blundered into the hunting territory of lions. Together the slave and he had watched as the huge cats closed on a small herd of camels. With his spear at ready and his heart beating in his mouth, Ela-nay had known that he would have died to protect the woman, for he loved her more than his own life.

"Come!" she urged him, moving on now. "Soon we will be among my people!"

She gave him no choice but to follow. With dawn ripening around them, he marveled at how well she knew the country. Sheela, avoiding herds of grazing animals around which predators would surely be lurking, skirted a place where the scars of war were still evident upon the land. He paused, brought short by a dark foreboding. The presence of the spirits of the dead and memories of his eager participation in war and killing made him uneasy.

"What is it, Ela-nay?"

"The ghosts of those whom I have slain are watching me."

"Perhaps."

"I do not think that they are welcoming me into the country of their ancestors, Sheela."

She stepped close and linked her arm through his. "You have no cause to fear the dead, Ela-nay."

He stared ahead at the hills. Wolves were howling again, and Ela-nay caught his breath. He had heard more than wolves across the land. In the thin light of morning, a party of spear-armed hunters appeared as though out of nowhere. He curled one hand into a fist three times, counting fifteen men. Tattooed, clad in ragged skins, furs, feathers, and the body paint of warriors, they were as hostile-looking as the dogs that were with them. Ela-nay instinctively knew that the men were more dangerous than the lions that he had seen on the kill the night before.

"Get behind me, Sheela. Do not be afraid."

Sheela gasped. "Put aside your spear, you stupid man! I need no protection from these warriors!" Before he could stop her, she raced forward. "Tsana!" she cried out and, weeping with joy, sped to the arms of one of the strangers.

Ela-nay stared, openmouthed. The warriors were before him now. Tall, big men, they towered over him. He stood straighter and puffed out his chest in the way of a horned lizard when, cornered by predators, it must make itself appear big and bold and capable of sticking in the throat of any attacker. He felt the glares of the newcomers boring into him, but he had no eyes for any of them except the man Tsana.

Although haggard as if from a long illness, the warrior was in his prime and physically impressive. He held Sheela as though he could not believe that she was in his embrace. Ela-nay assumed that the man was her brother or an old family friend. Then jealousy flared. Tsana was no brother! And surely he was more than a friend! He had his face against Sheela's, his nostrils to hers as he breathed deeply and hungrily of her every exhalation. In the way of a lover, his mouth found her lips, and his hands swept over her body. When she drew back in pain, he moved back and, fingering her cropped forelocks, looked at her battered features.

Ela-nay saw him stiffen, heard his intake of breath, and met the fury of his stare.

"You have done this to the one who was to have been my woman!" raged Tsana.

"I . . ." was all that came from Ela-nay's mouth before someone had wrested away his spear and Tsana was at his neck. A moment later Ela-nay was on the ground, staring up with his throat aflame and head spinning to see that he was surrounded by slavering dogs and men.

"No," Sheela told Tsana. "This man has brought me to you. It was another who did this to me."

"Name him! He will pay."

"Yes, I will name him. They will *all* pay." Then Sheela's voice took on a tone filled with concern. "Tell me, Tsana, where have you been since I was taken into captivity so many moons ago?"

The reply came from a burly man with a face painted completely black with ashes and grease. "Many times over these past long moons has Tsana's spirit drifted in and out of his body. The wounds he received in battle were many and great. Only the forces of Creation know how and why he did not die of them."

"And you, Ston?" Her voice was flat. "Why did you not come to free me and Rikiree? She was to have been your woman. Often she looked to the north and spoke your name and longed for you to come to her. Finally, in degradation and shame, she threw herself from the bluffs into the river."

A howl of anguish erupted from Ston. Bereft, he hung his head and wept openly while those at his side lay hands upon him in brotherly sympathy.

Anger tightened the tattooed jawline of Tsana as he turned Sheela toward him so that he might look once again into her face. "I would not have known you had you not called out to me." He tenderly kissed her swollen features. "Ston and others did search for you and Rikiree, and for all those who were taken. Your village was found burned, Sheela. Many were dead—old ones, children, even dogs. The bodies had been thrown into the burning lodges. There was no way for us to know that you were not among the slain. We raised the mourning songs and cut our flesh to show our pain for the passing of your life spirits into the world beyond this world."

Ela-nay attempted to rise. To his amazement, it was Sheela who reacted by kicking him so hard that he fell back, stunned and gripping his side. The pain of the unexpected blow was sharp and deep; his insides felt ruptured. Nevertheless, the pain was nothing when compared to the hurt he suffered because the woman of his heart had dealt the blow.

"How many have survived?" Sheela asked Tsana.

The man's face was grim. "We have become few—a tribe scattered across the Land of Grass, no longer what we were in the days when Ysuna, Daughter of the Sun, and Masau, Mystic Warrior, assured us that we would someday be as many as the stars and as invincible in our power as our totem, the great white mammoth, which has vanished from our land."

"The totem walks far to the south," informed Sheela coolly. "We will find it and hunt it all in good time. By consuming its flesh and drinking its blood, we take its power into ourselves. But for now, there is easier, closer prey. The hunting camp from which I have fled has been destroyed by the storm spirits. The bison hunters are weak with grief. In another day, perhaps two, the many bands that have come together for the great autumn hunt will go their separate ways. Many—perhaps *all* of the ones who have done this to my face and caused the death of Rikiree could be killed. The bodies could be left as our dead were left—burned beyond recognition."

The world seemed to tilt beneath Ela-nay. "Sheela," he reminded her, "my woman and children and mother are in that camp."

She glared at him with contempt. "They are nothing to me and less to you, Lizard Eater, or you would not have abandoned them!" She turned back to Tsana. "Besides those who stand with you now, are there other warriors who have survived the endless raids?"

Tsana nodded slowly. "A few. We are mostly a band of women and children. We have a shaman, and enough warriors to make new life on the women."

"Do they possess the heart and fighting spirit to attack Shateh's band?" she pressed.

The men of the People of the Watching Star exchanged meaningful glances as they murmured among themselves.

"I would go!" declared Ston boldly. "To avenge Rikiree, I would go!"

"Not alone," cautioned Tsana. "The People of the Watching Star have suffered enough deaths. It is time for our enemies to die. Return ahead of us to the stronghold, Ston. Inform those who await our return that one who shares the blood of Ysuna has come back from the world beyond this world to walk among the living once more. Let them prepare a feast in her honor. This will give them new heart. This will set fire to our warriors' spirits so that they will yearn to go once more across the land of our enemies."

As Ston trotted off toward the hills, Ela-nay could not take his eyes off Sheela. Disbelief numbed his mind. She was standing as straight and rigid as a pine tree. Her eyes were barely visible within her swollen lids, yet the pure, fixed radiance of resolve shone in them. Her mouth was set, and saliva bubbled at the corners of her once long, beautiful lips. Truly, he thought, shuddering, the blood of the murderous Ysuna *did* run in her veins. She had used him, then betrayed him.

"What you do is an offense to the forces of Creation," he spoke out as he managed to get to his knees. "My children, at least, deserve some consideration from you! I have given up everything to protect you, Sheela!"

She was not moved. "For my good, or in the hope of satisfying your own lust by owning me?"

He blanched, recognizing the truth.

"When your people raided my village, Ela-nay, did you protect *my* family?" She shook her head. "You and those loyal to Shateh and Dakan-eh stole me and my sister away into captivity and killed all others. With my own eyes, I saw you spear my old grandmother and fire our lodge. You took pleasure in the killing."

Ela-nay felt something begin to bleed within him; it was his hope. His life was over, and he knew it.

Still looking at Ela-nay, Sheela conceded to Tsana, "This lizard eater is not much of a man, but I *did* promise him a reward if he helped me reach my people."

Hope flared in Ela-nay's breast, then faded as he saw the look that passed among Sheela, Tsana, and the others. His reward was not to be life or the sparing of his family; it was to be a quick death. It came on the tip of Tsana's spear as, screaming for a reprieve that he knew would never come, he was struck through the heart.

4

"We will go now!" Siwi-ni, leaning against her backrest, stretched her skinny limbs toward the little cooking fire that the other women had raised. A morning meal of freshly snared birds and squirrels was being roasted by Ha-xa, U-wa, Mah-ree, and Ta-maya. "The day is young. Soon life will come forth again from this woman, and I would bear it in the new land!"

Kosar-eh eyed his woman with concern from the opposite side of the fire. She looked so shrunken and gray in the soft morning light. "The journey will not be easy for you, Siwi-ni. We should stay in this camp until the new life *is* life and you are well and strong again."

"Bah! I am not sick! I am wearied by this new life that grows in me; but I am strong enough to carry it, I can tell you that!" The wrinkled little woman clucked her tongue at him. "Do not look at me like that, Kosar-eh! You know better than most that nothing is easy. We cannot wait around for good things to come to us. We must go to them, even though the way be difficult."

"The way to the valley is not difficult," Cha-kwena said. Seated beside Kosar-eh, he yanked long, thin strands of underdone pink meat from the back of the squirrel that his mother had roasted for him. He ate them even though he wished that just once U-wa would cook something to his satisfaction.

"The trek may not be a problem for a young man," snapped Kosar-eh, "but for an old woman big with life, any walk is difficult!"

Cha-kwena was taken aback by the heat of the man's rebuttal. It seemed that Kosar-eh and he could not exchange even the mildest words without chafing each other these days.

Siwi-ni's denial was proud but pathetic. "I am not old!"

"You are not young!" Kosar-eh countered.

Uncomfortable, Cha-kwena set his underdone squirrel back onto the fire as he spoke out in the way of a conciliator. "We can go ahead, or we can stay here until Siwi-ni is finished with the ordeal of life bearing. Either way, this shaman will be content."

"Then we must go on!" Siwi-ni was emphatic. "Last night I sensed big meat eaters prowling close. I longed to be near our totem and within the protection of a big lodge with high ridgepoles and thick walls of wood and woven grass. Ah, how I have come to miss the comfort and security of a large settlement, where the many hunters and the scent of people and smokes kept predators away. I wish I did not have to worry so much about my boys."

"You do not have to worry about me, my mother," informed Gah-ti loftily. "I am a man now."

His younger brothers guffawed. He swatted out at them, but they ducked away in all directions. When his slap went wild, they shrieked with laughter.

"You had better be fast," Gah-ti warned them. "If I catch you, you will not like the punishment. I *am* a man, and the blows that I will rain upon you will prove it!"

"Threats of blows against children prove nothing of a man, except that he is no man at all!" Kosar-eh informed his eldest son sternly.

The youth stiffened, threw his half-eaten, roasted woodpecker into the fire, and, crossing his slim arms around his knees, glared belligerently at the flames.

Siwi-ni shook her head admonishingly at her other sons. "Do not tease Gah-ti, young ones."

"I, too, sensed prowling meat eaters and did not sleep well for fear of them," U-wa said as she rose, reached across the fire, picked up the skewered squirrel that she had prepared for Cha-kwena, and handed it back to him. Her expression told him to finish his breakfast.

"I am not afraid!" Mah-ree said. "You speak as though flesh eaters have never before come close to our encampments. As long as our shaman follows Grandfather of All, the totem's powers will protect us—in this camp or in any other!"

"Then let it be a permanent camp in the new land," said Siwi-ni.

Kneeling beside Siwi-ni, Ta-maya's expression revealed deep concern. "Listen to the wisdom of your man, my friend," she suggested gently. "A woman who is big with life must look to her own strength if she is to protect the child that grows within her."

Siwi-ni guffawed. "Ha! If I listened to my Kosar-eh's wisdom, there would be no new life in this belly at all. He has told me that I am no longer strong enough for baby making. But look at the five sons this strong, brave woman has borne to Kosar-eh! And if the forces of Creation are willing, I will soon bear him another and many more after that!"

Ta-maya looked to Kosar-eh. "You must speak reason to your woman, Dear Friend."

The man, embarrassed by Siwi-ni's boasting, had been staring down, idly massaging his crippled arm with his good hand. Now he met Ta-maya's glance and, as often happened when he lost himself in her soft eyes and lovely face, could not speak at all.

Siwi-ni's shrunken features tightened at her man's obvious longing, but she did not speak. She had seen the expression before—many times.

Now, suddenly, the dogs began to growl and snap over possession of some food.

Cha-kwena sat very straight. *Of course!* he thought. *Why have I not thought of it before?* He raised his hands and felt very much the shaman as he said, "The dogs have told us what we must do. We *will* go into the new land, but will prepare a litter. The dogs will carry the woman of Kosar-eh."

"Would you shame me, Cha-kwena?" Siwi-ni looked

horrified. "I will not allow myself to be dragged along like a crippled ancient!"

Kosar-eh's eyes burned upon Siwi-ni's face. "You will do as you are told!" He spoke so sharply that Siwi-ni, stunned by her man's unexpected hostility, clapped a hand over her mouth.

Kosar-eh's brow came down. His mouth was set. "Perhaps I have been wrong," he conceded at length, his tone tight, bitter. "Perhaps Shaman has spoken wisely . . . for a change."

Cha-kwena flinched against the statement, which offered both approval and criticism of his decision-making powers.

"My shaman *always* speaks wisely!" Mah-ree defended.

Kosar-eh's expression remained set, morose, brooding. A soft, cool wind had begun to blow from the north. Still massaging his lifeless right arm, he turned his gaze to high, thin clouds that promised a change of weather. "A storm is coming. Soon winter will be upon the land. We cannot stay in a camp that has drawn big meat eaters and that offers no nearby dependable source of water. We must go on."

In the days that lay ahead, Kosar-eh led the women and children, and Gah-ti guided the dogs pulling Siwi-ni's sledge. Meanwhile, Mah-ree hurried along, vainly calling out to Cha-kwena to wait for her.

Kosar-eh, watching the girl, could not fault Gah-ti for his infatuation with her. He felt a father's pride in all of his strapping boys and was certain that if Cha-kwena did not begin to take Mah-ree seriously, the young shaman would soon find himself with worthy competition.

As he walked, the clown recalled his own youth in the distant Red World. In those days he, not Dakan-eh, had been Bold Man of his band. In those days the women and girls of his people had smiled upon his physical perfection. Although he was barely fourteen at the time, when he had smiled back, more than a few of them, giggling, had drawn him aside and opened themselves for his—and their—

pleasure. He could have had any of them for his all-the-time woman, including the firstborn daughter of the chief.

"Ta-maya . . ." As he walked, he whispered her name, with the old, endless longing. He did not even realize that he spoke at all.

Ta-maya, striding at his side and beside her mother, looked up at him and asked what he wished of her.

He did not reply; he was lost in the past, seeing her as she had been in those long-gone days of his youth—a doe-eyed five-year-old, the most gentle and lustrous of children, for whom he had been gladly willing to wait. What were a few years? Nothing to a reckless, handsome young hunter who had his entire future shining before him. Perhaps he had been too reckless, too handsome? Old men had cautioned that sometimes the forces of Creation became jealous and spiteful; they had warned him to be wary, but he had been careless on a hunt, and to this day he was paying for that mistake. The handsome hunter was long dead. In his place was a scar-faced clown with a paralyzed arm that rendered him unfit to take any female except a broken-down old widow.

Kosar-eh sighed, disconsolate. Siwi-ni had been a good wife; he had come to care for her deeply, and he adored their sons. Now, however, as he turned to look where Gah-ti trudged along beside her sledge, the man knew that this latest gift was no gift at all. Male or female, this child seemed to be killing her.

May it be so!

Kosar-eh stopped in midstep, horrified by his thoughts. He knew that his longing for Siwi-ni's death had prompted him to allow her to make this trek. He was hoping against hope that the journey would kill her. If Siwi-ni died, he would have no woman, and Ta-maya would take pity on him. Perhaps, after all of these long, long years of yearning, the woman of his heart might yet be his.

He hung his head. Shame and guilt washed through him. To be at Ta-maya's side, he had willingly become an outcast from his people. To save her life, he had followed her deep into the country of those who had seduced her for purposes so vile that even now he could barely bring himself to think of them. He had turned his back on the prohibitions of his ancestors, taken up the weapons of a man, become a one-armed warrior against the People of the Watching Star, and earned the name Man Who Spits in the Face of Enemies. For him there was no life without Ta-maya somewhere near—if not as woman, then as friend. His heart bled, knowing that all he would ever have of her was the respect and gratitude he had won in the great war. Never having been unrealistic, he knew that when she showed concern for him, it was only a friend's kindness and pity for a cripple.

"What is it, Dear Friend?" she pressed, coming to stand beside him and slipping her hand through the perpetually crooked elbow of his ruined right arm. Because the rising north wind had blown his cloak back, the pallid flesh and atrophied muscles were exposed. "Your woman will be well. Siwi-ni will bear you another son . . . or perhaps this time a daughter to make your brave heart smile."

Dear Friend. Brave heart. He wondered if he had ever hated the words more. As for a daughter, he had never considered the possibility. Perhaps a daughter who might someday be as fine and lustrous a woman as the fair Ta-maya? His jaw tightened. He wanted no such child! He wanted the *woman!*

Their eyes met. Ta-maya smiled reassuringly. And suddenly, painfully aware of the press of her body against his, he looked down and gasped. His arm was bare! His ruined arm! And she was touching it, leaning into it, as though it did not revolt her as it revolted him. Disgusted by the thought of Ta-maya's unblemished hand upon his devastated flesh, Kosar-eh forced her hand away and frantically drew the robe over his arm.

He castigated himself. Siwi-ni deserved better from him. After all of these years, it was past time for him to accept that whatever might have been between Ta-maya and him had *never* been and was best forgotten.

Suddenly Siwi-ni got up from her sledge and began to point excitedly at a pair of fishing eagles circling in the sky. "It is the best of omens!" she declared.

When Kosar-eh came to stand beside her, she beamed up at him out of a flushed face, and her eyes sparkled with excitement. His left eyebrow arched with pleased speculation. The little woman looked much better than she had earlier. Indeed, she looked better than she had in days! He was relieved that the forces of Creation were not going to take him up on his vile, self-serving wish for her death.

"Do you see the fishing eagles, Kosar-eh? The forces of Creation are promising us that there is good land and much water up ahead! I will walk on my own two feet into this new land!"

"You will not." He was adamant. "When we reach the place where we may see down into the valley, then you may walk. Not before then."

As the People walked on, the eagles continued to ride the thermals. Broad, outstretched wings set shadows before the sun. Ta-maya looked up and, frowning, spoke of memories that caused a catch in her throat. "The sight of soaring eagles led the warriors of the People of the Watching Star to the lake country of the Red World." She trembled, then sighed, for the warriors brought war and death to the many bands there. "Had the warriors not come, I would never have known Masau, and perhaps he would be alive now, happy with his people and—"

"Looking to make war upon others!" U-wa snapped. "Looking for victims to seduce, for unknowing brides to be mated to him and then sacrificed to his cannibal sky god. How can you speak of Masau with longing, Ta-maya? He is better off dead. Because of him your father was slain, and at his hands old Hoyeh-tay was murdered. How many peaceful villages were washed in the blood of our people, then put to the torch at his command?"

Ta-maya hung her head and whispered softly, "You did not know him as I did."

"Praise the Four Winds I did not!" exclaimed U-wa.

Ha-xa was visibly disturbed. "I regret the day I set eyes upon Masau. Shateh knew what he was doing when he abandoned that son to White Giant Winter! We would all have been better off if Ysuna, Daughter of the Sun, and her murderous tribe had not rescued him from the storms." The woman paused when she saw that her words were hurting her daughter. "Do not bring the ghost of a manslayer into the new land," she said gently. "Forget him, Ta-maya. As long as you cling to his memory, you will never be free of him, and his ghost will be a cruel blight upon the memories of this band."

The distance slipped away beneath their feet until, at last, Cha-kwena crested the pass and loosed a great shout as he beckoned to the others to hurry.

The valley lay below, more wondrous and welcoming in the full light of day than when he had seen it washed in the pale blue colors of Moon and her star children. From the heights he could see the great white mammoth browsing in a lakeside meadow with others of its kind. An abundance of grazing animals was visible on the grassland that stretched between the hills at the eastern edge of the valley. As he stared down, breathless with excitement, a lone coyote emerged from behind a tumbled mass of boulders about three long strides directly ahead. Sag-hipped, its tail down and lower jaw agape, Little Yellow Wolf stared up at him. Its half-closed eyes glistened gold like pinesap in sunlight.

Cha-kwena stared back. Something about the appearance of this coyote troubled him, as it had the day when he had first viewed the blue mountains beyond the dry lake. Now he saw clearly that Little Yellow Wolf was in pain.

"Spirit Brother, what is it?"

The question was barely spoken before Mah-ree, with her favorite dogs running at her side, came scrambling up the slope. Gah-ti was right behind her. The coyote whirled around and raced off, with the dogs in hot pursuit.

"Call them back!" Cha-kwena demanded angrily.

Mah-ree obeyed, and in a moment all but Friend and Will Not Listen were back at her side.

"Ai yee!" exclaimed Gah-ti, eyes bulging as he stared past Cha-kwena to the valley. "Horses! Camels and elk and bison!" He was nearly overcome by delight. "If Dakan-eh could see this fine land, he would regret the day he placed his loyalty with Shateh and forced Cha-kwena and his followers to flee the country of their ancestors.''

Cha-kwena frowned at the unexpected reference to his old friend.

"What a stupid boy you are, Gah-ti," Mah-ree scolded. "No one has ever forced Cha-kwena to do anything. He does not 'flee' from anyone or anything. Those who 'flee' are those who fear! We are not afraid, are we, Cha-kwena?''

Cha-kwena did not answer. The euphoria he had enjoyed only moments before bled out of him. The wind was rising . . . the eagles banked and flew across the sun . . . a lion was roaring in the valley . . . what kind of omens were these? Good? Bad? He looked up, then frowned at the birds and the high, thin clouds. Kosar-eh was right about the clouds—these were the type that always ran before a storm. It would come on the back of the north wind in a day, maybe two.

A knot of uncertainty tightened in his belly as the eagles disappeared beyond the valley's eastern edge. Were the spirits of the ancestors warning him that the wonderful valley was not what it seemed? *No!* He would not believe that this was not a permanent resting place. He had come too far, endured too much, and was simply too tired to think of anything but settling into a permanent camp.

U-wa came to stand beside him. "Ah, it is all and *more* than you have promised, my son.''

In the valley far below, Life Giver trumpeted, turned its great head, and stared toward the height of the pass. When it raised its trunk as though in greeting, Cha-kwena felt relief. The sun was shining brightly, despite the clouds. The eagles were circling back out of the east and flying low over the lake. The day was one of exceptional beauty and promise. And the north wind was a low, steady tide of cool air that brought the good smells of fresh water, forest, grass, and game to those who gathered around their shaman. Kosar-eh helped Siwi-ni from the sledge so that she could stand with the others and admire the good land.

Head high, the young shaman assured himself that only a self-centered braggart like Dakan-eh would not have doubts at such a portentous moment as this. Briefly Cha-kwena found himself wondering if Bold Man still coveted the fair Ta-maya and searched for those with whom she had chosen to make her life. No, he assured himself, Dakan-eh and his mammoth-hunting allies were far away. If they had not found Cha-kwena and his band by now, they never would.

He drew in a deep, steadying breath of the north wind. It was cold, but it was also sweet.

Smiling, Cha-kwena led his people on.

5

Long after the other mourners had fallen asleep in little family groupings or collapsed into troubled dreams beside their dead, Pah-la's heartbreaking lamentations were echoed by the lonely song of wolves.

Shateh, sitting apart from his people and unable to sleep, listened wearily to the mother of Dakan-eh and was deeply moved. He exhaled heavily. Tomorrow he would have to ask that good and loyal woman to abandon the burned remains of her husband and walk with her new people into unfamiliar country, where the spirits of her ancestors did not know the trails and would not be able to follow.

He thought of the women he had outlived. Would they be wailing for him when his spirit left his body to walk the star trails of his ancestors? Of all of them, only one—the mother of Maliwal and Masau—stood out in his memory as a deep and abiding love. His lips stretched over his teeth. He did not want to think of that woman, but he did think of

her—and of Maliwal and Masau, the two best sons he had
ever sired. He had abandoned them as boys because they
had not fulfilled his expectations of bravery. Now, looking
back, he realized his goals had been too high for mere
children. Neither lacked courage as an adult.

A low moan of regret came out of him. Maliwal and
Masau would be waiting for him on the star trails. They
would be his enemies in the world beyond this world, as
they had become his enemies in this one.

The woman of the lizard eaters was still sobbing,
calling out the name of her lost man. As Shateh listened, it
occurred to him that Wehakna no longer wailed over
Kalawak, even though the time of mourning would not be
over until the next sunrise.

The chieftain's thoughts drifted to the bold, outspoken
woman of Dakan-eh. His loins warmed as he visualized her
flat belly, meaty hips, and bounteous, milk-swollen breasts.
Not since Ta-maya, the widow of his slain son, had briefly
shared his camp had he been so covetous of a woman.

Ta-maya was a woman he could have loved as well as
lain with again and again without wearying of her. She had
possessed the gentle grace and beauty of his lost Agrah and
had made his heart sing. Ta-maya had caused him to yearn
secretly for his lost youth.

Shateh shook his head and closed his eyes. "Soft-
hearted old fool," Shateh accused himself and, still sitting
upright, drifted off to sleep at last. . . .

He was hunting mammoth. Masau and Maliwal were at
his side. Together they pursued a small herd and threw
many spears. They suddenly, inexplicably, found themselves on opposite sides of a wide ravine, in which a
mammoth like no other was entrapped. It was the great
white mammoth, totem of his people, a creature that had
been born in time beyond beginning and whose blood and
flesh would grant the gift of infinite power and immortality
to those who killed the beast and ate it.

Shateh hurled his spear. It went deep.

Although he no longer held the weapon in his grip, he
felt the long, lanceolate stone head slice through skin and

muscle as the shaft went deep. The weapon's stem reappeared in the curl of his fist. He pulled back, twisted hard to the left, and removed the shaft for rehafting so that while one projectile point remained buried in the mammoth, he could use others to strike repeatedly at the animal. At last the mammoth fell dead. As his sons watched, Shateh leaped down upon the mountainous corpse. He tasted the hot sweetness of blood and flesh in his mouth. Suddenly he was young again, strong again—a man the same age as his boys, a man who would live forever.

The dream shifted. He was in a great lodge made of the skin of his totem. He was coupling with Ban-ya and Ta-maya at the same time, making new sons on both women as they howled like singing wolves and writhed beneath him, urging him on and on until . . .

"My father, wake up! Wolves have come close. You should not sit alone."

Shateh shook himself from the best dream that he had had in years. "Why do you disturb your chieftain's sleep?" he snarled, scowling up at Atonashkeh.

"The time for dreaming is over."

"Is it? And who made you chief since I left my fire circle to sit alone so that I might think and rest?"

Atonashkeh was upset. "When wolves come close to a fire circle, the only man awake must act as chief, and I—"

"I do not need you to warn me about wolves or to tell me of my responsibilities!"

Shateh paused, troubled, for at that moment, close to the band, wolves brought down what was probably among the last of the many orphaned bison calves. When the chieftain winced from hearing the death cries of the calf, the raw wound across his brow smarted cruelly.

The wolves are *close—too close,* he conceded to himself. Atonashkeh had been correct to urge him to retreat inside the protective circle of his band. He knew that he should thank his son; an expression of gratitude would sound like an admission to his own inability to make the proper decisions, though. Besides, Atonashkeh was too eager to have him admit to the infirmities of old age and become chief in his place.

Shateh averted his eyes from his son's face. He disliked Atonashkeh intensely. Of all of his sons, Shateh agonized, why had the forces of Creation left only the ambitious, mewling one alive? He wished that Atonashkeh and not the steady, loyal Kalawak had been consumed by the whirling wind.

"My father, I must tell you of—"

"You can tell me nothing that I do not already know, Atonashkeh!" He realized that he must have been asleep for a long time. Pah-la had ceased her ululations. The night was dark—too dark, unnaturally dark. When his eyes found the moon, he understood why and jumped to his feet with a cry of alarm.

"Yes!" Atonashkeh stood beside his father and stared up at the lunar eclipse. "This is what I have come to tell you! Never have I seen such a terrible thing! It is as I have warned! The presence of Lizard Eater in the Land of Grass offends the spirits of our ancestors and the Four Winds and has brought calamity upon us all!"

Under the black moon Tsana and his warriors accompanied Sheela across the land. They did not speak of omens; there was no need. No sign could have been worse. But was it for them, they wondered, or for their enemies? Only the forces of Creation could have answered that. Because there was no shaman in the group to interpret the dark portent in the sky, they hurried on even though Tsana had hoped to allow Sheela some rest.

"We will go on to the stronghold," she insisted. She had no more wish than any of the warriors to remain there while dark spirits fed upon the mother of stars. "If there is safety for us anywhere, it will be among our people."

The last sliver of the moon disappeared, and the world was plunged into darkness. A strange bloodred aureole pulsed in the sky. Were the stars crying out for their dying mother? Or did the cries belong to the travelers as they loosed their frightened dogs and prostrated themselves upon the earth?

Tsana pulled Sheela into a ferocious embrace. "I will not speak against Spirit Sucker if he comes to us now!" he told her. "The one who was to have been mine *is* mine! If this is all I am to have of you, Sheela, it is enough! If we cannot share our lives, then I thank the forces of Creation for allowing us to hold each other close in the moment of the death of the world!"

But the moment passed. The world did not die. Gradually the shadow passed across the face of the moon, and light returned to what was left of the night. Slowly, hunched and fearful, the travelers rose, summoned their dogs, and continued on.

Dawn was coloring the horizon to the east as they entered a high range of labyrinthine volcanic hills. Standing on the heights, armed spearmen raised their voices in a welcoming trill that reverberated within the canyon lands that lay beyond.

Sheela paused. "Long has it been since I heard that sound!" she exclaimed, exalting in it as tears stung beneath her lids. She raised both arms to the guardians of the ancestral stronghold of her tribe and, throwing back her head, released a high, keening, echoing cry.

The sun was rising as Ston re-joined them. Together they passed through the neck of a narrow canyon that was lined with the upended tusks of many a long-dead mammoth. Emerging into a broad, natural amphitheater of red, cave-pocked cliffs, they ascended by way of a series of bone ladders to the main cavern—a vast, vaulted, smoky chamber in which a feast fire burned and in which the survivors of the once-great tribe of the People of the Watching Star had gathered to greet their returning sister.

No one spoke. All stared. Sheela was stunned by the pitiful-looking assembly of men, many pregnant women, and dirty children who stared back at her, openly shocked by her brutalized face, shorn forelocks, and slave's garments.

"So few . . ." she whispered, incredulous and disappointed. She doubted if there were more than one hundred people in the entire cavern, even if she counted the little ones.

"Those who were once lions among the People are now reduced to what you see," Tsana explained.

"But there are others. They will come back now that you have returned." Ston's voice was tight with resolve.

Tsana nodded agreement. "The many bands that once composed the People of the Watching Star now run and hide upon the crags like so many flocks of frightened mountain sheep while those who have become wolves live free and unafraid upon the land below. They prey upon us when they can and take pleasure in our deaths. But no more! Now one who carries the blood of Ysuna has come back to us! Is it not so, Jhadel?" Hard-eyed, he appraised an older, sagacious man.

Jhadel's visage was hot with challenge; no one looking at the two men could have failed to see that they were in contention for leadership. For the moment, the older man was clearly in control of the assembly.

Sheela appraised Jhadel. Although not of her band, he was no stranger to her. He had been a shaman of great rank within the tribe until a clash of wills with Ysuna had sent him into hiding. Sheela had never liked the man. He had always made her wonder if he were not some strange sort of vulturine bird magically transformed into human form. His small, watchful eyes were condor's eyes. His prominent skull, set on a long, ever-swaying neck, made his bony face seem to be eternally sighting for prey. Beneath the huge thrusting beak of his nose Jhadel's wide mouth, almost completely void of lip seams, was always held slightly agape. And his entire face—including his ears, eyelids, and even his tongue—had been tattooed with ashes and grease so that it seemed as though someone had taken his head and charred it black in a smoldering fire pit.

Sheela tensed as she looked at him. His eyes, like tiny black lancets of obsidian, would single her out from among her friends and family at tribal assemblies and seem to stab at her hurtfully. She had always turned away, scurried off to someplace where his gaze could not find her. When word had come down through the tribe to her band that he had been forced to take to the hills and most likely would never be seen or heard from again lest he make of himself a victim of Ysuna's wrath, Sheela had praised the forces of Creation and hoped that he would die.

But here he was—alive, unchanged, apparently well and strong, and watching her with an odd, face-twisting speculation that caused her skin to crawl. He was adorned just as he had been years before, with a browband of raven's feathers and his gaunt body painted red with ochre. His well-remembered cottonwood staff had streamers of pounded mammoth hide, tufts of woven mammoth hair, and many tiny beads of bird bones, which clicked in the wind or whenever he shook the staff.

He was shaking it now in Sheela's face. She fought back the urge to knock it from his hands. She forced her eyes past it, to the medicine bag hanging from his neck.

Her gut contracted, for this was something new. Gone was the old wolverine skin in which he had kept the fetishes sacred to him. In its place was a much larger, elongated sack . . . made from a beautifully tanned, deboned human arm. Painted and heavily beaded with porcupine quills, the skin of the upper arm had been fringed, then folded to form a flap that closed the hollow, lower portion of the arm. A soft, unmistakably feminine hand remained attached. The long, translucent fingers, meticulously cured so that they remained uncurled, pointed downward toward Jhadel's bare belly. Sheela shrank from the sight of the human medicine bag and from the man who wore it.

Jhadel smiled, obviously gratified by her revulsion, then he shook his staff violently and held it tilted toward her. "Ysuna's blood was not so easily chilled," he taunted.

Sheela stiffened. If he had misconstrued her reaction as fear and weakness, she knew that it was important for her to correct the impression. Otherwise she would have no hope of holding her ground with him. But she did not have the chance as Jhadel turned his gaze to Tsana.

"Tsana and his hunting party have returned to us with strange and inedible meat," the shaman said. "How is the return of a single female of this tribe going to change things for the better? Another hungry mouth? Another pair of thighs to open to the rutting of our warriors? Another belly in which new life will take root? These things will weaken the People in the long, dark, hungry days that will soon be upon us."

"Forgetful old man!" Tsana accused forcefully. "This is not just *any* female! Behold Sheela, daughter of Sheehanal, who was brother of Quahnalay, who was father of Ysuna, Daughter of the Sun, high priestess and wise woman of the People of the Watching Star!"

"Yes, *young* man," Jhadel retorted, shaking his staff at Tsana. "I know this firstborn daughter of Sheehanal. I see now—as I saw in the long-gone days of her childhood— there *might* be some of the Daughter of the Sun in her. But Ston has told us how it was for her captive sister. If the power of Great Mother were in Sheela, she would have taken better care of Rikiree—would she not, Ston?"

Sheela saw uncertainty torment the warrior.

"My sister was weak," she proclaimed, then continued, despite the hurt in Ston's eyes, "Rikiree could not draw strength from my courage. She chose to throw her life spirit away upon the wind! Those among my people who have survived are fortunate to have found Jhadel to lead them. But if the power is in him, why did the great shaman not see the plight of the daughters of the Watching Star and send the warriors of our people against those who degraded us?"

The shaman's head went high. Obviously he had not expected Sheela to match his challenge.

Tsana smiled broadly at his woman as the assembly murmured restlessly.

Jhadel appraised Sheela warily from beneath tattooed lids. "Last night dark spirits ate the moon, then spat it out. As shaman I say that this was a portent of an ending of death. Yes—of *death*. So now I ask my people if the return of this woman is a good thing. Do you truly have power in your blood, daughter of Sheehanal? Or with your hair shorn and your face in ruins, are you merely another woman of the Watching Star who has been enslaved and degraded by our enemies?"

Swallowing her rising fear of him, she reminded herself that she was a grown woman who had faced many adversaries during the past many moons. This man was more dangerous than most, but she would match him step for step, word for word, challenge for challenge. He gave her no choice. "I have been a slave. True, my flesh was touched by degradation, but never my spirit. Always my spirit has been free . . . walking in the world beyond this world among the spirits of my ancestors—with Ysuna and Sheehanal, and with Masau and Maliwal. I have counseled with those who were slain in the great war. They have given me their strength, their purpose." She turned now as she spoke, addressing the people around her and igniting their confidence in her. "My face will heal. My hair will grow. My spirit is strong, for even though my enemies cut my hair in their need to weaken me, this they could not do. They could not weaken my will to escape from them and to bring the vengeance upon those who have reduced my tribe to what I see before me now. My invocations to the spirits of my ancestors have brought Thunder in the Sky to ravage our enemies. Now those who have made slaves of the daughters of the Watching Star mourn their dead. Now they fast and are vulnerable to attack. I can lead you to their encampment! And so I say that Jhadel is right! The dark portents that spoke to us out of the night sky *have* promised death—the death of our enemies and the beginning of a new life for the People of the Watching Star."

A great cry echoed within the cave. The young girl with the wild hair appeared spellbound, while the little boy by her side looked up at her worriedly.

Triumphant, Sheela glared at Jhadel. *There, old man! Match that challenge if you can!*

He strode forward defiantly. "You come to us with talk of battle and vengeance, Sheela. Battle is good—when it brings victory and spoils. Vengeance is good—for those who can take it and suffer no injury." He paused, allowing his words to settle. Then, with his free hand resting open across his grotesque medicine bag, he nodded darkly. "If only Ysuna's pride and ambition had been as limited as her ability to foresee where her goals must inevitably lead her followers! Then this tribe would have no enemies. You would not have been enslaved. And we would have no need to speak again of raids and battle and war."

Tsana was openly infuriated. "Ysuna was not to blame because other tribes did not share her vision or yield the sacrifices necessary for the favor of Thunder in the Sky! In starving times, her visions led her people to meat. Many mammoth died. The tribe rejoiced and grew strong. Our numbers were as many as the stars. When mammoth began to disappear and the storms of war came upon us, this was not the doing of Ysuna. Those who betrayed her were to blame. Now they are content to live as sheep while wolves claim their portion in the land of our ancestors. Is that not so, Jhadel?"

The shaman's contemptuous eyes speared the young man. "I was the one who first saw in Ysuna what she could and would be. I was her teacher. I gave her the knowledge that made her shaman. I did not betray her; I cautioned her. But Ysuna would listen to no counsel. Now she is slain by Masau, who—for love of a lowly lizard eater—turned on his adopted mother like a dog gone wild. He betrayed his adopted tribe to certain death when he reverted to his ancestral ties with the Bison People. Do you imagine that I do not wish vengeance against those who were his allies? Do you imagine that I do not grieve as much as any man for Ysuna's loss? But yes, Tsana, I would see my people live—as sheep if must be—until they are strong again, and many again, and may wisely dare to do what *can* be accomplished, not imprudently wished for!"

Sheela saw her dreams of vengeance slipping away. "Now *is* the time to strike against our enemies!" she insisted. "They will never again be as weak as they are now. Shateh and Dakan-eh guard against lions and wolves but not against men! Soon the time of mourning will be over, and the bands will go to their separate wintering grounds. Shateh will take his people along game trails that are familiar to me. Dakan-eh will be with him. If we come against them when they are on the trail and still weak from mourning and fasting and not expecting an attack, our warriors could come at them like hawks diving at rabbits!"

"And how many of our own number will die?" asked Jhadel.

"Thunder in the Sky will protect us." A wan young

girl stepped from among the others. Her long, thick, unkempt black hair fell around her shoulders and back like a cloak. Her eyes, huge in a face ravaged by hunger and grief, were fixed as though entranced, while a small, skinny, equally big-eyed and disheveled little boy took hold of her left wrist and tried to pull her back into the crowd. The girl would not be moved. She came forward, small and fragile looking in a worn dress of tattered elk hide. It hung over a gaunt body that showed only vague hints of impending maturation.

"Neea . . ." The little boy at her side whined and tugged imperatively at her wrist.

She shooed him back. "Be still, Warakan! I understand at last."

Sheela frowned. Neea was coming toward her, staring out of unnaturally wide, unblinking eyes. A moment later the child paused directly before the woman and reached to lay small, steady hands upon Sheela's forearms.

Sheela recoiled, recognizing madness in the girl's eyes.

"Ah, yes, it *is* clear now," Neea said as though she was in a trance. "My little brother, Warakan, and I are all that is left of our band, you see. The night raid against our village was swift and sure. Our lodge was close to the river, with trees sheltering it from the wind. Warakan had eaten too many berries and that night they made him sick. Mother was big with baby and near her time, so I did not want Warakan to disturb her. I took him into the trees above the river, so that he would not mess the lodge when he puked up the berries. We were under the trees when the raiders came. After they went away, we stayed in hiding. The village was burning. Mother and Father and everyone were dead. The raiders took no captives, not even the daughters of my father's brothers. Leruka and Plaki were my special friends. Their throats had been opened, like this, and there was much blood. For many days I stayed with them. Then Warakan cried that there was nothing to eat. And so we walked away, and walked and walked until Tsana and his hunters found us and brought us here."

Sheela, deeply moved by her own memories of capture and captivity, watched the reactions of those who listened to

Neea. The girl's suffering had been similarly endured by each of them. Sheela rested her hands upon Neea's narrow shoulders. "It is good that Tsana found you . . . and that the raiders did not."

"Yes," Neea said, sighing. "Although for a long time I did not think that it was. I would not eat, not even when Warakan refused to take food unless I did. Then Jhadel made me eat. For my brother's sake, he said. And so I did, for Warakan, not for myself. Why should I want to live when everyone I loved was dead?"

"I was not dead!" reminded Warakan.

Neea seemed not to hear; her eyes were on Sheela. "But now that *you* have come to us, I understand why the Great Spirit has allowed me to survive."

Sheela had no idea what the girl was leading to.

Neea stood to her full height and proclaimed in an unexpectedly dignified manner, "My people have suffered long and much! Our totem has turned his back upon us, but Thunder in the Sky *is* alive. He has saved you and brought you to us, Sheela, to speak through your mouth as he once spoke through Ysuna's. In you, Sheela, Ysuna has returned to live once more among the People! Now, because of you, we may take vengeance against our enemies. Thunder in the Sky will make our warriors invincible. We will be lions again. In gratitude we must make Thunder in the Sky strong in the way of our tribe. I am young; I have come to my first time of blood; I have not known a man. I have no mother or father to mourn for me. I am not afraid. I am the blood sacrifice for which Thunder in the Sky has been hungering. I will go to him consenting, at your hand."

The girl's words caused an instant reaction among the people; it was like a grass fire bursting to life. Jhadel was visibly shaken. Tsana seemed to grow taller, and Sheela was too stunned to move. "At *my* hand?"

"No, Neea!" Warakan grasped at his sister's dress.

Ston cried out, "Yes! In memory of Rikiree and all of those who have died, yes! Let it be as it was!"

Sheela, appalled by implications that had not occurred to her until now, remembered her warning to Shateh— words of blood and death, of the need for human sacrifice to appease the storm god of their ancestors. Events were unfolding too fast; she felt dizzied by them.

Jhadel looked around at the renewed energy and optimism that had transformed his people. The shaman appeared suddenly hopeful. He turned to Sheela. "Are you worthy of this, my daughter?"

Daughter? Sheela was incredulous. Had her enemy become an unwelcome ally? "I have returned to my people to be one with them beneath the Watching Star and to show them the way to vengeance," she said strongly. "But I am not Daughter of the Sun! I cannot take her place! I am *not* worthy!"

For an instant there was absolute silence.

"You *must* be worthy," Jhadel demanded, "for all that has been and all that is yet to be. I will stand at your side. I will teach you the way, as I once taught Ysuna before she recognized her own powers. Together we will lead our people to victory."

A shout erupted from the crowd. Sheela's eyes went wide. The survivors were closing around her now. All cried her name, chanted it, as though it possessed the power that Ysuna's had once held.

Warakan threw his scrawny arms around his sister's waist. "No, Neea, please! If you go to Thunder in the Sky, who will there be for me? Please, Neea, tell them *no!*"

Tsana put his hand on the boy's shoulder. "I will be for you. Your sister's sacrifice will give new life and strength—"

Warakan twisted away from Tsana's grip and stared up defiantly at the man. "I don't care about our enemies! I don't care about the People! I—"

Tsana struck him down.

Sheela felt a jolt of pity for the boy, but she would not look his way. She did not want to see the anguish and loathing in his face. Instead, she looked at Jhadel, who was opening his medicine bag.

Even before he drew from the hollowed arm a long, bloodstained dagger of bone, Sheela went cold. She knew the blade; she had seen it in the hand of Ysuna. She had seen the purpose to which it had been put and to which she would be asked to put it now. She knew what she must do if she was going to succeed in rallying her people. But *could* she do it?

"Ysuna will help you, my daughter," assured Jhadel, sensing her hesitation.

When she met his gaze she knew that he was waiting for her to weaken, to turn away from a duty that was almost too repugnant to bear; but bear it she would. "I will do this," she said coldly, strengthened by memories of Dakaneh's brutality, Ban-ya's meanness, and Shateh's toleration of her degradation. She accepted the sacrificial dagger from the man. "And Ysuna is not here to help me!"

"But she is!" Although Jhadel's mouth slid into a benign smile, his eyes were malevolent as he patted his medicine bag and then took it off and placed it around her neck.

Sheela gasped, recoiling as understanding suddenly exploded within her. "It is *Ysuna's* arm and hand that you have passed to me?"

"Yes. Hers. All that lions left of her. After I drove them from her ruined encampment, I found the sacred sacrificial dagger. Thunder in the Sky himself must have guided me out of the hills to follow Ysuna's forces as they moved against her enemies. I am the only shaman of the People of the Watching Star to have survived. But Ysuna has been with me, and with my people, here, close to my heart . . . waiting for you to come, Sheela, so that her strength and power could be reborn in you—*if* you are worthy."

It was all she could do to keep from retching; the weight of the "thing" about her neck seemed to be suffocating her. She held Jhadel's glance. "Let it be done, then," she said.

And it was done. To the shrieking curses of a little boy and the resounding acclamations of the People of the Watching Star, the sacrifice was made. By Sheela's hand, Neea died smiling. But only when the daughter of Sheehanal had, with the assistance of Jhadel and Tsana, flayed the corpse, donned the skin of the dead girl, and shared the meat of the sacrifice's heart with her people, did Sheela know that

she was indeed worthy to lead her people against enemies
who had so unjustly wronged them.

Bathed in blood she stood before them. The initial
horror of the events had numbed her. Now the numbness
was gone. Once the first cut had been made, the killing had
been so easy and quick. The flesh and blood of the sacrifice
had restored her strength. The weight of the medicine bag
around her neck and the warm, wet skin of the dead girl
upon her back no longer revolted her. She felt renewed and
strangely tranquil as she looked straight into Jhadel's eyes
and smiled. He had been a fool to put her to this test. He
could never frighten her again.

6

The black moon had spoken, and Shateh did not like what
it had to say. Throughout the eclipse, the tribe had gathered
in terror to shout, hurl spears, and throw handful after
handful of earth at the sky in an effort to drive the
moon-eating spirits away from Mother of Stars. The chieftain had attempted to assuage his people's fears by reminding them that he and all of the elders of the combined bands
had seen the moon go dark in their time.

"The shadow spirits will pass!" he had assured them.

But even after his word was proved true, few were
comforted by the sight of Moon returning bright and whole
and luminous to the sky. A predictable constant had been
taken from their lives and consumed by dark powers they
could neither see nor understand. Coming so soon after the
ravages of storms and stampede, the black moon had been
a terrible and mystifying omen. And so now, in the hushed

silence of morning, the shamans, chiefs, and hunters of the People of the Land of Grass called a council, even though the fifth day of mourning had not yet come.

"We should wait," a tired and deeply troubled Shateh told them. "Tomorrow, when the fourth day of mourning is complete, then we may join together in council. Not now. The spirits of our dead still walk the land."

"Do you wish to join them, Shateh?" The question came from Khutanay, chief of one of the larger western bands.

"I wish to *honor* them!" Shateh retorted.

"Then heed their warning. They do not want any of us to remain here. They want the bands to go their separate ways to their own wintering grounds—now, this day, not tomorrow."

"You are not a shaman, Khutanay! You cannot know this!" Shateh reminded.

"*I* am Shaman," spoke out Buhana, mystic of a small but important band from the hill country. His people controlled several quarries from which much fine, translucent, rich brown stone was cut, then brought to the other bands for trading. "I say that Khutanay is right. Has not Thunder in the Sky spoken to us out of the storms? Has he not scattered the bison to trample and crush our sons and brothers and fathers? Has he not sent the children of the angry sky to eat the moon?"

"Yes," Shateh agreed. "But the moon has *not* been eaten. Mother of Stars has returned in time to go to her rest beyond the western hills."

Buhana raised a telling finger. "As a warning! Next time she will disappear forever, and the bad spirits will come for us! We cannot stay in this country. We must go now, before the ancestors call us all to walk with them in the world beyond this world!"

"To leave now, before the time of mourning is over, is forbidden!" Shateh was aware that the others knew this as well as he; nevertheless he felt obliged to remind them.

"Then stay, Shateh," said Xiaheh, chieftain of one of the northern bands. "But we will not stay with you. Many times you have invited the bands of the People into this country to hunt bison with your band and to make the taking of much meat easier for all. We have been grateful. Good things do we trade at these autumn hunting camps, and much meat do we take back to our winter lodges. But now this land of Shateh's fathers is against us. The sky is against us. The herd is against us. We must take our women, children, and dogs back into the country of our own fathers before the White Giant Winter finds us with no meat to sustain us and no lodges in which to take shelter.''

Shateh was incredulous. ''You would separate the bands now? Before we have hunted meat for you to take with you? What will happen if you do not find game on the long trail back to your wintering grounds? The bison have gone south and east. Together we can track the herd, follow it, and hunt again. Many men can take much meat before the White Giant Winter comes to the Land of Grass!''

''I will not hunt that herd again,'' said Ylanal, one of the prominent chiefs of the eastern bands. ''That herd belongs to Thunder in the Sky. And I will not hunt in the land of Shateh. All the omens are bad here.''

Shateh was shaken. For the first time in more moons than he could remember, he was not controlling the vote. If he lost this vote, he would no longer be chief above all chiefs, but only one chief among many.

Atonashkeh, seated with the other hunters, was amazed. Never in his life had he seen the council turn against his father's will. He spoke out angrily and without thinking. ''The lizard eaters have offended the spirits of our ancestors and the Four Winds, not Shateh! The omens will be good again in this land once the People of the Red World have been forced to leave it!''

Shateh stiffened and glared with disbelief at his son, who was no doubt worried about his own status in the tribe. Atonashkeh's defense had been no defense at all. If Shateh had invited the lizard eaters, then he had also invited the turning of the tribe's luck.

Ylanal raised a telling brow. ''Shateh invited the strangers here. He did not ask the council. He simply said: 'Come!' And chose to name a lizard eater as Brother!''

A soft sighing went through the circle of men.

Ylanal gestured to where Dakan-eh sat with the others from the Red World, at the edge of the groves above the river. "Look at him! How can he rest when he knows that a lone man of his band is still upon the land, among wolves and lions? Perhaps Dakan-eh is afraid to search for him. And, now that I think of it, I have not seen that tall slave of his since he took her off into the trees on the first night of mourning. Maybe he killed her—not that she deserved better. But if he took off to lie on her on a night of mourning, then he has—"

Shateh's reaction was instantaneous. He snapped to his feet and stared down at Ylanal. "You saw a man take a woman into the groves on a night of mourning and did not speak against it?"

Ylanal flinched. "Not a woman—only a slave. And the man is no man; he is a lizard eater!"

Dakan-eh had never seen a man so angry. Shateh stalked from the council circle to the groves and, with the council members and most of his tribe following, came to stand like an enraged bear before Bold Man's stunned band.

"The man you call Ela-nay. He has not yet returned to this band?" The chieftain's query was more an accusation than a question.

Ela-nay's woman looked at Shateh out of reddened, hopeful eyes. "You have seen sign of my man? He has been gone so long, I fear for him."

Shateh's brow came down. He asked Dakan-eh pointedly, "You have not searched for this missing man?"

Dakan-eh was on his feet, defensive. "There is no need. Ela-nay is not missing. He will return when the sadness of mourning has left his spirit."

"He has been gone many days," said Shateh.

"His grief is great," Dakan-eh responded sourly.

Shateh's expression revealed nothing as his eyes scanned the band from the Red World. "The tall slave, the one called Sheela . . . I do not see her."

Ma-nuk had risen to stand beside Dakan-eh, as had the other hunters from the Red World. "That slave has not been seen in this camp since Dakan-eh took her into the groves for punishment on the night of the mourning fire," he informed coldly.

Dakan-eh was rendered speechless by the unexpected announcement; he cast a warning look Ma-nuk's way and was disconcerted by the glare of hostility that was returned. The man had been sullen ever since Bold Man had allowed Ban-ya to insult him, and even more so since coming twice to Dakan-eh to express concern over Sheela's absence, only to be rebuked by his headman and told to forget her. Bold Man castigated himself. He should have known that Ma-nuk would not forget Sheela; when the slave had first been brought into the band, Ma-nuk had offered to barter his own woman and eldest daughter for her. Dakan-eh had mocked his offer. Later, when the man had sulked, Bold Man had allowed Ma-nuk to lie on Sheela to assuage any feelings of enmity. Evidently his generosity had not been sufficient. So much for gratitude! Dakan-eh vowed to make Ma-nuk pay for this moment; but now all he could do was take comfort in the fact that no one but Ela-nay could prove that Dakan-eh had lain with his slave on that night. And Ela-nay was not here to speak against him.

But Ela-nay's woman was. "Perhaps the slave called my man into the groves," she mused, thinking out loud.

Dakan-eh assumed that the woman knew nothing about the prohibition against sexual union during ritual times of mourning and surely intended no malice toward him. Nonetheless, his heart sank as she opened her mouth again, her face contorting with suspicion and jealousy.

"The slave has wanted my Ela-nay. I have seen her eyes follow him, watch him . . . eyes that call to a man and suck at his spirit. I tell you, it is not like my Ela-nay to go off to grieve alone. Perhaps the slave tricked him into taking her to seek freedom among our enemies and—"

"Our enemies are long dead!" Dakan-eh interrupted, his face flaming with dismay at how close she had come to the truth.

Shateh raised a hand to silence him. "Is this true? There are *two* people missing from your band, and you have found no cause to search for either of them?"

Atonashkeh, standing to Shateh's right, fixed Dakan-eh with vindictive eyes. "Bold Man is afraid!"

With a sick, sinking feeling in his belly, Dakan-eh saw that every man, woman, and child of the Land of Grass was staring at him as if he was a coward. His tongue felt as though it had somehow become disconnected from whatever made it move; nevertheless he *made* it speak, and speak strongly.

"I do not have to defend myself! *I* ran before the whirling wind while Atonashkeh cowered in the ravine! And why is Shateh concerned for a slave? She is *nothing*! And she is *mine*! It is for Bold Man to be concerned for this slave, not for the chieftains and shamans and hunters of the Land of Grass!"

The chieftain's face remained set, but anger flared in his eyes, and something else, something that Dakan-eh found infinitely more threatening—disappointment. "It is a man's right to punish an unruly slave or to kill it. Have you punished the slave Sheela with death, Dakan-eh of the Red World?"

"To take a life on a night of mourning is forbidden!" growled Lahontay.

Dakan-eh could have kissed the elder; now Bold Man knew how to reply and maintain favor in the chieftain's eyes. "The woman has run away!" he stated. "She is trouble, so I have not gone after her. If wolves and lions have made meat of her, that is better than she deserves!"

Shateh was not pleased. "Among the People of the Land of Grass, if a dog strays unwisely across country in which it can have no defense against predators, the man who has kept that dog will track it and bring it back if he can, for the dog has served the man and earned its portion of meat and care. Should less concern be shown for a slave?"

Dakan-eh's face tightened; the wound across his brow hurt, but much less than his pride.

"Did you lie on the woman before she ran away?" asked Shateh evenly.

Dakan-eh was struck dumb, even though he knew that his silence was condemning him in the eyes of one who would never again call him brother.

Atonashkeh smirked. "We all know how this man chose to punish his slave."

Nakantahkeh nodded and, as always, affirmed the words of his boyhood friend. "Atonashkeh speaks the truth."

Lahontay shook his head. "The People of the Red World have stood with us against our enemies. Some have taken our daughters to be their women. But the lizard eaters have proved that their ways are not the ways of bison and mammoth hunters. Now the spirits of our ancestors and of the Four Winds are telling them to go from this land." He turned to gesture broadly toward the decimated plain. "My lodge has been swept away and the belongings of my family have been—"

"Better your lodges than those who dwell within them, old man!" Ban-ya proclaimed.

Dakan-eh could barely believe his ears as his woman spoke out in her defense. There was fire in her eyes as, holding her boy on her hip as was her way, she looked directly at the chieftain of the assembled bands of the Land of Grass.

"The great Shateh is wise! The great Shateh is *not* in disfavor with the spirits of the ancestors. Bad things come to all in this life—storms, hunger, thirst, the death of loved ones. There is not a man or woman here who has not suffered. Whom did you blame for your sadness then, when there were no 'lizard eaters' among you? Or did you look to your own mistakes, to your own oversights, and move on to better hunting grounds and better times? I say that this can be so again! If my man has inadvertently broken a taboo, then let him scourge himself. He has shown that he is unafraid to mourn as you mourn, to suffer as you suffer, to bleed as you bleed! Who among Shateh's warriors is as brave as my Bold Man?"

"It is so!" affirmed Dakan-eh, and then cursed himself for speaking at all; his voice had squeaked like a strangling hawk.

Shateh was eyeing Ban-ya with interest. "You have courage, woman of the Red World." He raised his eyebrow, appraised the strong boy sucking at her breast, then turned his gaze to Dakan-eh. "More than your man, I think."

"Never!" she replied, head high. "It is Dakan-eh from whom—and for whom—I draw my strength. You have seen his brave heart. You have seen him fight our enemies. You have seen him command the wind for the good of our people!"

Dakan-eh flinched. Ban-ya had said the wrong thing.

Shateh was scowling. "Is it possible for a man who is not a shaman to command the wind, woman of the Red World?"

"I . . . yes! With the inspiration of Shateh, it is and was possible!"

The chieftain's eyes narrowed. She was attempting to manipulate him, but he would not cooperate. "Your man ran before the wind to save those who were never in danger. Many died in the ravine because he challenged my command and slowed the steps of those who were torn between his will and mine. Will your Bold Man take credit for this as well?"

The question shook Ban-ya. Her face went blank. Her arms tightened protectively around Piku-neh as she sought an answer.

Hotly, angrily, without thinking, Dakan-eh answered for her. "Because of your command they lost their lives, Shateh, not because of mine! I told them to follow me! I . . ." His words stopped in midflow. He knew that he had erred badly.

Everyone was staring, aghast.

For a long time Shateh remained silent. He sighed and shook his head, spoke gently—not to Dakan-eh but to Pah-la. "I have listened to your lamentations, woman of the Red World. Your song of grief has touched my heart. Let it not be said that Shateh ever kept a brave man's spirit captive in a land where his ghost will walk forever among strangers and have no hope of ever being born again into the world of the living through his children. Take up the ashes of your man and of the youth Na-sei, then secure them upon a hide for traveling. It is time for you to take the bodies of your men and return with your people to the Red World."

Pah-la wept with gratitude.

"No!" Dakan-eh was livid. "We are no longer of the Red World! We have lived and hunted and mourned in the way of your people! Together we have fought our enemies. Together we have triumphed! Together we have suffered! Together we have grown strong! You have named me Brother!"

"No more. The spirits of my ancestors have spoken on the wind and in the storms and in the face of the black moon. Lizard Eater is no longer welcome in the Land of Grass."

Dakan-eh saw his dreams of a life as a warrior and eventual chieftain of this great people dissolving. In desperation he blurted, "The curse of Cha-kwena has twisted my actions and my tongue. Because of Cha-kwena death has come to the Land of Grass! None of us will know peace until we all seek him out—your people and mine—take his life, and bring Life Giver back into the lands of those who rightfully name him totem!"

"Perhaps," said Shateh wearily. "But now the great white mammoth is far away, and winter is coming. Lead your people home. Mourn in your own way, among the spirits of your ancestors."

"Our ways have become your ways, Shateh. If you send us away now, we will be as the dog you spoke of, bereft of pack, of pride, of honor—"

Ban-ya's words arrested the chieftain's gaze. He appraised and admired her.

Seeing this, Dakan-eh grasped at what he took to be his last chance at the life he so desperately longed to lead. "Allow us to remain, Shateh, and my Ban-ya is yours! She will give you pleasure and many strong sons!"

Ban-ya gasped. "I am your first woman! Your son draws life from my breasts! You cannot give me away!"

"I can and do!" Dakan-eh was afire with newfound hope. "I will hunt and bring meat to the fire circle of any man who will allow his woman to put my son at her breast! One milk-swollen teat is as good as another for such purposes. But the breasts and the body of Ban-ya, let these be for Shateh—as a gift from Dakan-eh, who would be his brother and hunt by his side in this land!''

There was dead silence among the people. Everyone was staring at Shateh, awaiting his decision. When it came, Dakan-eh was stricken, as though he had been hit by lightning.

''*I*, Shateh, decide who comes and who goes in the land of my fathers! My brothers among the many bands of the Land of Grass are right. This 'bold' man is an affront to our ancestors and the forces of Creation! Dakan-eh will take his people and go now! After he is gone, Shateh will see if Spirit Sucker follows. Then Shateh will know who walks in the favor of the Four Winds.''

The chieftain paused, taking obvious pleasure in the slack-jawed, disbelieving stare of the young man. Then he added disdainfully, ''You are right—Shateh could make strong sons on your woman. I will accept your parting gift as a sign that not all goodwill has been lost between us. You have been brave, Lizard Eater. You have put yourself at risk for my people as though they were your own. But Death has followed you into this country. I will give you your son and a woman with milk to feed him, plus another woman to spread herself for you on your journey to the Red World. But your woman, Ban-ya, will remain here in the Land of Grass to make new life in the form of strong sons for Shateh.''

7

A cold, hard, steady rain was falling upon the wondrous valley into which Cha-kwena had led his little band, but the individual family groups were warm and dry within shelters of brushwood and reed, hastily raised to the lee of a high range of cave-pocked hills.

Cha-kwena, however, sat alone and shivering within his own shelter and regretted not having had the time to explore the hills for a safe way to the caves; surely one or more of them might have proved to be a weatherproof refuge. He doubly regretted having refused U-wa's and Mah-ree's assistance with the raising of his weather break. He had never been very good at thatching. Now, chilling fingers of wind invaded his shelter and his rain-dewed robe of tightly twisted rabbit skins, and a maddening plop of raindrops fell upon his head. His mother would not be happy when she saw that the robe that she had meticulously stitched for him was as soggy as his scalp. He told himself that a shaman should not trouble himself over the opinions of women, but a rankled U-wa was not a pleasant prospect; his mother could pout for days, and her cooking, always less than tolerable, inevitably deteriorated to be completely unpalatable.

Irked, he rummaged in his traveling roll for the rain cloak of cured and oiled antelope intestines, which U-wa had also made for him. He slung it on. It fit him like a big, semitransparent tent, its finely stitched seams allowing no water or draft to penetrate. He sat quietly within it and,

171

glowering, listened to the wind and rain. The omens were bad, and he knew it.

"Clouds . . . rain . . . the north wind . . . and last night a black moon! *Why?*" Cha-kwena growled the question. In need of air, he rose and went out into the rain.

The wind embraced him. The rain pummeled him. Lowering the rain cape and holding it closed below his chin, he welcomed the cold wash on his face and scalp. A woman's singing came to him from the shelter of the widows of Tlana-quah and their daughters. He recognized Ta-maya's voice. A child giggled in response; it was little Joh-nee. Ha-xa joined Ta-maya in song. U-wa and Mah-ree followed. It was an old song, a round, a learning game in which a question was asked and as many answers were given as the singers could think of:

"Who comes to the meadow when Sun goes down?"
"Deer comes to the meadow when Sun goes down."
"Wolf comes to the meadow when Sun goes down."
"Fox follows wolf when Sun goes down."
"Coyote watches fox when Sun goes down."

Cha-kwena was well aware that the women were attempting to distract themselves and the children from the terrible fear that had settled over the band with the rising of last night's black moon. Now he clearly heard little Tla-nee sing out: "Moon come back?"

Cha-kwena felt grateful when he heard Mah-ree reply, "Mother of Stars always comes back when Sun goes down, little sister! Except on those nights when she is sleeping on the far side of the sky, of course! She came back last night, didn't she? Just as Cha-kwena promised! Now stop asking silly questions, Tla-nee, and let us continue our song!"

Cha-kwena shook his head. Mah-ree had so much faith in him! This was, at times, unnerving. When the moon had gone dark, he had been as appalled as everyone else. Old Hoyeh-tay had spoken to him of many things when Cha-kwena had shared the old man's sacred cave. But if his grandfather had instructed him in the ways a shaman must behave when Moon was attacked by black sky spirits, he could not remember. Admittedly he had not always listened very well, and the old man had died before a fraction of his knowledge could be passed along. And so, in the waning light of a dying moon, Cha-kwena had stood paralyzed by fear until Kosar-eh had given him a sharp nudge and told him what to do.

"Dance, Shaman! Sing! Invoke the forces of Creation! The power of the totem is yours! Prod the sky with your spear! Show our people that the magic of Cha-kwena is all that is needed! Promise them that Mother of Stars will not die and that the black sky spirits will not come down out of the night to feed upon the people!"

Cha-kwena had obeyed. He danced, he sang, and he made up the words as he went along. As so often happened when he hoped that the spirit of his grandfather would be with him, the spirit of the old man had obliged. Emboldened, Cha-kwena had shaken his spear at the black sky spirits.

For one terrible moment, Moon had disappeared and the sky around her had turned red with her blood. The children of his band had clutched at their mother's corded skirts, and even the dogs had howled in confusion. Siwi-ni had fallen to her knees and, sobbing that her infant had ceased moving within her body, had wrapped her arms protectively around her belly and begged Cha-kwena to save the life of her unborn child.

"The battle of wills is not over!" Kosar-eh had shouted at Cha-kwena. "Command the black spirits to abandon the sky, and it will be so!"

Certain that he had nothing to lose, Cha-kwena had obeyed. And slowly, the black sky spirits had moved across the face of Mother of Stars, then disappeared. Moon had returned to gaze down with gray, never-blinking eyes at him and the People. And in that moment Cha-kwena's eyes had met Ta-maya's. He trembled when she had smiled with transcendent gratitude at him. He doubted if he had ever felt stronger in his power or prouder to be called Shaman.

Now, through slitted eyes, he scanned the encampment of little conical shelters. His gaze rested on one empty hut sitting apart from the others—the birth shelter that awaited Siwi-ni.

Cha-kwena sighed. The frail, aged woman had collapsed after the moon-eating spirits had run away. Ta-maya had rushed to her side, but Kosar-eh had waved the young woman away, then carried Siwi-ni into the hut that he had raised for his family. He and his sons had been with her ever since.

Cha-kwena's right hand rose to press against his medicine bag and the sacred stone that lay within. As always, the touch of the talisman reassured him. Also, the rain was lessening. The clouds began to thin, revealing wide patches of blue. He squinted not against rain, but against the sudden bright, warm, and welcome light of the sun—a good omen!

He felt better, too, because despite the terror of the black moon and the sudden onset of the rainstorm, this campsite was the best of places. Timbered hills provided protection against the full impact of the north wind, and a nearby warm spring would provide a winter-long source of ice-free water. Across broad, grassy meadows was a reed-thick lakeshore, beyond which Life Giver and a small herd of mammoth bathed and browsed within the shallows.

Cha-kwena and the band had exclaimed with delight at the sight of the reed beds and lush meadowlands, for many of life's most important staples could be obtained from them: game, waterfowl, fish, and precious eggs; tall stands of camas, whose sweet roots were among the most prized of tubers; several varieties of reeds, which could be woven into matting for lodge covers and floor cloths, while their roots, shoots, seeds, and pollen could be eaten. Even their brown spiky seed heads were useful as torches and kindling and, when pulled apart into a downy fluff, as an insulating lining for winter shoes, garments, and cradleboard padding.

Now, though, as he stared across the sodden meadow to the lake, Cha-kwena could see no sign of mammoth. Life Giver and the little herd with which he had been grazing had gone their way. Was this another bad omen, he wondered, or merely a gathering of tuskers wishing to get out of the cold rain?

"Cha-kwena?"

Mah-ree came to stand beside him. Her favorite dog, Friend, was at her side; its left ear was torn, and the fur above its eye was nicked in several places.

"Will Not Listen is still gone from his brothers," she revealed sadly. "And Friend has been bitten by a little yellow wolf, I think. I have salved his hurts."

Cha-kwena gave his attention to the dog. If Friend had caught up with Coyote, it was not surprising that the animal had returned with a few nicks for its presumptuousness. As to Will Not Listen? Either the dog would return or would not. Mah-ree was the only one who cared about the creature; its willfulness made it the least useful dog in the pack.

Cha-kwena cocked his head. The unmistakable trumpeting of mammoth from somewhere to the east was a balm to his spirit. As long as Life Giver walked before him, what was a little rain and thunder, or the flash of a few lightning bolts, or any other ill-defined omen? He was foolish to question any signs that came to him at all.

From high above and far away, the sound of a lion was heard.

"Cha-kwena, he is close, this lion."

"No, Mah-ree. The hills bend the sound of his voice. He is far. Do not be afraid. The magic of this shaman has driven away the black sky spirits. If Lion threatens, this shaman's magic will drive it from these hills. If it will not be driven . . . this man has hunted lions before."

"You speak as boldly as Dakan-eh."

"And so I am!" assured Cha-kwena. "But you must forget Bold Man. He is far away. He will not come into our lives again."

In the Land of Grass, the sun stood high in a cloudless sky, but the wind carried the promise of an early winter. Dakan-eh's mood was as dark and threatening as any of the storms that had passed across the plains. In a turmoil of rage and frustration, he led his people away from Shateh's hunting grounds and toward a drought-ravaged land where survival would be difficult. Morose and silent, they followed without looking back.

In the way of the People of the Red World, they carried their few belongings on their backs and the remains of their dead on sledges that were dragged by the women as the man of each little family group walked ahead.

"Your son should have taken the dogs," complained a sullen Cheelapat to Pah-la. "They were Shateh's gift to Dakan-eh's band when you first came to the Land of Grass." Bent forward under the weight of her backpack, she plodded along beside the headman's mother and well behind Dakan-eh. "I am not used to bearing burdens upon my back like a dog!"

"Get used to it," Pah-la advised the much-younger woman. Pah-la dragged a double-poled sledge. On it were her meager belongings, plus the hide-wrapped remains of her man. "Carry your new man's possessions with honor. Besides, your load is light compared to that which I have seen Ban-ya proudly carry. She was able to save only a few things, so why do you complain? You are Dakan-eh's woman now, Cheelapat!" The women walked on in silence for a few more paces before Pah-la added angrily, "My son could not take the dogs with him to the Red World. My son has too much honor to accept such a gift from one who has shamed him!"

"He accepted *me!* And he accepted Rayela! Look at her as she strides at his heels ahead of us! She carries no burden—except the headman's son."

Pah-la shook her head at Cheelapat's ignorance. "Milk women are allowed to carry no burdens in the Land of Grass. Why do you imagine that it would be different among the People of the Red World? And you and Rayela were *not* gifts. You were given in trade for Ban-ya. A man must have a woman into whom to pump the milk of his need, and a son must have a woman from whom to suck the milk of life! When Shateh took Ban-ya, he deprived my Dakan-eh of both." Again she shook her head. "Despite all that has happened, I do not think that Shateh is an unfair man. You will ease my son's hunger for a woman. Rayela will satisfy the hunger of my grandson for milk. And Shateh will have Ban-ya. But what are dogs to this band? In the Red World we do not roam about the land, following the herds and carrying our shelters on our backs. We dwell in settled villages and have no need of dogs!"

"They would ease our way until we get there!" moaned Cheelapat. "I was the woman of a chieftain! I have been honored! Many dogs were mine! I—"

"You are still the woman of a headman, Cheelapat!"

The woman snorted with contempt, then fought against upwelling tears. "I have done nothing to deserve being given away to lizard eaters!"

Pah-la was indignant. "You have fared better than Ban-ya! You were only a third woman within Shateh's lodge. You gave him no sons, so it was his right to trade you for another. He has not dishonored you! Your new man is young and strong. Perhaps he is better than you deserve—we will see. Now you will live in the way of the People of the Red World. Our ways are good ways, and I am grateful to Shateh for sending us back to them! My burden grows lighter with every step that I take toward home!"

Cheelapat might have offered further complaint, but in that moment she was distracted by a mumbling, disheveled old woman who came up from behind them, calling Pah-la's name and begging that she wait.

"Kahm-ree?" Pah-la looked with open concern at the woman. "Where is your pack, old friend?"

The grandmother of Ban-ya moaned and shook her head. As if in a daze, she said not a word to Pah-la. Instead she lengthened her stride and called out to Dakan-eh. "Bold Man! I would speak with you."

"Not again, old woman." He increased his pace, but she managed to match him stride for stride.

"Ban-ya has been the heart of my life for many a long moon, Dakan-eh. If you will not go back for my Ban-ya, then again I must ask to be allowed to remain behind with my granddaughter."

As Dakan-eh looked down at the fat, sag-fleshed old woman, his contempt was obvious. "Your mind has gone as flabby as your skin, Kahm-ree! It is Shateh, not Dakan-eh, who refused you permission to stay in the Land of Grass."

"Yes, but if you are *still* Bold Man, if you are *still*

Brave Hunter, you will go back and take my Ban-ya away from the one who has stolen her from her people!''

"*If* I am still Bold Man? *If* I am still Brave Hunter? Old woman, you risk too much with me!''

"For my Ban-ya I would risk everything!''

"And so you have!''

She ignored his threat. "I am not afraid—not of you, not of Shateh. I fear only never seeing my Ban-ya again.''

"Then you must learn to live with this fear, old woman. If I were to do as you suggest, Shateh would have his entire tribe after me! We are outnumbered. We cannot make war against Shateh and his tribe for the sake of a woman! Now go away. The sight of you offends me!''

Kahm-ree's wrinkled face crinkled into an angry, ugly clot of cysts and spots and seams. "And the sight of you offends the forces of Creation, Dakan-eh! What kind of man gives away his best woman and deprives his son of a mother? What kind of man would separate his woman from her son?''

"The choice was not mine to make!''

"If you had not tried to buy Shateh's favor with the body of my Ban-ya, she would be with us now. My little Piku-neh would not be sucking milk from the breasts of a stranger and—''

Dakan-eh stopped dead and yielded to the urge to shove her hard on her shoulder. Kahm-ree fell and landed hard on her capacious buttocks, with her fringed buckskin skirt up and her fleshy limbs splayed before her. Bold Man glared down at her with eyes that held a warning. "Do not speak to me of Ban-ya again, old woman, or I vow that you *will* remain behind—alone, cast out of this band, and unwelcome among any of the bands of the Land of Grass.''

Dakan-eh walked on. Soothed by having vented his temper against the old woman, he felt better for a while. Then he found himself agonizing once more over all his shattered dreams and broken ambitions. He remembered how Ban-ya had looked at him just before he had turned his back on her and walked away, and of how she had cried out piteously for her son. He cringed at the memory. How she had shamed him and herself! But Shateh had paid no heed to her misery. Dakan-eh clenched his jaw. He would never forgive Shateh for that moment—never!

And he would never forgive Ma-nuk for informing the chieftain that he had taken a slave into the groves on a night of mourning. If only the man had not spoken! Bold Man's stride was long, his footfall angry. He had not set eyes upon Ma-nuk since the man had betrayed him. There had been no sign of Ma-nuk when the band had begun the trek southward to the humiliating "good riddance" chants of the People of the Land of Grass.

And if Sheela and Ela-nay had fled this way, Dakan-eh had found no sign of them, either. Frustration twitched beneath his skin. Perhaps in time he would find them. He *longed* to find them! To *kill* them! To make them pay for all that they had brought upon the head of such a brave and honorable man as himself.

Suddenly the voice of K-wok brought him to a stop.

"Look who follows!" the hunter called. "There is the one who should be cast out of the band—and now, as an example to any who would speak against our headman."

Dakan-eh turned. The entire band had stopped. His brow came down. K-wok was gesturing back along the way they had come, past Kahm-ree, Rayela, Pah-la, and Cheela-pat. Bold Man found himself snarling again. Ma-nuk! Solemn and repentant, the man appeared with his weary-looking woman and children. When had the traitor decided to follow?

"Stop!" Dakan-eh cried, and raised his spear menacingly. He would have hurled the weapon had he not remembered that the projectile point was of rare brownstone quarried in far hills that he would probably never see again. Ma-nuk was within range, but unless Bold Man made a perfect throw, the spearhead might be damaged in the kill. Dakan-eh lowered his arm. Ma-nuk was not worth the risk. Besides, it had occurred to Bold Man that it was within his power to give Ma-nuk a more demeaning death.

"You will not walk another step with my people!" he shouted.

"Dakan-eh's people are Ma-nuk's people!" Ma-nuk shouted back. "Ma-nuk *must* walk with Dakan-eh."

Dakan-eh studied the man. "When Shateh and his shamans came to accuse me, your words worked to assure their enmity toward me and my people. Because of your willingness to speak against your headman, this band has been cast out of the Land of Grass and now must return to the Red World! You have chosen with whom you would walk, Ma-nuk."

"Bad spirits ran loose within my mouth at that moment. From where they came, I do not know! But they will not speak against Dakan-eh again!"

Ma-nuk's woman looked up at her man sourly; from her disgusted expression it was evident that she bore no affection for him. "How controlled is Ma-nuk's tongue now that Shateh has refused to allow him and his family to remain in the Land of Grass?" she asked loudly.

Ma-nuk gave his woman a hard, openhanded shove.

She withstood it.

Ma-nuk swallowed hard and, with obvious strain, demeaned himself before Dakan-eh. "Please, Headman! This man has acted badly! This man's spirit bleeds because he has spoken against you. But the bad words were the fault of the slave. Yes! From the first day Sheela set bad spirits between you and me. But now she is gone, and Ma-nuk is himself again. Dakan-eh *must* allow Ma-nuk to walk with him to the Red World! A man alone in this land is a man soon dead!"

"You will not be alone," Dakan-eh responded coolly. You will have your woman and your children."

The hands of Ma-nuk's woman flew to her face as she wailed, bereft.

Ma-nuk was aghast. "If I am killed or injured, how will my woman and little ones survive?"

"Your boy Hah-ri can hunt for them. You have chosen their fate and your own."

A restless murmuring rippled through the band. Irritated by it, Dakan-eh snapped hotly, "Is there a man here who will defend Ma-nuk? He has spoken against his headman in hope of remaining as an honored warrior among the big-game hunters of the Land of Grass while his band was banished in disgrace. Is there a man who cannot see this? Is there a man here who will walk with such a traitor?''

The silence that followed was broken only by the rasp of Ma-nuk's strained, shallow, frightened breathing. Then Pah-la spoke out, pleading not for the man but for his woman and three children.

"They have done nothing against the band," she reminded softly.

"Nor will they contribute to it on the long trek ahead with only a youth to hunt for them," Dakan-eh countered.

Hah-ri, Ma-nuk's elder son, stepped forward hesitantly. "If this *must* be, then I will hunt for my family and for my band.''

"Be silent, sloth brain!" a suddenly infuriated Ma-nuk commanded.

Bold Man raised a speculative brow. Hah-ri had not displayed any particular courage on the day of the stampede, and he was cursed with an undeniably slow wit. But the youth was strong and agile, and—unlike his deceased friend Na-sei—had always been loyal to his headman. Neither had young Hah-ri seen Bold Man cowering in the ravine, pissing and puking and screaming in terror.

Dakan-eh's mouth tightened as he forced himself to face the situation at hand. His eyes settled on the youth's sister. Ili-na was no beauty, but she was of an age to take a man. But Ma-nuk's woman, Ghree, was comely. Appraising her now, Bold Man recalled the time when Ma-nuk had shared her with him in exchange for a night of pleasure on Sheela. Ghree had demonstrated a surprising eagerness to satisfy him.

Acknowledging possibilities that were not at all displeasing, it occurred to Dakan-eh that perhaps the spirits of his ancestors had not abandoned him. He had left the Red World with two women and a son; he would return to it with four women and three sons. Despite the deaths of Owa-neh and Na-sei, his people could hardly perceive him as a man who had lost his luck. Perhaps, when all was said and done, he would be looked upon as a chief of great wealth and status after all—if not in the land of bison- and mammoth-hunting strangers, then at least in his own.

"The family of Ma-nuk may walk with this band," he said benevolently, conceding to the anticipation of new-found status and the sating of future lust. "I will hunt for the women and children of Ma-nuk. I will offer them the protection of my spear arm and the warmth of this head-man's fire. Ma-nuk's woman and daughter will be Dakan-eh's women, his sons will be Dakan-eh's sons."

Ma-nuk exploded with rage. "If I go from this band, my woman and sons and daughter will go with me! You will not shame me by naming them yours!"

Dakan-eh found the moment sweet. He smiled. "Let them choose, then—solitude and a lonely death at your side, or life within a band at the fire circle of their headman."

"I choose life! I choose Dakan-eh!" declared Ma-nuk's woman without hesitation as she slung off her wood-framed backpack.

Ma-nuk was incredulous as he watched his woman kneel and untie the traveling roll that held his belongings. "What are you doing? You ungrateful woman! Since the day I brought gifts of fur and feathers and fine hunting nets to your father, I have hunted for you! I have made sons on you! I have—"

"Since coming into the Land of Grass you have beaten and shamed me! Here! Take the belongings that I have saved from the storm for you. I will carry them no longer."

He was aghast. "I have done no more to you than is a man's right. And who could blame me? Your mouth has proved to be as big and loose as the opening between your thighs!"

"You were willing to trade me and your daughter for a slave!" Ghree retorted hotly. "I have not forgotten or forgiven the humiliation of that, or of being passed around among the hunters of the Land of Grass as though I were a slave and of no more concern to you than a bladder flask that might be filled and sucked dry and enjoyed by all!"

"It is the way of men in this land!"

"Then I praise the forces of Creation for allowing me to leave it!" Ghree glared hatefully at Ma-nuk. "From this moment, I am favored by the Four Winds to walk as a headman's woman at Dakan-eh's side, free at last from an unworthy alliance that I regret ever having made!''

Ma-nuk's face twisted with rage. "Do you think that he will not beat you and share you and—"

"May you die alone, Ma-nuk!" Ghree interrupted with the speed and venom of a striking rattler. "May your name and life spirit be lost forever as penalty for the shame that you have brought upon this woman!"

It was an appalling curse. Even Dakan-eh was shaken by it.

Stunned, broken by humiliation and the unexpected viciousness of his woman's words, Ma-nuk was rendered unable to speak or move. He remained where he was, alone, as his woman urged his daughter and two sons forward. Then he watched in silence as the band walked on without him.

The land rolled ahead like waves on a storm-tossed lake turned gold in the bright, cold light of day. Ma-nuk's form grew smaller and smaller against the horizon. Then he was gone.

Hah-ri paused, looked back, and spoke his father's name.

"You must not look back. You must not speak his name," Bold Man commanded immediately lest the youth's pity for his father weaken the resolve of the entire band. "By his own actions, he has put himself outside the band! Forget him, but remember always why he was cast out. Do not repeat his mistakes lest you end your life as he will end his."

The youth's face was tight, unhappy.

"Be obedient to our headman in all things," said Ghree, coming to stand beside her son but looking at Dakan-eh. "My sons and daughter and I will honor and seek to please you in all ways. Never doubt that this woman will be forever grateful to you!" She lay a tremulous hand upon his forearm, allowed him to see deference—and something else—within her eyes. The clear sexual invitation startled him. "May the forces of Creation grant many sons to Bold Man through this woman and her daughter."

His loins stirred, heated.

Ghree smiled, lowered her lids, then linked an arm through Hah-ri's. Pulling her son along with her, she deferentially fell back to take her place beside her daughter, Pah-la, and the two new women of the band, Cheelapat and Rayela.

For a moment Dakan-eh looked back over his shoulder to watch Ghree before glancing forward again across the empty land ahead. Ghree was no Ban-ya. Nor could her adolescent daughter even begin to compare to the woman whom Shateh had stolen from him. Nevertheless, when the band paused and rested for the night, he would penetrate them both, along with Cheelapat.

His jaw tightened. Unexpected resentment flared within him. He realized that he did not want these new women. He wanted his brazen, big-bosomed Ban-ya. What a partner she was! Memories of past matings with her riled him. How he had longed for the moment when his son was weaned and her body was available to him again. Now, with her son taken forcibly from her breasts, Shateh would have her.

A slow, dark rage rose within him as he stalked on. If there were a way in which he could oblige old Kahm-ree and launch a successful raid against Shateh's tribe to win back his Ban-ya and his battered pride, he would do so! But there was no use longing for what could not be—at least not for now. His loins ached. He paused, looked back again, appraised his women, and knew that there was no necessity for him to wait until nightfall to sate the leading edge of his need. He loosened the waist thong of his loin cover.

Pah-la frowned, and Cheelapat scowled. Rayela, however, looked interested as she appraised the state and size of his penis. Ili-na blushed and hung her head. Ghree smiled and licked her lips.

Dakan-eh gestured to Ghree.

Smiling, she came to him.

The band moved on, then paused just far enough away

to allow the twosome some privacy, but also some protection from predators.

After Dakan-eh was done, he brought the woman back to the others and walked on. How eager Ghree had been, how ready to be taken, how quick to howl and yip with delight as he penetrated her body with his own and began to move on her. And yet he felt on edge. Ghree's words followed and troubled him.

"If only he could see the way it is with us!" she had said. "How much I want this with you, no longer with him. Put life into me, Dakan-eh. Let me be your woman now!"

The apparent ease with which the woman had been able to turn her affection to him and against Ma-nuk was disturbing. Were all females capable of holding such malevolent grudges against their men, of turning to other mates in a moment and never looking back?

Of course, he soothed himself, Ma-nuk's woman had every cause to consider herself fortunate. He was Bold Man! He was Brave Hunter Who Chases the Whirling Wind to Save the People! Was there a woman in all of this world or the next who would not prefer him to any other man?

Ta-maya. Sheela. Memories of their rejection shamed him. He wondered bitterly where those two women were now.

May they be dead! No! May they be alive! And may the Four Winds grant me the pleasure of finding them, of making them and all who have stood with them against me pay with their lives for the misfortune that their disloyalty and ingratitude have brought to me and to my band.

Squinting across the plain, a disconsolate Ma-nuk watched the band disappear until, with grim resolve, he decided to follow. He suspected it was a mistake from the first step he took and was sure of it when, crouching in the storm-broken grasses that furred a long, rolling stretch of high hillock, he looked across the land and in hate-filled silence watched his woman give herself to Dakan-eh.

He heard her hoot and yip when the moment of release came to Bold Man. Growling, Ma-nuk realized that it had been many a long moon since Ghree made noises like that under him. He debated his options: He could continue to follow, then sneak up and kill her and Bold Man in the night. Or he could go back to Shateh and once again throw himself upon the chieftain's mercy.

"No—never again. None of it," he decided. He refused to humiliate himself again before either man. Ma-nuk chose a third course: He would make the best of what had happened to him.

He eyed the sky. Winter would come early to the Land of Grass. He rose, turned, faced into the wind, and headed north toward distant mountains, where he could hunt and find a sheltering cave and survive alone. When spring came, he could come down from the heights and try to find some far-flung band among the People of the Land of Grass that did not ally itself with Shateh; if his pelts and trading items of bone and bead, of claw and tooth and lengths of sinew were good enough, he might be welcomed if he made up a clever enough story about who he was and whence he had come.

He walked on and on until he came to the river. He was not much of a swimmer, but feeling reckless, he crossed to the far shore at a wide, stony place that offered little threat to a surefooted man. His thoughts grew lighter with every step as he decided that things were not going to be too bad for him after all. He had his spears, his tool-making supplies, and the makings for fire. He was resourceful, brave, and next to Dakan-eh, the best hunter in the Red World. Now he would be the *only* hunter in this part of the Land of Grass. Spring would bring its reward. He was sure of it.

He found himself laughing softly as he walked. Let Shateh fight the omens and the bickering indecisiveness of his fellow chiefs and shamans! Let Dakan-eh take Ghree and his sloth-brained children back to a life of eating lizards. He, Ma-nuk, would make a new life without help from any of them. He might just come across Sheela wandering lost and alone and in need of a man to hunt for her and keep her warm during the coming winter.

"Now there's a thought!" he exclaimed, then stopped short, realizing that he had been walking very fast and had come very far. He would be in the foothills soon. Dusk was settling. The air was growing colder. His eyes sought some cover under which he could take refuge during the night. There were boulders ahead, and soft, high islands of green showing around what appeared to be a creek running between a deep cleft in the rolling land.

He strode out again, thinking of Sheela. "Ah, daughter of the Watching Star, did my headman kill you and give your body to the river? What a waste that would have been. And what happened to that fool Ela-nay? Did he feed himself to meat eaters as he wandered alone in his grief? I should have run away with you that night! If I find you alive, I will suffer no other to be your man!"

It was nearly dark by the time Ma-nuk reached the trees. He drank deeply from the creek, set up a small stone weir and a few snares and deadfall traps for passing nocturnal mammals, then settled down for the night. Considering his circumstances, he slept well and heavily.

Ma-nuk rose before dawn, retrieved his snare lines, along with a wood rat and a rabbit, then drew the largest fish from the little pool that his weir had made. Hunkering on his heels, he made a small fire over which he roasted the fish and rat.

Soon it was dawn. Picking the last morsels of meat from his kills, Ma-nuk watched the sun rise.

Beyond the trees, the grass was whitened by frost. He relieved himself, observed his urine and fecal matter steaming in the frigid morning air, then—after gutting the rabbit, attaching it to a length of sinew, and slinging it over his shoulder for a later meal—took up his belongings and went on, striding under the light of a cold sun. The foothills were near. If he could keep on at his present pace, he would reach the flank of the hills before sunset. He broke into a trot and ran easily across the land until he was at last brought up short by the need to rest and eat. He knelt, preparing to skin and eat the rabbit. But he found himself staring at the ground, across broken grasses and disturbed earth. He leaned closer to sniff at the grasses and broken soil. He was certain that he had come upon the tracks of a man and woman. Sheela and Ela-nay! They were headed for the mountains!

He rose again, no longer of a mind to eat, and followed. His spirit sang until he saw the carrion-eating birds circling and settling ahead. He paused. Something was dead, and whatever had attracted meat-eating birds to a feast would draw water carnivores as well. Frowning, he turned his steps slightly to the north and continued on until the flight of startled birds alerted him to danger. He fell flat and hid within wind-stirred tall grasses as a small group of men in war paint passed close by.

Breathless with terror, he nearly screamed. He recognized these men, knew them by their height and bearing, by their long hair, by their body paint and tattoos, and by the look of the tall, deadly-looking spears that they carried.

"Warriors of the People of the Watching Star . . . But how can this be? You were all slain in the great war."

He swallowed. The men were real enough, as were the big wolflike dogs that ran with them. From the direction in which their long, earth-eating strides were taking them, and from the way they paused now and then to study the ground, he knew that they were following Sheela's and Ela-nay's tracks toward Shateh's ruined village by the river.

But what had happened to Sheela and Ela-nay? Heart pounding, Ma-nuk told himself that he must worry about himself now. He thought hard about what he should do. If he hurried downwind and ahead of the warriors, he could return to Shateh's people in time to sound an alert. Surely, he thought, the chieftain would be honor bound to accept him back into the tribe. But, Ma-nuk thought, there was great danger in solitary heroism. He might be better off racing after Dakan-eh to offer warning; Bold Man might be so pleased by news of an enemy attack against Shateh that he would forgive Ma-nuk. Hopeful of winning Ban-ya back and regaining favor in the eyes of Shateh, Bold Man might decide to fight with the chieftain's people against this unexpected and potentially deadly enemy.

Resentment hardened Ma-nuk's heart. *Why should I risk my life for Shateh or for Dakan-eh?* he asked himself. *They have chosen to walk apart from me. And for now the Four Winds have placed me beyond danger.*

He smiled smugly as he decided to lie safely hidden in the grass until Death passed on its way.

Suddenly Ma-nuk's smile faded. Something was moving in the grass behind him. *No!* Ahead of him! *No!* All around him! He made to rise, but it was too late. Death was closing on him. And now Death spoke out of the mouth of a woman.

"No, Ston!" she commanded. "Wait!"

But the order went unheeded. The point of a spear drove straight through his back. A single scream ripped out of Ma-nuk. His breath exploded as another spear struck him through a lung. A third went into his pelvis. He turned his head to see that Sheela, with a warrior on either side of her, was standing over him. Ma-nuk's eyes bulged.

His assailant looked down at him with loathing. "You said that he was one of the many who shamed my Rikiree," the warrior said to Sheela. "He will die slowly."

The other warrior was scowling. "Why is he so far from the others?"

"Let us ask him." Sheela knelt.

Ma-nuk was gasping, fighting for breath and clarity of mind. His vision blurred, and blood filled his mouth. "Sheela . . . followed . . . wanted . . ." He barely recognized the sounds as his own. And things were unnaturally bright and quavering. For a moment, as he attempted to fix his gaze on Sheela, he was appalled at the condition of her battered face. He knew Dakan-eh had done that to her; he wished that he could form the words to say that he wanted Bold Man dead.

Sheela was bending close, whispering vindictively. "Are you trying to tell me that you have been following me, Ma-nuk? Searching for a *slave*? Ah, I remember: You offered to trade your woman and daughter to Dakan-eh for me. But I also remember that when you had your chance to lie on me, you did not turn away in pity and allow this slave her pride. You took me as did all the others, carelessly and with no concern for my humiliation." She appraised him out of eyes that were devoid of compassion, then rose and said coldly, "Finish him, Tsana, as you finished Ela-nay."

"He is finished already," replied the man named Ston as he stepped forward.

Ma-nuk felt one of the man's moccasined feet placed hard against his back just below his shoulder blades. With a yank, the warrior retrieved one of his spears. The second projectile was not as cooperative. Ston twisted it brutally, but the point had lodged in Ma-nuk's shattered pelvis and would not be withdrawn. Ma-nuk's garbled screams and retchings did nothing to deter the man from making further efforts. With a snarl of disgust, he bent and loosed a dagger from a leather sheath that was attached to his belt; at first Ma-nuk was sure the man was going to carve the spearhead from his pelvis. Instead Ston slit the thongs that held the stone point to the shaft. In a moment the shaft was free. He stood and glowered down at Ma-nuk. "The death of this lizard eater has cost me a good spearhead. But it has severed his spine, so, in memory of Rikiree, I consider its loss a trade well made. He will lie here, unable to move, until he dies."

"Let us join the others before the carrion eaters come to feed upon him," said Sheela. "I want to be with the raiding party when Shateh's camp is reached. With my own hand I will take the life of Dakan-eh, and before he dies, he will know that we have made his woman, Ban-ya, a slave." Her face worked with her need for vengeance. "I will cut her hair and kill her spirit. And then, while Dakan-eh is forced to watch, you will enjoy his woman. All of the warriors of the Watching Star will enjoy her! Ban-ya will be for Jhadel, as Rikiree was for old Nachumalena. Then Dakan-eh will die." She was smiling now, her mouth tight and twisted. "We will see how long it takes before the woman of Dakan-eh runs screaming into the night." She drew in a deep, steadying breath, then exhaled it with pure and venomous resolve. "We will bring slaves, stolen spears, and the dogs of our enemies back to the stronghold. Then Jhadel will know that the blood of Neea has not been wasted and that Thunder in the Sky is smiling upon those who walk with the daughter of Sheehanal."

"The many bands of our tribe have gone their separate ways." All morning Shateh had been restless and irritable.

The break-fast meal of small animals, birds, and fish that the women had snared and stoned in the first light of dawn had done nothing to lighten his mood. Now there was desolation in his voice as he looked across the once-teeming encampment. "We must prepare to follow the bison, to hunt, to make meat and hides and sinew and fat before White Giant Winter finds us with no food and no lodges."

The chieftain moved past Ban-ya, to walk among the other fire circles and urge each family to hurry. Shateh's women and children worked to assemble the pitiful remains of their once-copious belongings; but Ban-ya stood motionless, staring southeastward in the direction in which Dakan-eh and her people had gone.

"You! Lizard-eating woman! Lend a hand!" commanded Wehakna.

Ban-ya ignored her. Her milk-heavy breasts ached and burned for want of a child, but they did not hurt her half so much as did her heart when she thought of Dakan-eh and the son who had been so cruelly taken from her arms.

"He will come back for me," she murmured, not realizing that she had spoken aloud. "He *must* come back." Her mind ran wild, trying to understand how he could have left her behind. "He must have had a reason . . . a good reason."

"Forget him," snapped Wehakna. "That 'bold' man has given you away."

"To a better man than you deserve," said Senohnim.

"My father is your man now!" reminded nine-year-old Oni. She sat with her two younger cousins, Khat and Tinah. "The lizard eater did not want you anymore! And no one here wants you, either!"

The girl's words stung. Ban-ya turned and angrily faced the child. "Your father wants me!" she said loudly, and was gratified when Oni shrank from her.

"Watch the way you wag your tongue at my daughter, woman of the Red World, or you may soon find that you have no tongue at all!" Wehakna glared with open animosity at Ban-ya. "You are not without enemies in this band. My Atonashkeh is right to hold you and your kind responsible for the death of my Kalawak!"

"And for all that has befallen this band!" added pregnant Senohnim, gesturing to her two daughters as she ordered sternly, "Khat, Tinah, do not look into the eyes of this lizard eater lest her spirit turn your skin to scales and—"

"Watch your own tongues," Ban-ya warned, "lest your chieftain learn of the way you speak to me and against his good judgment whenever his back is turned."

This said, she pulled her coyote-skin robe tightly around her shoulders. Holding the garment closed at her throat, she headed for the groves and the river beyond. Soon Ban-ya was within the trees. Breathless with hope, she walked quickly, with every intention of running away.

"Woman of the Red World, stop!"

But Ban-ya did not stop. Recognizing the voice as Shateh's, she broke into a run. As she attempted to leap over a downed tree, her left foot came up short, and she went flying. She reached out to break her fall. Instead, her momentum sent her open palms raking forward through wind-downed branches, and she landed hard, facedown, with all of her weight on her breasts. She lay still, stunned, trying hard not to sob.

A moment later Shateh was extending one wide, long-fingered hand down to her. "You will not run away. Get up."

Ban-ya raised her head and looked at the chieftain. There was no use trying to resist him. She rose without accepting his assistance. Wincing from pain, she saw one of his eyebrows arch. He was staring at her chest. From his expression, she could see that man need was awakened in him.

She looked down. Her robe had fallen over one shoulder; beneath it she still wore her nursing tunic with the upper flap unlaced. She angrily grabbed at the edges of her robe and pulled them together.

"It is the fifth day," he said huskily, and reached to draw her hands away. "The time of mourning is over."

Her fingers closed into fists around the fur and would not allow him to part it. But he did part it, so roughly that she heard some of the fine stitching tear.

He did not speak as he took her down. Straddling her, he laid the robe and tunic wide and began to handle her great, hot, milk-laden breasts.

She stiffened, catching her breath because the pain was so great. "I am Dakan-eh's, always and forever."

"He has given you to me."

"To one he trusted as a brother . . . to one who betrayed his trust by accepting his gift, then turning him out of the tribe."

"You speak as boldly as your last man, Ban-ya of the Red World. If I had allowed him to stay, did you imagine that I would have shared you with him? What is mine, I keep—for as long as it pleases me."

"And do you imagine that I would even try to please you after you have stolen me from the man of my heart and sent my son away?"

"For too long did Piku-neh suck life from you, woman. It was past time that one was weaned." His hands were under her breasts, lifting them, working them until milk rose to bead the nipples. She flinched. Tears squeezed from her tightly shut lids. "I cannot ease the pain in your heart, but I can take the heat from your breasts and place it where it belongs as I make new sons on you," he said as, bending, he began to mouth her breasts.

She was startled, and her eyes flew open. She gasped and strained against him and against the fulfillment of his words. But as he drew the milk from her breasts, the pain and heat did lessen within them. Fire burst free within her loins. The intensity of her reaction appalled her; it was all she could do to keep her thighs clenched and her hips still as Shateh knelt back and, after removing his loin cover, stared down at her.

"Open yourself to me, woman of the Red World. In your milk I may well have found the blood of my youth. Not since the woman named Ta-maya walked briefly among my people have I set eyes upon a female who stirred me more. I *will* make a son on you. Now."

"Your woman Senohnim is big with child! She may give you sons!"

"Not like the sons you will bear me, Bold Woman!"

With a sudden upward lurch of her hips, she attempted to unseat him and roll away; to her surprise, she succeeded. As she got to her knees, she realized that he had allowed the movement. His reaction to it was sudden and powerful and adroit. In a moment she was on the ground again, but facedown with the chieftain behind her, positioning her hips for penetration, then, with no attempt to ready her, driving deep.

"My father, the band is ready to move on."

It was Atonashkeh. Shateh paused, enraged. "Go, then! Lead them south along the river to the place where the two waters meet and fork. The bison will have gone there. I will follow after I have put life into this new woman."

"The people say that we should not seek that herd again," said Atonashkeh. "There is much talk against this woman. For the tribe, drain yourself, then kill her. Leave her in this place of death."

8

A baby's first cry was heard in the valley within the blue mountains to which Cha-kwena had led his people. Siwi-ni had given birth within the small hut of bent willow branches, which Kosar-eh raised for her. Cha-kwena listened with amazement to the cries of the newborn, for despite the old woman's frailty and everyone's worst fears after the rising of the black moon, Siwi-ni's labor had been no labor at all. U-wa and Ha-xa had escorted her into the hut, and suddenly the child was squalling.

The shaman sighed with relief; all had gone well. Even the weather had cleared.

Nevertheless, as he knelt upon the sacred calling-upon-the-favor-of-the-spirits-for-the-good-of-the-mother blanket, which he had inherited from his grandfather, Cha-kwena felt disconcerted. He had had no time to work any magic on behalf of the infant or its mother—no dances, no smokes, no chants, so the forces of Creation would grant Siwi-ni an easy delivery and a strong, healthy child.

He had positioned the sacred blanket, and then the baby had cried. Apparently Siwi-ni and the forces of Creation needed no help from him this day. She had made her own magic, the most impressive magic in all of this world—from out of her body she had brought forth new life.

And now, to everyone's surprise, Siwi-ni herself emerged from the birthing hut. Wrapped in a deer-hide cloak, she looked pale, and gray half circles shadowed her lower lids. But she was steady on her feet, and her eyes were bright.

With a beaming Ha-xa beside her, Siwi-ni held her baby high. "The woman of Kosar-eh offers this newborn to the band and to her man. Will Kosar-eh accept this child?"

Surrounded by his boys, Kosar-eh came to stand before her. He took the child and cradled the tiny naked form in the fold of his one strong arm. As he appraised the latest addition to his family, the baby's small arms flailed, and its bowed little limbs kicked vigorously against the lifeless hand that lay against his chest, hidden beneath his cloak. He winced, then caught his breath. His brows expanded, then furrowed. His mouth tightened. After a moment he turned, lowered his arm, and allowed his sons to look upon . . .

"A girl?" exclaimed Gah-ti, incredulous.

The boys were clearly befuddled by the idea of having a female among their ranks.

"The newborn is not a son," Siwi-ni admitted, uncertain now of her man's acceptance of the child.

Kosar-eh shook his head in gentle remonstration. "Five sons has Siwi-ni borne to Kosar-eh. It is time she had a daughter. A strong daughter who kicks at her father and fills him with—" He paused and seemed distracted. "Kosar-eh accepts this child!" he declared at last. Then, mindful of time-honored rituals, he commanded his boys, "Now let the sons of Kosar-eh name this girl child Sister!"

"She will not want to hunt with us, will she?" asked Ka-neh, frowning with worry.

"Don't be stupid! Girls cannot hunt!" put in Kiu-neh.

"Mah-ree has hunted, and with her own spears!" reminded Koh-neh.

"Not anymore, she doesn't!" Gah-ti silenced his brothers, then said forthrightly, "In this new land Gah-ti proudly names this new child Sister! Gah-ti's brothers will do the same. Now!"

The other boys echoed their brother. Cha-kwena, meanwhile, stole a glance at Mah-ree. The girl was glaring at Gah-ti as though she longed to kill him with her eyes.

Kosar-eh faced the band now and asked his people if they would accept his newest child as one of their own. Without hesitation the group replied in happy affirmation. "Gladly we accept this child!"

"See baby!" said Joh-nee.

"Me see baby!" piped Tla-nee.

Kosar-eh carried the infant to the two little girls. He knelt before them. "See the newest sister of this band, little ones," he invited.

The toddlers' eyes grew big as, with pudgy baby fingers, they reached tentatively, lightly, to touch the arm of the infant. Kosar-eh, knowing that they were afraid, assured them that it was all right. They patted the infant's brow and cheeks until Kosar-eh rose and held his child for the viewing of Mah-ree and Ta-maya.

The sisters were as rapt as the little girls had been.

"She looks like Siwi-ni," observed Mah-ree thoughtfully.

Cha-kwena wondered if she had intended an insult or compliment. Hoyeh-tay had once told him that Siwi-ni had been a pretty girl, as quick on her feet and as delicate of face and form as the tiny brown-streaked birds called pine dancers. It was difficult for Cha-kwena to believe this; if she resembled the little finches for which she had been named, in his mind the similarity had more to do with her pesky, aggressive personality rather than her looks.

He stared at Siwi-ni and tried to imagine her as a young, pretty girl. He failed. Besides, why look at an old woman when Ta-maya was nearby? He shifted his gaze and was transfixed by the beauty's smile as she raised her eyes and spoke to Kosar-eh.

"Ah, Dear Friend, a daughter will lighten your days and bring a smile to your heart," Ta-maya predicted. "If the forces of Creation allow, she will mature to ease the work of your woman and make your sons bold for her sake. She is so tiny, so beautiful. See how strongly she grips my finger and kicks at your chest!"

Kosar-eh had the oddest expression on his face. "She may well be more special than you know," said the cripple.

The man was looking at Ta-maya, and she was looking back. Her smile softened. There was unmistakable and unstinting love for him in her gaze.

Cha-kwena frowned; she never looked at him like that. Annoyed and jealous, the young shaman strode forward and eyed the newborn. He had to admit that the baby *was* pretty. And in her delicate, perfectly formed features there *was* a startling resemblance to Siwi-ni. Sudden sadness touched him. As he looked into the face of the infant he realized that even the loveliest of living things must someday wither with age until they became only shadows of their former selves, and then even the shadows must fade, until they were no more than memories within the dreams and thoughts of those who had once known and loved them.

Distressed by the unwelcome swing of his mood into solemnity, Cha-kwena forced himself to remember his duties as shaman. He cleared his throat, stood as straight as he could, and asked, "By what name shall this band's new daughter and sister be known? Let it be spoken now, so news of this child's birth may be carried on the Four Winds to the forces of Creation, to First Man and First Woman, and to all of the spirits of the ancestors who watch us from the world beyond this world."

"The one from whose body new life has come forth

shall choose and speak this name,'' replied Kosar-eh with a nod of deference to his woman.

Unlike male infants, whose birth names were replaced by new names when they came to manhood, a female's birth name was hers for life and therefore of critical importance. For this reason it was traditionally the right of the father to name his daughters as he saw fit, choosing names that would call down the blessings of the spirits upon them and strengthen them against the rigors of a woman's lot in life. For a man to allow his woman to choose this name was a sign of utmost respect and trust in her wisdom and judgment—qualities that were considered to be absent in all but the most exceptional females.

The old woman stood as tall as her meager height would allow, then released the child's name upon the soft wind of the sunlit day. ''May the Four Winds carry the name Doh-teyah to the ancestors! May the spirit of the mother of Kosar-eh smile in the world beyond this world and rejoice in the birth of this daughter who shall carry her name and honor her spirit in this life.''

Cha-kwena saw that Kosar-eh was deeply moved.

''It is good!'' exclaimed the cripple to his woman. ''It is the name I would have chosen! The life spirit of this man's mother will smile in the world beyond this world, as she once smiled upon his son when many turned away in disgust at the sight of him! May the wise and loving spirit of Doh-teyah guide and protect this little one, who will now bear her name forever in this life, and in the spirit life beyond!''

''May it be so!'' Cha-kwena offered the obligatory response, and was caught off guard by a lump in his throat that made his voice crack.

As was expected at this point in the traditional introduction of a new baby into the band, the gathering repeated the shaman's words in one voice. ''May it be so!''

And now, as Kosar-eh gently returned his newborn child into the eager arms of his woman, he placed a long, hard kiss upon Siwi-ni's brow, then proclaimed loudly and ferociously, ''May the woman of Kosar-eh live *long!* May this man be at her side when this child comes to her mother

and father as a woman with her firstborn in her arms!
And . . ." He stopped and shook his head, too overcome
with emotion to go on.

"Ay yah hay!" exclaimed the two widows, U-wa and
Ha-xa, hugging each other as they wept openly and happily
for their band sister. Both women had borne their last
children with no man to welcome the births.

Cha-kwena snuffled, blinking back tears of gladness
for the couple. But the tears held sadness, too; in his heart
he doubted that the old woman would live to see this child
even half-grown.

Kosar-eh straightened, faced the band, and for the first
time in many a long moon he smiled a broad, white smile of
such gladness that despite his scars, he was handsome.
"This man rejoices! Come now, Cha-kwena! Come, sons of
Kosar-eh! While my Siwi-ni rests with our new daughter,
while the women and little ones attend her, we will set our
nets and snares for whatever game the forces of Creation
may send our way! Tonight we will celebrate as we have not
celebrated since leaving the Red World! All of the spirits in
this world and the next will know that we give thanks for
the gift of new life that they have given to this man this
day!"

Then, to the young shaman's amazement, Kosar-eh
came forward to sling his good arm around Cha-kwena's
shoulders in a powerful hug. "You have been right all
along, grandson of Hoyeh-tay! Indeed, you *are* Shaman, for
you have brought us all into this good land where, despite
rain and wind and the rising of the black moon, the omens
are far better than you know!"

"The *totem* has led us," reminded Gah-ti sourly.

"Only because Cha-kwena had the wisdom to follow!" countered Mah-ree.

Kosar-eh was still beaming. "Let there be no words to
shadow this day. We will hunt in this good land to which
Shaman *and* Life Giver have led us."

And so it was. But even as the hunt began, a lion was
heard roaring in the hills, and Cha-kwena realized that he
had not seen the totem since the rain had begun.

*   *   *

When darkness at last came down upon the valley there were rabbits, fat-thighed hares, and squirrels on the spits. The music of wooden flutes, bone whistles, resoundingly beaten drums, and the high, hissing and clacking sound of rattles of antelope scrotums and tortoiseshells filled the night. At Kosar-eh's urging, Cha-kwena led his people in dance and song while the cripple, in full body paint and the feathered raiment of a clown, performed joyous panto-mimes that made the women and children laugh with delight.

From far across the benighted land, wolves and coyotes echoed the songs of the people, and the solitary lion that had been heard earlier roared again in the hills. But tonight Cha-kwena feared nothing. With the sacred stone around his neck, he danced and whirled and raised his arms and voice in bellowing thanksgiving to the forces of Creation. Never before had he felt stronger in the power of his calling! Not since leaving the Red World had Cha-kwena been in a more joyous encampment.

And now, from somewhere far away, he heard the trumpeting of mammoth. His heart soared; somewhere in the darkness the great white mammoth grazed with others of the mammoth kind. *Tomorrow I will search for them,* he decided. But now he was too happily intoxicated upon the moment to think about the morrow. Instead he wondered what Mah-ree and the women had mixed into the celebra-tory brew; the more he drank, the better he felt. His eyes were full of starlight, and his body was as light as the wind. His mind wandered across bright flashes of light as he danced, whirled, and suddenly threw back his head and howled. The Four Winds embraced him. He spread his arms in welcome as Owl swept toward him from out of the stars and came to rest upon his back. Its pale, broad, raptorial wings spread wide.

"Ay yah hay!" Cha-kwena exclaimed in awe, for somehow the bird and he were one, and his arms had become wings, stroking the air. The ghost of his grandfather appeared out of the night to dance with him, guiding him through complex, half-remembered ritual steps and turns and intricate risings and fallings of his voice.

"Dance, Cha-kwena! Sing, my grandson! Truly you are Shaman now!"

"Yes! Surely it is so!" replied Cha-kwena ecstatically.

"Come!" invited Owl. "Why do you wait? It is time for Cha-kwena to fly upon the back of the winds!"

How could he refuse? "Yes!" he cried and, with a resounding hoot of pleasure, leaped into the embrace of the Four Winds and was borne upward on the wings of Owl as he flew away across the world and into the night.

Kosar-eh lowered his swan-bone flute and paused in his own dancing to stare at Cha-kwena. Never had he seen the youth in better form. Tonight, for the first time, Shaman seemed to *be* Shaman, strong in the power of the totem, no longer a hotheaded boy in constant need of the guidance and goading of a clown.

"Ish my shaman not wonderful?" asked Mah-ree. He shpeaks to the shpirits! They ansher from hish mouth in their own voishes!"

He looked down, startled as the girl came tottering close. She held a limp bladder flask. The dog Friend was at her side, as was Gah-ti. Kosar-eh frowned. His son was nearly as tipsy as Mah-ree. "What *have* you and the others put into the celebration drink, girl?"

Mah-ree smiled. "Good thingsh. Sheecret things! Hoyeh-tay taught me of them long ago: rootsh, leavesh, and after the rain, magic mushroomsh! They are all here in thish new country. Ish not Cha-kwena wonderful to have brought ush into thish fine land?"

"How many times," Gah-ti asked, all out of patience, "do you have to be told that he only follows the mammoth. The mammoth is totem! Cha-kwena is—"

"Wonderful!" She sighed euphorically and raised her flask to Kosar-eh. "Here! Drink! I will share!"

"I thank you, but no," he said. "Such is my happiness tonight that I need nothing to enhance it. Besides, while our shaman communes with the spirits on our behalf, one man must remain clearheaded in this camp."

"I am a man!" Gah-ti's voice was made belligerent by drink. "My head is clear. Almost." He looked imploringly at Mah-ree, and his tone softened. "Why will you not see that I am a man?"

Mah-ree looked him up and down. "I shee nothing when I look at you, Gah-ti. No one at all!"

Kosar-eh was annoyed. "This is a night upon which the forces of Creation have smiled upon this band. Out of respect and gratitude to them, stop your constant bickering and smile at each other!"

Mah-ree, unable to deny the wisdom of Kosar-eh's words, forced the corners of her mouth upward into a tight little crease that was there one moment and gone the next.

Gah-ti, on the other hand, smiled broadly and eagerly. "You will be my woman!"

Kosar-eh rolled his eyes. The boy was obnoxious in his single-minded desire to win the girl. If there was a chance of Mah-ree's affection being turned in his direction and away from the shaman's, Gah-ti would ruin it if he kept on like this. *We'll have to talk soon,* Kosar-eh thought. *Father to son, man to boy.*

He found himself brought up short, startled as he appraised his son. When had Gah-ti grown so tall? Only yesterday, the boy's eyes had been at the belly level of the father, and yet now Kosar-eh had only to bend his head a little to meet the hard, steady gaze of his son. And although Gah-ti was still as leggy as a yearling colt, when had his upper back and shoulders grown so broad? Was it possible that the boy was *not* a boy? Was he, as he claimed, a youth not only on the brink of manhood but well over the edge of it?

Wide-eyed, he looked long and hard at his eldest son. *Yes.* It *was* so! Soon Gah-ti *would* be a man. Already the youth had proved himself an adept worker of stone and setter of snares, and his spears flew with an ease and accuracy that would soon make him a hunter in whom any father would take great pride! Yet his proprietorial, aggressive manner with Mah-ree was shameful!

Kosar-eh shook his head, disgusted with himself. Since leaving the land of the ancestors, he had been so preoccupied with the journey, he had allowed all of his boys to grow up wild. By now, in the Red World, his three eldest sons would have taken up residence in the boys' lodge to be instructed in the ways of the hunt, weapon and tool making, and the proper manners to use when courting females.

He fixed his eyes upon his other sons. Things would change for them; he would see to that. As soon as the band found the perfect site to raise a permanent village, a boys' lodge would be raised! And a girls' house, too, in which Siwi-ni, as eldest woman, would serve as teacher and wise woman.

Kosar-eh was jerked from his reverie by Gah-ti's imperious proclamations.

"Make Mah-ree dance with me, my father! Gah-ti will hunt for her and bring her gifts of meat and fur and feathers and beads!"

The youth, strutting proud, circled the girl and tried to take her hand.

"Get away from me, you shtupid boy!" Mah-ree threw herself against Kosar-eh and, to the amazement of the clown, hugged him hard and planted a firm kiss on his robe where it lay over his lifeless right hand. "I love my clown almosht ash much ash I love my shaman! If Gah-ti were more like hish father I would love him, too. Not like a woman lovsh a man, of coursh, but like a brother!"

Gah-ti was livid. "You *will* be my woman!"

"Never ever never!" Mah-ree, nose atilt, ran off to join the others.

Gah-ti was hot on her heels. He cursed and kicked at Friend as the dog took off after him, nipping at his ankles, catching a tooth in the ties of one sandal, and dragging along behind until the youth tripped and fell flat.

Looking back over her shoulder, Mah-ree laughed at him. "You will not be a hunter of thish band, Gah-ti! You will be a clown like your father!"

"Mah-ree!" Ha-xa scolded.

But Kosar-eh was not offended. He knew that the girl was too intoxicated to have thought about what she was saying. Besides, at the moment, his heart was pounding, his mouth too dry for words, his thoughts were too wild to focus. He stared down at the fur that covered his ruined hand.

Had he felt the press of Mah-ree's kiss? After half a lifetime of dreaming and yearning for feeling to return to his arm and hand, he could not fully believe that it was possible. Yet, earlier in the day, his newborn daughter's tiny foot had kicked him, and he could have sworn that he had felt her heels pummeling the back of his hand. Then, as now, it had seemed too much even to think about. Nor had he been able to bring himself to touch his ruined arm and hand lest disappointment prove too bitter to bear! Yet, all the long day, hope had been a constant tease in his thoughts.

Now, with his heart leaping in his chest, Kosar-eh slowly raised his good hand. Trembling, he positioned it across his robe to press the atrophied flesh and muscle that lay beneath.

Yes? Yes!

Kosar-eh gasped. He had not imagined it! There *was* feeling in the hand! He pressed harder, then harder still. The atrophied muscles and lifeless bones would not flex, but feeling was there, like a band of invisible ants moving beneath the surface of his skin, tickling his flesh with the prick of thousands of minuscule antennae.

Tears smarted in his eyes as he fought back the impulse to shout his news. It was too soon. Jealous spirits might overhear and spitefully reverse the healing process. For now he must wait and be content to wonder why, after so many years of longings and silent, secret invocations, the forces of Creation had answered.

He looked up at Cha-kwena. Had the young shaman induced the forces of Creation into taking pity on him and returning life to his ruined arm when every other shaman in the Red World and beyond had failed? Surely it was too much to hope for! And yet Kosar-eh did yearn as, head spinning, he was tantalized with the possibility of being a whole man again.

He stood tall, drew in a deep, steadying breath, and strode through the circling dancers to where Ta-maya stood beside the sleeping Siwi-ni. Let his woman sleep! She was not fit for dancing this night, and he would have a lifetime to dance with her old bones! Now, with a confidence that had not been his since his youth, Kosar-eh forgot his scarred

face and took Ta-maya's wrist within the strong grasp of his
one good hand.

"Come!" he said, and led her boldly to the dance.
"Tonight our shaman invokes the forces of Creation!
Tonight Siwi-ni sleeps with a new life at her breast! Tonight
my children sing of gladness in a new land, and the great
white mammoth grazes with his own kind! Smile, daughter
of the Red World. It is time to put past sadness behind us.
The omens are better than you know! Dance with me,
Ta-maya, for only the Four Winds may say what magic
powers are awakening within the stars this night!"

9

Shateh awoke with a start. The wind was up, from the north.
And something was moving within it. The chieftain sat up,
listening. The men who kept watch at the peripheries of the
traveling camp had not raised an alert; the dogs were silent.
Tense with foreboding, Shateh squinted into the frigid
darkness but could not see more than a few paces in any
direction. Clouds had settled upon the earth, obliterating the
stars and turning the night into a flowing river of mist that
moved eerily around him. Somewhere far away a nighthawk
keened—or, Shateh wondered, had he only imagined the
sound? He could not be sure. One of the dogs barked once,
then was still.

The chieftain pulled his heavy bearskin traveling robe
over his head and huddled within it. A storm was coming;
he was certain of that. The unmistakable taint of ice was in
the wind. He breathed it in and recognized the presence that
had roused him from heavy, dreamless sleep: White Giant

Winter had awakened in the north and was now advancing across the world.

Much too soon, he thought. *My people have yet to find the herd, to hunt, to take meat and hides for new lodges. It is not good!*

Beside him, Ban-ya moaned in her sleep and shivered under the bison hide he had given to her. He regretted forcing her to part with her own cloak of coyote skins; it had greatly distressed her and added to her misery. But what else could he have done to silence the venomous tongue of Atonashkeh and to pacify his son's equally poisonous wives? They had all seemed surprised and upset when Ban-ya and he had returned to his people from the grove. Atonashkeh had no doubt told them that he had advised the chieftain to kill the new woman.

His son repeated his conviction that Ban-ya's presence would cause their misfortune to continue. Shateh had seen the deeply troubled looks of distrust, envy, and hatred in his people's faces. The chieftain immediately realized that the only way to keep Ban-ya with him was to reduce her status in the band. So he had slapped her, then had commanded his two wives to cut the forelocks of her hair. She had tried to escape, but he had held her pinned against him with her arms behind her back. And when Nani, Atonashkeh's pregnant second woman, covetously eyed Ban-ya's robe and said that it was much too good for a slave, he had taken the garment from Ban-ya's back and given it to the other woman.

Shateh growled at the memory. His son's constant challenges vexed him. Even if Ban-ya failed to please him, he would keep her alive just to irritate Atonashkeh and to make certain that there was no doubt as to who—he or his son—was in control of the band. But the woman *had* pleased him enormously. Just thinking of lying on her hardened the bone of his manhood and made him feel young and virile.

Now Ban-ya moaned again in her sleep, and Shateh felt ashamed. He knew he had used the woman badly. It was not his way; nor would it be again. Already he had sworn this to himself. But as chief and shaman, he could not demean himself by revealing the oath to her—not to a female, and never to a lizard eater.

All day he had watched her as she had followed him in stoic silence, several steps behind Wehakna, Senohnim, and their daughters. Ban-ya obeyed him and his women but refused to react to Nani's taunting. "Look at my new robe, slave! Don't you wish you had such a fine robe as this? See how perfectly it fits me? As though it were made just for me!"

When the dark had come down and weariness finally brought his traveling band to encamp, Shateh, ignoring the glaring eyes of Atonashkeh, had led Ban-ya away from his other women and had shown her how it could be with him. He had been gentle with her this time, once again sucking milk from her swollen breasts to ease the pain that the sudden forced weaning of her son was causing her. His slow, methodical, invasive fingerings had never failed to set fire to even the most unwilling partners, but Ban-ya had not caught fire. In the end she had been a passive receptacle for his passion.

He had been disappointed, but the long day's walk had wearied her, and the trimming of her hair indeed deprived her of spirit. He led her back to the night's encampment. Then, after a scant meal and yet another coupling, she fell asleep on her side, naked under a heavy wind-ruffled bison robe, facing away from him.

He frowned now. Her breathing was shallow, erratic. He raised her robe and, drawing his bearskin over them both, lay down against her. Drawing her close, he ran his hand along the curve of her side and hip, then forward over her belly, and upward to fondle her breasts. Their great weight and heat roused man need in him, until Ban-ya responded to his touch with a long, tremulous sigh of misery.

"Dakan-eh . . . Piku-neh . . ." she moaned.

Shateh exhaled in annoyance. His need was extinguished. He exhaled again, closed his eyes, and tried to sleep. Now and then he heard a low groan come from Wehakna, who slept behind him. His spirit hurt to hear her. The mourning time was over, but Wehakna still grieved for the loss of Kalawak, as Ban-ya grieved for want of Piku-neh.

Did his women imagine that he had left his own grief in the devastated village by the river? Did they believe that because he was a man, a chief, and a shaman that he suffered less over the loss of a son? Over all of his lost sons?

He tried to comfort himself, but his thoughts were burdensome. The wind spoke to him of coming snow. If and when it came, it would probably be a brief storm—a thin fall, a mere promise of the earth-burying blizzards. His people could endure an autumn storm. The returning sun would soon warm the land, and his band could move on, searching for the bison along familiar seasonal migration routes. Soon they would find the herd, and life would be good again. Soon his people would be secure again, rich in meat and hides and pride. And when at last the tribe gathered for the great autumn hunt—in whatever band's territory might be chosen—he would lead his people brazenly among the many bands. All the chiefs and shamans who had turned their backs upon him in fear that he had caused them to lose their luck would cringe and look away in shame. They would know that *he* was their luck, their power, as he had been since his youth, when he had first inspired them to stand up to Ysuna and the People of the Watching Star, to abandon their lives as mammoth hunters in a mammoth-poor land, and to turn instead to bison as their major source of meat.

At last sleep came. It was untroubled. With one long, strong arm holding his new woman close, Shateh dreamed of his youth and of a white mammoth plodding into the burning face of the rising sun.

The raiders, invisible within the clouds, came with the snow. They were absolutely silent and undetectable in the darkness and the rising wind until the scream of a dying woman betrayed their presence. Every man, woman, dog, and child within Shateh's encampment leaped up to the defensive, but by then it was too late. With wind and cloud and driving snow as their conspirators, the raiders disappeared as quickly as they had come.

And now the women and children of Shateh's encampment wailed and cried, while the warriors gathered and assessed their losses. Two men were dead, several others injured, and a child was missing.

"Aiyee! My Wila! Has anyone seen my Wila?" cried one of the women of Nakantahkeh.

"Perhaps she is hiding?" suggested another woman.

"Yes! Come, we will look for her. We will find my Wila and—"

"You will stay where you are!" Shateh was emphatic. "No one will leave this encampment until the warriors of this band have made certain that no 'wolves' are lurking near."

"Oh, bad spirits . . . bad spirits . . ." moaned Wila's mother. In a daze, she called her young daughter's name again and again until Atonashkeh told her to shut her mouth.

Shateh turned. Something in his son's voice sat on the edge of madness. He moved slowly through the wind and falling snow, until he could see Atonashkeh clearly. His son knelt before a snowy mound of fur through which a spear had been driven. Slowly, with shaking hand, Atonashkeh drew back the coyote-skin cloak that covered his second woman. Nani lay motionless, curled into a fetal ball around the mound of her pregnancy, impaled, lifeless, staring gape mouthed, her throat opened from ear to ear.

Cha-kwena descended through the night on the wings of Owl, zooming through long, vertical, spiraling rivers of stars that seemed to whisper his name as he came back to earth. His head was swimming. Where was he? He did not remember leaving camp.

He found himself on the rough, lichen-crusted top of a broad monolith. A solitary lion was roaring in the cave-pocked hills. Disconcerted and feeling vulnerable, the young, nearly naked shaman shivered. Afraid he might fall into the darkness below, he planted his sandaled feet firmly. His head began to throb. He rubbed his eyes and looked around.

The night sky told him that he had been away from this

world for a long while on his journey through the stars. Again the lion roared. He scanned the benighted hills. Then his eyes settled on his two favorite spears and the traveling sack that held his flint blanks and knapping tools, and the heavy parfleche that held the magic spearheads. He felt an upwelling of relief and gladness to have brought his weapons and sack.

He knelt, then unfastened the thong that closed the larger carrying case. Inside were the three individually hide-wrapped projectile points. He wondered why had he brought them out of the encampment. He touched the talisman around his neck and asked the night, "How have I come to be in this place with the things that are sacred to me? And why?"

Slowly, barely knowing that he did so, he laid bare the first of the three spearheads. The pale, starlit perfection of a leaf-thin blade of chalcedony was as wide as his palm and nearly as long as his thigh. He shivered again.

"Only with these blades can the totem be killed."

Who had spoken? Above, a winged form swept across the stars. "Owl? Is that you, Owl?"

"The one who takes the life and blood and flesh of the totem becomes the totem . . . immortal!"

"Owl?" He hastily rewrapped the magic blade, closed the parfleche, got to his feet, and peered at the sky. "Where are you, Owl?"

"Keep them safe, Cha-kwena, Brother of Animals, Guardian of the Totem. Keep them safe in the power of the sacred stone and of the ancestors until the time that has been foretold!"

"Grandfather? Is that you, Grandfather?"

"Cha-kwena!"

Breathless, his head pounding, he squinted down to see that Mah-ree was calling to him from the base of the great boulder.

Friend and several other dogs were with her. The animals settled themselves, but she clambered up beside him. Smiling adoringly, she handed him his robe of twisted rabbit skins and a limp little flask of drink.

"Oh, my shaman, you were wonderful tonight! The

way you danced! The way you sang! Hoyeh-tay would have been so proud!''

The words soothed him less than the warmth of the robe and the warming drink; he sat down and with no thought of sharing thirstily drained the flask.

She made no objection. ''I saved the last for you,'' she confided, smoothing the short little cape of rabbit skins that she wore around her otherwise bare torso.

''How did you find me, Mah-ree? And where am I, anyway?''

She shrugged. ''Just behind the camp. When you walked off after the others went to sleep, I thought that you might be cold, so I brought your robe. You did not go very far—not like you usually do. Why must you always find such hard-to-reach perches upon which to talk to the spirits, Cha-kwena?''

''I seek solitude. Someday I will find a 'perch' that you will never find!''

''Ha! I will always find you. Together we can be alone.''

He rolled his eyes, determined to ignore her.

But she leaned very close and asked flirtatiously, ''Are you angry with me for following?''

''Yes.'' It occurred to Cha-kwena that he was not telling the truth. He was grateful for the robe and knew that he should thank her, then send her away; but in that moment mammoth trumpeted in the darkness, and he listened, rapt, trying to differentiate among the calls.

''I hear Life Giver,'' Mah-ree said in a hushed and reverent voice. ''Listen. Others of his own kind invite him to walk with them across the new country, to drink from hidden pools, to graze in fine, wide meadows where the mammoth kind browse and bear their young in peace and safety. He answers that he is more glad to see them than they can possibly know. Now they talk to him of all that they have seen and heard since he has been traveling toward them across the long—''

''You cannot know what they say, Mah-ree!''

''But I do! The tuskers' language is one of sounds and sighings, of touch and swayings, not of words. . . . But it

is a language all the same, much as people can talk to one
another with movements and exhalations and with their
eyes—like this.''

He looked at her and was startled as she moved closer,
amazed as she sighed and smiled and, with eyes that were
filled with starlight, told him without uttering a single word
that she loved him.

"You love me, too. I know you do!"

He was about to snap a denial, but the calling of the
mammoth stopped as suddenly as it had begun, and Mah-
ree, visibly concerned, listened intently.

"Grandfather of All is tired," she whispered. "He
says that he will rest now. What have you seen for him and
for us in the stars, Cha-kwena?"

He looked up. His gaze followed the misty rivers of
light in which he had bathed this night. His eyes sought the
bright points of incandescence that did not shiver like the
others; Hoyeh-tay had taught him that these were the sign-
posts that marked the way to the encampments of the
ancestors in the world beyond this world. He frowned. What
had he seen in the stars this night? Strange . . . he could
remember nothing about his journey.

"Ah!" Mah-ree exclaimed, pointing.

He caught his breath. He had seen it, too—a falling star
blazing out of the northern quadrant of the night, and then
another. Both flamed across the one star that maintained a
relatively constant position in the sky—the Watching Star.

"What does that mean, Cha-kwena?"

He blinked, disconcerted. As shaman, he should know
how to answer the girl. Meteors had been common enough
occurrences in the clear night skies of the distant Red
World. Hoyeh-tay had taught him that they were a sign of
both life and death to the People and viewed as either good
or evil, depending upon the omens that accompanied them.
But tonight he had seen two stars fall almost as one. Since
they had streaked across the northern sky, Cha-kwena could
not help but recall his enemies, the People of the Watching
Star. He was troubled even though he knew that they were
far away, in another world, vanquished by other enemies, by

those who had once named him Friend. He scowled, thinking of Dakan-eh.

"What is it, Cha-kwena?"

Cha-kwena did not respond. He continued to ponder the meaning of two stars falling at once and wondered if perhaps, no matter where he led his people, he might never find a land of peace where they might hope to live forever in harmony. Perhaps, in all the world, no such place existed for the children of First Man and First Woman.

He remembered the Creation story of the ancestors, of how First Man and First Woman had come from the north, from out of the Watching Star, from beyond a Sea of Ice, through a magical and terrible Corridor of Storms, and into a Forbidden Land where they had given birth to monsters— the twin gods of war and divisiveness, who were fated to dwell forevermore among the People.

Perhaps, wherever the People went, the twin monsters of the sky watched them from out of the night and awaited their chance to descend and feed upon the cohesiveness of the band. He shivered, not wanting to believe it—not tonight.

Beside him, Mah-ree had been considering her own thoughts. "Did you see, Cha-kwena? The stars have fallen toward the southeast. Surely it must be a sign from the ancestors, an omen that affirms the rightness of the path along which you and the totem have led the People. Things will be good for us now. I know they will!"

And in that moment, overwhelmed by her enthusiasm and grateful for her optimism, he did the strangest thing. He took her pretty little face in his hands and kissed her—a man's kiss, hard on the mouth.

Without so much as a breath of hesitation, she threw her arms around his neck and kissed him back—in the way of a woman, passionately. And then, sighing ecstatically, she drew back. "I will be a good woman for you, Cha-kwena! You will see!"

He felt amazed, disoriented. The pain in his head was gone now, but the stars still shone in Mah-ree's eyes, and the essence of oil of purple sage that she had combed through her hair was heady in his nostrils. Had she always smelled as sweet and looked as fair? She appeared not at all like a little girl, but so much like her sister that it was almost like holding the fair Ta-maya in his arms. He shook his head to clear it; it would not be cleared. His body was reacting to the sight of her. "How much like your sister you look this night—too much. You had best get back to camp, Mosquito."

"You promised to stop calling me that, Cha-kwena!"

"Yes, so I did. Long ago."

"I am not such a pest, am I? You are glad for the warmth of the robe and drink?"

"Yes . . . for the warmth of the robe and drink."

"And not too sad to see me, either, I think! Oh, Cha-kwena, I am for you. You know I am!"

"Gah-ti does not think so."

"I care nothing about Gah-ti! He is an untested boy who will have to wait for Joh-nee and Tla-nee to grow up. Why should I have to even think about him? Have you forgotten that you once tried to spear a lion for me and risked your life to save mine and—"

"I have not forgotten. But that was long ago. Besides, the lion was old and perhaps not of flesh and blood."

"You were brave and wonderful," she disagreed and, snuggling close, kissed him again.

He accepted the kiss while telling himself that he should break it. But her mouth was as sweet as her hair and breath, as moist and open and inviting as—

The bark of one of the dogs startled them both. The kiss was broken. Mah-ree clung to Cha-kwena as they listened, suddenly tense, frightened by the possibility of predators closing on them from out of the darkness. When the dog did not bark again, Cha-kwena relaxed and assured Mah-ree that they were safe upon the monolith.

"I have my spears."

She nodded, wide-eyed, still upset. "Will Grandfather of All be safe in this new land, Cha-kwena? He sounded so tired tonight. Will beasts who do not know that he is totem look at him as meat?"

The question wafted smokelike through Cha-kwena's mind. Distracted and strangely transfixed by the girl, he did not answer; indeed, his eyes were lost in hers again. Her resemblance to Ta-maya was confusing. Perhaps she was Ta-maya? The premise was foolish, and he knew it, but he was too intoxicated to care. As a moment passed, then another, she slowly relaxed within his embrace. Enveloped in a mutual enchantment, they kissed again, lay together upon the stone, and were soon one beneath the stars.

The mammoth were silent. The lion had long since stopped roaring in the hills. The dogs kept vigil against predators at the base of the monolith. . . .

In the encampment of the band, the women, children, and Siwi-ni and her new daughter slept. Kosar-eh, having honored his eldest son by allowing Gah-ti to keep solitary watch, yielded his long-troubled mind to the most hopeful dreams that he had known in half a lifetime. . . .

With Mah-ree dreaming in his arms, Cha-kwena smiled as he drifted off to sleep. The north wind combed gently through the fur of his robe. Barely feeling the chill, he drew the garment over himself and the girl. He felt confident that the forces of Creation were smiling upon him this night, for surely after so many long, bitter moons, he dwelled in good country, with the fair Ta-maya in his embrace, safe from his enemies at last.

Hidden within a clump of red-barked shrubs not far from the base of the monolith, Gah-ti hunkered beside the dogs. He had seen it all between Mah-ree and Cha-kwena. Gah-ti's hand tightened around the haft of his spear. Tears of frustration, disappointment, and anger welled in his eyes; he would not allow the tears to fall as he rose, turned, and started back toward the encampment.

If this is what she wants, let her have it, and him! And to think that I risked myself to follow and protect her against predators! Never again! Never! If the lion that was roaring in the hills should come after her, let Cha-kwena kill it! He is Lion Killer, too, it seems, and not only Shaman in her eyes!

He stopped, his thoughts in a sudden, roiling turmoil of reassessment as he whirled and stared not toward the monolith but beyond and upward, across the dark range of hills in which he had earlier heard the lion. He had already fixed the location of the sound, and certain that distance canceled any threat from that beast to him or the band, he had abandoned his responsibilities as watchman. Instead Gah-ti had brazened off on what he viewed as a more important duty.

Now, looking at the sky, he remembered the two falling stars. Hope flared within him, driving away his fear.

"Mah-ree will *still* be mine," he vowed to the stars. "Never again will I hear her call me Untested Boy! Never again will she dare to say that Gah-ti is not a man! Cha-kwena may be Shaman, but the firstborn son of Kosar-eh will be Lion Killer!"

In wind and snow-stung darkness, Sheela, angry and defiant, faced her warriors. "I have killed the woman Ban-ya with my own hands," she said. "But it is not enough. I wanted to take her captive, but I dared not allow her to scream and wake the others. Now I tell you that I will *not* return to the stronghold until Dakan-eh is dead!"

Tsana shook his head. "We are not clothed adequately for fighting in this storm and cold. Be grateful for the success of the night's raid. I, for one, am content that it—"

"Success?" she exploded. "Until I slay the one who shamed me and caused the death of Rikiree, I will not be content. Nor will I consider our raid successful!"

The other men remained silent. Their young captive stood among them. Her head was down, and she trembled from cold, exhaustion, and fear.

Tsana reasoned quietly, "We have come away from this assault with no fatalities or injuries. Jhadel will say that the forces of Creation are indeed with the daughter of Sheehanal. Thunder in the Sky has protected his people. The presence of the captive will prove it. Truly, we have done well this night."

Sheela looked down at Wila; her hatred of the girl twisted her ash-darkened features. "Why so quiet, daughter of Nakantahkeh? Never before have you hesitated to mock and speak against me. Talk! Let me see how bold you are now when it is *you* who are enslaved to enemies!"

The girl burst into tears. "My father is a great warrior! He will come for me. And when he catches you, you will be lucky if all you have to complain about is enslavement!"

"Is that so?" Sheela taunted, bending now, forcing the girl to look into her face. "I will tell *you* how it will be, daughter of Nakantahkeh. In the days to come, wherever your people travel along the game trails, we will follow to harry and hunt them. When they least expect us, there we will be. They will learn to live in terror of us, as they have forced us to live in terror of them. At our pleasure they will die—all of them—and you will watch their deaths. Yes, Wila. I will make sure that you see them die—your mother and father and sister . . . as I have watched my family die. Then, after the killing is finished in this land, the People of the Watching Star will go south to seek other enemies. We will find those who have driven our totem beyond the edge of the world. We will fulfill the vision of Ysuna, Daughter of the Sun. We will hunt the great white mammoth and kill it, then feast upon its flesh and drink deeply of its blood. Its power will be ours. We will be immortal, invincible. And anyone who tries to stand against us will die."

Wila was trembling violently as Sheela rose and, veiled in wind-driven snow that made her and the others partially invisible in the howling darkness, turned her attention to her warriors once again.

"Listen!" Tsana's deep voice bit into the wind.

Sheela stiffened; at her side the dogs began to growl. "Yes, I hear."

Ston nodded in grim affirmation. "Our enemies come after us."

Wila screamed. "Nakantahkeh! I am here! I am *here!*"

Ston hefted the child and slung her belly down over his broad, hard shoulder.

"Come! Quickly!" urged Sheela.

As the group broke into a trot, Wila screamed again, "Nakantahkeh! I am here! Please help me!"

It was awhile before the war party stopped. Sheela came over to Wila as the girl was lifted from Ston's shoulder and set on her feet. "Did it not occur to you," the woman asked sweetly, smiling in satisfaction, "why no one tried to silence your cries? No? Stupid girl, we were using your calls as bait to lure your would-be rescuers into a trap.''

"Atonashkeh! Wait!''

But the chieftain's son did not wait. Shateh was angry but not surprised. Atonashkeh had to be half-blinded by wind and snow and was surely made heedless by pure, mindless rage. Brandishing his spears, urging Nakantahkeh and the others to follow with their dogs, he ran forward into the storm. "For those who have died! For my slain Nani and for Wila, we will not be turned from vengeance—not even by the power of White Giant Winter!''

Brash, unthinking words, Shateh thought, fuming, doubting if even Bold Man of the Red World would have been so uncaring of his fellow hunters or of his own life. Only a handful of older warriors and their dogs remained at the chieftain's side. He knew the men well enough to be confident that they had chosen not to race forward out of respect for the wisdom of their chief, not out of fear. Their blood was up for killing.

"I do not hear the cries of the girl anymore,'' said Teikan, the eldest of the loyal few.

"They have taken her far ahead, old friend.'' Shateh's hand tightened around the haft of his spear. "They are drawing us on, running to the left, then right, back, and forward. They are trying to confuse us in the storm so that we would not know where they are leading. I cannot see through the storm to mark the rise and fall of familiar hills and valleys, but my legs and feet know the rise and fall of this earth that is my mother. Now our enemies will be cutting hard to the west, into the bad country of many breaks and draws. In our youth, Teikan, you and I often ran horses and antelopes to their deaths there, in tests of speed and daring!''

Teikan stiffened. "Then those who follow are asking to die! The broken hills are the best country in all of the Land of Grass for an ambush!'' He paused, shook his head, allowed an exhalation of incredulity to hiss through his teeth. "Your son is leading the others into those broken hills for the sake of an ungrown woman, Shateh!"

"My son is a willful, disobedient fool!" snapped the chieftain, inwardly cursing the day of Atonashkeh's birth, then cursing himself for having such thoughts. "But he *is* my son—my *only* son. I will go after him."

"This man is not afraid!" Teikan said, although his stance betrayed his bravely spoken lie.

"No, I will go alone," Shateh told him and the others. "If I do not return, take the people north and seek welcome in the lodges of Xiaheh. Tell him to send runners to all of the chiefs, so that they may know that the black moon *was* a sign of death, that somehow our enemies have been reborn to come against us, and that he was right—this land *has* turned against Shateh, a man who by then will be chief and shaman no more."

"You will return!" Teikan was emphatic.

"May it be so!" Shateh replied.

Now Indeh, one of the other warriors, spoke out hesitantly, "And if it is not so, then, Shateh, what of the lizard eater? Xiaheh will proudly honor your wives and daughters, but Ban-ya will not be welcome among the northern bands."

"You are right. She will be seen as a bringer of bad luck," conceded Shateh.

Once more he regretted his separating her from her people. Without his protection, she would die. If he had not taken her robe from her and given it to Nani, she would have been dead already. His brows expanded, stressing the unhealed wounds on his face; he felt no pain because a staggering thought occurred to him. Could Atonashkeh have been correct about her and her kind? Were the lizard eaters summoning death? First the whirling winds, then snowstorms, and finally man- and woman-slaying enemies came to steal the children of his people and strike terror in their hearts.

"Shateh? . . ." Indeh pressed for an answer to his question.

The chieftain gave it. "If I do not return, then you must kill her. If I do return, then I will kill her."

* * *

"Dakan-eh . . ." Kahm-ree's voice rasped through the darkness.

Bold Man stirred, shifted his weight under his sleeping robe, and, propping himself onto an elbow, looked past the old woman into the night. High, thin clouds veiled the stars, and an occasional flash of lightning illuminated a massive storm front. He squinted into the wind. It was strong from the north. He did not like the smell of it, and it was much too cold for this time of year.

"Thunder in the Sky is coming for us," Na-sei's young widow said.

He turned, startled by the statement, and saw that Lehana was staring at him. She sat bundled in her traveling robe beside her dead husband's sleeping mother. He knew that the girl missed her family and had no wish to be with his people; her advanced pregnancy had decided her fate, however. Since she carried the child of a lizard eater, her father, Nakantahkeh, had turned his back upon her. Although her mother had wept and her younger sister, Wila, had hugged her as though she would never let her go, her father had been unmoved.

Dakan-eh scowled. Nakantahkeh was a hard, ambitious man. By spurning his elder daughter because of her association with lizard eaters, he had won approval from Atonashkeh, who someday would be chief. Bold Man's mouth twisted. He wished the man an early death—wished them *all* an early death, painful and hideous, as punishment for the ruination of a bold man's pride.

"It is not too late to go back for Ban-ya," Kahm-ree whispered.

Bold Man, glaring at the old woman, ordered her to hold her tongue. Why must she constantly shadow him to recall one whom he was trying so hard to forget? He rose, drew his sleeping robe up with him, stared into the wind, and shook his head. He was worried about the coming storm. "We cannot stay in open country. If we move now and quickly, we will be able to shelter in the forested hills that flank the mountains between the Land of Grass and the

Red World. Enough game will be there to see us through the weather until we can continue into warmer country."

His people were stirring. He urged them to prepare immediately to move on.

Old Kahm-ree sagged and sighed in pathetic acquiescence. Then she ambled away, muttering, "My poor granddaughter . . . will I ever see my Ban-ya again?"

Dakan-eh's heart was hard toward the old woman. His brow worked with resentment when he saw Pah-la go to Kahm-ree and wrap a bison's hide around her drooping shoulders. He knew that his mother must have taken the extra hide from his father's winding shrouds. Frowning caused pain to flare in the self-inflicted wound across his forehead. What purpose did the wound serve now? he wondered bitterly. In the Red World men did not mutilate themselves as a sign of grief. In the land of his ancestors the scar would have only one purpose—to remind Dakan-eh that he had failed in his attempt to become a warrior and chief in the Land of Grass.

"My son." Pah-la's voice was warm with affection as she came to stand beside him. "I thank the storm gods that drive us from this land. Think ahead to the warm, welcoming valleys of the Red World. I know that the life spirits of your father and of Na-sei rejoice with every step that brings them closer to our village beside the Lake of Singing Birds."

"I do not rejoice," he snarled.

Nearby, young Hah-ri, son of Ma-nuk, was assisting his mother and siblings. He looked toward Dakan-eh and reminded, "Cha-kwena warned us not to join with the People of the Land of Grass. He told us that it was not our way to hunt bison or to take mammoths and to eat of the meat of our totem. Perhaps you should have listened to him, Dakan-eh. Perhaps you should not have broken with the ways of the ancestors and—"

Dakan-eh roared, "You will not speak the words again! Never again speak the name of Cha-kwena! Everyone knows that your thoughts come slowly to you, but can you be so stupid that you do not understand that the curse of the grandson of Hoyeh-tay has turned the Four Winds against me?''

Ashamed, Hah-ri hung his head.

Dakan-eh felt the eyes of everyone in the band upon him. He did not mind. His outburst had soothed his mood. ''Come,'' he commanded his people evenly. ''Thunder in the Sky can have Shateh and those who do not see the wisdom of our ways. We will go on into the Red World and never look back!''

''But what of my Ban-ya?''

He whirled at Kahm-ree's question; had the old woman been within striking distance, he would have killed her. ''Take comfort in the son that she has borne to me—a son that this Bold Man has bravely brought out of the Land of Grass! Yes! That is how it was! All must see this! Shateh thought that it was by his own will that Piku-neh was given into Bold Man's hands; but it was because of Bold Man's wisdom and clever talk that Shateh was tricked! Yes! That *is* how it was!''

The old woman lowered her chin and eyed him. ''If Bold Man is so 'wise' and 'clever,' why did he not trick Shateh out of my Ban-ya as well?''

In that moment Dakan-eh resolved that old Kahm-ree was not going to be with his band when he returned to the land of the ancestors. He measured her with contempt and loathing as he replied coolly, ''Because Bold Man was wise and clever enough to trick Shateh into giving him new women, more women, *better* women! Ban-ya is dead to me and to her people, Kahm-ree. Do not speak her name again!''

This said, he turned and walked on. His new women would follow with his belongings, just as he had told them to do. But in his secret heart, he knew that not one of them would replace Ban-ya . . . not one of them would be able to draw the ache and the frustration from his spirit. Thinking of his bold, loyal, big-bosomed Ban-ya with Shateh filled him with rage and shame. And despite his proclamation to the contrary, he knew all too well that if any man had been clever, it had been Shateh, who had used Bold Man's own words to win Ban-ya away from a mate who had been too afraid to fight for her.

Dakan-eh drew in a deep breath. *No!* he rationalized. *To have fought for her would have been to die for her, and she is, after all, only a female!* He would not think of Ban-ya now. Whatever her fate, he would not hold himself accountable for it.

Alone within the broken hills, Shateh had one regret: He had been given no time to purify his body and spirit for what might well be his final battle. But in the end he realized—and sooner than he would have dared to hope— that the greatest battle was to be with his own shame, and with the sadness that he was now forced to endure, as Nakantahkeh and the others emerged through falling snow. The men carried an unconscious, seriously wounded Atonashkeh and spoke of four other warriors—and as many dogs—lost to the spirits of the storms.

"We never saw the enemies. We heard their sudden laughter from around and above us and felt the death sting of their spears and of the stones they hurled upon us." Nakantahkeh grimaced. "They pissed upon us! They shamed us! They boasted that my child would make the sky god smile. I called out to my Wila, but if she was still with them—or still alive—I heard no word. I would have gone on, followed, tried to bring her back, but we found ourselves at the back of a draw with no way out and—" His voice broke; he hung his head in shame.

"She was long gone by then," Shateh guessed grimly, squinting into the wind and snow. "But only the storm spirits of the night can say where they have taken her. We cannot follow—not in this weather."

"They told us that we would see them again when we least expected them and that before they came to us, we should sweeten the flesh of our women and daughters with good meat and oil so that they would be savored when taken as slaves."

"It was a trap," said Shateh dully. He went to his knees and examined his son's injuries—a deep but minor shoulder laceration and a lower wound, one that caused the older man's hand to shake as he drew away the hastily made packing and bandages. The chieftain cried out despite himself, appalled and devastated by the grotesque amputation that met his eyes.

"He is strong, young. With care he will live," said Nakantahkeh.

"I do not want to live," rasped Atonashkeh.

"You must!" encouraged Nakantahkeh. "To taste and enjoy the death of those who have done this to you!"

Atonashkeh began to sob like a woman. "My woman and unborn child are slain!" he cried. "With my own hand I have obeyed the laws of my people and have strangled my firstborn son because he was delivered during a time of mourning! Now I can make no sons on any woman ever again!"

Those who heard Atonashkeh looked away, aching because of his grief and humiliation. Shateh took his son into his arms and held him as though he were a boy, as though his embrace might somehow undo the terrible damage that the forces of Creation had made upon his only son. Atonashkeh's penis had been cleanly severed from his groin. Never again would he put a child into the belly of his women and give hope of rebirth to a father who was growing old with no newborn sons of his own to take his name. From this moment Shateh had no hope of grandsons. If he were to die now, he would die forever.

Shateh quaked against an inner desolation that was as cold and dark as the night. Then hope flared, wan but bright. Senohnim might bear him a son. She had yet to birth a male child. Her infant was due soon. Perhaps this time she would not disappoint him.

"She has brought this upon us!" Atonashkeh's assertion was a high, thin shriek of rage. "She must die, my father! Ban-ya and all of the lizard eaters must die! It is the willful arrogance of Dakan-eh that has caused . . . *this!*" Unable to find the words to describe the magnitude of his loss, he turned his face inward, against Shateh's chest, and giving vent to the agony of his heart, once again he began to sob.

The chieftain's mouth turned down. The forces of

Creation, he decided, knew what they were doing by depriving Atonashkeh of the ability to breed; regardless of the extent of his son's bereavement, his behavior was inexcusable. With strong, unsympathetic hands he put his son away from him and got to his feet, then looked down with disgust at Atonashkeh. "Your man bone has been cleft from you because, once again, you dared to challenge the command of Shateh! By your own will you led others into an ambush in the broken hills, Atonashkeh! Because of your defiance, men are dead, their bodies abandoned to the wind and storm! How are you any less arrogant than Bold Man? How are you less willful? Bah! If you had held back when I ordered you to stay your ground, you would still have all of your parts! But maimed or not, you are still a man. Now act like one. Or are you no longer my son?"

Backhanding tears from his eyes, Atonashkeh looked up, sobered. But then, suddenly, he teetered on the brink of panic. "*You* will name a future son for me, so that when I die my life spirit will not be lost forever!"

Bitterness filled Shateh's mouth. Even now Atonashkeh presumed to command his chieftain! What a disappointment was this son! He could feel neither sympathy nor empathy even though he realized that, at last, he and the impetuous, all-too-ambitious Atonashkeh shared something in common other than blood: Without sons, both were condemned to die forever.

The thought of sharing eternity with Atonashkeh at his side was not pleasing. The chieftain scowled deeply. Of course, Kalawak and his other sons would be with him, all of his many fine, strong, long-dead sons who had sired no sons of their own. And the most courageous would be at his side again. "Maliwal, my Wolf . . . Masau, Mystic Warrior . . . do you wait for me to come to you upon the winds? Will you be my enemies in the world beyond this world as you are in this life? Will you seek to kill my spirit, as you sought to take my life? Will we be forever at war with one another in the world beyond this world?"

"Maliwal? Masau?" Atonashkeh's face expanded with incredulity. "Surely you would not name sons for them and bring the life spirits of such murderous marauders back into the world of the living when I, Atonashkeh, have lost all hope of—''

Shateh silenced him with a snarl and an upraised hand. He stood tall, but he was deeply shaken; he had not intended to speak aloud. His mind had wandered, and he knew it.

Atonashkeh reached up to Nakantahkeh and was assisted to his feet. Standing, but bent and fighting against pain, he declared, ''I *am* the son of Shateh! I *am* still a man, a warrior of the Land of Grass! As soon as the weather clears, we will seek the raiders! We will find Wila! But first we will follow the lizard eaters and slay them for turning the forces of Creation against us! And after we return to our encampment, I will slit the throat of the woman Ban-ya, who has called down the wrath of the Four Winds upon us and—''

''That woman is mine,'' Shateh reminded him angrily. ''Because of your disobedience this night, you have been maimed in a way that assures that you will never be chief, Atonashkeh! So shut your mouth and remember your place lest you find yourself missing your tongue! I, Shateh, determine what we will and will not do to our enemies.''

This said, he turned and stalked away into the storm, back toward the encampment. He did not need Atonashkeh or any other man to tell him that Ban-ya must die. Now.

10

Since before dawn Gah-ti had been hunting lion. All morning the lion had been watching Gah-ti.

''I know you're here,'' the boy said to the unseen presence of the beast. ''I feel your eyes on me. But I am not afraid!''

The last statement was questionable—so much so that Gah-ti had continuously repeated it on his way high into the hills. Soon the words had overridden his doubts and soothed his spirit. Doing his best to think like a lion so that he might find the whereabouts of his prey, he had walked in and out of dead-end draws and up and over slag-sided ridges before finally making his way along a promising creek bed, through thick woodlands, and up an easily sloping gully that opened onto a broad incline. Now, having just come across lion spoor for the first time and locating an easy ascent to the caves before him, he actually believed in his courage. His goal lay ahead, and he was *not* afraid! The cry that had just issued from his mouth expressed triumph and vindication.

"Gah-ti is coming for you, Lion! Mah-ree will regret giving herself to Cha-kwena when such a brave and clever hunter as this firstborn son of Kosar-eh could have been first with her! Are you listening, Lion?"

From somewhere far below and at a considerable distance, a worried voice called to Gah-ti. The youth smirked. Kosar-eh had been shouting his son's name since dawn. Gah-ti had chosen not to reply.

Let him worry. Let him wonder where I am. He treats me like a suckling! He shames me! Soon both Kosar-eh and Mah-ree will be amazed when I return, dragging the carcass of a lion!

A slight constriction of Gah-ti's belly and bowel reminded him that what he had set himself to do was not going to be easy. Nevertheless, he was not about to turn back now.

The cloud cover briefly thinned and parted. The youth squinted upward across the cave-pocked cliffs—pale, bare, heavily striated, sunstruck rock. The glare hurt his eyes. Again Kosar-eh called, more anxiously than before, and this time Ka-neh and Kiu-neh echoed their father. Gah-ti looked back. Neither Kosar-eh nor his two eldest brothers were to be seen. *Good.*

He turned to the caves again and craned his neck so that he might see them all. Some were mere breaks and hollows in the face of the cliffs; several were large and deep enough to shelter large mammals; one was a huge, corniced lateral fissure that looked big enough to contain a herd of mammoth. The caves seemed to stare back at him from the wide gray face of the striped cliffs.

Gah-ti swallowed. *The lion is in one of those caves.* His throat was dry, and his belly churned in a constriction of fear that mocked his earlier boasting.

His eyes narrowed at whitish bands of stone in the main body of the cliff face. They looked promising; he would need Kosar-eh's practiced eye to affirm his evaluation, but to Gah-ti the intrusions looked to be of a kind of rock from which spearheads, scrapers, and blades might be made.

"Ay yah!" he exclaimed in great excitement, for the discovery of a ready source of workable stone would be of even more value to his people than the killing of the lion! "Two gifts will Gah-ti bring from these hills this day!"

The idea made him feel strong and bold. But then, somewhere above, the lion roared, and Gah-ti was sobered instantly.

He hefted his spears, his best weapons, and looked at them long and hard. Under his father's strict tutelage, he had fashioned the shafts of second-growth hardwood, which he had cut during the previous winter when sap was thin. After long, slow smoking over a constantly maintained fire to drive out all wood-eating insects, the wood had been worked. Greased with fat that he had pounded himself, Gah-ti had meticulously smoothed and straightened the shafts with his prized stave-straightener of elk antler. Once again the wood had been smoked and heated and hardened over the coals of his painstakingly attended fire. At last, after scrupulous polishing with gritty reddish stones that Kosar-eh had carried with him from the far side of the Mountains of Sand, the shafts were as sleek as the belly skins of horned lizards.

The projectile points were Gah-ti's true pride, for although he boasted otherwise, the flaking of stone did not come easily to him. He had reduced many a prized flint nodule to rubble before he had managed to produce the fluted points that were now hafted to his spear shafts. He ran his left thumb along the cutting edge of one of the spearheads; with only the slightest pressure, it was sharp enough to draw blood. He nodded, satisfied.

He looked down to make certain that his spear hurler— that simple but deadly device, which could add both strength and length to his throw—was attached to the thong around his wrist. It would be ready to use at a moment's notice. He left his tool bag still attached to his thong belt. In it were extra spear points, a roll of sinew for binding, and a selection of burins and gravers, necessary for shaft repair and rehafting. In a separate carrying pouch were his bow drill and kindling for the making of fire and, in a leather sheath that Siwi-ni had made for him, his bone knife. In yet a third pouch were leftovers from last night's feast.

He reached into the food carrier and brought up a charred squirrel forelimb and popped it into his mouth. He liked the way the little bones crunched between his teeth. Still hungry, he pulled out a tiny remnant of rabbit rib cage and ran the bones one by one through his teeth to strip them of meat. He was glad that he had gone back to the encampment after leaving Mah-ree and Cha-kwena alone to their rutting on the monolith. A man could not hunt lion on an empty stomach and with only one spear. And he had wanted to bring the makings of fire since he intended to use it as his major weapon against his prey. With fire as his ally, he could smoke the lion from its den, spear the beast, and kill it before it knew that the great hunter Gah-ti was after it. It seemed like a good plan.

He readjusted the load across his back—dry grasses and sticks of dead and green wood bound together with a cross-tied length of thong, which he had fashioned into a double shoulder sling. What a fine, hot, smoky fire he would make at the entrance to the lion's cave . . . when he found it.

From far below within the trees, Kosar-eh's frantic voice shouted back to him. "Gah-ti! Wait! Not even a man can hunt lion alone!"

Not even a man. Resentment hardened Gah-ti's resolve. "I *am* a man! Still you do not believe me. But this day I will prove it!"

He turned to his purpose, ignoring further calls of his father and brothers and, to his surprise, the cry of a woman.

"Gah-ti! Please come back to us!"

"Ta-maya?" he spoke her name, wondered what she was doing with the others. Disappointment touched him. Why had Mah-ree not come? Was she still with Cha-kwena? Again resentment hardened his resolve. The way to the caves was an easy walk from where he stood—several more long strides, and he would be there. His heart was pounding. His mouth was still dry. In which cave would he find the lion?

There was only one way to find out.

"Life Giver! Grandfather of All! Great white mammoth, totem of my people since time beyond beginning, may your spirit be with me now!" Gah-ti implored as, hefting his spears, he went on his way without looking back.

With the first soft blush of a clouded dawn, Cha-kwena was awakened by the distant trumpeting of mammoth and the high, frenzied yapping of coyotes. He grimaced. His head ached as though a herd of tuskers had walked over it.

Fragmented recollections of dreams intensified the throbbing in his head as he sat up and looked around. What was he doing on top of a boulder in the midst of unfamiliar country? And what was Mah-ree doing there, wide awake and kneeling beside him?

"Listen, Cha-kwena," she whispered imperatively.

"I hear," he replied irritably. "Mammoth and coyotes."

"No!" she corrected sharply. "It is what you do *not* hear that troubles me."

"And just what is it that I do not hear?"

"Life Giver! I hear coyotes and other mammoth—of cows and calves and a pair of young bulls, I think—but I have not heard our totem since his trumpeting awakened me before dawn. He sounded strange—startled and then frightened."

The last word caused Cha-kwena to exhale through his teeth. "What a silly girl you are, Mah-ree. He is *totem*! What could frighten him?"

"I do not know, but a few moments ago Friend took off into the far country with most of the dogs as though something had summoned them. I called them back, but they would not come. And last night Life Giver sounded so tired when he spoke to others of the mammoth kind. Do you think Grandfather of All is all right, Cha-kwena? He is so old that . . ." She stopped, obviously upset and hesitant to speak her mind.

Cha-kwena was annoyed. "Life Giver was old in the time beyond beginning. He was old when First Man and First Woman put their backs to the Watching Star and came out of the north into new worlds. He was old when their children came walking across the mountaintops into the Red World. He was old then; he is old now. Do not trouble me with useless words! My head aches too much to listen to them."

Her eyes were very wide as, with lowered voice, she spoke her heart to him, "For many a long moon I have had a secret fear, Cha-kwena, about Grandfather of All. And I have just dreamed a terrible dream, in which the great one was not leading us to new and better hunting grounds but searching for that place the ancients spoke of—the land where mammoth go to die. Our totem may lie down to rest his ancient bones and sleep the forever sleep."

Cha-kwena was appalled. "He is immortal!"

"First Man and First Woman died. Those of their children who first came walking across the mountains into the Red World died. Perhaps, in the end, all things die, Cha-kwena. Perhaps that is what the falling stars were telling us last night. Perhaps they were dying, as we must all die someday—even our totem."

"Be silent, foolish girl! North Wind could carry your words to the forces of Creation! If, somehow, they were to take the life spirit of Grandfather of All, the People would die forever!"

The girl hung her head. "I meant no harm. But it troubles me that I have not heard our totem since—" She paused, looked at him shyly, then lowered her gaze and confided softly, "Not since we were one together."

"Since we were *what?* You and I? Shaman and *Mosquito?* Ha!"

She stared at him. "We *were* together, Cha-kwena," she insisted. "I cannot believe that you do not remember how it was!"

Something tightened in his gut and in his spirit. It roused memories of last night's fragmented dreams. But they were about Ta-maya—passionate, warm, and yielding Ta-maya. His eyes went round. Could the dream have been more than dream? Through pounding temples and aching head, he looked at Mah-ree. "It could not be true. And it could not have been *you!*"

She looked hurt. "Who else?"

"You go too far in your attempts to win my affection, Mah-ree. How could we have been one together? You have yet to become a woman!"

"So?"

"*So?*" he echoed, incredulous. "Has your mother taught you nothing about such things?"

Mah-ree looked at him as though he was an idiot. "After the way it was between us, I would have thought that you would wish to congratulate my mother for all that she has taught me about pleasing a man!"

"A man cannot join with a female who has yet to shed moon blood, Mah-ree! A girl—*a child*—is forbidden to a man by the laws of the ancestors!"

Mah-ree cocked her head to one side. "I do not remember Ha-xa telling me anything like that." She thought for a moment, then informed him with an apologetic little shrug, "If that is so, then I am afraid that we *have* broken the laws of the ancestors, Cha-kwena."

He stared at her, disbelieving. "I would not have done such a thing! And certainly never with you! As Shaman, I have sworn to keep the ways of the ancestors! You should not be here, Mah-ree. You must learn to stop following me! I do not want you at my side!"

She hung her head again. "I will always follow you. I am your woman now."

He was rendered speechless. In the silence he became aware that the coyotes and mammoth were quiet now, too.

Somewhere in the cave-pocked hills on the far side of the encampment, though, a lion roared. And from within the camp itself, Kosar-eh was shouting Gah-ti's name.

Mah-ree rose. "Something is wrong! Listen to his voice, Cha-kwena."

Cha-kwena listened. The clown sounded furious. And now he was calling Mah-ree's name, then Cha-kwena's.

"We have been gone too long from the encampment," Mah-ree said. "We must get back."

"*You* should not have left in the first place!" Cha-kwena reminded nastily. "Take your dogs and go. I will follow at my own pace. I do not want to look at you!"

Tears filled Mah-ree's eyes. "I swear to you, Cha-kwena, if there was a prohibition against our lovemaking, Ha-xa did not speak of it to me."

"Lovemaking? Ha! If anything passed between us in the night it was in your dreams!"

Mah-ree informed him tightly, "There is blood on my thighs, Cha-kwena. It is the blood of first piercing. Look. You can—"

"No!" he shouted.

But she drew aside the knee-length braided-cording strands of her skirt and, adjusting her stance, allowed him to see the truth of her words.

But he did not want to see, did not want to believe. "Get out of my sight!" he raged.

Tears spilled down Mah-ree's face. With her head held high, the girl obeyed.

Cha-kwena watched her go. How small she was! How graceful and light on her feet! And so utterly, pathetically dejected that he almost felt sorry for her. When she reached the base of the monolith and was welcomed by a wagging Scar Nose and One Ear, Mah-ree did not pat their heads, nor speak a word of greeting to the dogs. Head lowered, shoulders slumped, she vanished into the trees and scrub growth.

Cha-kwena's brow came down. Had he lain with her last night? Yes, it must be so, he reasoned. Mah-ree would not lie. He did not remember their joining, but he knew in his heart that his dreams had been more than dreams last night and that, inebriated, he had broken with the ways of the ancestors.

"I did not mean to," he rationalized, but as he got to his feet, he knew that intent did not matter. What was done *was* done.

He felt cold. He bent, snatched up his robe, and slung it on, then stood into the wind with both hands curled around his medicine bag. Between his palms, the sacred stone grew warm inside its leather pouch. The young shaman stood transfixed, remembering the night upon the mountain when the great white mammoth had come to him from the far side of the pass to enfold him within the embrace of its trunk, to exhale the moist, hot stench of its breath upon him. Its breath did not carry the scent of clouds and mists or of the mystical spirit food upon which the totem was said to feed; instead it held the stink of an old, sick animal—a dying animal?—and Cha-kwena nearly lost the contents of his stomach.

"The totem *cannot* die!" He shouted the denial to the rising sun and wind and to whatever spirits might be listening, then caught his breath as a lone coyote walked slowly out of the trees and stood poised at the base of the monolith.

"Come, Cha-kwena! Come with me, and the totem will not die," said Coyote.

The unnatural sound set the hairs rising across Cha-kwena's scalp. He tensed when he saw blood on Coyote's snout and a long, gaping wound on its shoulder. "Little Yellow Wolf, are you speaking to me in the light of day?"

"Do you not know me for who I am, Cha-kwena? Ah, soon . . . if you will follow!" Then, in what seemed less than the blink of an eye, the animal turned and was gone.

In the next moment, the north wind gusted so strongly that it nearly swept Cha-kwena off the monolith. He threw himself forward, belly down. He listened to the wind for the yapping of a coyote but heard the roaring of a lion, and then the high, defiant cry of a boy.

Cha-kwena climbed to his feet and listened, straining to hear. But the lion roared no more, and the youth did not cry out again. From the encampment, though, U-wa was calling his name.

"Cha-kwena! Where are you, Cha-kwena? We have need of you! Hurry!"

"The totem has greater need, Shaman!"

Startled, Cha-kwena looked down to see that Coyote was back at the base of the monolith.

"Come!" Little Yellow Wolf urged grimly.

"Time for what?" asked Cha-kwena, not liking the sound of this. "My people are calling. I must go to them."

"If they are ever again to walk in the way of the totem, you must not! You must walk with me. Now!"

Cha-kwena followed Coyote through the intermittent brightness and gloom of the morning and into the face of the rising sun. Raven and his clan were circling up ahead, just over the crest of the low range of wooded hills through which Coyote was leading him. As other carrion-eating birds joined them, Cha-kwena paused, troubled by the distant barking dogs and the trumpeting of mammoth.

Coyote looked back over his shoulder. "Come, Cha-kwena!"

"To what are you leading me, Spirit Brother?"

"You will see!" informed Coyote, and ran on.

Cha-kwena jogged on with North Wind strong at his back. He shivered as he ran. The omens were dark, so dark! Briefly he thought of Mah-ree and of the way he had ignored his mother's imperative summons. Something was wrong in the encampment; he knew it, *sensed* it, and ached to return and find out what it was. But he could not turn his back upon Coyote now. He was Shaman, and the spirits were leading him.

On and on he followed Coyote until at last he passed through the narrows of a short canyon and came out on the other side of the hills. He stood buffeted by North Wind on an overlook that stole his breath away.

The little yellow wolf loped down a gentle incline into a portion of the valley that Cha-kwena had not seen before—and now wished that he had never seen at all. Under the misted sun, under the shadow of circling ravens, vultures, and white-headed eagles, and in one of the most beautiful landscapes that even a shaman's mind could imagine, uncountable skeletons of mammoth littered the earth in great tanglings of white bones and skulls and tusks.

Cha-kwena gasped. This was the place that Mah-ree had seen in her dream, the legendary land of which the ancients had spoken, the place where mammoth came to die, the country of the dead toward which the totem had been leading him all along!

"It cannot be!" he cried.

"But it is!" whispered North Wind. "Once, I tried to turn you from this, but you would not be turned. You would follow the totem!"

"As he must!" affirmed Coyote, looking back over a tawny shoulder. The little yellow wolf raced downhill, skirting and leaping over piles of bones on his way toward a wide, boggy arm of the lake that all but filled this distant corner of the valley.

And now Cha-kwena was shaken by a horror so appalling that his mind could not fully grasp it. The great white mammoth was down and mired in the center of the lake. Savaged by predators, the totem, torn and bloodied, lay on its side, surrounded by a circling herd of females and young of its own kind.

Terrible waves of desolation and despair swept through the shaman as the cries of the mammoth came up from the valley. He understood the language of the tuskers.

"We will not leave you, Great One!"

"We have driven away the predators that have done this to you."

"Rest . . . rest. . . . we will not let them near you now."

"Here in the shallows at the center of the lake your spirit will pass in peace from this world into the world beyond, for you are safe from the predators' claws and teeth. Those that would make meat of you will not swim out as long as we are with you."

"And we shall stay with you, Great One . . . until the end."

"No!" Cha-kwena shrieked. "It cannot be! As long as

I hold the sacred stone and spearheads, the totem *cannot die!*''

He squinted across distance to see that Coyote was prancing lightly along the shore amid the crushed carcasses of several carnivores—coyotes or wolves or dogs, he could not tell from where he stood. Nor did he care, until he remembered Mah-ree's telling him that Friend and several of the dogs had run off into the valley before dawn. *No*, he thought, *they could have had no part in this; they are of the band, of the People. And yet they were given to us by our enemies, by those who sought to hunt the great white mammoth and kill it so that they might consume its blood and flesh and take its power into themselves.*

The horror was rising in him, until he raced screaming toward the lake. Hurtling madly over mammoth bones and tusks and skulls, he waved aside a gathering of vultures that had perched along the extended tusks of a mammoth skeleton half-buried in the muck of the shoreline. Heedless of his own safety, Cha-kwena cast aside his spears and parfleche and, braced against an expected chill, threw himself into the water.

The water was startlingly warm, almost hot, as he swam toward the bastioning herd and the totem. He swam madly and desperately, uncaring of his own well-being, refusing to remember that he was no swimmer. His arms rose and reached, smashed into the water and drove deep, pulled back, again and again while his limbs kicked. Head down, he held his breath until, choking, he looked up to see that the largest of the cows had turned. She was facing him now. Belly deep in water, she raised her massive brown, freckled head and warned him back.

But Cha-kwena kept on swimming. He was not sure just when he chose to dive, head down and buttocks up like a hunting duck. As he kicked high and thrust himself deep, he gave thanks for the considerable depth of the water, which allowed him to propel himself through and around the massive limbs of the tuskers. He felt his way; the water was too disturbed and muddy to allow him to see more than a hand's distance ahead.

Hoyeh-tay . . . Grandfather . . . I know that your

*helping animal spirit was an owl, not a frog or a fish; but
if you have ever been with me, be with me now!*

He swam on, lungs burning, great forms pressing
close, the water churning and roaring with the sound of
mammoth. If the ghost of his grandfather was near, Hoyeh-
tay did not show himself until Cha-kwena was hopelessly
lost in the tumultuous depths. Then the shaman could have
sworn that the figure of the old man appeared out of
nowhere to swim ahead, to lead the way through swaying,
bending, pillaring limbs and roiling, aggravated water.
Cha-kwena followed. He broke for the surface only when he
was unable to remain submerged for another moment.

Choking and gasping, he stared up. An encircling wall
of mammoth stared down at him. He was surrounded and
too terrified to scream. He dived again and searched for
open water to allow passage to the center of the lake. But the
tuskers were pressing close, and in the brown, clouded
deeps Cha-kwena could see no way to swim past them.

"Hoyeh-tay, help me!" he cried, and on the following
instinctive intake of air, found his lungs and sinuses
assaulted by burning liquid. Pain and light flared in his
head. He exhaled again. The light and pain ebbed; nevertheless, the exhalation was a mistake—his last reserves of
air went bubbling to the surface. His body seemed to be
collapsing inward around his lungs even as his head felt
about to explode. Certain that he was drowning, he came up
for air and kicked madly, keeping his head above water just
long enough to fill his lungs. Then he dived again to avoid
questing trunks and sideward swings of deadly tusks.

Trunks and tusks dipped deep, searching for him.
Fighting for his life, Cha-kwena went to the bottom and,
once again, tried to feel his way past the mammoth; it was
no use. It was like trying to find his way through a forest of
ambulatory trees all determined to raise their roots from the
earth, come down upon him, and crush the life from him.
Blind, desperate, he swam in one direction, then in another,
turning and twisting his body until he knew what an otter
must feel like when hunters with fishing spears are closing
on it.

Suddenly something hard came up from beneath him.

It smashed into his belly and knocked out whatever air was left in his lungs. Stunned, he sagged forward, reflexively sucked water, and was instantly overcome as liquid filled his nasal passages and lungs. Drowning, in shock, he knew that Spirit Sucker had found him. As weakness and darkness threatened to overwhelm him, his hands reached out and contacted something at his sides. It was sleek and hard, something wide and curving away into nothing in front and behind him. Was this the shape and texture of death? Or was it the tusk of a mammoth? Did it even matter? He was a dead man either way.

"Gah-ti has gone there," said Ka-neh, pointing to a dark form moving upon the cliffs.

Kosar-eh stared upward as Gah-ti emerged from one cave, then promptly disappeared into another. "We must go after him." He turned to Ta-maya. "Go back to the encampment. Kiu-neh will accompany you. You should not have come."

"A boy of this band has run off to hunt lion alone, and the shaman of this band is missing," reminded Ta-maya coolly. "A man of this band who has been forbidden the use of spears has gone in search of them. The two boys who accompany him carry the short spears of youth. If called upon to use their weapons, I know that these boys will act bravely. But they are not experienced hunters. So I have brought my knife, my braining stick, and my sling with enough stones to arm it many times. I have no babies or children who will suffer if I meet Spirit Sucker this day, and I have no man to say no to me. I will walk with Kosar-eh."

The two boys looked puzzled.

"*I* will say no to you, Ta-maya!" Kosar-eh was emphatic.

"You are *not* my man!" Her retort was equally forceful.

"With no man to speak for you, *someone* must intervene!" He was insistent.

She would not be moved. "My man walks with the spirits in the world beyond this world, Kosar-eh. My spirit walked the wind with him on the day he died. My flesh and bones and blood and breath may live on, but I long for my spirit to be free to join him upon the winds. My life is nothing to me. *Nothing!*"

"I will not allow you to walk into danger, Ta-maya." Kosar-eh was more adamant than before.

"And I will not allow Brother of My Heart to walk unarmed into the cave of a lion."

"I am not unarmed. I have my dagger, and my own braining stick is here at my belt. I must find Gah-ti and bring him safely back to his people. You cannot stop me."

"Nor can you stop me from walking at the side of Dear Friend who once risked his life to save mine. I will give whatever assistance I can to Man Who Spits in the Face of Enemies."

"Assist me then, by returning to camp with Kiu-neh."

"If Gah-ti rouses that lion from those caves, Kosar-eh, you will need the spears of Kiu-neh and Ka-neh as well as the knife and sling and many stones of this woman if you or he—or any of us—are to survive."

"We will be all right, my father," assured Ka-neh impatiently, eager to test and prove himself.

"Where is the shaman?" asked Kiu-neh, the younger boy. "We could use his good spear arm now!"

Kosar-eh's eyes narrowed thoughtfully. "It is often his way to go off alone. Perhaps he communes with the totem. Perhaps—"

A lion roared loudly, dangerously. The sound seemed to be coming from all of the caves at once. And then, from within the great, gaping maw of the largest cave, the scream of a youth was heard.

Kosar-eh stiffened. "We must go now! Gah-ti is in trouble! Ta-maya, stay at my side and stand behind me when I command you."

"I will obey."

"As long as the shaman walks in the power of the totem, we *will* be all right, my father!" Ka-neh's statement had been boldly made, but his eyes were a little too wide, and his mouth had paled noticeably.

Kosar-eh laid a strong hand upon his son's shoulder and told the youth what he needed to hear. "And as long as the great white mammoth lives, we will all be strong in its power! Come now, all three of you. Gah-ti and the lion have called!''

One moment Cha-kwena was drowning; the next he was lifted out of the lake and held high above it. He came up sputtering and gasping, blinking and dripping, from the black abyss of unconsciousness. Head down, arms and feet dangling, he was hanging over the inwardly curling end of the tusk of a mammoth. He opened his eyes and recognized the huge, freckled cow below him and understood immediately that among her kind she was the preeminent female, leader of this herd, protector of the lesser females, and guardian of the young and old.

Despite Cha-kwena's intention to remain calm, the situation did not allow it. The mammoth had lifted him so high that she and the other mammoth and the wounded Life Giver seemed small to him. And now she was shaking him, swinging him back and forth in an excellent effort that must soon result in dislodging him, then hurling him to certain death. Having already encountered Spirit Sucker once this morning, Cha-kwena held on for his life and in a sudden fury of desperation screamed a sputtering, choking command.

"Do not throw me away into the sky, Mother of Mammoth! I mean no harm to you, to your kind, or to the great one who is totem to me! Put me down now—and *gently!''*

Even as he spoke, Cha-kwena knew that his command had been as ludicrous as his audacity. Yet, as had happened once before when he had dared to command the sun, the forces of Creation acceded to his will. Slowly the great cow lowered her head. She turned, then moved to place the half-drowned shaman exactly where he wished to be—on the shoulder of his prone totem.

The great white mammoth grunted and twitched in pain as Cha-kwena knelt and laid both hands upon its rough, bloodied, ravaged skin. "Grandfather of All," he said softly, surely, "you cannot die. You must be strong. You are immortal! Rise! I will walk with you to the encampment of my people. The spirits of the ancestors will protect us both from meat eaters. Mah-ree will tend your wounds with salves and much good medicine! She will make you well and strong again!''

The mammoth huffed, raised its great head and mutilated trunk, and tried to rise; it succeeded only in shifting its weight, in lifting its massive torso high enough out of the water to allow Cha-kwena a glimpse of wounds that had not been visible before.

He stared in disbelief and nearly fainted. Mah-ree had no medicines to heal what he saw now. The great white mammoth had been partially disemboweled; its innards lay exposed, and the vast, thick, pinkish coils of its intestines floated loose upon the fouled water.

''No!'' Cha-kwena shrieked as he slid back into the lake. He worked frantically to gather the organs of the animal and put them back into place, to close the wounds with his own bare hands, to work whatever magic he could to repair what the carnivores had done to his totem. But there was no magic to be found, not in the man, not for this.

At last exhaustion claimed him. He dragged himself onto the side of the dying beast. He lay sprawled, shaking and sobbing, across the shoulder of the great white mammoth. Cha-kwena's left arm extended upward, across the beast's neck below its jawline; his right hand clutched his medicine bag as he implored the forces of Creation, the spirits of the ancestors, and all the powers in this world and the next to restore life to his totem.

''Hear me, Grandfather of All!'' he begged the totem. ''You are more than mammoth, more than flesh and bone and blood! You are Life Giver, Great Spirit, and the source from which my people have been born! Live! You must live forever! If you die, the People will die with you!''

But the mammoth *was* dying. Cha-kwena felt its life force ebbing. Suddenly, still clutching the sacred stone, he closed his eyes, and a terrible calmness came to his spirit. He remembered falling stars and a young girl lying soft and yielding within his embrace.

By lying with Mah-ree before her moon blood made her a woman, he had broken the laws of the ancestors.

"I am Shaman. I am sworn to keep those ways," he said, sighing, echoing the past. "If I do not, then the power of the stone is nothing, the power of the totem is—" He stopped, opened his eyes, stared straight up into the sun, and implored, "Take me! I am Shaman! Of my flesh and blood and bone and breath, make new flesh and bone and blood for the totem! For the People! For all who have trusted and followed me! Take me instead!"

Gah-ti did not intend to scream, but then he did not intend to come unawares upon the lion, either. There it was: huge, poised with deadly intent, staring right at him, its head out and slightly up, ears back. Crouching in the murky shadows at the back of the cave, it was twice the size of a cougar or leaping cat, and bigger than any maned lion that Gah-ti had ever seen before.

With his heart pounding and fear surging in his veins, the boy quickly transferred two of his spears to his left hand and hurled the third with his right. There had been no time to use his spear hurler, which would have sent the spear arcing forward with deadly speed and force.

Even without the aid of his spear hurler, Gah-ti's weapon flew straight to its prey. The youth exhaled a congratulatory little hoot of pride—and relief—as he hefted and threw another.

The lion stood its ground. The first spear struck with a loud, chinking sound as the projectile point found its target and shattered just as the second spear made impact. Gah-ti winced, startled, as that spear bounced off the lion's shoulder. The projectile point exploded into fragments when the weapon hit the ground, and the shaft broke in two.

The youth froze, hesitant to hurl his last weapon. What kind of lion was this? Either one of the throws should have resulted in a killing wound, driving deep into the body and straight on through to its heart. Were the spears less worthy than he thought them to be? *Impossible!*

Gah-ti squinted through the shadows at the back of the cave to see that the motionless lion was, in fact, no lion at all but a trick of the light—or lack of it—playing upon a pile of stones.

Gah-ti exhaled a mocking laugh at his own expense as he lowered his spear arm. "Two spears ruined, and all to kill a stone lion!"

He shook his head in self-admonition and went forward to retrieve his weapons. Once closer to the mound of rocks, he saw that it did not look like a lion at all. He felt foolish; he had reacted with the panic and inexperience of youth and was glad that no one would ever know of it. "It will not happen again," he assured himself.

Kneeling, he examined the spears. Both were beyond repair.

"Ah, well," he consoled himself. "I have been clever enough to bring extra spearheads and tools to shorten and mend the broken stave."

As he rose, a sound distracted him. It was gone before he could place or identify it. Prickles rose along his shoulders and scalp. Was the lion lurking somewhere within the shadows?

The youth dropped his damaged spears and hefted his one remaining good one. He held his breath, waiting, listening, turning this way and that, ready for whatever must happen.

But nothing happened. Gradually his fear ebbed. Feeling foolish yet again, Gah-ti reminded himself that he had just vowed not to fall victim to panic. He drew in a deep, deliberate breath. Looking around, he was entranced by the beauty of the vast, labyrinthine hollow into which he had come. Odd rock formations hung from the ceiling, reminding the boy of giant teeth. A quick sniff of the air and scan of the earth assured him that there was no lion about—at least not in the outer reaches of this cave—although there had been lion sign in two of the three smaller, tunnellike hollows that he had investigated as far as the morning light had allowed.

Feeling more secure but fatigued, Gah-ti put down his spear, slung off his load of sticks and grass, and stretched his back and shoulders. As his eyes wandered, he recognized the cave's potential as a permanent residence for his people. Wide and dry and deep, it opened to the southwest and would welcome the long, low rays of the winter sun while offering cool shade in the summer. And was that water that he heard dripping and splashing somewhere within the darkness at the back of the cave? *Yes!* He could hear the drops plopping and splattering.

"A spring!" he exclaimed. He realized that he had overlooked bringing a water flask; he was very thirsty. "This son of Kosar-eh thanks the lion and the spirits of the ancestors for showing me the way to a cave such as this! Cha-kwena should be ashamed that he did not find it first! He is not the only one who is strong in the power of the totem! If the water that I hear is drinkable, then this cave is even more perfect than it looks!"

Feeling bold and as motivated by thirst as by curiosity, Gah-ti ventured deeper across the rock-strewn floor into the cave. Spear in hand, he reached the back of what was the first of many chambers. From where he stood, several drafty openings led into long, vaulted tunnels stretching into the heart of the hill, into darkness so thick and heavy that he dared not proceed into it.

Gah-ti cocked his head. Kosar-eh was calling to him, but the boy did not answer. He had a source of water to discover and a lion to kill before he faced his father again.

He knelt, scooted forward on his knees, and listened for the water, first at one opening, then at another, until he was brought up short by a growl. He turned.

"*Lion!*" he shrieked, staring in wide-eyed horror.

The beast lunged forward and raked a great paw hard across Gah-ti's head, shoulder, and arm. The boy curled into a tuck and somehow managed to scramble away into darkness, deep into the hollow of the hill.

With blood dripping hot in his eyes, with his heart pounding, and with his right arm nonresponsive, Gah-ti burrowed like a mole, deeper and deeper into a small opening through which no lion could follow.

"It will be all right. . . . It will be all right. . . ." He sobbed and spoke aloud to calm his fear. The great cat roared in frustration behind him. "As long as the band walks in the power of the totem, it *will* be all right. It *has* to be!"

There was no sign of the lion when Kosar-eh, Ta-maya, and the boys ascended to the cave and peered inside.

"Stay behind me, all three of you," Kosar-eh told them, then called out to Gah-ti.

There was no answer.

"Look, my father, over there! A bundling of sticks and grass and—"

"Those things are Gah-ti's!" Ka-neh interrupted his younger brother and started off across the cave, only to be brought short by the extension of Kosar-eh's good arm.

"You will obey me, or you will go back to the encampment! The choice is yours—make it now. If you disobey me again in the midst of what we must do, your misbehavior could well bring the wrath of the forces of Creation down upon us all! Is that understood?"

The two youths nodded, grim faced.

"They will obey," assured Ta-maya.

Kosar-eh eyed her with discontent. "If only you would do the same! You should go back to—"

Gah-ti's low moan brought Kosar-eh to instant silence. With his burl-tipped ironwood braining stick grasped in his good hand, he cautiously advanced across the cave, following Gah-ti's moans to the edge of darkness. The smell of blood was strong in the air, and the color of it was thick on the shadowed rocks around the narrow opening into which the boy had crawled.

"Gah-ti . . . come from your hiding, boy!" said Kosar-eh. "And tell me that this is lion's blood, not your own!"

"Not a boy . . . a man," came the feeble response. "Can't move . . . bleeding . . . hurts . . . so much!"

Kosar-eh commanded Ka-neh and Kiu-neh to guard his back while he climbed in after Gah-ti; but it was impossible. He was too big a man to force himself through the entrance. With his good arm extended forward, he strained to reach Gah-ti, begged him to try to work himself back along the cavern floor. "If I could take hold of your leg, I could pull you out!"

Ka-neh was standing close, eager to prove himself. "Let *me* try, my father!"

"No! I will go!" said Kiu-neh.

"Someone must go, and quickly," injected Ta-maya severely. "There is much too much blood here. Gah-ti's wounds must be seen to immediately."

Kosar-eh sat up. Briefly, he cursed Cha-kwena for his absence. The shaman's lean but powerful young body would have had no difficulty extracting Gah-ti from the side of the hill. But instead of a competent hunter to help him rescue his son and stand against the marauding lion, Kosar-eh had an eleven-year-old boy, an eight-year-old boy, and a woman!

He made his decision. "Ka-neh, you are the strongest. Go after your brother."

Without hesitation, Ka-neh laid his spears down and obeyed.

Kosar-eh got to his feet.

"Someday you will let me go first?" Kiu-neh asked, solemn and resentful.

Kosar-eh had had quite enough of thin-skinned, vainglorious young boys. "Someday," he snapped at Kiu-neh. "If any of us live long enough!"

"Kosar-eh! Look!" Ta-maya's voice had been no more than a whisper. Yet, somehow, it had been a scream.

Kosar-eh turned his head. The lion had emerged from one of the side tunnels to stand between them and the cave's entrance.

Kosar-eh's heart went cold as the lion snarled and lowered its head meanacingly. The animal was enormous. Black-maned, as tawny as the Land of Grass in autumn, it stared at him out of milk-colored eyes. The man's brows expanded. A milky-eyed animal was a blind animal, or nearly so! He looked closer. *Yes!* This lion was old and sag bellied and nearly blind! Hope flared, then faded as the beast raised its head, opened massive jaws, and roared, showing its teeth. They were sharp enough to pierce a man's skull and rip him open from throat to crotch. If this was the animal that had attacked his son, then Gah-ti was lucky to be alive. "Ta-maya, Kiu-neh . . . move slowly. Stand behind me," he urged softly as, slowly, very slowly, he set down his braining stick and reached for Ka-neh's short spears, and the one long spear that Gah-ti had set aside.

"My father, they are forbidden to you by the forces of Creation," Kiu-neh reminded.

"Not during war against our enemies," Kosar-eh countered. "An enemy stands before us now, Kiu-neh, and I cannot hope to win without the use of a spear. The forces of Creation will look aside."

Now, tucking Ka-neh's lightweight spears under his bad arm, he held Gah-ti's weapon in his good arm and used it as a prod to distract and draw the lion to himself. Slowly, feinting to his left, speaking low and evenly all the while, he told Ta-maya what she must do now, for it was his intention to maneuver the animal into a position that would open a way by which she might flee with Kiu-neh to safety. He would, he hoped, survive this game, although he knew that there was little chance of it.

"Do as I tell you, Ta-maya. When the lion has its back to you, run to the camp with Kiu-neh. Bring Cha-kwena and the women and, if I am no longer able to help you, save Ka-neh and Gah-ti if you can."

Ta-maya made no reply. With narrowed eyes she watched Kosar-eh speaking to the great cat, drawing it to himself and away from her. With a strength of will that overwhelmed Kiu-neh, she suddenly snatched the boy's spears from him and shoved him down, commanded him to crawl into the opening in the cave wall with his brothers. "Stay there until it is safe to come out! If your father and I do not win this war, use these to save yourselves if you can!"

Two of the spears went clattering to the ground; the third she tucked under her left arm as she loosed her birding sling from her belt.

"Ta-maya, what are you doing?" Kosar-eh was frantic. With the lion advancing on him and swatting at his spear, he could only glimpse her in his peripheral vision as she stood her ground, heedless of her own life, calmly arming her trithonged stone hurler, and Kiu-neh had not budged.

Ta-maya raised the weapon and adeptly whirled it overhead. He heard the thongs hissing in the air, and then, to his horror, he heard her call the beast.

"You! Look here, Lion!"

The creature turned.

"See what this woman has for you!" Ta-maya taunted as she snapped her wrist and loosed the stone missiles from her sling.

Two of the stones struck against the wide bridge of its snout, breaking skin and cracking bone as the third embedded itself in the right eye of the beast. The lion bellowed and reared back onto its hind legs, its front paws wiping at its face.

Kosar-eh watched breathless with amazement as the lion circled madly. It rolled over once and then came up roaring, focusing its rage and pain through its remaining veiled eye. Then it charged straight at Ta-maya.

Kosar-eh charged after it, hurling one spear, then another and another before drawing his dagger. The lion went down just short of Ta-maya and Kiu-neh. Having had no time to rearm her sling, the woman had positioned herself in anticipation of the beast's charge. With Kiu-neh's short spear held at the ready in both hands, she did not quaver. But Kosar-eh knew that despite Ta-maya's courageous heart and brave intentions, when the lion rose and charged again, it would kill her and the boy. Screaming, Kosar-eh leaped upon the beast's back and drove his dagger deep, straight between the ribs, then withdrew it, only to drive it deep again and again and again until—

"Kosar-eh!" cried Ta-maya.

"My father!" exclaimed Kiu-neh.

He looked up, stunned, shaken, confused, to see his son and the woman of his heart standing to one side of him as he straddled the motionless downed beast. They were much too close. "Get away!" he shouted. In a moment the lion would rise again, come for them again. With one hand he pulled one of Kiu-neh's short spears free from the body of the beast and levered himself up with the other.

They did not move.

"Run!" he commanded, fixing his gaze on the lion, ready for the moment when it came up out of its momentary torpor. He placed himself between them and danger, knife in one hand, dagger in the other.

They did not run.

"What is the matter with you? Move, I say!"

"The lion is dead, Kosar-eh!" Ta-maya said. She dropped her weapons, shuddered, and uttered a little cry as she raised her hands to her face.

"You have killed it, my father!" exclaimed Kiu-neh.

Kosar-eh stared down. With slowly dawning incredulity, he saw that they spoke the truth. The lion lay in a heap, head out, tongue lolling, forelimbs lost to view beneath its chest, wounds and bladder extruding blood and fluid. Against all odds, a one-armed clown had killed it! A wave of relief and pride swept through him.

Ta-maya was laughing and crying all at once, and Kiu-neh gaped at his father.

"What is it?" Kosar-eh demanded, suddenly offended. "What is the matter with you? This man was a hunter once—the best of hunters. Why are you so amazed that it should be so again?"

"This is not it, Dear Friend!" declared Ta-maya through tears of gladness.

"Then what?" snapped Kosar-eh, struck to his heart and beyond by her mockery. "I have just slain a lion! Even now must I be a clown in your eyes?"

Seeing his pain she rushed to him, embraced him, kissed him on the mouth, and then stepped back, running her hands down his arms. "Kosar-eh, I do not laugh at you! I laugh with joy *for* you!"

He did not understand. He looked down at her, unable to speak, to think, even to breathe; her kiss, her nearness, and her touch had unmanned him.

"My father . . ." whispered Kiu-neh. "You hold two weapons—a spear in your right hand and a dagger in your left! You have used *both* arms to make this kill!"

Kosar-eh looked down and was so stunned by what he saw that he dropped both weapons. It was true! For the first time since the hunting accident that had maimed him, his right arm was fully extended. The pale, atrophied muscles were flexing under the movement of Ta-maya's hand. He could feel her touch! There was no question about it! Almost afraid to do so, he willed his arm to rise, his hand to move, his fingers to flex . . . and they obeyed—stiffly, unsurely, but they obeyed. "Can it be?" he breathed.

"It *is*!" affirmed Ta-maya and, ecstatic in her gladness, went on to proclaim, "Cha-kwena has been right all along! The forces of Creation *are* smiling upon this band, and we *are* strong in the power of the totem!"

Suddenly mindless of all but the moment, with a great, resounding whoop of joy, Kosar-eh had Ta-maya in his arms. He whirled her around and around, and all the while his mouth was on hers. He was kissing her as he had so often kissed her in his dreams, or when he lay upon his aged Siwi-ni and secretly yearned to give the gift of his love and life to Ta-maya. Fiercely, passionately, he kissed her, drawing the substance of her breath and heartbeat into himself, and then returning them with a power that had her gasping in his arms, accepting his kiss with an ardor that filled him with an almost unbearable joy.

Truly, he thought, the forces of Creation *were* smiling upon him once more! His days as a cripple were over! He could hunt again! He could be a man in the eyes of his people again and dare to envision the day when he would take Ta-maya as his woman! *Soon! let it be soon!* he yearned. *My Siwi-ni cannot live forever!*

The last thought ruined the moment, for even as it invaded Kosar-eh's mind, Ka-neh's voice brought him to his senses.

"Is someone going to help me with Gah-ti?" the boy asked. Bloodied and dripping with sweat, he emerged from the wall of the cave.

A moment later Kosar-eh was lying on his side, reaching into the opening, taking hold of Gah-ti's foot and pulling the unconscious youth from the darkness and into the clouded light of the cave. What he saw shook him so badly that he nearly swooned as Ta-maya caught her breath and Kiu-neh vomited.

"It will take the forces of Creation to heal that!" Ka-neh said in revulsion.

Kosar-eh was numb, shaking his head. "No . . . no . . ."

Ta-maya pulled in a deep, steadying breath, then took

control of the moment. "Ka-neh, take your weapons and go back to the encampment. Tell Mah-ree and my mother what has happened here. Have them bring whatever medicine things they can, as quickly as they can! Kiu-neh, stop retching. Take your brother's fire-making pouch and his bow drill and raise a fire with his grass and sticks. His wounds must be stanched. Go, boys! Do as I say! Kosar-eh, help me to stop your son's bleeding before Spirit Sucker draws the life force from him!"

Kosar-eh looked up at her. Hope was dead in him. The forces of Creation had, in the cruelest parody of kindness, once again made a clown of him. They had given back to him the use of his arm and hand, but they had not made a gift of the usage—they had made a trade, a grotesque and hideous trade. Nearly overcome by frustration, he took the mauled, nearly scalped Gah-ti into his embrace, and with his right hand pressed the gaping stump that was all that remained of his eldest son's right arm, effectively stopping the bleeding. "It is not a fair trade," he sobbed. "Not one that any father would have made. . . ."

Gah-ti's eyelids fluttered open. "Has . . . the lion . . . killed me?"

Kosar-eh trembled as he spoke. "The spear of Gah-ti has slain the lion!"

"It . . . is so?" The youth's lips worked into a wan and tremulous smile.

"It is so!" assured Ta-maya. "It would take more than a lion to take the life spirit of the firstborn son of Kosar-eh!"

"Mah-ree will say that I am a man?"

"She *will!*" said Ta-maya, blinking back tears.

"Then I will not speak against her and Cha-kwena." Gah-ti sighed. "I . . . will keep . . . their se . . . cret." The youth closed his eyes; he was shivering violently from the pain, losing consciousness again.

Kosar-eh and Ta-maya looked at each other as Gah-ti went limp in his father's arms.

Ta-maya's face twisted with sorrow. "Sleep eats pain. This, at least, is a good thing. Perhaps Cha-kwena will come soon. We could use his magic. He must be with the totem.

And as long as the great white mammoth walks before us in this good land—''

"Magic?" Kosar-eh interrupted bitterly. "Ah, yes! It *will* take magic to make this firstborn son of Kosar-eh whole and strong again in this 'good' land to which Shaman and our totem have led the People. The forces of Creation have at last smiled upon us out of the mouths of man-eating lions under the light of the black moon! Tell me, Ta-maya, with the totem leading the way and Cha-kwena interpreting the omens, what other good things can possibly lie in store for us?''

Her face was stricken, the sadness back in her eyes. "Only the Four Winds and the forces of Creation can tell you this, Brother of My Heart," she said softly, then turned away.

But before she did, he could see her tears.

11

All morning long Ban-ya fled across the snow-covered land in hope of finding Dakan-eh. Exhausted, she walked on in misery. Snow turned to rain, then to sleet, and finally to snow again. The wind, still hard from the north, tattered the cloud cover and granted her tantalizing glimpses of the sun. Its position told her that it was nearly noon. The landscape, on the other hand, told her that she had probably been walking in circles since running away from the encampment after the raid. Worse than that, it allowed her to see that she was not alone: Shateh and a small group of runners were following with their dogs. She should have known that they would come after her the moment her absence was discovered. She began to run. Stumbling forward on frost-numbed feet, she was certain that the chieftain would blame her for the attack against his people—Atonashkeh would see to it.

The land rolled ahead of her. She kept on, slipping and slogging through tall grasses until the hem of her dress and her moccasins were soaked. Only her coyote-skin cloak, which she had snatched from Nani's body when no one was looking, remained waterproof and served to keep her upper body warm. She clutched the forepaw ties tightly at her throat and forced herself to think of the man who had brought the pelts to her. How she longed for him!

"Dakan-eh!" Ban-ya called, and begged the wind to carry the name to her man. Perhaps it would. Who knew? She had nothing to lose. He was out there somewhere, traveling with her precious little Piku-neh and her beloved old grandmother. No doubt they grieved for her. No doubt her baby boy, old enough to suffer her loss but too young to know why she was gone from him, cried for her. Even now Dakan-eh was no doubt planning a way by which he would rescue her.

"Woman of the Red World! Stop!"

Ban-ya recognized Shateh's voice, but she did not obey. She ran faster until, with a start, she saw a small group of men and dogs appear at the crest of the rise directly ahead of her. Her heart leaped. "Bold Man!" she shouted her hope as loudly as she could, only to have it shrivel as she remembered that Dakan-eh had taken no dogs from the encampment. The men were Shateh's hunters, and they were coming toward her.

She stopped and turned. Her race for freedom was over. It did not matter. With a deep, ragged breath she ran perpendicular to the closing parties until the dogs were leaping at her and savaging her moccasins. She heard the rasp and wheeze of a man's breath at her back and, a second later, was grabbed from behind and jerked backward so hard that she fell in a heap.

"Kill her!"

Nakantahkeh's voice . . . Ban-ya would have looked up, but whoever had grabbed her robe had pulled the ties so tightly against her throat that she was choking. She was trying so hard not to be sick that she merely hung her head and, gagging, willed herself not to retch. If she was going to die, she would die like Bold Man's woman, not like a hair-shorn slave! At last he let go of her. Rubbing her throat, Ban-ya fought to calm the bruised muscles.

A man spoke. "We picked up sign of a recent resting place of the lizard eaters just beyond the rise. There were no tracks to show that the raiders had crossed their path. Beyond that place the weather prevented us from seeing where the lizard eaters had gone."

Now Ban-ya looked up. Teikan had spoken, and his words revealed that his men and he had not been searching for her; they had been looking for Dakan-eh. She eyed him through the thickening snowfall, then turned to see Shateh glaring down at her from the men surrounding her. She hated the chieftain even more than she feared him. Because of him she would never see her baby again or stand proudly at Dakan-eh's side. Because of him she would soon be dead, doomed to walk the spirit world in a land far from the country of her ancestors, lost forever to those whom she loved.

Certain that all was finished for her, she replied contemptuously to the chieftain, "The raiders will not touch my Dakan-eh, and you and your men and dogs will never find him. He walks in the favor of the Four Winds, just as he told you. You should have believed him. Now your people, not his, suffer and die. Is that why you track him instead of your real enemies? So that you may steal his strength and the favor of the spirits from him, as you stole his woman?"

"Silence her, Shateh!" Nakantahkeh's fur-hooded face was convulsed with loathing. "*She* is the one who called the raiders down upon us!"

Ban-ya glared up at him with equal loathing. Certain that she was to die, she feared nothing but the loss of her pride. "How long have you been a blind man, Nakantahkeh? And when did your ears cease to serve you? The spears that the raiders left behind were clearly marked by their tribe, and after the attack there was talk in the camp that the enemy wore the paint of the People of the Watching Star. They were *Sheela's* people, not mine.''

''Sheela was the slave of your man, woman of the Red World,'' Shateh quietly reminded. ''If she escaped to bring others of her tribe against us, the fault was his.''

''And when we find your lizard-eating man, he will pay with his life and with the lives of his band!'' assured Nakantahkeh.

Teikan's expression was thoughtful. ''When the storm is finished, this woman could show us the way that her people came into the Land of Grass. We could follow without being slowed by the necessity of tracking.''

Ban-ya's eyes narrowed. ''Fools! Do you believe that I would lead you to my people so that you could slay them? Can you not see what has happened? Do you not see how luck was with me and with my people? Sheela's hatred would not be for only you; it would be for Bold Man. She brought raiders to your camp to seek out those who enslaved her. They did not find the ones they sought because Shateh sent my people away. The women have said that a raider called my name as his spear was thrust into Nani. That woman would be alive now and I would be dead had Shateh not given my cloak to her. Even as we speak, my Dakan-eh walks strong in the power of the Four Winds. The storm spirits hide his trail from those who would follow to harm him. If you wish to find yourself in the favor of the forces of Creation, Shateh, you have only to walk into the rising sun with Dakan-eh as your brother, not as your enemy.''

Nakantakeh was nearly hopping with disbelief and impatience. ''Finish her, Shateh, before her words twist and confuse our spirits and we forget what we have come to do this day!''

Ban-ya's voice expressed her incredulity as she said, ''How well you speak, Nakantahkeh! And here I had begun to believe that there were no thoughts of your own in your head and no words in your mouth unless Atonashkeh spoke first and allowed you to be his echo.''

The reaction to her insult came instantly, but not from Nakantahkeh. Shateh moved so quickly that Ban-ya suddenly found herself grabbed by the ties of her cloak, yanked to her feet, and then swept off them as she was lifted and held face-to-face with the chieftain.

"My only remaining son lies gravely wounded this day as reward for bravely pursuing our enemies, woman of the Red World! You will not speak his name. You will not mock him!"

Ban-ya dangled in the chieftain's grip. His hand was pressing so tightly against her throat that she could not breathe or protest against the pain that he was causing as his fist pressed the muscles of her neck inward against her larynx.

"The wind grows stronger, Shateh," said Teikan, eyeing the darkened sky. "There will be much snow before this storm blows itself away across the world. If we do not return to the encampment now, we may not be able to find our way back."

"Let us return, then," Nakantahkeh growled, "and leave this woman here as dead meat for the carrion eaters that will follow the storm."

Ban-ya, still nose to nose with Shateh, was growing faint, and her vision was blurring. But what was it that she saw within his eyes? Hatred? Yes. Distrust? Yes. But were there not also pity and regret and a deep, twisted admiration? *Yes!* she thought, realizing that this man did not want to kill her.

"Finish her, I say!" Nakantahkeh urged again. "Let us return to our people before the storm makes travel impossible!"

"You *are* an echo of Atonashkeh, Nakantahkeh!" shouted the chieftain. "Would you presume to command *me?* Have you not had enough of death and killing this day?" With a sudden growl, Shateh released his hold on Ban-ya's robe.

She gasped harshly, rasping, able to breathe again. Despite her efforts to stand, her knees buckled, and she slumped forward against the chieftain. A broad, strong arm enfolded and supported her.

"Teikan is right!" declared Shateh. "It would not be a good thing to kill this woman. She can show us the mountain pass through which the lizard eaters have gone.

Perhaps Bold Man and his band *do* walk in the favor of the Four Winds! Perhaps Dakan-eh spoke the truth when he told us that our enemy is not in this land. Perhaps it *is* time for us to turn away from hunting bison and seek the great white mammoth, totem of our ancestors, so that, strong in its power once more, we may fight those who have seen fit to use it against us.''

Nakantahkeh's face was livid. ''One enemy is here in your arms, Shateh, and the other hides in the hills. Do not listen to this woman! She is bad luck! The raiders who have attacked us cannot be many! Now that we know they are still a threat, we will be strong against them! We can go to Xiaheh and the other chiefs, and together we can hunt the People of the Watching Star. Together we can make our enemies regret their decision to attack us! The days of the mammoth hunters are over. We are warriors and bison eaters in this Land of Grass in which there are no longer enough mammoth to feed the People! Shateh himself was the first to lead the hungry tribes to strength and unity as bison hunters! Bison are totem to us now! For this reason the great white mammoth has gone across the Mountains of Sand and beyond the edge of the world! Men cannot follow it!''

''Cha-kwena and his people have followed,'' said Ban-ya. Looking up into the face of Shateh, she saw his age and weariness. Insight and then hope flared within her as she added softly, ''Cha-kwena is the true enemy of the People of the Land of Grass. With Bold Man and Shateh at her side, this woman and the son she now carries in her belly would not be afraid to seek the totem beyond the edge of the world or to see vengeance done against those who—''

Shateh flinched, then stared down at her with disbelieving eyes. ''What did you say? It is too soon for you to know *if* or *what* you carry!''

''A woman *always* knows these things from the first moment,'' she said calmly, authoritatively, as though she believed it.

Nakantahkeh snorted a derisive laugh. ''She lies! Her words are tricks with which she hopes to save her life!''

''Kill me and cut me open then, Nakantahkeh,''

Ban-ya challenged. "By the thickening of my womb see the truth of my words as Shateh observes the death of yet another son—this one at your hand!"

Nakantahkeh's gloved hand tightened on his spear. He looked to Shateh, waiting, yearning, for the chieftain to command him to act on Ban-ya's challenge.

Instead Shateh shook his snow-whitened head. "We must return to camp, to take our turn at watch. Once again we have dead to mourn and wounded to attend. This woman will come with us. Time will reveal the truth of her words."

Ban-ya trembled with relief. She was not going to die today! Gladness filled her heart. Perhaps she might yet convince Shateh to believe that his luck lay with Dakan-eh; if she could do this, then she might yet see her man and Piku-neh again. By then Shateh might have tired of her and let her go. The thought was sweet, but bitterness inevitably followed it. If she succeeded in becoming pregnant and managed to give Shateh a son, he would want more, not less of her. And how long could she stay alive with such enemies as Nakantahkeh and Atonashkeh in Shateh's camp?

Ban-ya continued to worry as she walked on with her shoulders gripped tightly in the fold of Shateh's arm. How powerful he was! How long and sure his stride! Was she being foolish to believe that she could manipulate him? Not even the hard, stern-eyed Nakantahkeh could sway the chieftain's mind. And what if one of his women told him that it was all but impossible for a nursing woman to conceive a child?

Her heart sank. She should not have risked such an untruth. Now, so that her milk would cease to flow, she would have to think of a way to stop Shateh from handling her breasts and drawing a man's pleasure from them. She needed to come to her time of blood again, although, when she did, she would have to make certain that no one knew of it. After she was cleansed and ready for life making again, she must become pregnant, and soon!

She curled her hands into fists as she walked. *Dakan-eh, my Bold Man, why have you not come for me? Ah, what a selfish woman I am! I know that you cannot, for the band's sake and for my little Piku-neh's sake. You must lead our people home. Then you will come. Yes! With fighting men from the Red World, you will come for me!*

Deep within Ban-ya's memories, a recollection stirred of a brazen adolescent with whom she had fallen hopelessly in love, despite his self-serving nature. Surely she could not have faulted him for the latter. How could Dakan-eh not seek to please himself in all things? By his very superiority over others he had that right. What joy there had been when she had finally won his smile, and when he had accepted a gift of food from her even though he had already spoken for the band chief's daughter. Ta-maya had not been right for him; Ban-ya had known that and she had provoked him into realizing it, too, by displaying her body, by inviting his touch, by allowing him to be first with her as she had spread herself for his pleasure. He had not refused her; he had taken her offerings of affection as hungrily as she had given them. And she had known then that she would live for him—and die for him, if it came to that. But to live *without* him? The thought was unbearable.

Somewhere far to the south and east, the great white mammoth walked with those whom she had abandoned when she had chosen to follow Dakan-eh into the Land of Grass. Bold Man might have been right when he claimed that Cha-kwena had stolen the luck of his people. But the mammoth was still totem to Ban-ya's tribe, and it held great power for her.

She formed a silent plea. *North Wind, take this prayer across the skies so that Grandfather of All may know the heart and needs of this woman of the Red World! Be strong in your power, Life Giver, and wherever you are and whatever you are doing, give me the strength to make new life. May I live long enough to be here when my Bold Man at last comes for me!*

Raven and his clan were gathering on the shore. The great white mammoth raised its head and tusks at the sky and trumpeted as though in answer to a distant call.

Cha-kwena, still sprawled upon the shoulder of the totem, came up out of a daze of exhaustion. The circling herd of sentinel mammoth had divided into two smaller groups, allowing the young shaman to stare across the open water to the ravens on the shore, then up at a pair of circling eagles. His mouth flexed with bitterness. He had been so sure that the fishing eagles had called him to a new and better life. But the dark omens that he had chosen to ignore had been the relevant signs after all, and the eagles had not been beckoning him to long-yearned-for hunting grounds— they been summoning him to this . . . the death of his totem.

Beneath him the great mammoth shivered as it lowered its head and exhaled in exhaustion and pain. Cha-kwena's spirit bled as he heard and felt the agony of the animal. The sacred stone was still around his neck, and he had been chanting and murmuring prayers to the Four Winds and the forces of Creation since first climbing onto the shoulder of the totem. They were not listening. The mammoth was dying, and he could do nothing. He had offered his life, but what was that worth? True, he was Cha-kwena, grandson of Hoyeh-tay, and last in a line of holy men that went back to the time beyond beginning and to the children of First Man and First Woman. But he was also a callow youth who had never wanted to be a shaman, and now that he was, he was ineffective at best and an offense to the ancestors at worst.

He closed his eyes. *Dakan-eh! Bold Man of the Red World, you warned me to turn from the old ways and accept the new. If you could see what has befallen me now, even you would weep for me.*

The shadows of the circling birds drew his eyes upward again. He frowned. Soon it would be high noon. Old Hoyeh-tay had taught him that noon was a mystical time, with the morning dead, and the afternoon yet to be born. And beyond the edge of the world, night waited to swallow the sun so that it might give birth to it again with the coming of dawn. Then the cycle of light and life could begin anew.

Cha-kwena stared through narrowed eyes and his thick, stubby, filtering eyelashes at the sun. Hoyeh-tay had also taught him that the sun was the watching eye of Father Above.

"Have you gone blind up there beyond the clouds? Have you no ears to hear the chanting of those who name you Father? I am doing my best to be Shaman! Maybe it has not been good enough! Maybe I have made a few mistakes! Sometimes I act before I think. It is not my fault that Spirit Sucker took Hoyeh-tay from this world before I could learn from him all that he had to teach me! So you must *help* me! It has been said by great shamans that as long as I remain guardian of the sacred stone, only the magic spearheads can end the life of the totem. But look at him! Can you not see that he is dying? If you *are* one of the forces of Creation, if you are a great and powerful spirit, then give the great white mammoth back his life! He is totem! He is not supposed to die!''

Long, silent moments passed. The unblinking, compassionless eye of the sun continued to stare down, blind to the plight of the young man and the mammoth.

Then, slowly, from all along the sunstruck shore, the forms of other predators crept from behind the skeletons of the many mammoth that had come to this place to die. Startled, Cha-kwena wondered if his eyes were tricking him. *Bear? Puma? Wolf? Leaping Cat? Lion?* These were the phantom creatures he had encountered upon the mountain. The predators came together now in silence, as they had on the night when he had sensed them moving as shadows in the darkness, to watch him out of eyes that burned his consciousness.

They cannot be real, he told himself, and shut his eyes. Colors flared and swam beneath his lids—the colors of sun blindness, pulsing red and yellow and white, with brilliant flarings of blue and purple that took shape and leaped like vaulting cougars in pursuit of deer. He pressed his eyes; the display of light warped and twisted until cougars became lions, then leaping cats, then bears and wolves. Finally they exploded into a thousand unidentifiable patterns and were gone.

Trembling, Cha-kwena was afraid to open his eyes. Had the colors been the gift of a shaman's vision or the curse of Father Above, visited upon him as punishment for speaking so rashly to the sun and daring to stare too long into its watching eye? When he ventured to raise his lids, would he see the lake and this long, narrow, terrible arm of the valley, or would he be a blind man?

He needed to draw in several long, deep breaths before he dared to find out. Slowly he opened his eyes. Light and vision poured into them. He exhaled with relief. He could still see as clearly as before, although an odd, tiny circle of black light remained fixed in the center of each eye, like a dark bird hovering before the face of the sun.

The predators that he had seen prowling the shoreline were gone. He frowned. A lone coyote had replaced them. Watching him from across the water, the little yellow wolf sat beside a large mammoth skull. A single raven perched atop the skull and busily pecked at something held fast beneath its claws.

Cha-kwena's heart lurched. Was that the parfleche within which the magic spearheads lay? *Yes!* He had forgotten all about it. And his spears—where were his spears? There they were, on the shore where he had cast them aside.

The great mammoth suddenly shifted its weight and moaned as it tried to rise. Failing, it fell hard on its side again, its skin and muscles rippling with pain and sending Cha-kwena sliding into the lake. He went down gasping, swallowed water, came up choking, spitting bits of matter from his mouth as he tread water that was unnaturally warm and red and fouled by the mammoth. Suddenly the horror had him again. This was not water; he was swimming in what had become a lake of blood and gore. He had drawn into his mouth the flesh and blood of his totem.

Appalled, revolted, he shrieked as he lurched forward and grappled madly for purchase on the mammoth's side, to lie stunned as the totem heaved and moaned beneath him.

Cha-kwena was shaken to the depth of his spirit by two horrible epiphanies: The great white mammoth was only a mammoth after all; and he, grandson of Hoyeh-tay, had failed as a shaman—not because the spirits were deaf to his pleas but because there were no spirits. Bleakness consumed him. "It has all been lies," he murmured, feeling betrayed. "In all of this whole world and the world beyond, there is no magic. There is nothing more than flesh and blood and death for all living things!''

The mammoth shivered, sucked air, slobbered, and twitched. Perceiving the animal's pain, Cha-kwena looked to the shore. The coyote was gone. Even Raven and his clan had flown into the sky to circle with the eagles. The young man's brow furrowed as he stared at his parfleche and knew what he must do—Life Giver was only a beast of flesh and blood, but it had given heart and hope to the People. Cha-kwena could not allow the animal's suffering to continue any longer.

In a daze, numb in mind and spirit, he swam to shore. The sentinel mammoth let him pass. He clambered onto dry land and paused before the mammoth skull upon which the raven had been perching. He looked around and saw the mutilated corpses of several coyotes and two of Mah-ree's runaway dogs. Remembering the bloodied snout of the coyote that had led him to this place, he knew that the animals had attacked the totem as it had lain weary and sick and partially mired upon the shore. They had disemboweled it before it had found the strength to rise and grind them into the muck; only after that it wandered into the lake to collapse and begin to die of its wounds.

Bereft, Cha-kwena opened what was left of the tattered parfleche. With the sun shining in mockery of his bleak mood, he unwrapped the thong bindings that protected the spearheads within. He stared at them. How beautiful they were! Cha-kwena shook his head at the bitter irony. Now Life Giver would indeed die by the legendary blades, but not by the hand of one who sought to steal his power. He would be slain by the hand of one who had sworn to be his guardian.

He took up one of the three spearheads. It was heavy in his hand and sharp against his palm as he returned to the mammoth and climbed once more under its shoulder. ''And so now I *will* guard you, old friend, from pain and from those eaters of the dead that would tear you to pieces while you still live.''

The mammoth raised its trunk and sighed in a way that made Cha-kwena wonder if it understood what he had said.

"Forgive me, old friend," he whispered.

Ignoring the restless movements of the sentinel mammoth, he took the long, massive spearhead into both hands and did what must be done. Cha-kwena drove the exquisitely sharp chalcedony dagger deep.

The mammoth made one high, short exhalation as the great neck vein was found. Blood fountained. The blade fell away from the shaman's hands. As the sun slipped past noon, Life Giver relaxed into death and, with a grateful sigh, breathed its last.

"It is done," said Cha-kwena with bowed head, and wished that he had died with the totem.

There was a single moment of absolute, eardrum-crushing silence. Then the sentinel mammoth trumpeted, Coyote howled, and clouds rode upon the back of North Wind to block the light of the sun.

Awash in the blood of his totem, Cha-kwena looked up. He was beyond tears, devastated by guilt and regret as the ghosts of the ancient ones rose within his mind to speak to him of promises that he no longer believed: *On the day that Life Giver dies, the People will also die—except for the man who kills it. The man who eats its flesh and drinks its blood will take its wisdom and power into himself to gain immortality.*

"No." Cha-kwena shook his head. "I do not believe you." He was suddenly as weak as an infant as he dropped to his knees and spoke his heart to the wind and the clouded sun. "Nothing lives forever! *Nothing!* I, Cha-kwena, grandson of Hoyeh-tay, have slain the white mammoth. Great Spirit, Grandfather of All, totem of my ancestors, is dead, and I have taken its flesh and blood into my own body!" He was shaking. His sobs rent him to his spirit and beyond. "I am not a shaman! I do not want to live forever! I do not want to live at all!"

Cha-kwena did not know how long he remained kneeling upon the motionless body of the totem, or just when he first noticed the sentinel mammoth closing around the fallen giant. When he met the eyes of the great freckled cow, he was certain that she and her kind were going to kill him. And in that moment, he dove into the lake and swam underwater for his life. The mammoth did not try to stop him, and he was too relieved to wonder why.

When he reached shore, he saw that the lone coyote had returned to lie down beside the mammoth skull. When Little Yellow Wolf rose and looked at him, Cha-kwena could not have said what came over him, for it was the man and not the animal who growled.

"Get away!" he commanded, then gestured toward the dead coyotes and the slain dogs. "You share a common blood with them, not with me! You have hunted my totem, and I tell you now that you have killed more than a mammoth this day. You have killed a shaman, too!"

The declaration made, he leaped past the coyote, snatched one of the spearheads from his parfleche, and hurled it at the little yellow wolf.

The spearhead struck a glancing blow, then rebounded into the lake. The coyote yipped and whirled and ran away.

Shaking, Cha-kwena watched it go. "We are brothers of the spirit no more, you and I!" With grim intent, he picked up his parfleche and the remaining blade and hurled them both into the water. "It is finished," he proclaimed, and raised his hand to rip the medicine bag and the sacred stone from his neck. But in that moment the wind stayed his hand as it drew his eyes to the clouded sun. The White Giant Winter was awakening in the north. He knew that he and his people must leave this cursed land before it was too late.

It was obvious that in the days and nights that lay ahead, the band would need faith in magic and in the spirits if the People were to survive their travels across unknown country ahead. He could not tell them what he had done or that when he had taken the life of the great white mammoth, the part of him that they had come to rely upon as shaman had died, too.

Despondent, he took up his spears and returned to his band. Darkness had nearly fully settled. He found the encampment deserted and was puzzled until he saw the flickering light of a beacon fire burning in the hills and followed it to the cave.

Rain was falling by the time he ascended the wide,

gravelly sand bench. The young shaman was determined not to tell his people about the death of the totem but to say instead that his first instincts about this new land were correct and that they must prepare to leave it. He was greeted by a tearful Mah-ree.

"Oh, Cha-kwena!" she cried as she ran to him, threw her arms around his waist, and pressed close. "Where have you been? Gah-ti has been hurt! And on the way to the cave Siwi-ni began to bleed and, and, and—" She stopped, pulled in a calming breath, then blurted all that had happened since he had been away. "But it will be all right now that you are back! My shaman's magic will heal what my medicine cannot! Oh, Cha-kwena, tell me that you have found the totem and that all is well with Grandfather of All!"

"Yes, I have found the totem," he replied obliquely, and followed her into the cave. Stunned by what was left of Gah-ti and by the deathly pallor of old Siwi-ni's face, Cha-kwena knew that it would be many moons before his people would be able to leave this cursed land to which he had led them and in which the mammoth and the totem had come to die.

PART III

FOUR WINDS WAILING

1

In the Land of Grass, Shateh listened to wolves howling in the early morning cold. He rose and stood facing the rising sun. His hair and robe were stirred by strange, troubling winds that blew first from one direction, then from another.

His eyes narrowed. As the shaman, he knew the omens were bad. As the chief, he knew that to stay in this open, unprotected camp was madness. The weather was threatening, there was nothing to eat, and the likelihood of another raid was strong. But there were wounded to be considered, and the time of mourning for the recent dead was not yet over. To move on now might incur the wrath of the forces of Creation. But what would happen if his people stayed?

Shateh's jaw tightened. He had obeyed the laws of the ancestors: He had honored the dead; he had cast out all but one of the lizard eaters. But Spirit Sucker still came to feed upon his people. Perhaps Atonashkeh was right about the woman? He exhaled in frustration. *No!* He would not concede to that, not yet! A day's walk or two to the south would bring them to a more readily protected place along the river where his people had camped many times before.

"We will go there!" he announced to the wind.

Although the camp dogs looked up and the few women who were ambling about searching for who knew what to burn and cook for breakfast stared at him, Shateh was completely unaware of having spoken aloud.

Ban-ya kept her head down and her back bent under her traveling burden as she trudged along with the other women.

Having feigned the morning illness of early pregnancy, her load was made lighter than that of the other women, except for those who were with child; but nothing else was easy for her. She watched the snow fall and fall and wondered if it would ever stop. No one except Shateh's wives and daughters would speak to her, and they were abusive. The chieftain saw to it that they did not kick her or strike her. He made certain that she was as warm and well-looked after as any of his wives. Since robes and hides were scarce, he allowed her to keep her coyote-skin cloak, even though this won resentment toward her from the other women.

At times Ban-ya found herself wishing that he would not be so concerned for her; it was not easy to hate a solicitous master. To keep her heart hard, she remembered that Dakan-eh had rarely been as thoughtful and, angered by the comparison, despised Shateh for causing her to make it. Furthermore, if he allowed the other women to strike her, then she would have an excuse to hit them back on occasion.

Now, as they followed the men into the new campsite, removed the browbands that helped to distribute the weight of their backpacks, and slung off their loads, Ban-ya saw Senohnim approach her.

"The baby in my own belly is quiet now," Senohnim whispered. "It has moved into the birth position. Soon I will bear the chief a son, and then there will be no room in this camp for a bad-luck woman. Shateh will not want you anymore. He will put you out of the band to die!"

Ban-ya did not cower from the threat. "If you bear a son, how then will my presence be seen as bad luck? You have given birth only to daughters before. I was not here to take the blame for that, Senohnim. If you have yet to please your man by giving him a son, it is not my fault!"

Senohnim's pretty face contorted with scorn. "May the 'thing' in your belly wither and die, woman of the Red World!"

Atli, Atonashkeh's sole surviving wife, had just come to assist the other women after leaving her man moaning in pain on the tripoled sledge upon which he had been dragged across the long miles by Nakantahkeh. Having overheard the gist of Senohnim's comments, Atli leered dangerously at Ban-ya. "It was you the raiders wanted when they slew Nani. It was you who should have died. If the raiders come again, I will tell them where you are!"

Wehakna silenced Atli with a clucking of her tongue. "Do not trouble yourselves, sisters. Even if she bears a son to Shateh, it will be half lizard and never accepted among the People of the Land of Grass. In time Shateh will turn away from the thing and from her, and both shall be abandoned to be food for meat eaters!"

Ban-ya trembled, but she stood tall within the thick furs of her cloak so that the others would detect no weakness in her. "Shall I ask Shateh if this will be so? And shall I tell him everything the three of you have just said, and how dearly you long for the death of a child of the chieftain?"

Senohmin glowered. "I, too, carry his child!"

"I would deny any words that you would speak against me!" Atli retorted, shaken.

Wehakna, older and wiser, realized that she had said too much. She took thoughtful measure of Ban-ya. "Shateh would never believe this of me."

"May he never be asked to hear them," responded Ban-ya, thinking that if she held her tongue and gave the women cause to be grateful for her generosity toward them, she might at least have three fewer enemies in camp.

But it was not to be. The days wore on. No one except Shateh spoke to Ban-ya. She kept to herself, which was not difficult. She had only to plead queasiness or the welfare of the nonexistent child, and Shateh would seek his rest and ease beside Wehakna. With her aching breasts bound tightly with strips of buckskin to slow the upwelling of unwanted milk, Ban-ya missed the chieftain's touch. Often she lay awake in the night, longing for her lost Bold Man and Piku-neh and hoping that they were faring better than those with whom she was living now.

"Look back, Dakan-eh," urged Pah-la. "The storm has settled on the Land of Grass and the far ranges. It has not followed us into the mountains that stand between us and home. Truly, my son, now that we walk toward the Red World, the forces of Creation are smiling upon us once more. And see here, young Hah-ri has found our Kahm-ree for us! She was not lost in the dawn wind after all! I knew that Hah-ri would bring her back to us!"

Dakan-eh stared at the old woman and tried hard not to show disappointment and disgust. He had seen her wander off alone, babbling mindlessly about returning to her granddaughter. He had let her walk on until she was well out of sight, then he rose to obliterate her tracks. Only then had he wakened the band with talk of enemies following them in the wind. He had them up and moving so quickly that he hoped no one would notice the old woman's absence. He should have known better. Pah-la would never abandon a friend. "Ah, Kahm-ree! There you are!"

"Have you seen my Ban-ya?" she asked Dakan-eh.

"No, old woman. Nor do I expect to see her, ever again."

"You are too harsh, my son," said Pah-la sadly.

"I would go back for her," said young Hah-ri with the eagerness of a dull-witted pup that is all too ready to race into danger if it thinks that this will win praise.

"My son is brave!" exclaimed Ghree proudly.

"Your son is a fool!" Dakan-eh told her, and did not care when the woman and the boy wilted in his shadow. "Look!" he pointed angrily back along the way they had come. "We must go on now and take advantage of this break in the weather. The storm wind might yet rise again and follow!"

Life was hard and cold in a camp without lodges. The people of Shateh blamed the banished lizard eater and his woman for bad luck, but they did not speak these accusations to their chieftain. They cut trees and branches and braced them against the embankments of the river above the high-water line. After covering them with the few hides they had managed to save from the whirling wind and chinking the interior walls with mud, they lived like wood rats within these nests of sticks. Their only good luck came when a small herd of dwarf pronghorns was located and driven over an icy deadfall to be butchered and skinned and feasted upon. The mother of Wila keened for her missing daughter as yet another search party returned without success.

"We will not see that girl again," murmured the women of the band.

Ban-ya's worried eyes were not the only ones turned fearfully toward the cloud-covered mountain vastnesses into which the raiders from the People of the Watching Star had disappeared.

Shateh appointed watchmen for every moment of the night and day, and the dogs were kept on the edge of hunger so that they would be irritable and alert for the slightest sound or scent of potential threat.

"If they come, you will have called them down upon us!" Wehakna accused when Shateh was away from his women; it was the first time in days she had spoken to Ban-ya.

"And would I also call them down upon myself?" Ban-ya protested.

"We should not have banished your people," injected Senohnim. "We should have killed them all. Given the opportunity we should still do so! We were a great people before the lizard eaters of the Red World came and brought their bad luck and the storms of the angry sky down upon us!"

"The People of the Watching Star were your enemies long before you ever knew there was a Red World! And the storms have saved you, stupid woman!" Ban-ya retorted. "Bad weather drove the raiders into the mountains and has kept them there, allowing us to travel to a new camp. Our tracks have been covered by snow, so our direction is something that our enemies can only guess at!"

She saw the hatred, jealousy, and disbelief in their eyes and knew that her more lethal enemies dwelled in her own lodge of sticks. Her life remained in jeopardy as long as the women continued to focus their animosity upon her. She knew she had to do something to change their attitude before they managed to harden Shateh's heart toward her also. Desperate, she recalled the words that she had spoken in Dakan-eh's defense, and she spoke them now in her own. "When Shateh chose to keep me as his woman, he also saved his people, just as my Bold Man saved you when he risked his life to run before the whirling wind. The forces of Creation smile upon my people. There is enough luck in me to assure you that had I not been in the encampment when the raiders came, you and all of your people would have died! I *am* your luck!"

The outrageousness of her assertion shook her more than a little; she waited for the other women to speak out in challenge, but in that moment a cry went up from Teikan. A small herd of bison had been seen. The call to hunt went out to the men of Shateh's band.

Ban-ya took a deep breath and brazenly dared to state, "If the people feast tonight it will be because Ban-ya has called these bison to prove her good intentions toward the new band!"

"And what if we do not feast, or if men are injured on the hunt?" Wehakna demanded.

Ban-ya drew in a deep breath and, knowing that she had very little to lose, spoke out menacingly, "If bad things happen, it will be because the women of this band have offended me!" Yet even as the words left her mouth, her hands were knotted into fists behind her back as she silently implored the Forces of Creation, *Please, for the life of this woman, let things go well upon the hunt this day!*

And it was so.

The women continued to mutter suspiciously against Ban-ya; but for the first time since the bitter and unprecedented autumn weather had begun, the men found cause to speak in gratitude to the storm spirits. Despite the presence of Lizard Woman within the band, the hunt had gone better than any dared to hope. Snow and wind allied themselves with the hunters, enabling them to track their prey virtually undetected. Using snow walkers—some salvaged from the storm-devastated camp, others newly made of bent willow cross laced with sinew—Shateh led his men with relative ease over deep, soft drifts of snow. Approaching downwind of the herd, the hunters maneuvered the animals into a blind, snow-choked draw within which the bison were soon mired and exhausted. Shoulder-deep in snow, the massive animals had no defense against hunters who came howling at them from across the top of the drifts, hurling their spears deep into the hearts and lungs and diaphragms until the entire herd was slain.

The women and children with their meat-making tools followed the hunters. The bison were skinned and butchered on the spot. Before the best meat and skins were dragged back to the river camp on hastily contrived sledges of bison bones and skins, the people of Shateh gorged themselves on raw, fatty hump steaks and sweet, soft-textured livers and tongues. The band cracked bones and scooped marrow, and the children were given eyeballs to suck. The "good glands" of the cows were taken and portioned among the women, while intestines were laid out and slit open so that everyone could dip fingers into the pungent, slimy green pudding within.

Now all agreed that had it not been for continuing foul weather, the people would still be hungry and without bison hides. Nakantahkeh had enough food in his belly now to insist upon traveling north, in hope of overtaking Xiaheh and convincing him to bring his warriors south again, before the weather cleared and mountain-dwelling marauders found it possible to venture from the ice-blasted heights to begin their raids once more.

"When Nakantahkeh returns, he will bring the chiefs and warriors of the northern and western tribes," assured Teikan. He and several of the men of the band gathered with Shateh in the stick house of Atonashkeh, to cheer the wounded man with their fellowship. "They will come when they hear that hunting is good in this land again."

"Together we will go into the mountains and seek our enemies as soon as the weather clears," added Indeh. "You will be well and strong by then, Atonashkeh!"

"*If* the weather ever clears," drawled a surly Atonashkeh. Feverish and in pain, he pulled in an angry, impatient breath and choked on the mouthful of meat that Atli had just served to him from a bison-bone platter. Hacking the offending mass into his hand, he threw it at the woman who knelt beside him. "Do I not suffer enough?" he raged loudly enough for the entire camp to hear. "Must you gag me with your badly cooked meat? Is it any wonder that my wound will not heal? Get away! Get out of my sight! Someday you will kill me with your cooking!"

Atli, mortified, scuttled away on her knees. All of the men except Shateh looked down, embarrassed by Atonashkeh's display of temper.

"A man of the Land of Grass should not gulp his food unchewed or speak until it is fully swallowed," said the chieftain evenly but with visible annoyance. "You have taken on the eating habits of a lizard eater, Atonashkeh . . . although after having spent time with us, not even Bold Man of the Red World continued to bolt his meat like a dog."

No one moved. No one even breathed.

Chastised and humiliated, Atonashkeh stared at his father for a moment, then fell back onto his bed furs. "How can you speak to me like this? It is not fitting! It is not good! It is not *right!*"

Shateh's face tightened as he eyed his son and thought that the man deserved to choke. Nevertheless, the chieftain was disturbed because he could not remember what he had said. Actually he was not aware of having spoken at all. Confused and ashamed, he rose abruptly and walked out into the continuing snowfall and left the younger men to their restless talk.

Atonashkeh glowered after him. "I tell you, he speaks his thoughts aloud these days like an old woman. The lizard-eating female is calling bad spirits upon him and us."

Teikan shrugged. "My woman has told me that she has heard it said that Lizard Woman claims to have called the bison and the snow and has willed the raiders to stay away from this camp."

Atonashkeh would not hear of it. "Then let Lizard Woman will the spirits to bring the girl Wila safely back to her people. Let her command the spirits to undo what the raiders of the Watching Star have done to me!''

Again Teikan shrugged. ''That night in the snow . . . we heard their taunts and felt the sting of their spears, but we never saw them.''

''So?'' snarled Atonashkeh impatiently.

Teikan lowered his voice. ''So perhaps it is ghosts and not living men who have come against us, Atonashkeh. Perhaps it is not Lizard Woman who has called the bad spirits upon us. Perhaps, when the slave woman Sheela ran away, she died out there in the night. In death she might have been reunited with the spirits of the many slain warriors among her people. Perhaps she has brought *them* back into the world of the living. Perhaps, through her . . . the Daughter of the Sun has been reborn.''

There was dead silence among the assembled hunters. Furtive, fearful glances were exchanged. And then, as one, they raised their hands, palms out, as a sign against malevolent spirits.

Indeh shook his head and whispered, ''For the sake of Nakantahkeh's grieving woman, we must not even think it, Teikan.''

''It is *because* of Nakantahkeh's grieving woman that I *do* think it!'' answered Teikan. ''Why else would they have taken her daughter and no other slaves? Wila was young and had yet to come to her time of blood or to be pierced by a man!''

Atonashkeh was scowling. ''The stink of their piss was real enough! They were not ghosts. And if the woman Sheela was with the raiders, she would want to hurt that girl. Many was the time when that child came forward to taunt the slaves. Besides, in spite of her nastiness, Wila would be considered a prime captive for some man!''

''Or be offered as sacrifice to the sky god of the People of the Watching Star. It was their way,'' reminded Teikan in a low, worried tone. ''Through deceitful trade or in many a raid, they took the young girls of other bands and tribes to live among them—to gentle their fears and earn their trust, and then to mate them with their god, to Thunder in the Sky, through the sacrificial blade. The woman Ysuna, Daughter

of the Sun, danced in the skin of her victims and vowed that
only through such blood—and eventually through the blood
of the great white mammoth totem—would she and her
people live forever!''

"Ysuna is dead," said Atonashkeh grimly. ''And most
of her people with her. The rest are scattered bands of
renegades. When Nakantahkeh returns with the warriors of
Xiaheh, we will finish the threat soon enough and take Wila
back from whatever man amuses himself with her now!''

Teikan was staring at the painted bison hide that had
been hung as a weather baffle across the cross-braced
entryway to Atonashkeh's lodge of sticks. The hide's
patterns and pictographs recounted many past battles in the
great war against the bloodthirsty Ysuna and her People of
the Watching Star. ''Yes,'' Teikan said, nodding. ''You are
right. Ysuna *is* dead, and it is good. I would not want to live
those days of war again.''

In the mountain stronghold of the People of the
Watching Star, Jhadel shivered in his winter robe of tawny
bearskin. His eyes narrowed as he stared into the falling
snow and howling wind. The intensity of the storm was
troubling him. For many a long, cold day and night he had
sensed a change in the wind. Instinct told him that something terrible had happened, but what was it? Irked, unable
to gather his thoughts, he turned from the fury of the
elements to observe the fury of Sheela as she paced and
loudly cursed the weather.

"The choice of this high place as stronghold was a bad
decision!'' she declared, striding around and over the seated
and reclining forms of her people. Gathered into little family
groups, they were watching her in silence.

"It was chosen by Ysuna herself!'' reminded Tsana,
following her like a fur-clad shadow.

"What good is it if in weather like this it prevents the
warriors of the Watching Star from setting out on other
raids?'' she demanded, still pacing, her face tight with
concentration.

"It allows us to come together in safety to rest and

regain our strength,'' said Jhadel, crossing his arms over his chest and observing Sheela thoughtfully.

Utterly transformed and revitalized in her new role as successor to Ysuna, she did not even remotely resemble the battered creature whom Tsana had returned to the cave. Her face was no longer swollen and discolored; but her mouth and brow would carry scars for life, and the bridge of her high, straight nose had been broken. It was wider now and slumped in the middle, giving her nostrils and the tip of her nose a slightly downturned and flattened appearance. No man would ever again remark on her perfect beauty, but somehow—in Jhadel's eyes, at least—the minor disfigurements added to her looks rather than detracted from them; they were the scars of a survivor.

"I was not aware that we had *lost* our strength!" she snapped. As she paced, the bone-beaded fringes of the worn elkskin dress that one of the women had given to her clicked like teeth in a cold man's head.

"There are many strengths, daughter of Sheehanal," replied Jhadel. "The least of these is the physical strength of the body."

She stopped and stared angrily. "Speak with a straight tongue, Jhadel. If you want to say something, be direct."

"Ah, but all things, even talk, must be shaped to conform to the sacred circle, daughter of Sheehanal. Beyond that circle lies the world of spirits . . . of the dead . . . of the Great One who made all things in the time beyond beginning." His tattooed head went high. He had more than the attention of Sheela now. His people were listening.

He nodded, gratified. Even after the raid and sacrifice, he still had them. They were afraid of the woman, but they trusted him. He smiled; it was what he had intended, what he had led her to accomplish for him and for herself. Someday she might be leader of this people, but he was—and would always be—shaman. As such, his power would be as great, if not greater than, her own. Even as old age crept into his skin and bones, he would have a place within the tribe for as long as his people had need of magic. In this tenuous, often baffling condition called life, his people had good cause to fear the future. He had learned long before that a fearful people had as much need of magic as of meat.

He nodded. "Yes, daughter of Sheehanal, from birth to death, all living things drift in the web of the eternal orb spider, round and round until the net is closed and that which was young is old, and that which was dead is reborn and—"

"What are you saying, Jhadel!" she demanded, clearly aggravated.

"I am saying that you must not be so eager to lead another raid. Praise the spirits for the success of the last one. Do not be so eager to risk death. It will come to us all in time—even to you, daughter of Sheehanal. And afterwards, which one of us can say what will be until the circle of our own life closes and—"

"I do not speak of death!" she interrupted hotly. "I speak of life! I speak of blood! The *life* of the People of the Watching Star! The blood of our *enemies!* It is on this that we will grow strong! With my own hand I took the life of the woman Ban-ya, but her man, Dakan-eh, the man who did *this* to my face, still lives."

Jhadel raised a hand to silence her. His small, black eyes darted to the far corner of the cave. There, half-hidden amid a jumble of old, rank furs that had belonged to the sacrifice, the captive had looked up with interest at the mention of Dakan-eh's name. Jhadel smiled benevolently in Wila's direction, then extended an arm toward Sheela. "You and I must talk together, daughter of Sheehanal," he said, and although her expression gave him no cause to believe that she came eagerly, she joined him in that part of the cave that he had made his own behind high wood-framed partitions of woven strips of hide and long ribbons of feathers.

"If you would let me sacrifice the girl, the storms might end," she snapped with lowered voice, eyeing the ceremonial belongings he kept hidden behind the partitions. Under the blanket of raven skins lay the human-hand medicine bag and the skin of the last sacrifice.

He clucked his tongue. "You must learn patience. Soon all that you yearn to accomplish will *be* accomplished;

but you know as well as I that runners have gone ahead of the storms to seek those survivors among our tribe who have not yet come to join their brothers and sisters in this sacred place. Soon the few will be many. You still have much to learn before you are ready to command them.''

"You have said it yourself—the blood of Ysuna is in me! I am the only one fit to walk in the footsteps of the Daughter of the Sun!''

He chuckled indulgently. ''So eager you are! Did you enjoy the raid so much, and the taste of the sacrifice's flesh and blood, and the feel of the dead girl's skin against your own? Are you so eager to sate yourself in death again?''

Her face was wary. ''I would avenge myself upon the killers of my sister and upon the man who has done this to my face. I cannot rest for want of killing him. If the death of that girl will hasten this, then yes, I am eager. It will please me greatly to give her the gift of death.''

"You speak only of your own needs and of your own pleasure. This is not good. This was not the way of Ysuna. If you are to walk in the footsteps of the Daughter of the Sun, you must remember that she was also called Woman Who Gives Life to the People. Where Ysuna walked, there also walked many mammoth, and upon the meat of our totem animals, our people grew strong. Only when the mammoth began to walk away from this land did enemies come against us. Only then were the sacrifices made, so that Thunder in the Sky would smile upon his people and assure them victory over their enemies and everlasting meat in return for the meat that was given to him.''

"I know all of this, Jhadel.''

"But you seem to have forgotten that sacrifices must come *consenting* to the god lest their hesitance to embrace his power offend him and turn his wrath upon those who name him Great Ghost Spirit.''

"I have not forgotten.''

"Then listen to the wind and to the voice of the storm, for the Great One speaks. Now I understand that he is telling us what we must do: We must wait until the raid upon the encampment of our enemies seems like a long-forgotten dream to them . . . until they have begun to cease to fear us or to search for us. Then, when they least expect us, we will bring Spirit Sucker into their camp and give them cause to mourn their dead—a woman here, a child there . . . first an old one, next a watchman. Again and again, over the passage of many moons, we will strike at them until a slow bleeding away of courage will begin in the hearts of our enemies. One by one they will die. Then, when they despair as we have despaired, when they fear the dawn of each new day as we have feared it, then and only then will we prepare the sacrifice. When the blood of the captive has been shed, the great raid will begin. Let Shateh and Dakan-eh be the last to die, for then, daughter of Sheehanal, will your vengeance be sweetest.''

"Yes! You *do* speak wisdom, Jhadel!''

Although he heard her words, her eyes told him that she would continue to be driven by blood lust and impatience. He tried again, hopeful that some of his words would sink in. "And let there be no talk of this in front of the captive. She is to be treated as a daughter and gentled into trust until the day comes when, unsuspecting, she will walk willingly to her death, never guessing her fate.''

Sheela frowned. "What of the boy? What if he speaks of it to her?''

"Warakan? The brother of the last sacrifice? Ah, he is so young! Already he is being mothered by Oan. He understands that what has happened to his sister was not a death but an honoring. He will not speak of it to the captive. Indeed, since the sacrifice, he has not spoken at all. But he is of the People. In time, with Jhadel and the daughter of Sheehanal to lead him, he will be a great warrior.''

"If the snow ever stops so raids may begin again,'' said Sheela.

"It will stop. All things must end, daughter of Sheehanal, so that there may be new beginnings for us all!''

2

Far across the world, a much younger shaman stood in another cave and contemplated the future of his people. At the mouth of the great hollow in the hills, a sullen and troubled Cha-kwena looked across the "wonderful" valley. The rain had stopped days before. The skies had long since cleared. Now the sun was rising over the eastern mountains, bathing the forests, grasslands, and vast, sweeping blue lake in the soft colors of another perfect morning. All around the valley, the great, ice-capped ranges folded away into distances that caught the light, then threw it back in tones of brilliance that should have taken his breath away.

But the colors of the new day failed to touch him. His spirit remained in darkness. The totem was dead. He had killed it. And now, with Siwi-ni wan and sickly and Gah-ti lying maimed and suffering from wounds that would require many moons to heal, he could not bring himself to tell his people that they must leave this land before it was too late. But too late for what? Memories of dark omens pricked him, but he did not know what they meant. With the totem dead, they were all doomed, no matter what they did. They might as well stay, he thought, and face whatever came.

Not for the first time since he had returned to the cave, strange thoughts accosted him—if the great white mammoth had been only a mammoth after all and not a supernatural creature born of the forces of Creation to protect those who named it totem, and if there were no spirits moving in the winds and clouds to shape and define the destinies of men, then perhaps it did not matter what the people did, or where they went, or where they chose to settle. They would live, and like all creatures that drew breath, they would eventually perish. It might as well happen there, where the mammoth and the great white tusker that they named Totem had come to die.

"All will be for the best!"

U-wa's proclamation startled him. He turned. His mother was up and shaking her bed furs. "You must stop brooding, my son. Now that the lion is dead, this cave has proved to be a dry, comfortable place. Siwi-ni can regain her strength, and Gah-ti can recover here. Women always bleed after bringing babies into the world, and with proper care Gah-ti's arm will grow back!"

"That is not likely," he told her. "I do not know where you and the others have come up with such an idea!"

Genuinely amazed by his doubt, she folded her bed furs over her bent forearm and came to stand beside him. Drawing in a deep, contented breath of the morning, she smiled beatifically as she looked out across the valley. "There is good hunting in those hills and lowlands, and good fishing in that lake. In this fine cave the band is protected from the weather and from predatory animals. Despite all that has happened, our totem and our shaman have led us well! My son has worked great magic in this camp. Life has returned to the arm of Gah-ti's father. With my Cha-kwena as shaman, why should it not also be so with the son?"

Cha-kwena eyed his mother. *If only she knew the truth!* he thought. Her pride in him was a source of shame to him now. He looked around their shelter. He had never liked caves, probably because he had been forcibly taken from the boys' lodge of his village after his father's death had made him the only living male descendant of the village shaman. The memories were bitter. It had been Cha-kwena's duty to be apprenticed to his grandfather and to share old Hoyeh-tay's cliff-side aerie. He had felt trapped within it, isolated from his friends, deprived of his hope of someday becoming as great and fearless a hunter as Dakan-eh.

And when he had needed help in trying to save the totem, where had the ghost of old Hoyeh-tay been? Absent?

Off on some fanciful dream flight with Owl? Or non-existent, a figment of his grandson's fertile imagination?

Looking down, he eyed his medicine bag. Cha-kwena's hand strayed to the sacred stone, then released it as though it had burned him. What folly was this? There was no magic in the stone! It no longer soothed him, and he no longer sought vision while he touched it. He was certain that whatever gifts it had once bestowed upon him must have been born in the same imagination that had conjured the ghosts of Hoyeh-tay and Owl.

He scanned the interior of the cave and felt trapped within it, just as he had in Hoyeh-tay's, during those long-gone days of his boyhood when the old shaman had kept him to his lessons and snared him in endless hours of storytelling. Nevertheless, U-wa was right about its suitability as a permanent habitation, even though her thanks were due to Gah-ti—or perhaps, he thought ironically, to the lion, whose roars had fired the youth's need to prove himself. Now that the lion was dead and skinned, the people owed it thanks yet again, for its hide had been fleshed and stretched and pegged to the floor of the cave to cure, and much of its meat had been consumed. The rest was sliced thin and set to smoke over drying frames, which the women had made from segments of the lion's own bones after they had been cracked and scraped free of precious marrow.

Lion flesh was not the only meat being cured in the cave. Since the rain had stopped, the people had gone out on hunting and gathering forays. Rabbits and hares had been taken, and many fish and waterfowl. The women had gathered great, gray-leaved, tawny-flowered armfuls of sagebrush with which to smoke the meat. The sagebrush would also make many good medicines. Mah-ree had been delighted to discover that the rain had not destroyed all of the grass and sunflower seeds, and there were still rose hips and a few chokecherries to be picked and stored. The women dug edible roots and waded into the reed beds along the shore, to harvest ripe cattails and cut lush reeds, which were now stacked in neat piles for later weaving.

"Greetings to Shaman on this new day!" said Mah-ree as she rose from her sleeping place. Bundled in her sleeping robe, she blushed with uncharacteristic shyness when U-wa gestured her forward. She paused before him. "Are you still unhappy in this good place?" she asked in reaction to his grim expression. "Soon Gah-ti will be healed, and Siwi-ni will be strong again! You will see, Cha-kwena! Won't he, U-wa?"

Cha-kwena scowled; the girl's words had been uttered with the extra enthusiasm of one who hopes to convince herself of something that she does not fully believe.

"Soon. Yes! It *will* be so!" U-wa replied. Then she turned and left them to speak privately.

Mah-ree looked up at Cha-kwena. Her eyes were soft, expectant. "Will you not wish me the goodness of morning, Cha-kwena?"

He did not oblige her. Things had changed between them since the night on the monolith. He felt a tension between them that had not been there before. An undeniable reserve and shyness in her stance and expression embarrassed him. It seemed to proclaim to everyone who observed her as she looked at him: This man and I have been one together!

And have broken the laws of the ancestors, he thought miserably. *And have brought the wrath of the forces of Creation down upon the People. And have caused the totem to weaken and die.*

His jaw tightened. *No.* He did not believe this anymore—not in the laws of the ancestors, not in the forces of Creation, not in the powers of a totem that he could kill with his bare hands. If he had, in fact, lain down as a man with this immature girl, it did not matter to anyone—except to her.

She picked up a basket and brought it to him. Its contents smelled strongly of pine. She had spent her evenings pounding new-growth bark from several species of saplings and from tender young pines, then heated the pulverized bark and strips of buckskin in a boiling bag. She then used the medicine-impregnated strips to cleanse Gah-ti's wounds. And while the youth had smiled wanly, adoringly, through intermittent delirium, she spoke to him of how quickly he was healing and assured him that he must have hope in the future. If feeling had at last returned to his father's arm, she said confidently, then Gah-ti had every reason to hope that his own arm would soon grow back.

Cha-kwena winced against his recollections. He had wanted to talk privately to her about this. Now was as good a time as any. Indicating her medicine basket with a downward nod of his head, he said, "You must not expect too much of your skills, Mah-ree. Gah-ti may be healed by your medicine, but his arm will not grow back."

"Why not? I have seen the tails of lizards grow back after they have been torn away by hawks."

"Gah-ti is not a lizard."

Her chin quivered. "He saw us together, Cha-kwena."

He did not respond. The revelation was not as unsettling as it should have been; somehow Cha-kwena had suspected it all along.

"He hunted the lion to prove himself to me. He was *so* brave. And I was so . . . uncaring of his feelings."

As I have been of yours, he thought. He was so startled by that revelation that he flinched.

"He deserves to have his arm back, Cha-kwena. Make extra magic for him. You are strong in the power of the totem! Surely you could—"

"I can do nothing, Mah-ree!"

"I do not understand."

"I do not expect you to. Go away. Your place is not with me. You are Medicine Girl. Take your medicine to Gah-ti, and then to Siwi-ni. They have need of you. I do not."

She withered. "You have not been the same since you came back to the cave, Cha-kwena!"

"*Nothing* is the same!" he shouted.

The others were waking now. The dogs were stretching and yawning. At the sleeping Siwi-ni's breast, little Doh-teyah began to fret and cry.

Downcast, Mah-ree turned away and then, after only a few steps, turned back to speak pleadingly. "Everything will be good for us again, Cha-kwena. I know it will. And Friend and the other dogs will return, won't they, my shaman?"

Cha-kwena stiffened. He had tried not to think about the dogs, for they represented yet another betrayal. The animals had been raised by his people, yet the dogs had run with coyotes to savage the totem and, with it, everything that he had ever believed and found holy. But could he tell her that? Or that they had been crushed into the muck of the distant arm of the lake? "Forget them," he said bleakly.

She was as shocked as the others who heard his words. "How can you say this, Cha-kwena?"

He sneered; the bitterness in his heart was so vile that he nearly wept. "Do I not know all things? Can I not heal all wounds? Am I not *Shaman?*"

3

Nervous sentries guarded the river camp of Shateh as the birth cries of Senohnim rent the night.

Ban-ya cowered at the back of the chieftain's lodge of sticks. She was alone. Shateh had gone out to stand birth vigil. Wehakna served in the birth hut as one of several midwives to Senohnim, while the daughters of the chieftain had been sent to pass the night in the lodge of Senohnim's father and younger sisters. Ban-ya listened, desperately afraid, to the on-again, off-again screams of Senohnim and to the deep, steady beating of the drums that were simulating the heartbeat of the earth, of Mother Below, the great, all-knowing female force whose strength and sympathy must now rise up and enter the heart of the childbearing mother to give her strength and courage throughout her travail.

In an effort to keep herself from shaking, Ban-ya

tucked her knees beneath her chin, wrapped her arms around her legs, bent her head, and willed herself not to yield to despair. It was no use. She was doomed, no matter what transpired. Tears smarted beneath her closed lids. If Senohnim brought forth a daughter, the women of the tribe would say that because of Lizard Woman's evil influence, Shateh had again been deprived of a son. If Senohnim brought forth a male-child, the chieftain would no longer have cause to look to a less worthy woman of the Red World to give him the sons he so desperately yearned for in his old age.

And if Senohnim brought forth a dead child, or herself died in the delivery, all eyes would turn in accusation to Ban-ya, and not even Shateh would be able to stand up to the many who would demand that Lizard Woman be put out of the band to die. She would, of course, argue in her own defense, as she had already done so many times. The band was now well fed on the meat of bison, which she had claimed to have called to the hunters; but Wehakna would no doubt remind the band that Lizard Woman had also claimed to bring the early winter storms, and all knew how difficult it was to prepare hides and sinew and fat when the days were cold. The fingers of the women grew stiff and could not work the needles or the fleshers with any ease, nor the scrapers or the awls without being cut. Wehakna would hold up her bleeding fingers and would speak of all that had gone before—the whirling winds, the deaths of Kalawak and of so many others, the raid, the missing girl.

Ban-ya moaned in abject misery. *My beloved! Why have you not come for me? Had it been you, I would have come in the snow and wind and would have taken you away before anyone could prevent me!*

She forced herself to stop these thoughts because they were unfair to her Bold Man. And worse than that, they reduced her to a sniveling, self-pitying weakling who could not stand against the winds of change. If she faltered now, she would die. Her life spirit would be lost forever, and she would never see her little Piku-neh again, in this life or any other.

The drums stopped abruptly. Ban-ya looked up, listened intently. Senohnim was no longer screaming. Breath-less, Ban-ya waited, wondering what would happen next and agonizing about when she might know what must happen next.

"Ai yah hay!"

A man's cry—jubilant . . . but followed by a long and heavy silence.

"Yah nah!"

A woman's cry, equally jubilant. "A son is born to Shateh!"

"Shateh accepts this son!" The chieftain's voice was loud and strong. And yet, somehow, it was as bleak and cold as the wind.

The drums began to beat once more. Whistles were sounding. People were singing and clapping. Ban-ya knew they would begin the nightlong dances. She swallowed. Her mouth was dry. She swallowed again. The tumultuous rejoicing of the river camp passed easily through the hides and sticks that made up the walls of the chieftain's lodge. She put her head down onto her knees, and a strange calm passed over her as she closed her eyes. Senohnim had given birth to a male-child. Shateh had a son. He would not want her anymore. Tomorrow, sooner perhaps, she would be put out of the band. She wondered if she should gather up all the warm clothing that she could find within the lodge and flee now.

"No." She sighed in quiet resignation. Dakan-eh was far away; it was unlikely that she could ever catch up with him. The night was so cold. She had heard wolves howling to one another before the drumming had started. And Sheela and the raiders of the People of the Watching Star were out there somewhere in the dark. "I will not feed myself to wolves or put myself into the way of the People of the Watching Star! I am Dakan-eh's woman. I will not be afraid. Perhaps even now my Bold Man is coming back for me. I will wait. I *will* live—for him!"

Darkness found Dakan-eh on the far side of the great pass that divided the Land of Grass from the Red World. He was not thinking of Ban-ya. Instead he was pondering the fact that he had brought his people far. Now, with bellies full of roasted rabbit, squirrel, and pinyon jays, they slept around a smoldering fire within a sheltering grove of ancient junipers high on the Blue Mesas. This massive, flat-topped range of gorge-cleft buttes was the last obstacle between them and home. Tomorrow they would fill their water flasks at cold, snow-fed streams, heft their belongings, and begin the final phase of their journey—the long trek down from the highlands and across the great red valley toward their abandoned ancestral village by the Lake of Many Singing Birds. What would he find there? he wondered.

Now, hunkering alone on a bare, windy overlook, Dakan-eh scowled across the parched and ancient land of his ancestors. His eyes had grown used to the darkness. He could see the terrain below—the broad, white salt flats, the small remnant lakes sparkling with reflected star glow here and there, the towering buttes and cinder cones and long volcanic hills that would show red and black when the light of day struck them. He frowned and, squinting, looked for the expanse of water that was Big Lake. He saw only a broad, well-defined flat area of unbroken gray. The great lake was completely dry again, he realized. Drought still lay upon the land. He cursed, then looked up, startled to see that K-wok and the other hunters of his band had come to stand on either side of him.

"Bold Man need not be ashamed of having been banished from the Land of Grass," said K-wok. "Bold Man is not alone. We will stand tall beside our headman in the days to come, and it will not be so bad for us."

"At least the whirling wind will not come here to eat of our people, eh?" added Xet with his usual optimism.

K-wok nodded, somber. "Perhaps, after all is said and done, it is best that we return to the land of our ancestors. The ways of our people are familiar to us." He sighed. "But I will miss the great hunts and the way the bison ran before the dogs and hunters, and the way our women looked at us when we returned to the villages with—"

"When we return to the Red World, it will *not* be as before!" Dakan-eh interrupted, adamant. "And let no man say that we have been banished! Of my own free will I have put my back to the bad-luck encampment of Shateh. Too long have we hunted in the way of the men of the Land of Grass. We return to the country of the ancestors, but never again to live as lizard eaters!''

"How else shall we live in the Red World?" asked K-wok. "Long has it been since the great herds—"

"We shall live as warriors!" vowed Dakan-eh, giving voice at last to a determination that had been stewing in his mind for days.

Dubious, the hunters exchanged glances.

"Whom shall we make war upon, Bold Man?" Atl queried.

"Upon all who oppose us!" replied Dakan-eh.

Again the hunters looked at one another.

"The great war between the tribes of the north and south is over," reminded K-wok. "And the bands of the Red World have always been peaceful, Dakan-eh."

Dakan-eh cringed. "It is time for them to learn new ways," he growled.

"But we have slain our enemies in the great war, Bold Man. There is no one left to fight!"

Dakan-eh was on his feet now, glaring, snarling through clenched teeth. "There will always be enemies, K-wok! Think about drought . . . storms . . . a changing world that drives the game from the land! Shateh has stolen my woman; but he has made me see that although I may not become a chief in his land, I *will* be one in mine! A great chief. Using the ways and weapons of the bison and mammoth hunters of the Land of Grass, I will soon become chief over all chiefs."

"But whom will we *fight*, Bold Man?"

Now, for the first time in longer than he could remember, Dakan-eh found himself smiling. He reached out and gave K-wok a friendly shove. "You miss the point, K-wok. In the land of the lizard eaters, who will there be to fight *us?*"

Once again the hunters traded blank-eyed glances.

Dakan-eh clucked his tongue at their lack of imagination. "Our spears will assure our will as we take the best hunting and watering grounds and women as our own. The chiefs and the shamans will turn up their necks like dogs and say yes to us. Because the men of the Red World are afraid to fight, we will have whatever we want, whatever we need of them."

K-wok's brow furrowed; he was clearly uncomfortable with the sound of this. "They will name us Enemy. They will hate us. The women will weep when we take them. The watering places will dry up, and the game will not come."

Dakan-eh shook his head. "The watering places are already drying up, and the game has long since ceased to be plentiful in the Red World. Far beyond the Mountains of Sand, a shaman sends the ill will of the forces of Creation against our people! Cha-kwena is the enemy. Cha-kwena has stolen the sacred stone of our people and driven our totem before him. All men know this. We will affirm that it is so even as we gather men and teach them to be strong warriors against Cha-kwena. Maybe someday we will seek him. Maybe someday we will find him and kill him. In the meantime we will live as chiefs and warriors in the land of our ancestors and—"

"And maybe someday we will have enough warriors to go back into the Land of Grass and make Shateh pay for dishonoring us!" interrupted an excited Xet. "And then you will have your Ban-ya again and—"

"Yes! May it be so!" Dakan-eh cut in on the man's enthusiasm, but he did not share it. Xet's reference to Ban-ya had reminded him that for all of his valorous talk of soon-to-be-acquired chieftainship, he was still a man in retreat, a Bold Man who had been afraid to challenge Shateh for his woman.

Dakan-eh squatted, balancing his weight on the balls of his moccasined feet, and, with his forearms resting on his thighs, stared across the vast, disgustingly familiar land that lay below. Thunder was growling in the storm clouds that remained bulked high upon the northern horizon, but he barely heard it. He had no doubt that his life's ambition was about to be achieved. Tomorrow the shamans and lesser headmen of the Red World would take one look at his spears, and trembling like leaves in the gale of his arrogance, the men would accede to his every whim. Soon he would be a great chief, a feared and respected leader of his people! But the lizard eaters of the Red World were not the people he longed to command.

His eyes narrowed as he gazed across the world of his youth. It seemed empty without Ban-ya. Suddenly he hated her. Thinking of her called to mind too many incidents that shamed him. Although he would soon return to others of his tribe as Bold Man of the Red World, and Brave Hunter Who Runs Before the Whirling Wind to Save the People, he had earned other names in the Land of Grass: Sits in His Own Puke, and Man Who Kicks Father and Makes Him Die, and Fearful One Who Gives Away Best Woman!

Dakan-eh never wanted to see or think of Ban-ya again. Already little Piku-neh was transferring his affections to Rayela and calling her mama. Dakan-eh had other women now. And he would soon have more. Ban-ya was nothing to him! *Nothing!* He wished her death in that far land, which he was loath to put behind him. He wished them all death! Shateh . . . Atonashkeh . . . Nakantahkeh . . . and all of those brave men who were what he could never hope to be: hunters and warriors in the Land of Grass.

Ban-ya slept, then awoke with a start. She was no longer alone in the lodge. How long, she wondered, had Shateh been there, sitting cross-legged on his piled sleeping furs and staring solemnly into the dark? He ran his long, strong fingers absently through the wind-tangled lengths of his hip-length hair. Even in the darkness she could see the exhaustion in his face and in the stoop of his shoulders.

Drums were still sounding, and the people were still singing—that hard, flat, nasal, and atonal noise that was alien to her own tribe. Dakan-eh had secretly mocked it, had imitated it with mirthful derision. But she had heard Shateh's people say that the drums were the heartbeat of the world, and now, alone with the chieftain in the darkness of his lodge, her own heart was responding to the weariness in the man and something else—a sadness . . . an almost desperate, raw-edged need for solace.

Beyond the song and drumbeat, wolves howled again.

Ban-ya watched as Shateh stiffened and his eyes narrowed at the sound.

A tremor of fear ripped through her. What were the wolves feeding upon this night? Would it be her flesh that sated their hunger tomorrow? She caught her breath in horror as she imagined her flesh being savaged, heard her own screams—screams that no man would heed but that would bring satisfaction to Shateh's women. She exhaled sharply, shivered, and tried to rid herself of thoughts of her own death but could not. Then she felt the chieftain's eyes on her. Her exhalation had caused him to look in her direction.

Although the heartlike beat of the drums went on and on, Ban-ya was certain that her own heart had stopped. This man was all that stood between her and the wolves, but since coming to live with him she had done nothing to win his affection. *Nothing.* The word was a lance to her spirit. She had yet to be anything more than a sullen, recalcitrant slave or to yield her body to his with any sign of pleasure; even in her feigned pregnancy, she remained hostile and aloof. *Foolish woman!* she scolded herself.

She raised her head and spoke slowly, softly, so her words would be like medicine smoke—fragrant with her desire to heal the wounds between them. "Shateh has a son. All has gone well with the birth?"

"All has gone well."

"It is a good thing. This woman is glad."

He studied her face. "Because now you think I will let you go back to your lizard eater?"

"He is of the past, far away beyond the storms of this early winter. I am Shateh's now."

"Hmmm." His expression did not change as he looked away; his thoughts were his own.

She sensed that there was something that he was not telling her. It did not matter—he was her chieftain; she was his slave. There was no cause for him to share his thoughts with his women. There were other things to be shared— more important things that could not be shared among warriors or other hunters, or even with wives whose bodies and sexual responses had grown predictable under the passage of many moons.

As Ban-ya looked at him now, she knew that the sharing would not be unpleasant. Despite her initial determination to hate him, she had been moved by his capacity to mourn for his people and by his willingness to take full responsibility for what had befallen his tribe. Dakan-eh never had seemed capable of doing either.

Slowly, willing herself not to tremble, Ban-ya reached beneath her cloak and loosed one of the shoulder thongs of her dress. Then she quickly unwrapped the wide buckskin swath that compressed her breasts and stuck it under the bed furs.

Now, with her heart pounding and her breath shallow at the back of her throat, she shook off her cloak and approached him on her knees, moving to kneel at his back as she gently removed the robe that he had draped around his shoulders.

"Allow this slave to ease you," she whispered huskily, and, before he could protest, began to massage his broad, hard back and shoulders. She resolved to please him now as no other woman had ever done, to make herself indispensable to him in all ways, to cause him to savor and yearn for her nearness and compliance so that when others spoke against her he would refuse to hear the words. Her hands worked slowly, deftly, her palms and fingers pressing and curling into the muscles, rousing blood and warmth until she felt him relax and heard him sigh with pleasure.

"It is good?" she whispered, leaning forward, pressing her breasts against his back while sending her hands downward over his chest, then his belly. As she stroked him, moving her hands up and then down again, lower each time, she leaned into him, allowing him to feel the soft, urgent press of her body against his back. Her fingers drifted beneath his loin covering, lingering to fondle the warm extension of his manhood, caressing until it grew and throbbed and went hot and hard. Suddenly, with an unexpected growl, he grabbed her by one arm and jerked her forward. She went sprawling.

"Woman. Get away from me. You carry life within you, I cannot join with you."

She moved quickly to crouch in abject deference before him. "Ban-ya is Shateh's slave, not his woman. Look. My hair is shorn. My spirit is weak. This night Shateh's woman Senohnim has given him a son. The life that a slave carries is nothing compared to this. But the gladness that this slave feels for her chieftain is great. She wishes only to add to his joy."

This said, before he could command her away again, she reached to undo the thong ties that held her dress by one short run of lacing. One twist of the ties, and they were undone. As the garment collapsed around her hips, she straightened, tucked in her lower back, extended her chest, and slowly moved for him. She cupped her great breasts and extended them with her palms. "These are for Shateh on this night of pleasure. Why should the chieftain deny himself release within this willing slave?"

She saw his face tighten and heard his intake of breath. His eyes devoured what she offered. She sat back, her knees widely parted, and as she slowly lay back, the man followed to lie over her. As he penetrated, she knew that he was hers . . . and that she must love him as though he were Dakan-eh . . . as though it would be the last loving she would ever give to a man . . . a loving that would take the haunted look from this chieftain's eyes and make him believe he was young again.

He took her. Holding her wrists, looking into her face as he drove deep, Shateh moved toward climax on the writhing woman, then pulled back, poised motionless to delay the pleasure. He saw the desperation in Ban-ya's eyes and knew that all that she was yielding to him now was not truly for him, but for herself—a mad, despairing, hungry reaching out to life. Could he fault her? Only a dull-minded woman would have failed to see the threat that the birth of Senohnim's son presented to her. But then, no matter what Ban-ya did or said in this band, there was always a threat to the continued existence of Lizard Woman within it.

But he could allow no harm to come to her now. Senohnim's newborn son was so puny and pale, it might not live until dawn. For this reason the drums beat on and on,

and his people danced and sang and clapped their hands
with what appeared to be resounding joy. Spirit Sucker must
be tricked into thinking that the child was strong and fit for
survival. Then Death would go on its way this night to feed
in the footsteps of wolves. If Spirit Sucker was not fooled,
the child would die, and the people would blame Ban-ya. He
had no doubt that Wehakna would make sure of that, as
would Atonashkeh.

And Shateh had no doubt that his woman of the Red
World would stand up to their hatred and accusation as
boldly as she had before, desperately and brazenly conjuring
lies in which to shield herself from their desire to see her
dead. What a bold and magnificent woman she was! What
sons she would give him!

His mouth tightened. But how could he keep her? She
was a source of antagonism between his people and him.
Guilt moved within him to dull his pleasure . . . but only
a little as he began to move again. He knew he should not
have taken her from her man and son; he should have
foreseen what must await her among the women of his tribe.
They would never accept her. Even if Ban-ya gave him a
son equal to her bold nature, she would be resented and
hated for it, and the child would never be accepted unless
taken from her breast and raised by another. Impatience
touched him. This was no time to think. It was a time to act.
His hands moved to cup her buttocks, to open her wider as
he pulled her hips high so that, at the moment of ejaculation,
he would be deep enough to touch that magical place within
a woman from which all life and pleasure came.

In answer her body opened like a flower in the sun,
took him deep, then closed and flexed, rousing sensations of
such exquisite delight that they bordered on pain as she led
him in the dance that no woman had ever performed for him
with the perfection that she was dancing it now.

Release came with a ferocity that stunned him. With a
gasping cry she brought him to the heights, then fell with
him sobbing as he collapsed onto her—not like an exhausted old man but like a youth who has discovered the
immediate capacity to seek more of that which has just
drawn the fire of life from him. He rolled to one side and

stared at her as she lay beside him in the darkness. He traced the contours of her face and body with his hand, then frowned as his fingers encountered the moisture of tears on her cheeks and the warm wetness of milk upon her breasts. Tears he could understand, but the presence of milk puzzled him; once life had taken root within her, milk should have ceased to flow.

"Still? Even now?" He bent his head to mouth her breasts as he whispered gently, "I know that it was cruel of me to take your son from you, but a woman with a suckling at her breasts does not take new life into her belly. And it is life that I seek from you—a son as strong and bold as his mother. A son to make Shateh proud! A son to—" He paused, disturbed not only by the sudden vehemence that had come into his voice, but by the fact that he had spoken his thoughts to the woman at all. Had she seen into his heart? Had she guessed that the newest offspring of Senohnim was a grave disappointment to its sire?

She was shivering violently. From fear of him or from the cold, he could not tell; but it *was* cold within the lodge. He sat up, reached for his robe, and then, seeking to please her, retrieved the coyote-skin cloak and placed it over her as he lay down beside her. Watching Ban-ya pull the cloak close and draw it around herself, he found himself frowning again.

"This robe . . . why is it so important to you?"

For a moment she did not speak. Then, in a whisper, she said, "It is mine, something of my own people. I have made it from the finest skins that Dakan-eh had taken for me—skins stripped from the bodies of animals that were sacred to one who was our enemy. As long as I wear this robe, his power cannot touch me."

"Whose power, woman?"

She sat up and pulled the robe tightly around her shoulders. When she looked at him, her eyes were flashing bright, even in the darkness.

"Cha-kwena!"

He shook his head. "You truly believe this, Ban-ya? I remember Cha-kwena from the days when our peoples briefly encamped together in the country of your ancestors.

He was a boy with a brave heart. When the fighting was over and the peoples went their separate ways, it must have taken courage for him to part company with Dakan-eh and follow his totem beyond the edge of the world.''

"After he had stolen the sacred stone of our ancestors, what need had he of courage?" she asked bitterly. "He was Shaman! With his bad magic he drove our totem before him and left my people nothing!'' Her face worked with loathing and with something else that Shateh could not identify in the darkness. "If Shateh would speak of courage, let him speak then of Dakan-eh, who dared to lead his people north when he had no totem, no sacred talisman, no shaman to speak for his band! Only a man of great heart would have been so brave for the sake of his people that he would dare to seek the fellowship of Shateh and his warrior tribe.''

"I have not come into my lodge this night to speak of Dakan-eh, Ban-ya. It is *life* I seek—a *son* before I die forever! A strong, *worthy* infant through whom I may be born again into this life. Give me such a son, and I swear to you upon the Four Winds that I will take you to your people. With my own hands I will put your firstborn boy to suckle at your breasts again and stand aside while you lie again with your bold, lizard-eating first man. Give me a son, Ban-ya, and this man, Shateh, will ask nothing of you ever again . . . and whatever you may ask of me in the days and nights to come will be accomplished.''

"Then I ask you to join with Dakan-eh to seek our true enemies beyond the edge of the world, and bring death to Cha-kwena and all those who followed him.''

"It will be so," Shateh promised. "Just give me a son, and it will be so.''

4

Cha-kwena was puzzled because things seemed to be going reasonably well for his band. But the totem was dead. The shaman had lost all faith in magic. No longer did he look to the sacred stone for vision. When he chanted and raised smokes upon which he sent a shaman's prayers to the forces of Creation for Gahti's sake, he did so because it was expected of him. His heart was not in his words, for he held absolutely no belief that anyone or anything existed beyond this world that could hear, much less heed, his prayers.

Nevertheless, Gah-ti's wounds were healing—slowly, but they *were* healing—and Mah-ree still insisted that with the proper care his arm would grow back. Siwi-ni also assured her son that this was so. The little woman of Kosar-eh remained wan and tired, but she had milk enough for her fretful infant. The newest addition to her prodigious family brought delight to little Joh-nee and Tla-nee. The two girls spent their days watching as Siwi-ni changed swaddling and bathed the child's bottom with cleansing washes made by Ha-xa and U-wa from recipes handed down through the generations of the band's mothers and guaranteed to prevent "bottom redness" in babies. Ta-maya rocked the baby while Siwi-ni slept, kissed her when she fussed, and scolded away the dogs when they came close.

Although Mah-ree often called for her lost Friend and the other missing dogs, none returned. Scar Nose, however, had whelped a litter of thirteen pups. Four among the litter were stillborn, and the rest were suffering from suppurating eyes as well as diarrhea. Neither condition was unusual in puppies, and Mah-ree made special poultices for their eyes and tended to their needs with the same love and concern that she showed to the sick and wounded among her people.

Already the cave was stocked with nearly enough provisions to ensure survival during the harshest winter . . . but the weather had stabilized, so the band enjoyed the warm, fragrant days and cool, dry nights of autumn. Hardwoods flamed red, yellow, and orange among the evergreens. Goldenrod shone in the wetland meadows, and rabbit bush exploded yellow on the sage flats. Crisp grasses crackled in the wind. Great wedges of birds winged from the north to feed upon ripe seeds and to settle upon the lake in vast flotillas of honkings and quackings and cheepings. There were herons in the shallows now, and great, long-necked, high-plumed cranes. At all hours of the day and night the sounds of birds talking and splashing on the water came up to the cave.

Since Gah-ti's injury, Kosar-eh had been solemn and introspective. He spoke rarely in relaxed conversation and avoided words with Ta-maya entirely; but he worked his right arm and hand constantly until slowly, painfully, he was able to put them to many tasks that he had learned to accomplish without them. He set himself to teach his younger boys how to fashion birding decoys out of wood and reeds, an art that had been useless to them once they had traveled beyond the Mountains of Sand and left the many saline lakes of the Red World behind them. When skillfully placed and accompanied by his masterful birdcalls, the little wooden-headed, reed-bodied decoys drew many a gullible waterfowl toward the shallows where U-wa, Ha-xa, and Ta-maya waited with their birding slings.

At Siwi-ni's urging, Kosar-eh also had the youths wading shoulder deep into the lake as he instructed them in the age-old game of "catch-a-coot." Disguised as clumps of vegetation in high hats of reeds, they overcame their fear of water and learned to swim as they followed their father well out from shore to insinuate themselves among great, gibbering rafts of black, red-eyed coots. It took a few days before they mastered the sport, but soon each boy—except for Klah-neh, the youngest—was fully capable of floating amid the unsuspecting coots, and then, at just the right moment, of grabbing the feet of a bird with one hand and jerking it underwater, then breaking its neck with his free hand. In this manner, one boy could loop as many as six coots to a line attached to his waist before frog kicking back to shore and striding manfully back to the cave. There the women would promptly skin, then spit, boil, or roast the stringy, red-fleshed little water birds, and the boys could be sure that Siwi-ni would boast of their hunting prowess as energetically as she boasted of their lion-hunting older brother.

Waterfowl were not the only birds to be smoked or roasted for winter eating. Every day the women set snares and net traps for small seed and insect eaters. Once scorched free of feathers, the little birds made crunchy cooked snacks for the children. U-wa supervised the women in the weaving of quail-catching baskets—long, narrow, tubular devices closed at one end that were baited with seeds and berries, then set out upon the land in invitation to any foolish quail that would bow in for an easy meal, only to find itself unable to straighten or turn around. Holes carefully spaced in the top of the basket would encourage curious quail to poke their heads up and through for a look around. Even though escape from the predicament would have entailed merely bending their heads and backing up, the birds' inability to reason held them fast. U-wa, Ha-xa, and Ta-maya brought their baskets back to the cave laden with dull-witted quail haplessly peeking through the holes and made them a source of education.

"Do not be like Quail!" cautioned Ha-xa. "Always be wary of that which comes too easily in life!"

"And before you lead your brothers blindly into trouble, look around so that you may avoid dangers that you do not see!" added U-wa, then looked over her shoulder, hopeful that Gah-ti had not overheard.

"And if you do get into trouble, make sure that you look around doubly hard, for there may be an escape route if you will only use your head!" embellished Ta-maya.

As for the quail, they lost their heads. Their softly feathered skins and their curling little topknots were taken, cured, and set aside for future sewing into children's clothes, and their succulent, meaty, pink bodies were spitted for immediate eating or slow roasted and then smoked with sage under special cones of hide so that they might be preserved for future enjoyment.

Many a day saw Cha-kwena, Kosar-eh, and the boys off on hunts for deer and antelope. In the way of their ancestors the hunters set deadfall traps for rabbits, squirrels, and whatever small game might blunder into the deadly snares. The sun never set before they successfully carried home the edible and preservable portions of their prey. By night, in the fire's glow, the men and boys worked at stone knapping while the women dressed skins, made thread out of fiber, and sewed. They talked and talked, and all seemed to agree that Cha-kwena and their totem had brought them to a very fine land—everyone, that is, except Cha-kwena.

While the women and children laughed and spoke happily—even Gah-ti and the moody Kosar-eh found heart to join them in occasional boisterous rounds of song—Cha-kwena remained desolate, sleepless, tormented by secrets. He tried to understand why he felt so restless while everything was going so well. Yes, he had killed the totem; but Life Giver had been only a mammoth after all. Even though it now lay dead in that hidden, bloodied arm of the lake beyond the hills, the People prospered. Obviously its death meant nothing. Grandfather of All was only one less mammoth in a world where mammoth were rare, anyway.

Why was he constantly possessed by the need to break and run, to rouse his people and tell them that they must leave this "wonderful" valley? With Gah-ti and Siwi-ni unfit for travel, how could he speak the words? And what would their reaction be when he told them that he had killed the great white mammoth and that their shaman was a shaman no more? Would they believe him? And more important, would they ever forgive him?

He was hostile to Mah-ree when she shyly came to him with questions about what was troubling him, and when she asked if he had seen or heard the totem, he assured her with a nasty snarl that he saw and heard Life Giver all the time—but that he saw it only in his dreams. Soon even U-wa, who was used to his moods, avoided conversation with him. Often he found Kosar-eh watching him from beneath speculatively lowered brows, and not even the soft words of the fair Ta-maya could bring a smile to Cha-kwena's face.

He was often silent on the hunt. Even when he worked with the others to clear away the rubble of an ancient rockfall to expose and widen the access to the spring that Gah-ti had discovered, he found no joy in his labor. When the dogs came near, he drove them away. Whenever Coyote came to sit silently below the cave in the night, Cha-kwena, sensing its presence, would hurl stones at it until it ran away.

Now, often in the night when the others slept and he could not, he passed his time exploring the deepest recesses of the cave by the light of a stone tallow lamp borrowed from U-wa. Carrying extra fat-impregnated wicks, oil, and flints, he ventured into tunnel after tunnel, dead-end hollow after dead-end hollow, and into several passages that led him out of the cave entirely and into the starlight on the far side of the hills. By these tunnels the lion had come and gone. Then, one night, following a narrow, unpromising fissure that he had overlooked before, he came into a wide, low ceilinged cavern that stole his breath away. There, barely discernible upon the pale back wall, was the form of a mammoth—massive, head high, tusks reaching into darkness. Cha-kwena gasped and stared in disbelief, ready to whirl and flee if the beast broke out of the rock and ran at him. With an exhalation of relief, he realized that the thing was only a trick of the torchlight as it flickered across the uneven contours of the stone.

Cha-kwena moved closer, held his lamp high, and slowly traced his hand along the wall. Memories came to him—for a change these were gentle, soothing memories of the long-gone nights of his boyhood, when he had stood with Hoyeh-tay at the back of his grandfather's sacred cave and watched the old man as he painted upon the wall images of the history and legends and day-to-day lives of their people. After Hoyeh-tay's death, when Cha-kwena had become shaman and the cave had been ritually cleansed and made new for him by fire, he had made brushes of his own out of wood and cattails and animal hair and had revived Hoyeh-tay's images with fresh colors made of pounded mineral pigments mixed with animal fat and with white, red, and green clay brought from the shores of the Lake of Many Singing Birds. He had also painted new images and in this act had freed his spirit of the pain that had come to him after the old man had been slain.

Perhaps, he wondered, it might be so again?

And so it was that Cha-kwena, driven by a new purpose, returned to the main room of the cave. Dawn found him out and about the valley, collecting all that he needed to construct brushes and to fashion lamps of his own so that the cavern would be adequately lighted for the work that he intended to set himself to now. Painstakingly he sought the right plants and rocks that, when ground and mixed with fat and scrapings from newly taken skins, would yield moist, rich colors. These could be applied with ease and would not crack or chip away when the paints dried upon the stone. Along the lakeshore he gathered duck manure and set it to dry on a wide square of hide, which he laid in the sun at the lip of the cave. Later he would mix it with water, and the result would be a fine summer-sky blue. He collected kindling and small pieces of wood, which could be carried into the cavern to warm him in the long dark days and nights that he intended to remain within the hollow of the hill and from which he could take ashes and pulverized scorched wood to use as black coloring for his artwork.

His people watched him. They knew what he was about and, excited, offered to be of help; but although he accepted gifts of oil and wicks from his mother, he refused all other efforts of assistance and told his people that the painting would not be for their eyes.

"It will be for the eyes of the grandson of Hoyeh-tay only," he said.

Mah-ree nodded knowingly. "It will be a sign to the spirits of this land and to the forces of Creation that our shaman has found a place that is sacred and magic to him, and it will be his offering to the spirits of the ancestors in honor of the memory of First Man and First Woman and to Life Giver!''

Cha-kwena eyed her thoughtfully. How much faith she still had in him and in all that she had been raised to hold sacrosanct and beyond question! But then, what cause had she to question him? He was still Shaman in her eyes!

When Cha-kwena finished gathering and moving everything he needed, he entered the perpetual darkness of the cavern. He had already transferred his belongings, and U-wa had prepared enough food to last him for many days. For a long time he stood in the soft, dusky orange glow of the single lamp that had lighted his way, staring at the wall and at the strange formation in the rock.

The mammoth was still there. As Cha-kwena moved the lamp back and forth, the formation in the stone seemed to follow the light, to raise its massive limbs and tusks, and, sighing, it seemed to push against the rock as though . . .

Suddenly, with a ragged catch of breath, hope caught fire within Cha-kwena's spirit. He touched his medicine bag. Once again, as had not happened for all too long, the sacred stone within was warm against his palm. He closed his eyes. Was it possible? Was the totem somehow still alive? Was it here, within the cavern, trapped within the wall? Was he still, somehow, Shaman? And might he still hope to release the totem's power so that it might serve his people? Trembling, he placed his lamp upon the ground and prepared to find out.

Cha-kwena did not know how long he worked. For several days he did not take the time to eat. He was unaware that he raised a fire and kept it burning until his supply of firewood ran out. He refilled the oil in his lamps many times, even though he did not recall refilling them. He knew only that he began his work with a single touch of color—the imprint of his own right hand against the stone made first in white to signify the mark of a shaman, then overlaid in precious red ochre to verify the humanity of the artist who made the mark. After that his spirit bled away into the work, and he knew no more until, exhausted, he found himself standing in stunned silence before what had been a blank wall to see that it had been transformed.

It was alive with color and pattern, a vast intricately detailed depiction of the story of the People. It was all there, everything that he had ever been told about the ancestors, and somehow even more. In the center of the wall, in bold relief and as large as life, was the great white mammoth, the raised rock that delineated its form outlined in stark white. Within the body of the totem the story was told. Cha-kwena recognized First Man and First Woman as they led their children on their wondrous journey out of the north. The many children of First Man and First Woman were shown walking across the mountaintops into the Red World, and then the tale of Cha-kwena's band began and culminated in the coming of the People of the Land of Grass and the separation of the many bands. He frowned as he observed the bloody story of the great war and of the killing of many mammoth and men. He saw Dakan-eh walking away to take his place among strange tribes, then looked at the saga of his own flight across the Mountains of Sand, over the edge of the world, and into the wondrous valley.

Now his breath came fast and shallow. There were the painted renderings of the black moon, the early rain, the rising of the north wind, the circling of eagles, and the gathering of ravens. He saw the birth of Doh-teyah, and Gah-ti's hunting of the lion, and Kosar-eh's miraculous confrontation with and slaying of the beast. He saw himself entwined with Mah-ree upon the monolith beneath the streaking fire of shooting stars. He saw Coyote leading the dogs in the savaging of the mammoth, and he saw himself killing the totem in the lake.

Suddenly he was inexplicably shaken, light-headed, and then buoyed by inspiration. If all that had already transpired was on the wall, might he not also paint that which could be? The past could not be undone, but what about the future? Could it be made to happen?

Using the few paints that were left, he worked as though possessed. He painted Gah-ti with his arm restored. He painted Siwi-ni dancing. He painted the great white mammoth reborn and rising from the lake. He painted the totem whole and unscarred and powerful. And when the painting was complete, he sank to his knees and gripped the sacred stone and whispered to the forces of Creation. "Let it be!" he pleaded fervently. "Give me the heart to be Shaman again!"

He emerged from the cavern to find his people asleep. The cave was bathed in moonlight. His eyes strayed to where Siwi-ni dozed against her backrest, with her faithful attendant, Ta-maya, asleep close by. The old woman appeared to be breathing more easily than usual. Hope stirred within Cha-kwena as he moved his glance to where Gah-ti lay; but the shaman could not be sure whether or not the youth's arm had sprouted from its stump. *Perhaps!* he thought. *Perhaps even as I watch, it is growing back!*

Now, far across the land, the distant trumpeting of tuskers caused his heart to leap. The dogs raised their heads as, in absolute silence, he took up a spear and began a solemn nighttime pilgrimage back to the place where the mammoth went to die.

Ta-maya propped herself onto an elbow and watched him go. The moon was so bright, so beautiful. She sighed as disappointment replaced the joy that her ebbing dreams had brought to her. Her one love had been with her again.

"Masau . . ." She whispered his name with longing and inestimable sadness. It was only Cha-kwena's passage across the cave that she had sensed, not the longed-for coming of Masau's ghostly figure. She often sensed Mystic Warrior's presence close to her by day, and his frequent appearance within her dreams gave her the heart to greet each new dawn. She closed her eyes. Since her warm response to Kosar-eh's kiss, her dreams had been troubled. No longer did the ghost of Masau come close to enfold her in his arms, assure her of his love, and breathe upon her in the wind so that she would know he was beside her, waiting for the moment when she would come to him. She knew that she had offended him. Now he stood at the edges of her dreams. His long, powerful arms were extended, and his face was set against pain as he called to her across the misted distances between the worlds of the living and the dead and begged her not to forget him.

"Masau . . . Masau . . . you must know that I would come to you if I could." She sighed as she lay back and tried to sleep again, hopeful of finding him in her dreams again, of reaching out to him and somehow locating a bridge that would accept the weight of her spirit and allow her to leave the confinement of her body and join him among the spirits.

A sharp nudge to her back caused her to sit up again. "What is it, Siwi-ni?" Ta-maya whispered. "Do you need water or—"

"I need to stop you from speaking the name of the dead in the night!" the old woman whispered. She looked pale and pinched in the moonlight, blue lipped and sunken eyed.

"But his spirit is with me."

Siwi-ni shook her head, then turned her face upward and spoke words that had Ta-maya staring, aghast. "If you can hear me, Masau, Mystic Warrior, son of Shateh, and warrior priest of the People of the Watching Star, remember that you once loved Ta-maya enough to give up your life for her! Now that you are dead, if you still love her, let her spirit go! Let her remember that life is sweet and all too short, that there are many who need her here, and that there is another who would fill her days as well as her nights with a man's love."

"Siwi-ni, stop!" Ta-maya's command was as softly spoken as it was emphatic. "I am the woman of Masau! I am in mourning. I will never take another man!"

"Hmm." Siwi-ni gestured weakly to where Kosar-eh slept beside Gah-ti. "There is one who wants you. And here is one who can no longer be a woman for the best and bravest of all men."

Ta-maya's face flamed in the moonlight. "No, Siwi-ni! You are the woman of Kosar-eh, always and forever! Soon you will be well and strong again for your man. You *will!*"

"*Someone* must be strong for him! He suffers much over poor Gah-ti. Kosar-eh tries so hard to pretend that what he feels for me is man-woman love, but I know that it has never been that. I was all that a one-armed clown might hope for in a woman, and he has loved me enough to have given me many children and to have been my friend."

"Siwi-ni, you must not speak so! You—"

"Who will look to my man's needs as sweetly as you look to mine, dear one? Masau is long dead. Someday, in another world, your spirits will walk the wind together. But now you are young and alive. If you care about this old woman, you will promise to look after her man when Spirit Sucker takes her away."

"Go back to sleep, Siwi-ni!"

"I will not sleep again until you promise!"

Ta-maya kissed the woman on her brow. Siwi-ni's imperious behavior seemed to indicate her imminent return to health. "Then sleep. I promise to care for your man. But I tell you, woman of Kosar-eh, you are stubborn enough to make yourself a bone in the throat of Spirit Sucker. If he ever comes for you, he will spit you out, and you will live forever!"

"You have been a good friend to me, Ta-maya," said the older woman. Content now, she snuggled down in her furs, kissed the top of her new daughter's head, closed her eyes, and said no more.

Cha-kwena walked lightly and in silence across the land. In his hand the sacred stone was warm within his medicine bag. His spirit was as eager as it was apprehensive. Now and then he thought he saw the shadows of a fur-clad old man and a coyote trotting on ahead, but he could not be certain. At last he came through the far hills and moved amid the moonlit skeletons of countless mammoth. Reaching the shore of the lake in which he had killed Life Giver, Cha-kwena hunkered down, disappointed that the corpse of his totem was still there.

The herd of mammoth browsed close by along the shore, continuing its watch over the body. The great freckled cow saw him, raised her trunk, and twitched her ears as she shook her head and trumpeted a warning . . . or a welcome.

Emptiness pervaded Cha-kwena's spirit. Under the cold, compassionless face of the full moon, his hope was now as dead as the totem. He rose slowly, feeling drained as he lifted the sacred stone from around his neck. As though in a dream, in a final act of utter futility, he hurled the talisman high over the lake.

"There is no magic!" he cried. "There is nothing here for me! Or for my people! Nothing!"

The talisman was about to hit the water and sink. But suddenly, in the light of the watching moon, an owl flew from out of nowhere to snatch it up and wing off with it.

"Follow me, Cha-kwena!" called the bird. "Bring the People! Follow me now in the face of the rising sun! It is not too late!"

"Winter is coming," Cha-kwena called back. "My people are sick. I cannot ask them to leave this place. And even if I could, where would I lead them?" He cursed himself for a fool. "You are not real, bird! Nothing that I have ever sought is real!"

"Life Giver will show you the way, Shaman!"

"I am no shaman! There is no magic. There are no spirits. Life Giver is dead! I have killed him, and he will not rise again!"

Suddenly the night was unbearably cold. The wind gusted hard from the north, and in the blink of an eye, Owl disappeared into the face of the moon. Cha-kwena glared after the bird.

"You are not real!" he cried, feeling even more despondent than before. "Go! Fly where you will trouble me no more!" He turned and trudged back to the cave.

Spirit Sucker returned to the cave before him. In Cha-kwena's absence Death had come to take the life spirit of Siwi-ni to the world beyond this world. For four days and nights the band mourned the loss of the feisty little woman. Cha-kwena fasted and prayed, as was expected of the shaman. Although his obligatory attendance to ritual was at first lackluster, it soon became ferocious with anger, bitterness, and disappointment. Those who watched were puzzled by his emotional display until U-wa shook her head and said that she had no idea that her son had loved Siwi-ni so much.

In the way of the ancestors of the People of the Red World, the women cleansed the body and anointed it with oil that had been colored with precious ocher, so that the blood of the living earth would be with Siwi-ni in the spirit world. They combed her graying hair and festooned it with feathers that would carry her spirit high into the world beyond this world. They adorned her with her favorite necklace and nose ring and with matching wristlets and anklets of tiny freshwater shells and bone beads dyed bright blue. They dressed her in her favorite sandals and skirt of knotted fibers, then wrapped her rabbit-skin cloak around her shoulders so she would be warm and presentable when she came before the ancestors. At last they enveloped her body within a woven shroud of reeds and carried it to the funeral pyre, which the men and boys had made at the entrance to the cave.

It had been no easy task bringing the deadwood up from the forest, but even little Klah-neh had carried his load without complaint. Everyone wanted Siwi-ni's body to have a great burning so that the essence of her living form would rise quickly to be united with her spirit in the world beyond.

Finally, in the first glow of the fourth dawn, the body was settled in a seated position upon the pyre, leaning against the beautiful backrest that Kosar-eh had made for her. Her belongings were placed beside her, and presents of food were brought in little funerary baskets and arrayed around her body, along with strings of feathers and beads, a bundle of beautifully cured rabbit skins, coils of fine fiber thread, and a quill case filled with fine bone sewing needles so that she might sew lovely new clothes for herself in the spirit world. With each offering, a good-bye was spoken, along with a ''watch over me from the spirit world, Siwi-ni, woman of Kosar-eh, for I will remember you until Spirit Sucker brings me to join you in the world beyond this world.''

When all was finally said and done, Cha-kwena knelt before the pyre and, with his bow drill whirling between his palms, roused fire from dry grass kindling. In a few moments the pyre was aflame. The band stood together in a half circle, facing the rising sun as their shaman raised his arms, threw back his head, and sang the traditional song that called upon the Four Winds to take the spirit of their sister Siwi-ni to dwell forever among the ancestors.

After the song was done and the people had turned away to sit in doleful silence within the cave, Mah-ree came to Cha-kwena and, with a gentle touch, asked him why he did not wear his medicine bag.

He glared. "The stone is where it belongs!"

"Where, Cha-kwena?" Her expression told him that he would have to offer a better explanation than that.

He frowned. He could never tell her the truth, but he would have to tell her something that would take the questions from her eyes. "In the Red World Hoyeh-tay kept the sacred stone enshrined at the back of his cave, didn't he? Now that I have brought my people into this 'wonderful' valley, should I not do the same?"

"But how will the spirits of the ancestors recognize your song for Siwi-ni's spirit if you do not hold the sacred stone up to the sun and let its powers sing with yours?"

"Will Medicine Girl tell Shaman the proper times to wear the sacred stone when she cannot make medicine to heal a sick old woman?"

Mah-ree caught her breath, hung her head, and turned away, ashamed.

Later, after the ashes of Siwi-ni's pyre cooled and while the people slept, Kosar-eh hunkered before the burned remains of his woman. The next day, with the rising sun, the people would sweep the ashes into the wind, and all physical evidence of Siwi-ni's life would be gone.

"She will live in her sons and daughter, Kosar-eh," said Ta-maya softly, kneeling beside him. "Come back to your fire circle now. Klah-neh cannot sleep and would be eased by the presence of his father."

"You need not trouble yourself with my boys, Ta-maya. Ka-neh will ease his brother until I—"

"I am now the woman of your fire circle, Kosar-eh. It is no trouble for me to be concerned for your sons or your daughter. Before Siwi-ni's spirit walked the wind, she honored me by asking me to take her place at your fire. To ease her heart I vowed to her that this would be so. Now I honor that vow. I will care for you and for your children as though you and they were my own.''

Too stunned to speak, he stared at her.

Misconstruing his gape-jawed silence for rejection, she lowered her eyes and confided in a whisper, ''I know that I can never be to you what Siwi-ni has been all these years. I know that your love for her is deep. I know that now, as you mourn her death, you long to be with her in the spirit world, even as I yearn to be with my own lost love. But until we both walk the wind and are reunited with our beloved, Kosar-eh, someone must be a woman for you and a mother for your children. I will keep your fire and cook your food. I will sew your garments and tend your children. I will spread myself for you when you have a man's need, and if there are children born to us, their birth will gladden my heart. I will obey you in everything you may command, Brother of My Heart. I will not break my vow to a dying woman. I am Siwi-ni's last gift to Kosar-eh. Dear Friend, I will be your woman.''

Brother. Dear Friend. The words cut deeply into Kosar-eh's pride. He remained mute, shattered by his emotions. Had there ever been a time when he had *not* wanted Ta-maya, longed for her, ached with need of her, desired her so much that he had wished his own woman dead! And now, with the stench of his woman's funeral pyre rising into his nostrils, Kosar-eh had his wish. Siwi-ni *was* dead. Ta-maya *was* his. But she did not want him as Man. He was Brother. He was Dear Friend. He had only to extend his hand, and bound by the vow that she had made to one whom he had wished dead, she would take him!

A deep tremor shook him to his spirit and beyond. In a turmoil of guilt and confusion, he turned away from the woman he had always wanted and still loved. ''Serve me with obedience then,'' he said. ''Leave me. I cannot bear to look at you now.''

5

Three times now had Shateh moved his camp farther south along the river. The raiders had not come again . . . until today.

Awakened by the low growl of distant thunder and by the cries of his people, the chieftain ran from his lodge to be informed by Teikan that a woman had been attacked and killed by wolves in the night.

"Wolves who walk upright on two legs," informed Indeh darkly as others gathered in grim silence around the mutilated corpse. "It was the snarling of feeding animals that drew me to her, but I think this woman of Nakantahkeh's was dead before the wolves found her. Even though I drove them off, there is not much left of her. But I think you can see that this gash in her throat is too clean to have been made by wolves. It appears to have been made by the blade of a man."

Shateh appraised the torn remains of the woman, then shook his head. "Too often did the mother of Wila wander alone from her sleeping furs at night to walk the peripheries of the encampment, where she wailed and mourned for want of her children. You have said that when you found her, her bloodied skinning knife was at her side. Perhaps in her grief, she cut her own throat? This has happened before among our people. In times of sadness and war and death, the life spirits of women are weakened."

"I tell you, Shateh, men did this. Men with knives," said Teikan with contained frustration and anger. "Nakantahkeh will have more cause than ever to convince the others to go with us against our enemies! When he returns with Xiaheh and the other chiefs and warriors, he will mourn again."

Shateh knelt, examined the wounds, and nodded in agreement. He commanded Teikan to take a small party of men and see what luck they would have in trailing the raiders. "I want to know from which direction they have come. Learn this, then return. When Nakantahkeh comes back from the north with Xiaheh and the others, we will put a stop to these raids forever!"

"*If* Nakantahkeh returns," snarled Atonashkeh venomously, fixing his feverish eyes upon Ban-ya. "Would that all of our women had life spirits as strong as Shateh's slave's—spirits powerful enough to send their hatred against those who have done this to Nakantahkeh's woman. Surely the lizard eater sends her hatred to work death upon the People of the Land of Grass!"

Hostile eyes turned Ban-ya's way as she stepped close to Shateh and waited for him to speak in her defense.

He did not fail her. "This slave carries a son of Shateh!" he reminded them all with a snap of temper.

"Perhaps . . . perhaps not," slurred Atonashkeh with a sneer that pulled his unnaturally sallow-looking features tight across his face. He slapped his chest. "Here is Shateh's son! And there, in the arms of the woman Senohnim, is another of Shateh's sons. Why should Shateh care what grows in the belly of a lizard eater?"

The chieftain's face tightened. "The son of Senohnim is weak and puny! The life spirit of Shateh cannot be reborn into the world through such a child. I have not given that son my name! I have given it your name instead, Atonashkeh, as a gift to one who has challenged his chieftain all too often and, because of this, has fallen from the favor of the forces of Creation and can make no more sons at all!"

Senohnim hung her head in shame.

Atonashkeh, leaning on a hardwood staff that allowed him to stand and walk in a way that lessened the pain of his wound, shook as though a gale had struck him. "Too often do you shame me without cause, my father!"

"Without cause?" Shateh's head went up angrily.

"Are you still man enough to threaten me, Atonashkeh? That is good. I had come to think that you had only enough courage left in you to speak against defenseless slaves. I have had enough of your bad talk against me and mine. This slave, Ban-ya, has called the bison to come to this people! This slave is Shateh's slave! You will not speak against her! Any of you! Now the trackers will go from camp! Now my people must prepare to mourn in the way of the ancestors—again!"

Shateh was torn. All day long, after performing the obligatory rituals of a shaman and chief, he brooded alone while his people mourned the death of Nakantahkeh's woman. Ban-ya watched him. She needed no supernatural vision to tell her what was on his mind. Until today things had been improving for his band. But the raiders had struck again, and Atonashkeh had, predictably, blamed her for bringing them. Shateh's people were restless, and the death of a slave might go a long way to appease their fears, even if the chieftain no longer believed that she was the source of their bad luck. As she went to him Ban-ya knew all too well that her life was still in jeopardy. Were it not for her feigned pregnancy, the chieftain would kill her with his own hands for the good of all, or put her out of the band to die within the storms of winter or to fall easy prey to carnivores.

"Shateh's son *is* here," she said, taking his hand and placing it upon her abdomen. "I feel him. He grows strong. Soon he will leap so boldly in my belly that Shateh will feel the movement against his palm. My chieftain must think of this and not weaken his spirit with grief."

Shateh looked at her out of tired eyes. "I am weary of death, Ban-ya. I long for the sun in these days of early snow and sadness."

Her heartbeat quickened. "Then take your people farther south! Bring them to winter in the Red World! For the past two winters you have done this. Dakan-eh has welcomed you and will welcome you again despite the hard words that have passed between you. Your people will bask and heal in the winter warmth of the country of my ancestors, and the People of the Red World will sing with pleasure to see the fine hump steaks and robes that Shateh would bring to them from the north."

"And Ban-ya would rejoice to be reunited with her Bold Man and her firstborn." He shook his head. "No. Not until you give me that which I seek from you. Not until I have my son—a *strong* son, a *bold* son, a boy in whom this man's spirit and name may live again in honor and pride after his death."

How much he yearned for that child! And how well he knew her—at least that part of her that longed for her Piku-neh and her homeland. *And yet,* Ban-ya wondered, *how well do I know myself?* For at this moment as she appraised the chieftain, a strange and unfamiliar softness for him lived in her heart. His scarred, weathered features were not unlike the land that had borne him: wide and high and handsome, harshly defined by the wind and elements, often hard and unforgiving. Yet sometimes—as now—his face was as soothing to her eyes as the curve of the gentlest hills. He was as old as he was handsome, and she knew that he could be merciless as he stood implacable before the bitter winds of his responsibilities as shaman and chief, as though he carried the world on his back. That was not because he wished to be cruel but because he knew that he alone was strong enough to bear the burden for the good of all.

But for how long? The question troubled her. What would happen to her if Atonashkeh succeeded in undermining Shateh's authority? The answer was clear enough: Shateh alone stood between her and the enmity of his people. A cold shiver ran up her spine. During these past days since the hunt and the birth of Senohnim's boy, the band's hostility toward her had not been as focused. She had gone out of her way to make herself useful, to be subservient and smooth-tongued to all, including Atonashkeh. Her efforts had won an occasional nod and grunt of begrudging approval from many, but no amount of deference had drawn the poison from the eyes of the chieftain's son, nor had kind words or thoughtful actions on her part lessened Senohnim's jealous loathing. Senohnim's hatred of her—and of the chieftain—had been obvious ever since Shateh, judging the newborn unworthy, had, in a magnanimous gesture that had reeked of contempt, named the sickly child for Atonashkeh. Equally obvious were Shateh's growing affection and concern for his slave.

Ban-ya trembled. The chieftain had been so good to her these past many days and nights that it was becoming increasingly difficult to hate him. Nevertheless, she *did* hate him, for despite his present benevolence, he had forcibly taken her from the man she loved and the son she adored and had raped her when she had refused to yield her body. Even now her beloved Dakan-eh must be sick with yearning, and poor Piku-neh must be growing cranky and colicky on the breast milk of a stranger. If she failed to keep herself in Shateh's favor, she would never see either of them again, and if things did not continue to improve for these people, Atonashkeh might yet succeed in bringing Shateh to believe that she was the cause of his bad luck. What would happen to her then?

Ban-ya felt suddenly light-headed. What if she were abandoned and fell victim to the raiders of the People of the Watching Star? Sheela was with them! A sudden vision of what they had done to Nani and to Nakantahkeh's woman caused her knees to buckle. Her hands strayed upward along the soft fur of her coyote-skin cloak. As long as the raiders remained a threat, she must keep it hidden within her traveling bundle. Sheela would know the robe and seek the woman who wore it, and Ban-ya knew all too well what her fate would be if she ever fell into the hands of her onetime slave! Briefly, solely out of concern for herself, she regretted her many past unkindnesses to Sheela, then wished her dead.

Out of terror and with grim resolve, Ban-ya slipped her arms around Shateh's waist and stepped close to lay her head against his chest. If she did not conceive a child of this man soon, he was bound to discover her deception. Then she would be dead at his hands or on the blades of their enemies long before he returned her to those she loved . . . if she gave him a son. *It is the son that matters more than the woman, more than the band. The strong, bold son that you must make for this man who, more than anything, fears that when he dies he will die forever!*

She began to spin a web of safety for herself and perhaps a filament of words along which Shateh's weary spirit might be drawn to follow a path that would serve them both. "I am glad that you still call me Slave instead of Woman," she whispered. "It is so cold in the Land of Grass of late, and I would not want to spend the nights alone beneath my sleeping furs with only an unborn boy to warm my belly when Shateh is near . . . forbidden to lie on a woman with child but welcome to place himself deep between the thighs of a slave."

His hands took her shoulders, then put her away from him so that his eyes might search her face. "It is forbidden during a time of mourning, and afterward I would not risk this son you will bear to me."

"He welcomes you into the 'lodge' in which he grows, as this slave welcomes you—eagerly."

Her words sent a tremor through him. "You make me feel young again, Ban-ya of the Red World."

"Shateh *is* young!" she told him, greasing his pride and, with it, her own hope of surviving. "When I am in your arms I sometimes wonder if Shateh has not gone beyond the Mountains of Sand and over the edge of the world in his dreams to seek the great white mammoth . . . to hunt it, to eat of its flesh and drink of its blood, to fulfill the legend of our enemies that says that the man who does this will be young forever."

He smiled drolly. "Then I would need no sons or a slave to make them for me." Enfolding her in his arms, he added softly, "I have dreamed many times of eternal life and youth, Ban-ya. With Ban-ya as my woman it would be a good thing, better even than a son to take my name when my spirit walks the wind—to live forever with a bold woman at my side."

She went cold. She had gone too far in her attempts to win his favor! He did not want to give her up! In a panic, she spoke without thinking, "Shateh has promised to return me to my people as reward for the son that I will give him!"

His brows arched upward. "Is it not good between us now, Ban-ya?" he asked quietly.

"Yes!" she affirmed, panic beating in her breast like

the wings of frightened birds. She realized that she must not only give this man a son, but she must take his life into her immediately, so that the time of the child's birth would not prove her to be a liar and deceiver in his eyes. Such betrayal would grant him an excuse to break his vow of honor and keep her forever in the Land of Grass as his slave. "It *is* good!" she assured him, and pressed provocatively close, moving her breasts and hips against him in a slow, unmistakable invitation to sexual union. "May the days and nights of mourning pass quickly so that this slave may lie down beneath her man and open herself to him again!"

"May it be so," he said.

But the days and nights passed slowly for them both. The weather worsened, then lifted only to worsen again. Snow turned to rain, and late in the morning of the second day, when the scouting party returned, the men were sodden, exhausted, and frustrated. They had found no sign of the raiders. Rain continued to fall out of an intermittent cloud cover until the dawn of the sixth day. The eastern horizon was colored with the promise of clearing skies.

In the dank mists of a cool morning, Shateh came to Ban-ya, and she lay beneath him and took him deep.

"It is good between us," he whispered.

"Yes, it is good," she told him, her body afire with his touch. But her spirit was rank with hatred for a young shaman. He had abandoned his people to lives that were now torn and shifting upon the Four Winds.

On that sixth day, under the first completely clear skies in weeks, Shateh led a party of men out to hunt. Ban-ya was called outside to join with the other women, who worked at the preparation of sinew and the pounding of fat from a previous hunt. She savored the welcome warmth of the sun, if not the work at hand. Since inexperience with the northern women's ways of crafting slowed her fingers, she was the last to finish her tasks. Already smoke was rising from the ventilation flaps of the lodges, and Wehakna was impatiently shouting her name from across the encampment, commanding her to come and help raise the bison paunch in which the chieftain's day's-end meal would be simmered.

Ban-ya sighed; there was no reason why Wehakna and Senohnim could not raise the paunch themselves with the help of the girls; but with a slave in their midst—even one favored by the chieftain—they never did it when Shateh was not around to watch them.

Ban-ya got to her feet, gathered her portion of the day's work, and—deliberately ignoring Wehakna—went to relieve herself. Not even a jealous first woman could deny her man's slave the right to void her body waste. With the exception of the littlest children who could not be expected to control such functions, it was not considered acceptable for any but the sick or elderly to make "water" or leave "warm piles" where others might blunder across them.

So, in the privacy of the squatting place of the women, Ban-ya relieved herself and, when she was certain that no one else was about, checked the soft length of deerskin that she kept between her thighs. She lived in terror of the onset of menstruation and in equal terror of its failure to appear. Moon blood would name her Liar. But she could not hope to conceive a child without it. In any event, the doeskin was clean now. Frustrated, she replaced it carefully, then smoothed her skirt. Despite her frequent joinings with the chieftain, there were no signs of pregnancy. Her breasts remained sore, and her milk was diminishing; but she was not sure what to make of this. The chieftain lay upon her so often and took such delight in handling her—often roughly when his passions were aroused—that of course her breasts were tender. As for the milk, if she were with child again, would they not be so? If only she could be sure! If only her grandmother could be with her! Kahm-ree would know.

"Lizard Woman!"

Ban-ya stiffened at Wehakna's bellow. The insult told her that Shateh had yet to return from the hunt. She hefted the hide that held her day's work and walked toward the chieftain's lodge of new, hastily cured bison hide. Halfway there, she was brought short by malevolent words from Atonashkeh.

"Someday perhaps my father will not return. Then I will be chief, and Lizard Woman will be meat for wolves and lions."

"You will never be chief, Atonashkeh!" she shot back hotly but quietly. The day had been long. She was tired. And she was suddenly weary to her bones of unsuccessful attempts to placate and soften his animosity toward her. She and the chieftain's son were well between the lodges. No one would hear their words unless they raised their voices, so she said with open contempt, "Your tongue spurts the poison of one who should have been named Snake! When Shateh welcomed Dakan-eh and my people, you saw the power of my man. You knew that Shateh would see that Dakan-eh was a better man than you could ever hope to be. So you coiled your tongue and struck at my man with lies! And now that my Bold Man is far away, you fear me—a woman—and the child I will bear to your father. My child will be the son to him that you have failed to be an—"

She stopped. Even in her weariness and need to spit the venom of her heart at him as he had spit his at her, she knew from his expression that she had been a fool.

"You carry no child," he accused. "My Atli has told me that since well before spreading yourself for my father, you did not enter the woman's place of moon blood. And look at the stains on your dress. How can a woman whose teats still spurt milk have taken life into a belly that has not prepared itself to nourish life?"

"Nevertheless, it *is* so!"

"Shateh may believe it, but he is old! He sees what an old man needs to see! But time will name you Liar soon enough, Lizard Woman. Until then watch where you walk because for you I *will* be Snake. And I will strike at you. Be sure of that. And know this: Either at my hand or at my instigation you *will* be meat!"

Stunned, she watched him turn away and return to his lodge. Now, from across the rolling, storm-sodden land, the flutes and whistles of the returning hunting party were heard. Dogs were barking. Women and children were running from their lodges to greet their returning husbands and fathers and brothers. The men of the band trotted forward to help the hunters drag in the tripoled, meat-laden sledges that they were pulling triumphantly toward their people.

"Tonight we feast on the sweet, red meat of horse!" cried Shateh in as jubilant a tone as Ban-ya had heard him raise. "Much horse! And the meat of mare and tender foal! Tonight we will praise the forces of Creation! The hunt has been good!"

Ban-ya found herself shaking as an idea took shape within her. Staring with narrowed eyes at the piled haunch meat and hooves and gut meats, she whispered under her breath, "Now I will feed you the meat of my hatred, Atonashkeh. Soon you will die of it—not like a snake but like a greedy wolf as you bolt your death and never know from whose hand it has come!"

She hurried off to prepare.

After so many days and nights of snow and rain, there was little dry wood for a large feast fire in Shateh's camp. The bulk of the meat was eaten raw, but not before the women worked together to butcher and slice it into manageable chunks before portioning it onto individual serving platters.

Under a clear night sky the hunters gathered into a feasting circle to tell the tales of the hunt while their women served them. Well-armed and well-fed men kept watch with their dogs; if the raiders of the Watching Star came tonight, the People of the Land of Grass would be ready.

No one saw Ban-ya deftly and surreptitiously add three pieces of meat to the platter that Atli had prepared and now placed before Atonashkeh. The men ate and talked of the hunt. The women and children "oohed" and "ahhed." Atonashkeh wolfed down his meat, as he always did, and licked the bone platter clean after raising it to his lips and noisily sucking the leftover juices. He was not the only man to belch, satisfied by the meal. But not one man, woman, or child at that gathering was as satisfied as Ban-ya.

No one would suspect that she had baited his meat with death. Some might look to her as a continuing cause of bad luck, but she had only to remind them of the improving weather and of their recent success upon the hunt, then add that if raiders attacked them, these were old enemies from the days of a long-gone war that had nothing to do with her;

besides, everyone had heard the chieftain repeatedly warn
Atonashkeh to stop bolting his foods.

Slightly apart from the other women, she hunkered
down when the serving was complete and ate her portion
with an enthusiasm for food that she had not known since
she had been separated from her people.

Later, in the lodge of the chieftain, she gave her body
to Shateh with extra care, and when the lovemaking was
done, she massaged him into sleep; she knew that he would
need to be rested for the ordeal of grief that would come
when his son began to react to her secret gift of death: three
tiny, meticulously fashioned coils of gall-soaked bone
slivers, each worked into the gristly portions of the meat that
she had placed on his platter. Usually used to kill wolves or
other large carnivores that came too close to encampments,
the coils were common methods both in the Red World and
in the Land of Grass. Softened slivers of bone were easily
curled tight when wet, then bound with strips of sinew that
held them fast until they dried. Once dry, the slivers held
their shape when the sinew was removed. Stored in
moisture-proof sacks, they were ready to be inserted into
meat used as bait. After sitting a few hours in the belly of a
beast, the bone splinters were softened by gastric juices until
they uncoiled like springs, effectively piercing the intestine
of any creature unfortunate enough to have consumed them.

That night Ban-ya dreamed of a gut-pierced man
howling like a wolf as he took many days to die. She
dreamed of Atonashkeh and of how she would soon have
one fewer enemy to contend with in the Land of Grass.

She awoke before dawn. Shateh sighed in his sleep and
drew her close, enfolded her in his strong arms, and lay a
hand protectively across her belly—and the son that he
believed to lie within.

Fool, she thought. *You think that you are defending me
when it is* I *who defends you from a neutered snake who
coils against you and puts us both at risk by striking at your
authority even to your face!*

She closed her eyes and heaved a sigh. She wondered
just how deeply Shateh would grieve for the loss of this
less-than-worthy son, then realized that she did not care.

What was done was done, and she was glad. Warm and at ease within the chieftain's embrace, Ban-ya smiled as she waited for the screaming of his son to begin. She hoped it would be soon. She hoped that Atonashkeh would die slowly. And she wished that Dakan-eh were here to appreciate how his woman had determined the death of one who was his enemy.

For three days the sun shone. It was still shining brightly on the day that Atonashkeh died. When Shateh stared up at the golden disk he saw not the benevolent eye of Father Above but the mocking eye of a malevolent, man-eating spirit leering at him through the blue robe of day. The forces of Creation were taunting him. He had begged for light and warmth, and at last they had come. But Spirit Sucker continued to ride the wind, and another son of Shateh was dead. Yet again it was time to mourn. Unable to bear it, the chieftain went into his lodge to be alone. He left Atli and Wehakna to wail and shriek over the body of Atonashkeh as his daughters stood aside and his people stared after him.

In the gloomy interior, he stared ahead, unseeing. *I must think about this,* he told himself. But he could not think and did not really want to think. Yet he knew that he *must* think, for he had never seen any man die as his son had just died. At first Atonashkeh, wincing, his brow sweated, had paced around the encampment as men will sometimes do when they need to walk off the belly distress of a poorly digested meal. For a while he had endured the teasing of companions who joked about his wolfish eating habits. But soon he was panting and gray faced, gasping and then screaming from pain. In an effort to confound the spirits of Atonashkeh's misery, the chieftain in his role as shaman had commanded the women to make medicine drinks and poultices. He had called upon every healing skill that he had ever been taught, even going so far as to attempt the most dangerous and selfless medicine magic of all—the drawing out of the evil pain spirits through Atonashkeh's navel and into himself by means of a special sucking tube made of the hollow wing bone of an eagle. It had been a heroic action and might have resulted in his own death had it succeeded . . . but it had not. Nothing had succeeded. In the end, Atonashkeh's cries had given way to convulsions. Salivating, bleeding from the mouth and rectum, he had begged that his misery be put to an end. A tremor went through the chieftain. What else could he have done?

Aside from baited wolves, he had seen this type of death occasionally among the band's dogs, when the animals inadvertently ingested bone fragments. Once the gut of an animal was pierced, nothing could be done but slit the throat of the suffering creature. But Atonashkeh was a man! He was not a dog or a wolf, even though he often ate like one! After three days, though, Shateh had been forced to do for his son what he would have done for a dog or a suffering wolf; could he have done less for a son?

His brow furrowed. Atonashkeh had been a disappointment to him, but he had not wished him dead. *What must I do to ease my people's fears now that Spirit Sucker has visited once again?* He exhaled in abject misery. There was nothing to do, except mourn the death and be rid of the lizard eater. The latter realization proved so upsetting that he flinched. "No! I cannot! I will not! She pleases me! I am young again with her, strong again with her! And she carries my child . . . perhaps the son I long for!"

"I am afraid."

Startled by Ban-ya's voice, Shateh squinted through the gloom and saw her kneeling in the shadows at the very back of the lodge. He had forgotten that she had retreated there when it had become obvious that Atonashkeh's condition was life threatening. He had heard her invoking the forces of Creation on his son's behalf in a high, plaintive ululation that would have moved a stone to pity. Everyone had heard her—except the forces of Creation.

"Your people will blame me," Ban-ya said to him now.

"There is no cause for them to blame you," Shateh told her gently.

"They need no cause. They will say that Spirit Sucker has come at the invitation of Lizard Woman. I am afraid, Shateh, not for myself but for our son."

His eyes narrowed. His sorrow was as cold and heavy as glacial ice moving upon the shoulders of a great mountain; he saw his many dead sons encased within it, and with a gasp, he saw himself entombed with them.

Ban-ya rose, and she came to him on bare feet across the hide-covered floor. Slipping her arms around his lower back, she pressed close to him as she said softly, ''You could not have saved Atonashkeh. Shateh is a powerful chief and a great shaman, but Shateh no longer walks strong in the power of the sacred stones and of the white mammoth. If the chieftain would be free of the ghost raiders of the People of the Watching Star and of the hauntings of Spirit Sucker, he must first be free of the curse of Cha-kwena. Cha-kwena has a stone and the protection of the totem.''

He held her away from him. ''My spirit bleeds, Ban-ya. This is not a time to try to lead me with your words of—''

''Will your spirit bleed for me and for our son when your band speaks against us and we are cast out to die?'' Her eyes were wide, sad, guileless. ''The spirits were smiling upon your people when you chose to keep me at your side, but no one will see this. I have not asked to be here. I have even tried to run away. Because I could not return to my own band, I have been obedient and tried to bring good things to those with whom I now share my life—snow to confound those who would hunt us, the warmth of the sun when we were weary of cold, the good red meat of bison and horse when we were hungry, and the birth of a son to Senohnim and Shateh! But now in the eyes of your people I have seen my death and the death of my son. They will say that Lizard Woman called the bad spirits into Atonashkeh's belly because he had no softness in his heart toward a slave who is not one of them. It will not matter that it was Atli who served Atonashkeh at the feast. No one will care that it was Atli who has secretly looked at Atonashkeh with hard eyes since he strangled her newborn son under a moon of mourning. Atli is not a lizard eater. No one will believe this woman if she tells them that she found *this* beside Atli's meat-making things on the night of the horse eating." Ban-ya raised her right hand and opened her fingers to display her palm. "In the Red World these bone coils are used by our hunters for baiting and killing wolves. In the Land of Grass perhaps Atli has used them for another purpose?"

Shateh grabbed her wrist and held her hand palm bent back and splayed so that he could stare a moment at the wolf bait before taking it into his own fist. "You found this near the place where Atli was preparing the feast meat?"

Ban-ya lowered her eyes and made no reply.

The chieftain, exhaling ill-contained rage, put a thumb under her chin and made her look at him. "By the Four Winds, Ban-ya, my people will have no cause to speak ill of you after this!"

She looked at him through deferentially lowered lashes. "I would not have it said that I have spoken against any one of them, Shateh."

"I will not name you in this! *I* will speak! Let Atli deny what *Shateh* has found!"

Atli could not deny it. Nor could she explain it. Nor could she defend herself against Wehakna when the bereft woman came flying at her, shrieking and tearing at her like an attacking raven. Stunned, confused, and more appalled than anyone by Shateh's accusations, Atli could find no way to convince the band that she had not baited Atonashkeh's meat with death. As a widow with no man to defend her, she had only the chieftain to turn to. When he turned his back to her, her fate was sealed. One by one every man in the band did the same until, bereft, Atli sobbed and threw herself at the feet of Lahontay, Eldest Hunter.

"Old Father, speak wisdom now and take pity, for I have done no wrong. Tell Shateh that what he has found cannot be! I have never . . . could not . . ."

Lahontay's brow wrinkled until it lay across his skull like a square of deeply corrugated pine bark. "Lahontay does not speak against Shateh for the sake of any *man*. He will not do so for a woman."

Atli crumpled.

"The children of Atli will reside in the lodge of

Shateh," the chieftain announced. "They will speak their father's name with pride. The name Atli will be spoken no more."

"Do you hear? The songs of lamentation come to us again!" Sheela was transfixed as she listened to the ululations on the wind. "I have commanded no attack," she said angrily. "Who among us has gone again to our enemies with Spirit Sucker as an ally?"

Jhadel, too, was furious. He turned on Tsana. "Not enough time has passed since the last raid. And after these many days of rain and sun, there would be no way to cover your tracks in the mud! Do you wish to bring death to our enemies or have them bring death to us? Could you not wait? Look at the sky! The high, thin clouds speak of yet another storm. Soon there will be snow again!"

Silence greeted the old man's tirade as the People of the Watching Star exchanged glances. Wila was so frightened by the look on the shaman's face, she moved back into the shadow.

Tsana replied curtly, "We may not possess the wisdom of shamans, Jhadel; but we warriors of the Watching Star are not fools. We have gone on forays to gather the many scattered bands of our tribe and bring them here, but we have made no new raids on Shateh's traveling camp. If someone is dead there, Spirit Sucker is responsible . . . although gladly would I have given Death my spears as assistance."

Jhadel did not miss the sarcasm in Tsana's cold response. "Just wait for the snow, Tsana. Then go alone, for all I care. Feed yourself to the coming storm, or to our enemies—you will be no loss to me!" He snorted and turned away, vanishing without a word beyond his woven, feather-covered screens.

Wila was relieved to see the old man go. The skinny, sharp-eyed, black-headed shaman was always kind to her, but his appearance was sobering. She had never been comfortable around Jhadel or any other old people. She was glad that there was less than a handful of "gray hairs" among the growing population of men, women, and chil-

dren who—despite the vast fluctuations of the weather—
continued to arrive at the stronghold from all across the
Land of Grass and the surrounding mountains.

Now, as she sat in her own little section of the great
cave, Wila looked around and knew who these people were:
They were the enemy. Yet not one of them treated her with
hostility. They were all cordial, sometimes friendly. She
knew that she should hate them. When they were not out
hunting or on forays that sent them searching for the
surviving bands of their own tribe, they made no secret of
their activities. They admitted to harassing her people, to
keeping them on edge and humiliating them as punishment
for atrocities that had been committed during the great war.
Her youth would not possibly allow her to remember or
understand these incidents, and Wila felt ashamed about the
pain and suffering her people had caused. The shaman had
told her that she had been stolen away to make her people
suffer in the same way that his own people had mourned the
many daughters that her tribe had taken from his. Wila
knew, however, that she was being treated much better,
almost to the point of deference, than the slaves among
Shateh's and Dakan-eh's people had been treated.

Wila had not been raped. She had not been beaten. Her
hair had not been shorn to weaken her spirit. True, when she
had begged her captors not to raid the encampment of her
people anymore, they had laughed at her; but Sheela had
taken her aside and, to Wila's amazement, had stroked her
shoulders and patted her head as though she had been a
favored sister. Sheela had sweetly asked Wila to describe
those among her band whom she most loved so that the
warriors of the Watching Star could recognize them on
future raids and grant them special consideration. Wila had
wept with gratitude. She had mentioned her mother first,
then her father and nearly everyone else—except old
Lahontay, who had castigated the meanness of Wila's
tongue once too often, and Wehakna, and some of the other
older women who were always telling her what to do. If the
People of the Watching Star wanted to kill them, Wila did
not care; besides, there was nothing she could do about it.
Wila felt grateful she had never informed Sheela that when

she had slain the woman in the coyote-skin cloak, she had not slain Ban-ya. That would have made Daughter of the Sun very unhappy. Nor had Wila said that if Sheela wanted to take the life of Dakan-eh, then she and her warriors had raided the wrong camp, for Bold Man and his tiny band had been banished from the Land of Grass. Lehana was with them! The girl's heart quickened with gladness for her sister, for surely Lehana was far enough south with her new people to be out of harm's way. Possibly Lehana had already birthed her baby.

Wila looked up now. Sheela had called her name. The woman was coming toward her with a horn of broth. Wila could smell the strong scent of sage and marrow. As Sheela knelt before her and proffered the horn, the girl accepted it greedily.

"You should thank us for stealing you away from those who have won the wrath of the forces of Creation. Shateh risked much by consorting with murderous, deceitful lizard eaters from the Red World. Here, among my people, you will be sheltered and favored by the spirits of the ancestors until the ending of your days. How well you look, Wila. Your skin grows sleek."

Wila drained the last of the broth, wiped her lips with the back of her hand, and returned the horn to Sheela. "Why are you so kind to me, Sheela? I was not nice to you when you were a slave to my people."

"You must not look back, Wila," Sheela replied. "Things will never return to the way they were."

"My father *will* come for me someday. My mother will not let him forget me. He will bring many warriors, and he will take me back to my people."

A strange, hollow-eyed expression moved across Sheela's face as she scanned the cave, then indicated the many warriors and women, all working at weapon and hide making. "Would you have your father come for you now, girl? We are many, and soon the scattered bands will be one—like this." She held up her free hand, curled her long fingers into a fist as a gesture of strength. "Soon I will take the life of Dakan-eh and of Shateh. Then we will leave this cave and seek the totem. Are we not your people now, Wila? Can you not be content with us?''

Wila sighed guiltily as Sheela rose and walked away. The girl realized that she *was* content. As the days and nights passed, she missed her family less and less. She could be completely at ease if only Warakan, the somber, mute youth who so often woke screaming in the night, would stop staring at her all the time. She turned her head. There he was, crouching on a ledge midway up the side wall of the cave, his eyes fixed on her. She stuck her tongue out at him. ''Have you never seen a girl before?''

Standing within earshot, a sturdy-looking man named Ston appraised Wila thoughtfully. ''I think you remind him of his sister.''

Wila frowned. ''So? Let him look at her, not at me!''

''She is dead,'' Ston replied.

Wila's frowned deepened; she felt a stab of sympathy for the boy. ''In the war? Was it a terrible death?''

Ston's face remained expressionless as he said, ''No. It was not in the war. But yes, her death was terrible.''

The people began their five days of mourning for Atonashkeh. On the first day the winds shifted. On the second day storm clouds obliterated the sun. Late on the third day a shaken Nakantahkeh returned alone; Xiaheh and the other chiefs had refused to come south with him. On his way back to the river, Nakantahkeh had been set upon by raiders, and he had barely escaped with his life. Shateh received this disappointing report with stoicism, then conveyed to Nakantahkeh the sad news of his own. Stunned and shattered, the man collapsed and, on the fourth day, joined the other mourners. Nakantahkeh grieved not only for two lost daughters but for a slain wife and a murdered hunt brother.

On the fifth day the woman Atli was still screaming, although her shrieks were weak and intermittent now, and she was mad with suffering after nearly five days of begging someone to end her life.

''Do not heed the howls of the baited wolf, little ones,'' said Wehakna, drawing her grandchildren close to her within the chieftain's lodge when the mourning time was over. "By the way Atli has offered death to your father, she has chosen the way in which she herself must die."

The daughters of Atli buried their heads in their grandmother's bosom. On her bed furs, Senohnim nursed her puny boy. The continuing lamentations of the chieftain were carried away by cold, blustering winds and returning snow flurries. Deep within the shadows of Shateh's lodge, Ban-ya sat alone, remembering the day when Atli had come close, calling her "vile," wishing her dead, and threatening to betray her to the raiders if they ever came again.

Now you will betray no one, Ban-ya thought, satisfied, and tried not to smile as she remembered the warning of the Ancient Ones, which the tribe's elders had often repeated to the sons and daughters of the distant Red World: *Speak against no one lest the helping spirits of the one against whom you have spoken hear your words and turn them against you instead.*

High above, where the newly cut lodge poles crossed and extended upward through the smoke flap of the hide-covered lodge of the chieftain, the wind was gusting erratically in the feather-adorned ends of the thong bindings.

"The spirits are restless," Senohnim observed fearfully, holding her baby close.

"Be at ease, sister of my fire circle." Wehakna's voice was so weighted by grief that it was beyond inflection. With a catch in her voice, she assured, "It is only the spirit of my Atonashkeh coming from the world beyond this world to see to the welfare of the new life that has taken his name."

"And to bring pain and suffering to the one who has killed him!" added a pinch-faced little Oni.

Ban-ya, suddenly wide-eyed with fear, looked up and wondered if the ghost of Atonashkeh would come for her now. And what about Atli? She was not dead yet, but she would be soon! *By the words of the ancients among my own people, Atli turned the spirits against herself when she spoke against me!* Ban-ya rationalized. *It was the same with Atonashkeh. I did not want to kill him, not really. His threats forced me to obey the will of the spirits. What else could I have done to save myself?*

She breathed again only after long moments had passed and she was certain that she had no need to be afraid. Atonashkeh's spirit might yet live again within Senohnim's pathetic excuse for a son, but for now that child was an infant incapable of speech or threat. As for Atli, she would be a long time dying, and Ban-ya was certain that it would be many a moon before any woman of this band would name a child for her. By the time Atli could be reborn, Shateh would have honored his promise to travel to the Red World with Ban-ya.

The wind was still moving around the ridgepoles. Far across the land, a coyote howled in the light of the ebbing day, and Ban-ya flinched. The spirit of Atonashkeh might not be the only phantom moving in the wind. A coldness stirred within her as she recalled the many times that she had spoken against Cha-kwena. Was he out there now, as Dakan-eh had so often claimed, an invisible force moving upon the back of the Four Winds . . . a vengeful phantom, working evil upon those who had refused to follow him beyond the edge of the world? Was he bringing bad things to them and spying upon one who had once named him Shaman? Was he preventing her from conceiving a child of Shateh's, and was he standing in her way of ever returning home to her man and beloved little Piku-neh?

Breathless, Ban-ya got to her knees, reached beneath the chieftain's sleeping furs, and pulled her coyote-skin robe from where she had hidden it beneath the other hides and skins. She shook it, slung it on, and, ignoring the disapproving eyes of Wehakna, Senohnim, and the girls, knew that for now, at least, she could wear it in safety. The raiders would not come into Shateh's camp while so many men and dogs kept watch. Only spirits could travel unseen across the land in such fine, clear weather. And in this cloak made of the skins and tails of the helping animal spirits of Cha-kwena, the power of the shaman and Yellow Wolf could not harm her.

At this moment Shateh came into the lodge. His eyes sought Ban-ya across the shadowy interior. "You have heard the voice of Little Yellow Wolf?"

"I have heard."

"He calls by day!" exclaimed Shateh.

Wehakna scowled at the rapt expression on her man's exhausted face. "It is late," she reminded. "Soon the sun will set, and the dark will come. It is not unusual that the mourning songs of men and the screams of a woman would summon coyotes and other eaters of the dead here. It has stormed for days; the beasts are sure to be hungry."

The coldness within Ban-ya turned to pure ice, but it was not the ice of fear; it was the ice of intense hope. It froze her where she was. With pounding heart and soaring spirit, she ignored Wehakna's logic and dared to lead the chieftain once more with words. "Little Yellow Wolf has come to mock Shateh for the death of his son—for the death of all of Shateh's sons. Look . . . behold the robe this woman wears. It is made of skins taken by Dakan-eh in far lands, and with each skin taken from the helping spirit animal of the shaman Cha-kwena, the power of the shaman was lessened. Dakan-eh hunted Cha-kwena across the Mountain of Sand and over the edge of the world. But how could Bold Man succeed? He was not a man of the Land of Grass in those days, and the men with him were lizard eaters. Had Shateh been with him, Bold Man would not have failed in his search for our enemies. If Shateh and the warriors of the Land of Grass had been at Dakan-eh's side, Cha-kwena would be dead now; the sacred stone would be around Shateh's neck; the totem would walk once more among the People; and the many chiefs and shamans of the Land of Grass would not have abandoned Shateh!"

Her words settled. Shateh looked with deeply measuring eyes at Ban-ya. Then, after a long moment, he spoke quietly but with great portent. "We will seek the sun in the Red World. We will winter once more with the lizard eaters. On the day I sent Dakan-eh back to the land of his ancestors, I said that we would see who Spirit Sucker would follow and by this know which of us walked in the favor of the Four Winds. This much is clear to me now: Spirit Sucker is feeding on my people. I will stay in this land no more."

6

Dakan-eh took his time crossing the Red World on the way toward his ancestral village by the Lake of Many Singing Birds. Everywhere it was the same: abandoned villages of pathetic stick huts, dry lakes, islands of dusty, dying greenery, small groups of people appearing from behind boulders, brackish seeps that had been good-sized spring-fed ponds when he had last seen them.

He observed everything with contempt. The people looked even worse than when he left them. After having hunted mammoth and long-horned bison on the great plains to the north, he felt like a foreigner. And the people—observing his great spears, strange clothing, scars, and the facial paint with which he had chosen to identify himself and his fellow travelers as men from the Land of Grass—stared at him with the wary eyes of prey caught unexpectedly in the shadow of predators. Haughty and amused, Dakan-eh stared back, basking in feelings of superiority. Pah-la went out among the frightened watchers and called to them by name, then asked them if they failed to recognize their old friends.

"Ah, woman of Owa-neh! I did not know you without your golden nose ring!" was the usual exclamation, and then there were many exchanges of hugs with tears of both sadness and happiness. Nearly everyone knew the woman of Owa-neh from communal gatherings of the tribe, and her pleasant and generous ways had made her one of the most popular of the matrons. The reputation of her bold son had given her great prestige. Now, as she followed Dakan-eh and his entourage toward home, Pah-la beckoned to people along the way and invited them to join with her and Bold Man in a great ceremony of mourning to be held in the abandoned village of her band.

"Owa-neh and Na-sei have lost their lives among strangers, but we bring their bodies home so that their spirits will live forever among friends!" Pah-la told them.

The news spread. At every village the travelers were made welcome. At every village their party grew larger as Dakan-eh's band was joined by an ever-expanding body of funeral observers. At first he began to worry about what he would feed them all after they reached his village; but after a while he stopped worrying. He reminded himself that he was back in the land of the lizard eaters; his people would eat anything.

Slowly, under gathering clouds and occasional rain showers, Dakan-eh made his way from one welcoming assembly to another.

"Dakan-eh returns!" the old men, hunters, and young boys cried, hurrying out to greet him.

"Behold! He brings the rain!" the women and girls shouted, adoring him with their eyes, just as they always had, and pushing their daughters of marriageable age forward.

"Yes! It is so!" Dakan-eh confirmed, measuring the girls with an eye to future matings. Since he was never one to miss an opportunity for self-advancement, he added with great solemnity, "Behold Bold Man of the Red World returning to his people! Behold Brave Hunter who has killed many bison and many enemies in the Land of Grass! Behold Man Who Dares to Chase the Whirling Wind to Save the People! Behold Dakan-eh! He comes with a great gift! Call him Man Who Brings Rain!"

Everywhere it was the same: meager food but generous hospitality and much curiosity about the newcomers from the Land of Grass. Since Na-sei's widow, Lehana, had given birth to a son en route into the Red World, the women wanted to see the baby. Invariably they were amazed to discover that the mating between a man of the Red World and a woman of the Land of Grass could have resulted in a

child that looked like any other baby they had seen. And
after the infant was admired by all, Lehana and the other
women of the Land of Grass were made to feel comfortable
among others of their gender as they were asked endless
questions about their garments, the length of their hair, their
favorite recipes for the boiling bag or the spit, or for the
seduction of a man, or for a teething infant, or for the
cramps of childbirth or moon-blood passage. Old Kahm-ree
mumbled about her lost granddaughter, but no one wanted
to listen; in the opinion of most of the women of the Red
World, Ban-ya was a forward, lusty, self-serving girl, and
because they had all envied her extraordinary figure and her
winning of a choice man, no one was saddened by the news
that Dakan-eh had kept the son she had given him and
traded her to another man for not one but two new women!

"So now he has *four* women!"

"Imagine! Four!"

"Tell us, Cheelapat and Ghree and Ili-na and Rayela,
is he man enough for all?"

"He is man enough!" proclaimed Ghree with pride,
for she had left the Red World as the woman of a common
hunter; she returned to it as the wife of a chief.

Ili-na eyed her mother through partially lowered
lashes. "He is disgusting. He is always ready for it."

Ghree shook her head at her daughter, then said, "She
is young. She does not know how lucky she is to have such
a man!"

Rayela raised a telling brow. "He likes the young ones
best. Lucky for us, or we would never sleep!"

Among the men it was much the same: talk of better
days, of hope for the future, of the need for rain, of hunting,
of women, boasts of matings and of prowess.

"Dakan-eh could always get the girls to spread themselves! But you never did find that pretty one—the one all
the men wanted? Tlana-quah's older daughter. Ta-maya,
wasn't it? The one that the raiders took away and who
Kosar-eh rescued during the war?"

The question took Dakan-eh off guard. The sound of
Ta-maya's name was an unexpected bruise to his spirit. He
remembered how he used to mock the old grandfathers

when they said that a man never got over his first love; now it seemed that they were right.

"She was promised to you, wasn't she? Before she ran off with the shaman, I mean. A girl like that—*hmm* . . . makes an old man rut like a goat in his dreams."

Resentment shadowed Dakan-eh's mood. "She was nothing. I let her run away, but only after I had her many times," he lied. "Believe me, she was nothing. I've had much better since her."

The talk turned, revolved around other women, other matings, other feats of masculine endurance; but in village after village all the men remembered the fair Ta-maya, elder daughter of the chieftain of the village by the Lake of Many Singing Birds. No one had forgotten the way in which she had spurned the legendary Bold Man and run off with a boy-shaman who had abandoned his people in those long-gone days after the great war.

"Do you think she still lives?"

"Yes," Dakan-eh would reply. "She is with him, with Cha-kwena. That shaman has driven the rain clouds and the game and the totem before him over the edge of the world. Cha-kwena has turned the forces of Creation against the People of the Red World. Although Dakan-eh walks with a band that has no shaman, Bold Man has returned from the Land of Grass, after many great hunts and many great battles, to be reunited with his people. Dakan-eh has stolen back the rain from the one who is our enemy!"

Far to the south, beyond the Mountains of Sand and over the edge of the world, mammoth trumpeted in the wonderful valley. In the darkness of the cave, a troubled Mah-ree dogged Cha-kwena's steps as he prepared to enter the inner depths of the cave.

"Where do you think you are going?" he asked in a perturbed whisper, not wanting to wake the other members of the band.

"To be with you. Every night you wake and go into the hill. Every night you are there alone. It is not good to be alone so much, Cha-kwena. It is—"

"How many times must I tell you that the interior of the cave is sacred. Only Shaman may enter it!"

She stood her ground, frowning as she listened to the mammoth. "They are sad. They cry just as Siwi-ni's infant has cried for her lost mother. The mammoth have been crying ever since Siwi-ni's spirit went to walk the wind. I think they are telling us to leave this place, Cha-kwena."

"Winter will soon be upon the land. Gah-ti is not fit for travel. Doh-teyah's eyes are as feverish and runny as the eyes of the few pups that have survived. The cave is well stocked. Why should we leave it? We must rest and grow strong. By spring Gah-ti will be healed, and with the help of the forces of Creation and your medicine, the baby will be well."

Mah-ree looked around to make certain that no one was listening, then said, "I have listened and listened, but I have not heard Life Giver since the night we were together under the falling stars, Cha-kwena. I think he has gone ahead of us. I think that my dear old dog Friend has followed. We must follow, too! There is sickness and death for us here—I can feel it. And Cha-kwena . . . why do you no longer wear the sacred stone?"

He glowered. "I have told you before—it is exactly where it belongs. Would you be Shaman as well as Medicine Girl, Mah-ree? Do you imagine that you could do better at one than you have done at the other? Surely you could do no worse!"

His anger intensified at the sight of her quivering chin. How could he tell her that never again would Life Giver lead them anywhere? How could he tell her that he had thrown away the sacred stone of their ancestors? His hand strayed to where the talisman used to rest within his medicine bag at his throat. For an instant its absence disconcerted him, then he felt nothing. The power in the stone died when the great white mammoth died. It did not matter now where it lay—at the bottom of a lake or in an owl's aerie. Even if he still had the talisman, and even if the totem still lived, with his band as weak as it was, Cha-kwena would not have considered taking his people from this high, dry, warm refuge.

"Perhaps if we were to go out together across the land, we might find where Grandfather of All has gone. If I could see him I would—"

"No longer doubt my word?"

She blinked, shook her head. "I—no, Cha-kwena. But . . ."

"If you no longer have faith in my decisions, take the dogs and lead the people back to the Red World!"

"You don't mean that! Not after we have been together as man and woman—"

"I have told you before, Mah-ree. Whatever happened between us was a mistake. Forget it. It is finished forever."

Mah-ree bit her lower lip as Cha-kwena whirled away and, stone tallow lamp in hand, disappeared into the depths of the cave.

"How can I forget?" she whispered to herself. "My shaman has made this girl a woman under the falling stars of night. Nothing can change that. Not even Shaman can make me say it is finished!"

She sighed. She loved him so much! Why could he not love her, too? She suddenly felt exhausted. She had not been feeling well of late. Perhaps if she had confided that to him, he might have listened. One more bad thing might have changed his mind about this place. But of course he was right: With Siwi-ni's infant unwell and Gah-ti in no condition to travel, the cave would prove a sensible refuge against the coming of the White Giant Winter.

Will it?

Who spoke? She did not know the voice. She turned and looked around to see Ta-maya, wrapped in her sleeping furs, awake and sitting up, rocking the fretful baby. Again Mah-ree sighed. It was late, and she must be more tired than she suspected if she was imagining strangers speaking to her out of the dark when all she had obviously heard was her sister cooing softly to Doh-teyah.

"Silly girl," Mah-ree admonished herself as she made her way back to her sleeping place and gently toed aside the three dogs that had come to take it over in her absence. After lying down, she patted their heads as they settled in beside her. "All right, Whimper and Thump Tail, you know you

are welcome. But shame on you, Scar Nose, for leaving
your pups! What kind of mother are you? And why are you
growling at me?''

She shoved the old female off and, after pointing the
way into the darkness, watched the dog sulkily obey her
unspoken command to return to her ''nest.'' Scar Nose had
been acting strangely of late, and her nose had been dry for
days. Mah-ree decided to try mixing oil of willow into her
meat tomorrow in an effort to cool whatever fever spirits
might be troubling the dog. Now, bundling herself in her
warm bed furs, Mah-ree closed her eyes and called for sleep
as she listened to Scar Nose settling down, to Ta-maya's
gentle crooning, and to an owl ''*oo-oo*ing'' somewhere in
the night beyond the cave. With a sigh, she smiled, drifted
into soothing dreams. . . .

She dreamed of long-gone days when the old shaman
Hoyeh-tay—with his perpetually molting, cranky old owl
perched atop his balding head—had honored Medicine Girl
by allowing her to enter his sacred cave so that she might sit
with Cha-kwena and learn with him of magic and healing
and of the history and legends of their people.

Mah-ree sighed and curled onto her side. Whimper had
moved closer. Mah-ree put an arm around the dog's
shoulder and, snuggling close, whispered reassurances—not
really to the dog but to herself. ''Old Hoyeh-tay has taught
us well. I must stop being a foolish girl who forgets that his
knowledge and magic has passed to Cha-kwena . . . not to
me. Cha-kwena is strong in the power of our totem. As long
as he remains guardian of the sacred stone of our ancestors,
he will keep his people safe. I know he will! He always has,
hasn't he?''

Dawn found a light snow falling once more in the Land
of Grass. Shateh had his people up and moving on, until
Nakantahkeh said that he would go no farther.

Shateh was brought short by Nakantahkeh's refusal.
''Come. We will and must go on,'' the chieftain said.
''When at last the weather allows the raiders to come down
from the mountains, they will not find us in the camps that
we have left behind; nor will they be able to track us across

a world in which snow will have covered all sign of our passage."

"To leave the Land of Grass will be to turn our backs upon our dead and upon my lost daughter. Regardless of where Shateh travels, how can he hope to find his luck as long as this bad-luck-bringing Lizard Woman walks among his people?"

"We have discussed this in council, Nakantahkeh. It has been decided. We will walk to the south in the way of Bold Man and his people, then winter in the Red World. Death did not follow in the path of Dakan-eh. It has come to us instead, as he foretold."

"Because of her!" Nakantahkeh glared at Ban-ya as he directed his words to Shateh. "Do you know what Xiaheh and the other chiefs said when I asked them to come south to join you? They have said, 'Better to join with the People of the Watching Star than with one who cannot recognize enemies even when they dwell among his people.' They say that Bold Man has tricked you! Because of the bad words that passed between you and Dakan-eh, he has left this woman here, so she might summon Spirit Sucker in the night. She welcomes Death and shows him how best to feed upon the people of Shateh!"

"He did not leave her. I *took* her from him. And because she is with us, we have found meat, Senohnim has borne a son, and the storms of winter conspire with us against our enemies."

"And Atonashkeh is dead! My woman is slain! My young daughter has been taken by raiders, and my chieftain has lost heart to fight them even though I have told you that I know where they are! I have seen their tracks in the soft mud of the river crossing while on my way back from the north!"

Shateh's face showed no expression as he said evenly, "And you have also told us of being forced to lie low while men traveling in escort of women and children passed you in the night. *Many* men, you said. All armed, you said. And I have considered your words. Yes, Nakantahkeh. I have lost heart to fight. I am weary of death. I am tired of songs of mourning. I have said this in council. You—and every other man here—are free to stand with me or go. Those who have named me their chief and shaman have always walked strong in the favor of the Four Winds. Until now. And so now I say that it is time for me to seek my totem and know why it and its kind no longer walk in the land of my ancestors. It is time for me to turn my back upon the storms of winter and to take this woman of the Red World back to that land where the forces of Creation smile upon her people—for surely they no longer smile upon me or mine in this land!''

"This is not the first time that winter has come early to the Land of Grass!'' Nakantahkeh stated angrily. "This has been the land of the ancestors of the Bison People since time beyond beginning! We cannot leave it.''

"In time within remembering we hunted mammoth in this land. Only when the mammoth became few did we hunt bison. In time beyond beginning the ancestors walked beneath the Watching Star in a land of ice and fire. When monsters came down from the sky to feed upon them, they learned from First Man and First Woman that in changing times, men must learn new ways or die.'' He paused, squinting in the direction of the snow- and cloud-shrouded mountains. Having alluded to the raiders of the People of the Watching Star, he now wondered aloud if monsters did not sometimes walk in the skins of men. "Before we came together for the great hunt of the Dry Grass Moon, I would have sworn before the council that we had killed them all. But now they live again, grow strong, and fall upon us like wolves out of the night and storms as we endure winter at a time when we should be enjoying the last, lingering warmth of autumn and hunting bison fattened from summer browse.'' He shook his head. "We live in changing times. The ancestors speak to me in my dreams. They tell me that it is time to lead my people away from our enemies. In the way of First Man and First Woman we will walk into the face of the rising sun and out of the Land of Grass before the Cold Moon rises and the White Giant Winter comes to crush the life out of this land.''

"And what if the White Giant Winter comes to crush you there? What if your enemies follow and find you?''

"Then I will remember that the woman Ban-ya has spoken of another enemy, a shaman. With Dakan-eh to show me the way beyond the Mountains of Sand, I will find the great white mammoth, then hunt this Cha-kwena. If he will not walk in the shadow of Shateh, I will take his sacred stone, and soon he will cast no shadow at all. Strong in the power of the totem, I will have heart to fight again, and those who have chosen to follow me with Spirit Sucker as their ally will regret the day that they ever named Shateh Enemy!"

"I will not live in the land of lizard eaters!" declared Nakantahkeh.

"Then stay and die in the land of the bison and mammoth hunters of the Land of Grass. I will not stop you."

Nakantahkeh watched the chieftain lead the band into the falling snow. He was not alone. "Let Shateh follow the call of his own spirit," he said to those warriors who had been hunt brothers of Atonashkeh. They and their families had fallen out of Shateh's band. "I will not stand with him. Xiaheh was right. The lizard-eating woman has turned his will to her purpose."

"But what will we do, Nakantahkeh, with the White Giant Winter on the land and raiders in the mountains?" asked Indeh, worried.

"We will journey back across the Land of Grass to join with Xiaheh and Ylanal and those of our people who have seen weakness in Shateh and wisely deserted him. Perhaps our enemies have not been wrong to make righteous war against one who would ally himself with lizard eaters. At one time the People of the Land of Grass and the People of the Watching Star were one. There was war between us only after Shateh turned to hunting bison, spurned the ways of our ancient ones, and made enemies of Ysuna and the mammoth seekers."

A troubled murmuring rippled among the gathering. "It was not solely a dispute over the kind of meat we would hunt, Nakantahkeh," reminded Indeh. "It was a war between opposing views as to how Thunder in the Sky could be brought to restore his favor to the People. Shateh would not sacrifice the daughters of the band in exchange for the meat of his mammoth children. Better to eat bison. Better to hunt in other parts of the Land of Grass and to make war upon those who would steal our daughters—as they have stolen your Wila.''

Nakantahkeh's face twisted as he nodded a bitter assent to the statement. Instead of addressing it directly, he said slowly, ''Mammoth have gone from the Land of Grass. Now the bison follow. So, too, does the power of the People. Perhaps Shateh is more right than he knows. In changing times men must learn new ways . . . or return to the old ones. All was good in the Land of Grass when Ysuna led the People of the Watching Star to offer sacrifice to Thunder in the Sky.''

The women among the gathering gasped and drew their daughters protectively close.

Nakantahkeh eyed them with impatience. ''If we had been loyal to the People of the Watching Star, my child would be alive now. They did not sacrifice the daughters of their allies!'' He paused, then turned his gaze back to the warriors. ''I will go back to Xiaheh. I will offer this counsel: Perhaps it is time for the tribes to be one again. Perhaps it is even time for enemies to unite against a greater enemy. It is the People of the Red World—not the People of the Watching Star—who have stolen our totem and driven it beyond our reach over the edge of the world.''

''And it is Shateh's desire to win it back,'' reminded Indeh.

''Yes,'' agreed Nakanatahkeh. ''But Shateh will hunt at the side of lizard eaters. With such allies, he cannot win. Together with the People of the Watching Star, though, the combined tribes of the Land of Grass must succeed!''

7

The soft warm days of autumn had ended in the wonderful valley. Now that the cave was stocked, there was little work for a hunter, or a shaman, to do. Cha-kwena occasionally sought solitude on long, overland pilgrimages to the place where the corpse of Life Giver lay within the lake.

The guardian herd had long since abandoned the body of the great white mammoth. The totem's bones had been stripped by carnivores. Morning saw ice in the shallows, but in the deeps where the water was warmed by hot springs rising from far beneath the earth, the lake surface steamed, and the bones of Grandfather of All protruded like the branches of ancient, leafless trees through a perpetual fog bank.

It was a desolate place; but it suited Cha-kwena's mood and spirit, and he was content to be there. Perhaps in some small, vulnerable, barely discernible portion of his heart he still had enough faith in the forces of Creation to believe that someday the bones would move, rise, and transform themselves into a living skeleton. Then, by some wondrous magic, the framework would clothe itself in flesh again and raise its head to trumpet at the sky. It did not happen, of course. Cha-kwena waited; he watched. Ultimately he mocked himself for being a fool.

Today, as on so many days before, Cha-kwena hunkered by the shore, leaned on his spear, and stared dolefully through the mist at the motionless bones. At length he sighed, turned his eyes away, and watched a pair of white-headed eagles circling before the sun. After a while

Raven joined them before flying down to settle upon the tip
of one of the dead mammoth's upwardly extended tusks.
Cha-kwena threw stones at the bird even though he knew
that he would indeed have to be a shaman to make a
successful strike from such a distance.

Cha-kwena watched Raven until the bird winged away.
The air was cool by the water's edge, so he pulled his
rabbit-skin cloak around his shoulders. Sleepy, he sat
glumly and listened to the *clee*ing of eagles, to the chatter-
ing and splashing of water birds, to the waves lapping at the
shore, and to the wind whispering in the reeds.

He cocked his head. The wind was restless, gusting
from all directions. He raised his face, closed his eyes, and
thought dreamily, *Four Winds, sacred winds, you are the
breath of the forces of Creation. You whisper around me
from the far corners of the world and sky. Yet I am alone,
empty of spirit, for I know that you are only wind, after all.*

His thoughts pooled and thickened, then took his mind
into the shallows of sleep and daydreams in which all of the
animals that he had ever named Spirit Brother came close
and sat beside him on the shore.

A lone coyote appeared to invite him from his dreams.
"Come walking into the rising sun, Cha-kwena."

"It is day, not dawn. And I will not walk with you ever
again. You have betrayed me."

"No, I have shown you the way to truth."

"Liar. With Wolf and Dog you have attacked and
eaten that which was sacred to me and to my people."

"Bad spirits have touched my kind in this land. They
have touched your people, too, and your pups and dogs. But
now the blood of the great white mammoth flows in us and
in *you,* Cha-kwena. We will survive. And as long as you
lead your people in his name, Grandfather of All will live
forever."

"I will *not* live forever! I will grow old. When I am
weak and half-blind with age, as Life Giver was, will you
come for me—you and the meat eaters of this world? Which
one of you will eat me as you ate him? Or will you all share
in the feast?"

"Life eats life, Cha-kwena," Coyote replied sagely. "But nothing dies forever."

Then the animal turned and ran off into the reeds to avoid the thrust of Cha-kwena's angrily hurled spear.

Cha-kwena awoke blinking, with a start. His spear was in his hand, but to his left, the reeds were still moving to reveal the place through which Coyote had disappeared.

Cha-kwena rose and moved cautiously forward. Broken reeds marked the way of an animal's passage. He followed, but after a while he paused and turned away. He knew that he would find nothing. Shivering from the eddying winds, he looked up to see that the sun was obscured by high clouds and encircled by a vast rainbow. It did not take a shaman's insight to know that a storm was coming. Cha-kwena walked on.

The cawing, shrieking, argumentative sounds of feeding ravens caused him to stop and turn again. Raven and his clan were setting into that portion of the reeds from which he had just come. He was driven by curiosity to go back and see what the ravens were eating. His stride was long and impatient as he used his spear to slash his way through the reeds and the ever-colder wind. His heart was beating hard and fast. A terrible dread was building in him, but he could not say why. Just ahead, the ravens flew skyward, and with a startled cry, Cha-kwena came through the reeds and into a small, beaten-down clearing and saw—

"Little Yellow Wolf!" He hurried forward, knelt, then reached a tentatively questing hand toward the half-eaten corpse of a coyote. "How can this be?" he wondered. Only moments before, the yellow wolf had been a part of his dreams, his imagination, flesh and blood, hair and bone. Yet *something* had caused the reeds to move and lead him in the way in which a living animal had recently gone.

"I do not understand." From the appearance of the desiccated remains, this animal had been dead for over a moon. From the smell of it, it had been sick for many a long day before that. He caught his breath as he remembered the sick dogs, the dying pups, the fretful infant, and the coyote on the mountain peak standing with tight flank and tucked tail and the look of sickness in the strange, fixed stare of the yellow eyes.

Bad spirits have touched my kind in this land.

The words of the animal in his dream came back to Cha-kwena. Was there a link among the sick coyote, sick dogs, and fretful baby? He snapped to his feet. Mah-ree was right! Sickness and death *were* in this land, and mammoth were not the only animals that came here to die. Coyotes died here, and dogs. And in the hearts of men, magic died along with belief in spirits. If he were still a shaman he would heed the omens and lead his people away from such a place, but now he was just a man. When he looked at the body of a dead coyote, he saw only that and no omens. But through the inner eye of purely human logic and inference, he saw much more.

Cha-kwena thought back. When he had first seen the coyote, it had been sick. The dogs had run with it. Scar Nose had returned to the cave and, soon sickly, had whelped a litter of stillborn and sickly pups. Little Doh-teyah, who was often licked by Scar Nose and the other dogs, was suffering from suppurating eyes, just as the pups were. And Mah-ree was making the same medicine for all, and using the same strips of buckskin to wash the eyes of pups and infant alike. Was it possible that the coyote had passed its sickness to the dogs and that the dogs had passed it to the baby? And what about Mah-ree? Was the girl somehow keeping the sickness alive as she soaked the buckskin rags in her medicine and then used them again and again to wash the eyes of the pups and the baby? Or was it possible that the dogs themselves were the root of the problem? They had, after all, been a gift from an enemy. Perhaps people and animals were not meant to live in the same camp?

There was only one way to find out. He felt much better just for having puzzled out the clues. Cha-kwena stood and faced the north wind beneath the darkening sun. He could smell snow in the air. A storm *was* coming. The White Giant Winter was moving southward. The young man had lost faith in magic and in the spirits but not in himself. "I will not run before you, North Wind. I will not lead my people into the storms of winter. We will stay in the cave. And we will not be afraid of whatever comes!''

Far to the north, the White Giant Winter brought snow once more to the Land of Grass. Jhadel agreed that it was time for Sheela, Tsana, and a handful of men to leave the stronghold and mount another attack against Shateh's people. But no sign of the chieftain at his last camp was found; the snow that had covered their own trail to the stronghold had also covered all evidence of the way in which Shateh had led his band.

Sheela grimaced into the wind. ''After the weather clears, we will be able to see their fires from our stronghold. Then we will know where to search for him.''

Ston was looking around the abandoned village site. ''There was good hunting here. By the bones that have been left, I know that much horse was eaten. Why would Shateh have left a camp in which there was no hunger?''

Sheela hissed at Tsana, ''Because someone among us ignored Jhadel's warning and raided alone, killed alone, and made Shateh nervous.''

Tsana cursed and kicked at the snow. ''We could have had him and the woman-beater Dakan-eh! Had I not been alone on the last raid, I would have been able to slit the throat of more than one aging woman!''

Nakantahkeh was not sure what caused him to command Indeh to lead the others into the country of Xiaheh while he turned alone toward the mountains in search of the People of the Watching Star. Perhaps it was a father's hope of finding a lost daughter alive or an ego-fed desire to test the potential of a daring new alliance. His hunt brothers looked at him in disbelief, then told him that the bad spirits had set up lodges in his head and were raising smokes to fog his ability to think. They were probably right.

Nevertheless, there he was, crouching within his heavy winter traveling robe, motionless in the falling snow, watching the raiders coming toward him as they returned from what he knew had been an unsuccessful attack upon an encampment that was no longer there.

It occurred to him that if he was going to place himself out of harm's way, this was the moment to do it. But the point was to put himself into harm's way. And so, as the raiding party approached him uphill, he leaped from among the boulders, his spear at the ready. "Ay yah! You will hold! I, Nakantahkeh, have come to seek council and alliance with the leaders of the People of the Watching Star!"

Hostile, fur-surrounded faces stared up at him through the falling snow. A woman's voice mocked him. "Ah, Nakantahkeh. We have not killed you yet?"

He recognized Sheela's voice. His gut tightened. So she was still alive! This was not good for him. He had used her. At the invitation of Dakan-eh they all had used her; sharing his slave had been Sits in His Own Puke's way of ingratiating himself to the big-game hunters of the north—as if anything a lizard eater could do might ever win anything but contempt from them.

Nakantahkeh raised his head with haughty defiance. "You have slain my woman. But death might have been a gift to her. She was not young, and she sorely missed Wila and Lehana. I will not know how it was for her until my spirit walks the wind with hers. But now I live, and I have come for something that belongs to me—my daughter Wila, whom you have taken from my people."

Sheela's voice came to him like smoke on the wind. "And if she is dead?"

"Already I have mourned for her."

The raiders looked at one another and murmured softly, impressed by his stoicism.

"What do you want of us, man of the Land of Grass?" demanded one of the tallest warriors. "Vengeance for the death of your woman and child?"

Again Nakantahkeh's gut tightened. So Wila was no more. He had been prepared for that. Besides, he had never had much feeling for his female children. Still, the finality struck him—now that his two boys were long dead and Lehana had been sent away, he had no children at all. His woman was dead, too. The realization was surprisingly liberating.

He repositioned his spear so that it was held upright, no longer an immediate threat to those who stood below. His head went higher. He had more than a daughter to think of now; he had a man's pride and the future of his people to consider. He was certain that whatever he said now would determine whether he lived or died. "As I have said, I seek council with the People of the Watching Star. I have come alone. But when I speak, my tongue speaks for many—for Xiaheh and Ylanal and for the many bands of my tribe that would now seek alliance with those who walk in the favor of the Four Winds."

"Why would you do this?" Sheela asked suspiciously.

"Because we will walk no more with Shateh. He is old. He is tired. He has said that he is weary of the ways of a warrior. He has abandoned the Land of Grass. Against the wishes of his band, he has taken the woman of the chief of the lizard eaters to make sons on, and now he has broken the trust of the ancestors by allowing his people to go their separate ways while he and those who walk with him follow lizard eaters into the Red World. He will seek that which is totem to us all, and when the power of the great white mammoth is his, who is to say that the legend will not be proven true? He may be made young and strong again and, remembering his enemies, return to make them flee before him."

"Then why not walk at his side until you see what the totem will make of him?" asked Tsana nastily, measuring the man with open distrust.

Nakantahkeh shook his head. "If Shateh hunts the totem, if he eats its flesh and drinks its blood, then the great white mammoth will be profaned. The one who will walk in its power will be a spawner of lizard eaters, and chieftain of the Land of Grass no more!"

Sheela had stiffened. Her head was down, her face extended like a cornered animal's. "You say he has taken a woman of the lizard chief."

Nakantahkeh sneered with contempt. "The one with breasts big enough to suckle a mammoth."

"I have killed that woman!" Sheela told him. "You lie."

Nakantahkeh frowned. "No, one who had taken her cloak of coyote skins was slain. Ban-ya lives. She carries Shateh's life in her belly."

Sheela rammed the butt end of her spear into the ground, and an explosion of frustration went out of her lungs and congealed as mist before her face. "And the one who calls himself Bold Man?"

"He has led his people into the Red World and taken the luck of the People of the Land of Grass with him. I know the way our enemies have gone. I could lead you there. Together we would be a force against whom no other band or tribe could stand! We could hunt and kill our enemies, take back our totem, then return to the Land of Grass. Mammoth and bison will follow. Life will be good again."

"Is it so?" Sheela pressed distrustfully. "You would lead us against your own people?"

"All was good in this land when Ysuna, Daughter of the Sun, led the people to offer sacrifice to Thunder in the Sky. Shateh opposed this, and because I was born into his band, I stood with Shateh. Now that my children and my woman are dead, I would ally myself with those against whom I have wrongly made war."

Tsana was not having any of Nakantahkeh's explanations. "He is Shateh's man! He could never be one of us!"

"I will live as you live, hunt as you hunt, and stand to any test to prove the truth of my words and the loyalty of my heart," Nakantahkeh said unflinchingly. Then, in a gesture that was both defiant and submissive he cast his spear into the snow. "Now I stand unarmed before the People of the Watching Star. Now I will take back my honor or will die. I am not afraid!"

"We will see," Sheela said after a moment's pause. "We will soon see."

With grim determination Nakantahkeh followed the raiders. He fully expected to be put to physical torture. As a warrior and big-game hunter, he had been tested before and was confident that he would not shame himself. He stood tall as he walked with the raiders into the labyrinthine hills. When the men led him through the narrows of a canyon that was unknown to him, he noticed fur-clad sentries standing on the clouded heights. Now he realized that he was being taken to the stronghold of the People of the Watching Star. He knew he must win their trust or die; no one whom they considered an enemy would ever be allowed to leave the stronghold alive. They trekked on in silence, with one of the raiders going before them.

When they came at last through the narrows and began to ascend to a great cave, the entire assemblage of the once-scattered tribe was there to greet them. Nakantahkeh looked up at the lean, war-honed men, women, and children. He had no idea that so many were still alive! Wolf-eyed and wary, they stared at him. Even the females and children looked dangerous, especially one wild-faced boy who placed himself to one side of the assembly, hunkering on his heels, appearing as though he was ready to leap to the attack. For the first time the man had second thoughts about his decision to come alone into these wild hills in a death-defying attempt to make an alliance with a stronger people than his own had proved to be. Nakantahkeh scanned the crowd and tried to remember how many raids against these people he had participated in and how many of their number he had slain. How many of his own band and family had they slain throughout the long years of war? His face remained impassive. It did not matter now. A hideous old man with a black, befeathered head and an ocher-stained body was coming through the crowd. Wila walked before him.

For most of the day the warriors of the People of the Watching Star sat in council with Sheela and the stranger while Jhadel listened with solemn introspection, nodded, and sucked at the ruins of his teeth.

"In time beyond beginning the People were one," the old shaman said at last. "If it were so again, perhaps Thunder in the Sky would fold his robe of storm clouds around himself, lay down his spears of lightning, and sleep content with the whirling wind."

"Together the many warriors of our combined tribes could go across the land and, like a flood, pour out of the mountains," Sheela said, rapt, afire with visions of vengeance. "Together we would have no need to go in stealth against our enemies. Together we could surge over those who have shamed us and kill them!"

Tsana was livid. "This Nakantahkeh has made war upon us! He has raided our villages! He has raped our women and daughters and—"

"Enough!" Sheela silenced him, knowing that Tsana was speaking out of fear of a possible competitor for power within the band. Then she eyed Nakantahkeh with cold speculation. "You can lead us in the way that Shateh has taken his band and his lizard woman?"

"I *will* take you," Nakantahkeh assured her.

The woman's eyes narrowed as she conceded, "It has taken a brave heart and bold spirit for you to come here."

"I have come into the hills many times in search of my daughter," Nakantahkeh told her. "What father will not risk his life for his child? And what warrior will not do the same for his new people?"

Jhadel's feathered black head was moving up and down in slow, thoughtful agreement. "Perhaps the circle of our lives in this stronghold is closing, and we should seek council with those with whom we have warred too long. Perhaps it is time for the People of the Land of Grass to be one again and to make those who stand against us tremble."

"How can you say this?" demanded Tsana, trying hard to control his jealousy of the stranger but failing. "This man is not to be trusted! He will never be one of us! He and his kind have no respect for the needs of Thunder in the Sky."

There was silence in the council.

Nakantahkeh looked earnestly at the assembled warriors, at the shaman, and then at Sheela. "How may I prove that this is not so?"

Sheela's eyes never left his face as she answered smoothly, "Submit to pain—a burning or tearing of your flesh . . . or a burning or tearing of your spirit. Choose."

Nakantahkeh frowned. His eyes met hers and held. When she had been a slave, he had shown her no kindness.

Now, in the stronghold of her people, she had somehow become a central force. He knew she would show no kindness to him.

She smiled. It was the smile of a constrictor drowsing with inestimable pleasure on a sunstruck rock while its recently ingested prey still suffers death paroxysms within its coils. "The choice is yours," she emphasized. "The pain of flesh or spirit?"

Nakantahkeh marveled at her wisdom. Whatever he chose now, he could not later say that she, or any of her people, had forced him to it. And yet, for all of her shrewdness, her own passionate nature and capacity to love—as he had witnessed in her attachment to her younger sister—had led her to misjudge him. "I choose the burning and tearing of my spirit," he told her.

The warriors drew in startled breaths; all knew that they themselves would never be as brave as this.

Sheela took thoughtful measure of him. "Do you know what you are choosing, Nakantakeh?"

"I choose the greater pain," he confirmed.

Jhadel's eyes had gone as small and sharp as obsidian lancets. "With your own hand you will take this pain onto your spirit?"

"Yes," said Nakantahkeh. "With my own hand let it be done. I will honor Thunder in the Sky in the way of your people. But when it is finished, let no man say that I am not one of you!"

With the night came a feast fire. There were dancing and singing and story chanting of bygone days, when mammoth were as plentiful in the Land of Grass as the grass itself. All the while the daughter of Nakantahkeh sat proudly beside her father, reminding everyone that she had told them that he would come for her.

Warakan watched fearfully from the little ledge that he had made his own. Now and then his body shook involuntarily. The cave seemed filled with fire and color and sound—so much so that his senses ached. He recognized the songs, the dances, the vibrant patterns of the body paint with which the People of the Watching Star had adorned them-selves. He knew all too well how this night must end.

"Here, boy, a few wedges of fat and a haunch of hare from the feast! Why do you not join us?" invited Oan, handing up the meat. "Sheela says that tonight we will reopen the circle of life in the way of our ancestors. Jhadel has agreed that the time is right. Come! We will partake of the mushroom now, and our shaman will lead us on the path of dreams."

Warakan accepted the wooden plate, then set it down, took up the haunch, and stared into Oan's wide, earnest face as he gnawed at the meat. She was kind to him. He did not dislike her, but she was one of "them," so he had not spoken to her since the night his sister had been sacrificed to the storm god. Warakan did not move. He continued to stare at Oan, making her uncomfortable. Soon she would go away.

"Have it your way," Oan scolded. "But I will bring you none of the mushroom. You will not know the joy of the dream path. And afterwards, when it is done, I will not bring you any gift meat. The power of the Great One shall pass you by!"

Warakan quaked. He put the haunch down, his appetite suddenly gone. Let the Great One pass him by! he thought bitterly. He would not eat of that meat again! This time Oan could not make him! He knew that she meant well, but he would bite off her hand if she tried!

He stayed where he was, watching, listening, as the woman walked away. That which he feared would not take place for a long while yet. First the girl would dance and make merry and be touched by all; then she would be prepared for her journey to the Morning Star, where the great cannibal Thunder in the Sky awaited her.

He squinted across the crowded cave. The weather baffles had been lowered because it had been snowing. If the skies did not clear, perhaps the celebrants would change their minds and merely go to sleep. Then, at dawn, the girl would still be alive, and Sheela would not be standing in her skin to greet the morning. Warakan thought about this for a long time. He closed his eyes and wished that the girl's life might be saved. Then, emotionally exhausted, he fell asleep.

When he woke, the celebration was building toward its inevitable climax. The people, including Wila, were dancing. The big, four-man drums were sounding. He felt sick. The drumskins had not been properly cured, and the sound was thick, as heavy as his heart. Suddenly he saw Wila come stomping close. Leaping like a young goat, he vaulted from the ledge and took her hands as he began to dance with her.

"Run away!" he whispered imperatively. "You must run away!"

Amazed to hear him speak, Wila stopped dancing and stared down at him. "You can talk!"

"Yes! I can talk! And you must listen to what I say!" But even as he spoke, Warakan looked up into her eyes and knew that he had little hope of convincing her. The centers of her eyes were enormous black pools that had sucked in all of the soft brown color that normally surrounded them. The mushrooms had already taken her on the dream path. "Wila!" he said, and pulled hard on her hands, drawing her away from everyone else. "You must run away!"

"Why? My father has come to rescue me. He likes it here so much that he has decided to stay!"

"He will kill you, Wila!"

She blinked, then burst out laughing. "He has risked his life to come for me!"

"And he will sacrifice your life at dawn to win his place among my people."

She sneered at him. "Go away."

"I will not! Not until you believe me. He does not care about you, Wila. I can see it in his face when he looks at you."

She yanked her hands from his, then slapped him hard across the cheek. "As long as my father is with me, I am safe. The People of the Watching Star are *my* people now! I am glad that Nakantahkeh has consented to become one of their tribe! Shateh was old, weak! I hope he dies! I hope you die, too!"

"He will," assured Sheela, appearing out of nowhere. "Now that he has found his tongue, it will surely kill him!"

Warakan cried out in surprise at the sound of Sheela's threat as she grabbed him by the hair and jerked him roughly aside.

"Come, Wila." Sheela placed an arm around the girl and led her back to the circling dancers.

Warakan was left to rub his aching scalp as the daughter of Sheehanal looked back at him. Her eyes reflected his imminent death. The boy gulped, then backed into the shadows and sought the solitude of his ledge. He was terrified, and not only for the girl.

For a long time he sat very still, immobilized by apprehension. He wondered what to do. He listened to the drums, to the singing, and after a while, when the movement and sound and firelight combined to reach a fevered pitch, he knew the answer: He could not stay. He *would* not stay. He would not witness another sacrifice. He would not watch Sheela dance in Wila's skin as she had danced in the skin of his sister.

Sickened and horrified by the memories of the killing and the ritual eating of the dead, and feeling certain it was to happen again, Warakan gathered his few belongings—a stone knife, a small graver for the piercing of leather, and a coil of sinew for the making of snares—and bundled them into his single well-worn sleeping skin, along with the wedges of fat and haunch of hare. He quickly pulled on his winter overshirt and leggings and his trisoled hunting moccasins, then slung his hunting gloves around his neck by their carrying thong. Finally he took up his two spears, then climbed down from the ledge, snatched up a pair of snow walkers and a winter robe—neither of which belonged to him—and left the cave. Not even the dogs saw him go.

A hard wind was blowing snow from the north. Donning his gloves and the robe—a hooded garment of wolfskins that had belonged to one of the more belligerent of the older boys—Warakan tied the snow walkers together by their bindings, slung them over his shoulder, and hurried down into the narrows. It took careful maneuvering to pass unseen by the sentries through the defile; but with the snow curtaining his every step, he soon reached the open grass-land and ran for his life.

The sounds of frenzied chanting, drumbeat, and the high screams of whistles were coming to him from the cave as he laced on his snow walkers, then hurried on. He felt warmed and satisfied in the weight of the stolen traveling garment and snow walkers; the youth from whom he had stolen them would be doubly vexed when he realized that Warakan, whom he had teased and intimidated, had been bold enough to take them from him. But after a while the satisfaction ebbed. The robe was heavy, and the snow walkers were too large for him. He had to stop repeatedly to adjust the bindings. He crouched in the wind and listened, suddenly realizing that he could not hear sounds from the cave anymore.

The boy stood and turned in a circle. He heard only the wind and the sound of stinging snow. The contours of the land were vaguely visible, unfamiliar. He had come far. For the first time the boy felt the weight of solitude and wondered how long he would survive.

Longer than if you had stayed at the cave, he reminded himself. *You have meat and fat. You have spears and sinew and a knife. You can make fire. You can keep warm.*

The wind gusted into his face; it held the smell of the north wind. He turned his back to it and headed south. The chieftain called Shateh was out there somewhere, moving along the game trails toward the distant Red World. He was old, they said, and weary of war and death; perhaps he would welcome a small boy who would warn him that one who had once walked at his side had betrayed him to his enemies and that even as he led his people south to live in peace, the few were forming themselves into many so that they might come against him in war.

But how to find him?

Warakan drew in a deep breath of the night. "North Wind, set me upon the right path. Show me the way to the Red World. And help me to find this man Shateh."

High above the Lake of Many Singing Birds, Han-da, shaman of the Blue Sky People, awoke with a start. He had been sleeping beneath a reed awning, which had been raised for him on the lip of the hillside cave he had appropriated

for himself. The aerie had once belonged to his old friend
Hoyeh-tay. Han-da thought that the spirit of his old friend,
long dead, would not mind that the Blue Sky People had
taken over the village after Dakan-eh had abandoned it to
travel to the Land of Grass. Han-da had seen fit to move to
Dakan-eh's village with his band after the waters of his own
lakeside settlement had gone up to the sun.

Han-da looked up. Water was dripping onto his head.
It was raining! he realized in jubilation. And someone was
calling his name.

"Han-da! Han-da! Get up! Dakan-eh is coming! Bold
Man returns with the rain! Even now he sleeps with the
people of Iman-atl in the Village of Many Reeds. Tomorrow
he will come here! Will he kill us all for taking over his
village? Aiee! What must we do?"

Han-da climbed to his feet and scooped up his
antelope-scrotum rattle. As he stared down at the runner
who was coming toward him, the shaman began to shake the
rattle violently; the action soothed him, even though it
would not save him from the wrath of Dakan-eh, chief of
this village. Nevertheless, as Han-da continued to shake the
noisemaker at the sky while the rain drenched him, the
sound of the rattle's clicking bones and bird beaks were
distracting. Perhaps, he decided, his ritual action was like
picking at a minor scab in order to avoid screaming in terror
of a much greater wound.

Fear, more than the chill of the rain, began to raise
goose bumps along the nape of Han-da's skinny neck as the
runner clambered up to the cave and stood before him.

"Shall we wake the band, Han-da? Shall we run before
one who will come to us as a savage warrior of the Land of
Grass? The People say he brings the rain, Han-da. They say
his powers are great and his spears fierce! Aiee! You were
no friend to Dakan-eh. When he called the men and
shamans to fight against enemies on the Blue Mesas, you
ran away. You threw away the sacred stone of our ancestors
and—"

"Enough! I do not need one who is not shaman to
recount the history of my people for me! I am not ashamed!
I do not regret leading my people away from conflict! In the

end I was not the only shaman to cast away my sacred stone rather than do battle with those who sought to steal the power of the stones! Now the stones are gone! Now the enemies have gone away to battle one another in their own world! Have you heard why Dakan-eh returns?''

The runner nodded his sodden head. ''To be a man of the Red World again. And to release the life spirits of his father and Na-sei into the winds that blow over the land of our ancestors.''

''Owa-neh is dead?''

''Killed in a great hunt! Na-sei, too! Ah, the stories that are passing through the villages! Aiee! Dakan-eh returns to us in great honor!''

Han-da frowned. He had never liked or trusted Dakan-eh, but the prospect of being forced to take his people back to their miserable little village on the shore of what once had been Red Butte Lake was much more intimidating. Many, including the village headman, had died of sickness after the lake had turned to salt. Han-da's frown deepened. He lowered his arm and let the rattle hang at his side. ''You say that Dakan-eh has brought the rain?''

''Dakan-eh says it!''

''He has a shaman with him now?''

''No. But he returns with four women instead of one, and with—''

''A headman with no shaman cannot long hope to command respect in the Red World.'' Han-da's eyes narrowed into slits of introspection as he shook the rattle and said, ''In a land without a totem, a shaman without a headman finds it difficult to make the decisions that will keep a band alive . . . and even such a bold headman as Dakan-eh will need a shaman now that he has returned to the land of the ancestors.''

''He has brought the *rain,* Han-da! What shaman has been able to do that?''

''You say he brings his dead back to the land of the ancestors! Without a shaman to speak for him, the People might wonder if he has brought the rain or if it follows him in sorrow. Who can say if this is a good omen or bad? A

shaman could tell them . . . whatever Dakan-eh would
wish them to hear.''

"Then you will not tell our people that they must run
away?''

"No. We will stay and prepare a greeting for those
who return. It is clear to me now that the Four Winds have
brought us here, not to usurp the village of another but to
await the coming of one who will now be headman of our
band.''

At last Dakan-eh and his great gathering of followers
came to pause before the Lake of Many Singing Birds. With
stern-eyed grace he accepted the greeting of Han-da. It was
obvious to Bold Man what the obsequious shaman was up
to; Dakan-eh was not taken in, nor did he fail to recognize
his own advantage in the situation. If things failed to go well
for him, he could blame his new shaman. He did not like the
man; but he did like the look of some of the younger women
in Han-da's band, and it pleased Bold Man enormously to
find himself suddenly chieftain of an enormous following—a
great headman in a land of little people.

The responsibilities of that position sobered him. The
rain had stopped. A closer look at the Lake of Many Singing
Birds brought shadows to Dakan-eh's spirit. The rain was
sweetening the blue waters that had once stretched for
miles. But since his absence, the shore had receded into a
quagmire of rotting, foul-smelling reed beds, and the
surface of the lake was brown in many places, revealing
shallows where deep, clear water had once reflected gentle,
benevolent skies. Soon the Cold Moon would rise over the
Red World. Would it bring much-needed rain or only thin,
dry snow or wind-driven dust until, eventually, this lake
also went up to the sun and he and his people could live here
no more?

People were gathering around him now. He was
grateful for the distraction of their asking for news of the
distant Land of Grass. He told them what they wanted to
hear: He and his fellow hunters had been great warriors in
that wondrous place, but now they yearned for the company
of their own people and for the land of their own ancestors.

When Cheelapat and Rayela looked at him out of disbelieving eyes, his glance warned them to keep silent and know their place. And when Kahm-ree grumbled about how her Ban-ya had been given away to strangers, he shook his head and said quite kindly, "The years of this woman are telling on her. I have given my Ban-ya to a great chief! A woman of the Red World will walk tall in the Land of Grass, just as the women whom the chief has given in exchange to me will walk tall here."

Mollified, the onetime women of Shateh did not speak. When Ghree was asked about the whereabouts of Ma-nuk she told them that her former man had chosen to remain behind. "But my children and I have chosen to walk with Dakan-eh, and he has chosen us! We are of the headman's fire circle now!"

Having listened in awe, a young woman of one of the bands that had been following Bold Man ever since he entered the Red World sighed with open adoration. "Truly, Dakan-eh is a man upon whom the spirits smile! It has not rained since he left us, and now that he returns to the Red World, behold the clouds on the far horizon."

"Yes, behold the clouds," said Han-da. "When will they come to us, Man Who Brings Rain?"

Dakan-eh, recognizing a trap, responded nastily, "*You* are shaman, Han-da. It is up to you and your fellow holy men to say when the rain will come. I can only summon it and hope that it will follow."

Bold Man's eyes turned northward. The minor rain squalls that had been advancing across the Red World were nothing compared to the vast, tumultuous storm clouds that lay over the land from which he had come. His brow furrowed; the new scar ached. He remembered other storms, and he wished Shateh dead in whatever storms were moving upon him now.

In days to come, the people of Shateh would remember the storm that forced them to turn temporarily from their southerly course so that they might seek the protection of the bluffs to the lee of the old bison wallows. There, in better times, they had hunted often and taken much meat.

With strong winds and blowing snow, travel had become a misery, and everyone was grateful for an opportunity to rest. They unpacked their sledges, raised their windbreaks, and settled in to wait out the storm. It passed in a single night and day.

Afterwards, the new mother, Senohnim, complained of bleeding. The children were irritable, old Lahontay was noticeably fatigued, and the pads of the dogs' feet needed attention.

"We will stay in this camp," Shateh informed them, restlessly eyeing the sky. "But only for two days. Then we go on."

It proved to be a good camp. Deer were taken. The people and their dogs ate well. For the sake of the new mother, a third day was spent resting.

"With tomorrow's sun we will go on," Shateh told them.

But with the rising of the sun, a wolf came blundering into the encampment. The dogs raced barking and snarling to the attack. The wolf screamed, and for Shateh and his people, nothing would ever be the same again. The wolf had screamed in the voice of a boy.

"No! Get back! Get away!"

"Raiders?" shouted Lahontay, rising and reaching for his spear as Shateh's band raced forward to see a young boy in a wolfish robe holding a pair of spears to keep the dogs at bay.

Shateh waded in among the dogs and drove them back. He towered over the boy. "Raiders?" He snorted at Lahontay. "If this is the size of the raiders who have come against us in the past, they all would have been blown away by the wind!" He looked down at the child. "Who comes uninvited into the camp of Shateh?"

The newcomer, exhausted and unsteady on his big snow walkers, exhaled a sigh. "It is Warakan, who has run away from the People of the Watching Star and who comes uninvited into this camp! It is a friend who has come to tell Shateh that the one named Nakantahkeh has betrayed you to my people. By now he has offered his own daughter to Thunder in the Sky to prove his loyalty to them. By now he is a man of the People of the Watching Star. Together with Tsana, Jhadel, and Sheela, he will make a great alliance with the bands that once named Shateh Brother. They will come to you. They will find and kill you. Then they will seek the totem and bring death to the one called Bold Man of the Red World!''

Standing not far from the other women, Ban-ya gasped.

Shateh did not miss her reaction to the boy's warning.

''Like the whirling wind they will come,'' said Warakan as, no longer able to stand, he collapsed to his knees. ''They will sweep Shateh away unless you run before them. Let Warakan run with you, Shateh! I, too, am tired of death!''

The chieftain's eyes narrowed; a few moments passed before he spoke. ''It will take time for the People of the Watching Star to make this alliance of which you speak. And then it will take time for them to seek Shateh. By that time Shateh will have reached the Red World and made an alliance of his own.''

''With lizard eaters?'' asked Wehakna, shaking her head dubiously.

''With Dakan-eh Who Walks in the Favor of the Four Winds!'' replied Shateh resolutely.

''With Bold Man Who Chases the Whirling Wind before Him!'' added Ban-ya with pride.

Shateh did not like her tone. There was dead silence among the People.

''Come,'' said the chieftain to them all. ''We must break camp and move on.''

''Warakan will come, too?'' The small boy's question was so full of hope that everyone was brought to pause by it.

''Leave him, Shateh. He is of the enemy!'' warned Lahontay. ''A time may come when the man who names him Son will—''

''No man names me Son.'' Warakan spoke his heart to them. ''No woman answers when I call Mother. My sister has been given to Thunder in the Sky. If I cannot walk with

Shateh, then I will walk the wind; I will be of the People of the Watching Star no more!''

Again there was silence among the people.

Then Shateh extended his hand to Warakan. ''Come, boy. You will stay with us.''

PART IV

THE EDGE OF
THE WORLD

1

A strange calm had settled upon Cha-kwena since he had discovered the death of Little Yellow Wolf. Life seemed easier for him now that he no longer believed in magic, waited upon the Four Winds, or asked the spirits of the ancestors what to do. When coyotes and wolves called across the darkness and the children gathered round to hear Shaman tell stories of the hunting creatures of the night, he no longer spoke of phantoms or spirit incarnations sent from the world beyond this world to guide men and women through their lives by way of omens and magical signs. He spoke instead of the true ways of the animals and of the inherent wisdom that was born into each living creature— the wisdom of instinct and reason, of the senses that would enable them to touch and feel, to hear and taste, to see and sense their own prey moving in the night or in the day.

Sometimes Cha-kwena would find Kosar-eh watching from beneath lowered brows. No doubt the man was wondering why the stories had changed. Then, lest his people begin to suspect that their shaman was no shaman at all, Cha-kwena would repeat the familiar tales that had been first told in the time beyond beginning, when the Ancient Ones had taught that the People and the animals were one. He had learned these stories from old Hoyeh-tay—tales of First Man and First Woman and of the totem, stories of magic and adventure.

It pleased Cha-kwena to see the young ones listening, wide-eyed with wonder, or laughing with delight, or shouting with satisfaction in the triumphs of First Man and First

Woman over evil shamans and the eternally warring twins, the Brothers of the Sky, who brought discord to the People. Often a bittersweet sadness would touch Cha-kwena when he spoke to the children, for he would find himself remembering the many times that he had listened spellbound and totally credulous to the same tales. Within him had grown a pride and strength as he felt united to the past and to all of the brave men and women who had walked before him in this world and whose lives had coalesced to give life to him. Then, as a child, he had believed it all. Now he believed none of it. If he wakened breathless in the night because phantom carnivores were stalking him in his dreams, he would calm down, knowing that this was what they were—dreams—and he would return to sleep, haunted but no longer tormented.

For the first time in his life, Cha-kwena knew the gratification that came with making decisions that had nothing to do with what others had done before or with what the omens might portend. If a thing needed doing, he saw to it that it was done; if a decision had to be made, he made it, accepting the fact that only time would tell if it was right or wrong. Whatever happened, the responsibility would be his, and he would accept it.

Cha-kwena rarely went into the heart of the hill. When he did, it was merely to add another scene to the painting. His effort had nothing to do with spirit calling or invocations to the forces of Creation; it was merely a recording of events, and now that things were going well and the People were prospering he derived pleasure from depicting simple things, day-to-day activities: the taking of a deer, the day Gah-ti was strong enough to leave the cave for the first time, and the baby, Doh-teyah, sleeping peacefully through the night at last.

Time was passing in a smooth succession of cold but windless days and nights. Mah-ree had been furious with him since he had commanded her to put the dogs from the cave. He had explained that the band had no use for them now that it had found a place of permanent settlement. The girl, however, had not been soothed by his argument. With her nose at a tilt, she had insisted that if the dogs went, she would go with them. Scoldings from Ha-xa had not intim-idated Mah-ree, but in the end her love for Cha-kwena proved greater than her affection for the dogs. In her need to obey her shaman, she had stood by, sobbing, when Cha-kwena drove them off. It was not until several days later that he discovered that she had been secretly hunting for them and bringing meat to them while sneaking down to minister to the sickly ones. In a rage, Cha-kwena had thrown away her medicine and rags and, after ordering her back to the cave, had commanded her to make new medicine for the baby and never to seek the dogs again.

"They are no longer of this band!" he had told her.

Mah-ree had not spoken to him since.

Now, standing at the edge of the cave and watching the sunset, Cha-kwena listened to the distant growl of thunder on the far horizon. The weather might change soon, but he was not concerned. Instead he found himself surprised to realize that he missed Mah-ree's hoverings and interfer-ences. He was sorry that she missed the dogs so acutely, but the animals kept to the woods just below the cave. They no longer howled at night, and when seen, they appeared healthy enough. Interestingly, Scar Nose and her sickly brood were not with them.

With the animals gone from the shelter, the place became cleaner, and Doh-teyah's eyes finally stopped oozing. Nevertheless, Mah-ree accused Cha-kwena of kill-ing her friends, and whenever she caught him looking her way, she glared at him hatefully and turned all of her attention to Gah-ti, fussing and doting and obviously attempting to make Cha-kwena jealous. The shaman raised an eyebrow in surprise, realizing that he *was* jealous.

Mah-ree was changing before his eyes, putting on weight and growing sleek skinned and high breasted. Very soon, she would come to her first time of blood and formally be recognized as a woman of the band. Ha-xa was already planning the coming-of-age celebration. He frowned. This should not interest him, but it did. Cha-kwena found himself smiling because of the irony. After all of these years of Mosquito's pesterings, now that he finally found himself considering her as a mate, she no longer wanted him.

*   *   *

"Kosar-eh?" Ta-maya came to her new man as he sat alone in the lengthening shadows of the dying day. He did not look up as he worked to put the finishing touches to a new spearhead. She cleared her throat softly to win his attention. "I have made a new knapping pad for you to place against your palm while you are working stone. The one you use is so worn and—"

"I do not want your gift," he said irritably. "I will use the old palm pad that Siwi-ni made for me."

"But it is worn through, Dear Friend. Look—you have cut your palm."

"It will heal. Go see to the baby, Ta-maya. Your presence troubles me."

"U-wa is looking after Doh-teyah."

"Then do something else. Sew a seam on the winter moccasins you are making for yourself. Or see if the boys need help. I do not want anything from you."

Tears thickened her voice. "You will not wear the clothes I make for you, and only begrudgingly do you accept the food I prepare. You turn your back to me in the night. Are my efforts to please you so unsatisfactory, Brother of My Heart?"

He looked up with a grimace. "I did not ask you to come to the circle of my family, Ta-maya. I do not ask you to sew or cook for me. I am grateful for the way you look after my children! But I do not want you to lie down beside me in the night!"

Ta-maya stood so stiffly that she looked about to break. "I must honor my vow to Siwi-ni. You may not want me, Kosar-eh, but you have no right to shame me!" She turned away, gathered up her bed furs and belongings, and walked to where her mother kept her things.

"What is this, Ta-maya?" asked Ha-xa, looking up.

Ta-maya put down her possessions and sat beside her mother. "Kosar-eh does not want me."

Ha-xa shook her head. "He wants you too much, dear one."

"I do not understand."

"He has always wanted you, First Daughter. Now that he has you, he is ashamed."

"Of what? His scars? They are nothing to me!"

Ha-xa shook her head at her daughter's failure to comprehend something that had been plain on Kosar-eh's face since Ta-maya had taken her things and gone to his fire circle. "He is not ashamed of his scars, my daughter! He has proved himself to be a great warrior despite them, even when he had the use of only one arm! He is ashamed because he knows that he has wanted you even when all the forces of Creation would only allow him Siwi-ni."

"His love for his woman was great!"

"True. Siwi-ni was a good wife to him, and a good mother to his children. She was a woman for whom any man would be grateful, but of whom no man would be proud, and in whom no man could find true satisfaction for the sating of his need."

Ta-maya was incredulous. "Five sons and a daughter did Siwi-ni bear to Kosar-eh!"

Ha-xa nodded, then lowered her voice and confided, "And if this woman's heart guesses true, every time he lay on that woman and made new life on her, in the eyes of his heart he was seeing and laying upon you!"

Ta-maya's face flushed. "Mother! He is Dear Friend and Brother of My Heart!"

"He is your man, Ta-maya! A man must be more than Dear Friend, and Kosar-eh has never looked at you with the eyes of a brother! Surely you know this!"

Ta-maya exhaled in abject misery. "I should never have come east with Cha-kwena. I should have submitted to being sacrificed by Ysuna to Thunder in the Sky. As it was between you and my father, so it was between Masau and me. I want no other man! After our escape and his death, my place should have been with Masau's father. Perhaps through Shateh I might have made a son through whom Masau's spirit could have been born again into the world. Shateh wanted me. He never spoke the words, but I saw it in his eyes."

Ha-xa's expression held deep concern. "Forget the past, Ta-maya! Shateh is far away, and Mystic Warrior's spirit walks the world beyond this world. Your life is here, *now,* with your own people and with one who will and *must* be your man!''

''Is this where I belong, Mother? If Kosar-eh wanted me, he would at least treat me kindly. As it is with him now, I have no life. My spirit walks with Masau. It would have been better if I had died with him. Or better yet, I should have gone to Thunder in the Sky as the People of the Watching Star intended. You would never have known of my fate, and Masau would be alive now—flesh and blood, not only a spirit moving warmly upon the wind of my dreams.''

This talk drove Ha-xa to her feet. Wrapped in the jaguar-skin cloak that was once a prized possession of her slain husband, she was an impressive figure as she strode across the cave and pointed furiously at Kosar-eh. ''Better men than you have fought and died to possess my firstborn daughter! How *dare* you send away in shame a child of Tlana-quah and Ha-xa? Ta-maya is a chieftain's daughter! You will not refuse to give to her what is a woman's due! You will eat the food she prepares for you, and you will wear the clothes she makes for you, and you will lie facing her in the night and make sons and daughters on her, as you have made many sons and a daughter on Siwi-ni. Ta-maya is your woman now. You will make her smile gladly in this life so that she will stop longing for the world beyond this world!''

Everyone in the cave stopped what they were doing and turned to stare.

Gape-mouthed, Kosar-eh stared up at Ha-xa. ''I . . . I have not sent her away.''

''You have not made her welcome!''

''I . . . I have been in mourning. I . . .''

''The time of mourning is over!'' Ha-xa shouted. ''It is time for Kosar-eh to rejoice in the many gifts that the forces of Creation have brought to him—the use of his right arm and hand, the returning health of his daughter, the way Gah-ti is regaining his strength, and the new woman at his fire. Siwi-ni lived a long life. Now she is dead! Let her spirit rest! Invite and welcome Ta-maya to your fire circle once

more—but this time do it not in solemn obligation but in the
way of a joyful man receiving his bride, lest she be shamed
before all who have looked upon her with honor! Do this,
Kosar-eh, and do it now, or by the ancestors I will say to
you that she will never be for you again!''

Kosar-eh was too shocked to speak.

Ha-xa snorted and threw up her head like an enraged
mare. "Too long has my eldest daughter been without a
man! And you are not the only man in this band who would
have her! Cha-kwena! Shaman! Come forth now and—''

"No!'' shrieked Mah-ree before a stunned Cha-kwena
could speak, but not before a sobered Kosar-eh was on his
feet.

Realizing what the mother of his beloved was rightfully demanding of him, Kosar-eh was breathless and
light-headed with fear of losing Ta-maya. He went to her.
Taking her hand he said, "I have not asked you to be my
woman because I, in more ways than you can know, have
not felt worthy of you. But I ask it now. I will welcome you
now. Come to me and be my woman, Ta-maya, and I will
shame you no more. You are the finest gift that Siwi-ni—or
the forces of Creation—have ever given me.''

Darkness . . . Kosar-eh waited for the darkness.
When it came, he welcomed it. As the others looked away
and pretended to sleep, he faced his new woman beneath
shared sleeping furs. Naked, as though in a dream, he
touched her bare body and began to love her as he had
longed to love her for more than half a lifetime. Slowly,
gently guiding her upon a journey of mutual pleasure, he felt
her tension dissolve beneath his touch, heard her breathing
become quick and ragged with expectation, felt her breasts
peak and harden as her pulse beat quickened. Gasping, she
joined him in a dance of ever-ascending fire until it seemed
that it was impossible to dance faster or higher. And yet the
dance went on and on to heights that he had not believed
possible until, suddenly, she cried his name with joy in the
moment of climax, and overcome, he joined her in an
ecstasy of release. Together they fell, plummeting in each
other's arms, and Kosar-eh quivered with an intensity of

happiness that he had not known since he was a youth
standing triumphant on his first hunt—young and whole of
body, with all of life's goodness and promise stretching out
before him.

Ta-maya awoke within Kosar-eh's embrace and lay
still, content. The pleasure that the man had brought to her
was exquisite. Because she had been intended as a virgin
bride for Thunder in the Sky, Ta-maya had not been pierced
by Masau. She closed her eyes and tried to remember
Mystic Warrior's face and touch; but it was so long ago, she
saw only Kosar-eh now—strong, gentle, and scar faced, but
loving and caring.

She touched his face in the darkness. "Dear Friend.
Brother of my Heart. My beloved. Kosar-eh."

He stirred and drew her closer.

As he did, she realized with absolute amazement that
she loved him not only as a friend and a brother but as a
man.

Thunder growled in the storm clouds that had settled
over the far mountains. *Thunder in the Sky is angry.* she
thought, trembling. *Masau is angry. I should never have run
away from his people. Perhaps I should have stayed with
Shateh. I should have given him a son. A son to take
Masau's name so that he might live again.* She looked
around guiltily. Yes, he was there. She could feel his spirit
hovering close around her as she whispered inaudibly to the
night. "Yes, my love. I feel your presence, and I hear your
voice in the thunder. Do not be angry. I am Kosar-eh's
woman, but not forever. I have not forgotten you."

2

In the village by the Lake of Many Singing Birds, the life spirits of Owa-neh and Na-sei had long since been sent to join the ancestors in the world beyond this world.

Now, in an enormous conical lodge framed of poles of bent willow and covered with thick mats of woven tule reed, Dakan-eh passed his time at leisure. At last he was a great chief. At last he knew the pleasure of seeing others offer homage to his strength and wisdom. How could they do otherwise? He was no longer Dakan-eh, Bold Man of the Red World; now he was Dakan-eh, Bold Man Who Brings Rain. He had only to suggest that he might withhold his favor, and his people shook with fear.

The intermittently heavy rains that had accompanied Dakan-eh into the land of his ancestors now stopped. There was water in Big Lake, in the Lake of Many Singing Birds, and in all of the minor lakes and ponds. For the first time in all too many moons, once-dry streams and rivers were running fast and sweet in beds and channels. In the upland woods and forests, trees and shrubs were washed clean by the life-sustaining gift of rain.

From the cave that had once been Hoyeh-tay's, then Cha-kwena's, Han-da had proclaimed that the snows of winter soon would come, and afterwards, the land would burst forth with the most abundant spring in more seasons than any living man or woman in the Red World could remember.

"*I* have done this!" Dakan-eh told his people, and sent emissaries across the land demanding tribute.

"Bold Man Who Brings Rain has returned to the people!" the runners were instructed to tell the headmen of the many bands. The messengers walked proudly among the long-suffering people and allowed the hunters and gatherers of snakes and lizards and grubs and seeds to see the height and weight of the deadly spears that Dakan-eh's followers had brought from the north—spears used for the taking of big game and for the killing of men. "Send gifts to Bold Man Who Brings Rain, so that he will continue to smile upon you and upon the land of the ancestors! If you do not do this, Bold Man Who Brings Rain will not summon the rain spirits again, and once more the curse of Cha-kwena will fall upon you!"

From all across the Red World, gifts were brought to secure the favor of Bold Man Who Brings Rain: blankets of twisted rabbit skins; wonderfully woven hunting nets, which, when unfolded, could be stretched across a distance of nearly a quarter of a mile and into which many a hapless hare and rabbit could be driven; choice flint and chalcedony from the White Hills; baskets of roasted seeds and grubs and insects; streamers of snake- and lizard skins and multicolored feathers and stone and bone beads; and the prettiest, most nubile daughters from the many bands.

Now, taking his ease upon a broad, thick expanse of the softest rabbit-fur blankets, Bold Man Who Brings Rain was stark naked and happily sating his appetite for food and females. He was not happy when young Hah-ri parted the feather streamers that curtained the entrance to his lodge.

"Shateh's band is coming toward the village from the north, Dakan-eh!" the youth said excitedly. "He comes once more to winter in the Red World!"

After hearing Warakan's warning, Shateh had wasted no time in taking his people through the mountains and into the Red World. Led by Ban-ya, they had quickly picked up Dakan-eh's route out of the Land of Grass. It was a long trek, but the weather had become clear, and the cold winds had swept the snow before them—almost as though the Four Winds affirmed the purpose of their journey. There were deer and other small game for the taking. Shateh's people knew no hunger.

The chieftain slept contentedly throughout the night, too tired to seek a man's ease upon his women. Ban-ya thanked the forces of Creation for this favor, for at last she had come to her time of blood and, though the flow was light and easily hidden, she rejoiced to know that she was soon to be reunited with her man and was not pregnant.

"You see!" gloated Ban-ya when the travelers entered the village by the Lake of Many Singing Birds. "Dakan-eh of the Red World does indeed walk in the favor of the Four Winds, as do all who follow him!"

And as do I! she thought in a rapture of happiness. Her heart was leaping in her chest.

With their destination reached at last, Ban-ya and her fellow travelers saw armed men from the many villages of the Red World appearing from hiding. The sentries blocked their passage to the village.

"You will not come to this land again!" said one of the sentries. "Bold Man Who Brings Rain has said that Shateh is no longer welcome in the Red World! He has said that Shateh must go away! Shateh will obey!"

Ban-ya's face flamed as Shateh raised a speculative brow. He eyed the short, small-headed hunting lances and forked snake-stalking tridents of those who had come to stand before him. The chieftain, she knew, must be feeling contempt for the poorly armed, pathetic race from which she had come. He towered over them. Even the women of his tribe were as tall as the Red World's tallest sentry. In their raggedly cut antelope-skin loin covers and cloaks of twisted rabbit fur, with their feet laced into sandals of pounded sagebrush fibers and their heads adorned with tufted head-dresses of dried grass designed to make them look taller, they filled her with shame.

Ban-ya lowered her eyes. With one sweep of his arm Shateh could knock half of them from their feet while the other men in the chieftain's band could lift their mighty spears and send the rest of them scattering like frightened quail. She waited for this to happen; she wanted it to happen. Such ignominious men as these did not deserve to live, much less to be recipients of the respect of Shateh.

Yet they received it. The chieftain nodded in deference to their command. Neither he nor any other man in his party raised a spear or made a single hostile gesture. Instead Shateh asked politely, "This Bold Man Who Brings Rain, am I correct when I assume that he is the same man who was welcomed among my people as Dakan-eh of the Red World?"

"The same. He is a great chief now!" Although the small man stood proudly, he was obviously relieved that his men had not been felled by the onslaught of the armed warriors of the Land of Grass.

Shateh nodded; his thoughts were his own. "Then the great chief will welcome Shateh when he learns that I bring him warning of many enemies who will soon come after him from the north. Shateh has come to stand with him— and with you—against these enemies. Move aside with your little spears and your snaking tridents, brave warriors of the Red World. Shateh, chieftain and shaman of the Land of Grass, goes before you to Bold Man Who Brings Rain."

Ban-ya almost laughed to see the expressions of the shaken, frightened men of the Red World as they fell back. Instead of preventing Shateh's progress, the sentries escorted him to the village by the Lake of Many Singing Birds.

But when Shateh came before the lodge of the great chief Bold Man Who Brings Rain, there was no laughter in Ban-ya's heart. Her old grandmother Kahm-ree came weeping to embrace her, but Ban-ya shoved the old woman aside. She caught her breath as Dakan-eh, wearing the finery of a man of both worlds, emerged from his lodge of woven grass. Never had her Bold Man looked more magnificent. With not even a glance her way, he glowered at Shateh. Ban-ya, having expected a joyous reunion with her beloved, felt a sudden chill despite the warmth of her coyote-skin cloak. Ghree, Cheelapat, and several naked young women emerged from Bold Man's capacious structure to stand behind him. Not far away, among a gathering of nursing mothers, she saw Rayela holding little Piku-neh to her breast. Ban-ya's impulse was to shout with joy and run to her child; but the boy was looking at her with only vague curiosity, and Rayela, head high, was smirking.

Has he forgotten me so quickly? Her heart bled, and regret bruised her spirit as she thought of the times that she had placed the boy into Sheela's care; he was used to being handled by other women. *Aiee!* she wailed in silent anguish. *Can he have forgotten that I am his mother?*

Bold Man was looking at her now. Again she caught her breath. Was that love that she saw in his eyes? She could not tell. Quickly he looked away to stare imperiously at the diminished size of Shateh's band. Ban-ya knew him well enough to be certain that he was now going to take the opportunity to repay the chieftain for banishing him from the Land of Grass.

"Has the Cold Moon risen early in the Land of Grass to cull the weak and otherwise unfit from Shateh's 'herd'? I warned you what would happen if you sent me from among your people after all I had done and risked for you."

Ban-ya's eyes widened. What was he saying? Could he not see that Atonashkeh was not among Shateh's warriors?

Dakan-eh apparently noted this now. He shook his head. "So Spirit Sucker has continued to feed upon the sons of Shateh. . . . This is not a good thing. But why does Shateh imagine that he would now be welcome here? Shateh is not welcome. Shateh must go. But before he does, I will have my woman Ban-ya. In return, you may have the two females given to me. I have found younger women to replace them, and my son grows pale on the thin milk of your woman from the Land of Grass."

Shateh's face tightened at the insult.

Ban-ya barely noticed. She nearly laughed out loud when, triumphant, she saw Rayela wither with shame and clutch Piku-neh close. But in the next moment it was Ban-ya who withered—not with shame but with profound disappointment, even though she had anticipated the chieftain's response.

"You may keep the women I have given to you," Shateh informed coldly. "I will keep Ban-ya. She is incapable of nursing your son. My life grows in her belly now. And you had best reconsider your hostile greeting and make this warrior chieftain and his hardened fighters welcome. Bold Man may have brought the rain, but he will need all of the men he can get if he is to stand successfully against the storm of enemies that will soon come after us.''

Ban-ya frowned as the shaman Han-da strode aggressively forward in the feathered, grass-tufted finery of his rank. He shook his rattle in Dakan-eh's face. ''Is this the rain that you have brought to us?'' he shrieked. ''An outpouring of enemies into the Red World?''

The right corner of Dakan-eh's mouth lifted into a dangerous sneer. Without hesitation, he pushed the man down.

Shateh, ignoring the incident, raised both arms in a gesture of peace and brotherhood toward Dakan-eh. ''Let there be no more words of anger between us. What has been cannot be changed. But be forewarned—a storm of men *is* building to the north. They seek vengeance against us for things done during the great war. An alliance of the surviving warriors of the People of the Watching Star and of the People of the Land of Grass soon will come against us. One who was once a slave to you is leading them. Her people say that the blood of Ysuna runs in her veins, and through her the Daughter of the Sun has been reborn.''

Dakan-eh was stunned. The villagers were silent, openly afraid.

Shateh took measure of them. ''I have thought much on this. When all is finished and our enemies are no more, it will be a good thing. Two people will have become one, and the one will be stronger than the two alone!''

Pah-la stepped forward from her place among the widows. ''How can this be?'' she asked tremulously. ''We of the Red World are not a warrior people. Once we fought with Shateh in a great war against the People of the Watching Star. But in those days we were strong in the power of our totem, and Shateh was allied with all of the chieftains of the Land of Grass. Now the great white mammoth has disappeared, and those who were once Shateh's allies are his enemies. How can we hope to prevail?''

With an upraised hand Shateh silenced the villagers' restless murmuring. "Our power to win lies in part in our weapons and our will to win. But we must also seek our totem in the land beyond the Red World."

Dakan-eh was scowling. "The great white mammoth walks with Cha-kwena beyond the Mountains of Sand."

"So you have said," affirmed Shateh. "It seems you were right: As long as Cha-kwena walks in the power of the great white mammoth, Raven and Death will follow us, and we cannot hope to stand against our enemies. So we will hunt and kill Cha-kwena, then take the sacred stone and walk in the path of our totem once more."

"It cannot be done!" shouted Han-da, jumping to his feet. "We must run away! There are places in this land to which the enemy will not come. We must go!"

"What is this small thing?" interrupted Shateh, eyeing Han-da with revulsion.

"It fancies itself a shaman," replied Dakan-eh. "I have allowed it to reside in my village."

Shateh eyed Han-da as though he were less than a flea on one of his people's dogs. Then he looked at Dakan-eh and, seeing the suspicious gleam in the younger man's eyes, stared straight into the heart of his ambition. "No longer does Bold Man Who Brings Rain need to look to the advice of such nits as this. I, Shateh, will stand as shaman with you now!"

The reaction among the villagers was instantaneous. Han-da shook his rattle in the chieftain's face. "You are not welcome in this land! Go!"

Now it was Shateh who shoved the little man down. "It is you who will go if you do not learn your place!"

Ban-ya saw an unmistakable tremor ripple through her Bold Man. She knew the moment was costing him. Shateh had come in friendship; but Dakan-eh was not one to back down from a confrontation. He stood as though at the edge of a deadfall and seemed to be debating whether he should plunge in or whirl around and leap to the attack. "And if I say no to you?"

Shateh shrugged. "Either way I will hunt the totem, as our enemies plan to hunt it. Whoever finds it first will win the power to challenge the Four Winds. The choice is yours, Dakan-eh. Stand with me or stand aside, but do not get in my way. I have come far. My warriors are a greater fighting force than yours. And I am weary of those who might try to stop me!''

At Dakan-eh's command, runners were sent across the Red World so that all might come to the village beside the Lake of Many Singing Birds to prepare for the journey across the Mountains of Sand, beyond the edge of the world, and into the unknown country where the totem had gone.

And in the darkness of that star-stung night Dakan-eh stood alone and brooded at the edge of the village. *But why,* he wondered. His life had suddenly become all that he had ever hoped it might be. He had become a great chief, and everyone had been obeisant to his every command. If he had regrets about being banished from the life of a warrior and big-game hunter to the north, his disappointment had been salved by the female game he had won to his bed furs and by the fear and awe in which he was held by the men of the Red World. Then Shateh had come with his talk of enemies and alliances. Suddenly, in the shadow of the older, greater man, he felt small again, less than a chief again.

Ban-ya came to him in silence. "Dakan-eh . . . I have waited, dreamed, *longed* for this moment," she whispered, touching his forearm. Then she opened her robe and showed him her nakedness. "I am yours, always yours. No other man can possess me." She slipped to her knees, raised her great breasts, then knelt back and spread herself in invitation. "Shateh need never know of this. No one need ever know."

Dakan-eh looked down at her. He had had many women since being forced to give this one away, but not one had a body to match hers. "You carry his child," he said, annoyed.

"I carry nothing but my love for you. Come. Lie with me before we are seen."

He looked around. Confident that no one was about, he obliged her with a quick and violent rutting.

Stifling sobs of joy, Ban-ya wrapped her arms and legs

around him and laughed deep in her throat. "Soon I will shed moon blood again," she confided into his ear. "When I do, I will weep and wail and say that I have lost Shateh's son. Then he will not want me anymore. Then I will be free to return to you and be first woman at your fire again!"

"What are you saying?" He knelt back from her and straightened his loin cover. "Have you not understood that a great force comes after us? A miscarriage would be seen as a bad omen. Go away, you stupid woman. You must be Shateh's now. He may not be the bold, brave man that I am; but he was once a great chief. His many warriors will train the hunters of the Red World to fight and use the weapons of war. Until this is accomplished, I need to stay in Shateh's favor. Be content with what you have! Go back to your man."

"*You* are my man!"

"No more. I have given you away!"

"Only because you were forced to." She sat up and pulled her robe around her shoulders. "I have killed Atonashkeh—for you. I have lied to Shateh—for you. And I have risked my life—for you, so that Shateh would come with his men and help you to fight your enemies. Shateh would never have come to the Red World had I not convinced him that his luck lay with Bold Man. It was for this reason that Nakantahkeh and the others betrayed him. I *am* your first woman, Dakan-eh! No one loves you as I do!"

Bold Man was not touched. He was angry. He felt cornered, trapped. Contemptuous of a woman who now claimed to have delivered to him all that he had been unable to secure for himself, he wanted to hurt her. "Soon we will leave the Red World and cross the Mountains of Sand," he told her cruelly. "If Ta-maya still lives, I will take her from Cha-kwena and Kosar-eh. Ta-maya will be my first woman. And you will still be for Shateh. Go away, Ban-ya! I do not want you anymore."

Hot tears burned her eyes as she stared, appalled. "I do not believe you! I will never believe you!" She rose hurriedly and, lest he see her cry, turned and ran away.

3

As time passed in the Land of Grass, enemies became friends. Indeh, having made alliances with the chieftains of the north, led them and their bands to the stronghold of the People of the Watching Star, as Nakantahkeh had instructed. The People of the Land of Grass and the People of the Watching Star set off together across the plains in search of Shateh. And in the Red World, lodges were abandoned as Shateh and Dakan-eh led their combined bands into the face of the rising winter sun, across the desert, and into the Mountains of Sand. A chastened and embittered Ban-ya trudged along. She was pregnant at last . . . but with whose child? she wondered grimly.

Beyond the Mountains of Sand, life was good within the cave of Cha-kwena. Mah-ree had come to her first time of blood, and as snow fell beyond the cave, she emerged at last from the seclusion of a little tent of woven reeds where she had passed the last four days. Now a joyous celebration took place as Mah-ree gave herself over to the happy ministrations of the other women and to the congratulations of the men and children of her band.

"A first-time woman in a first-time land!" declared Ha-xa. "We must allow the forces of Creation to know how glad and grateful we are!" She brought forth the coming-of-age gifts, which she and the others had been secretly making for her second daughter for many a long moon.

It was everyone's unspoken hope that Cha-kwena would step forward after the feasting and dancing and take

advantage of the ancient custom that allowed a man to speak
for the woman of his choice at the conclusion of her
new-woman ceremony. But long before the feast fire died
down, the shaman left the cave and went off alone.

"Soon, dear one, soon he will ask for you!" said
U-wa, touched by Mah-ree's obvious disappointment.
"Truly, I do not know what is wrong with my son these
days."

Mah-ree smiled wanly. "He cannot be blamed for not
wanting me. Since he sent the dogs away I have not spoken
to him."

"When my arm grows back and I can hunt again and
provide for a woman, I will be your man, Mah-ree . . . if
you will have me!" Gah-ti offered.

Mah-ree sighed. "Perhaps it will be so, Gah-ti. But
now I am tired. The night has been long. I would rest now
and dream of the coming-of-age dances and songs and
wonderful presents."

Mah-ree lay awake in the darkness for a long time,
sorely missing the companionship of her long-lost Friend,
of Whimper and Thump Tail, and of poor, sickly Scar Nose,
who, along with her pups, was no doubt dead. The old
resentment hardened Mah-ree's heart toward Cha-kwena,
but only momentarily; since the dogs had gone, she had to
admit that no one had become ill, and the baby was much
better.

Lying on her side and bundling in her new-woman
furs, Mah-ree looked across the cave to the now-happy fire
circle of Kosar-eh. Ta-maya was changing Doh-teyah's
swaddling while telling a story to the boys, and Kosar-eh
looked on with loving eyes. How Kosar-eh and his sons
adored her sister! But then, everyone adored Ta-maya. . . .

Mah-ree closed her eyes and wondered what specific
quality her sister possessed that never failed to win the
affection of others and captivate the hearts of men. Whatever the secret was, Mah-ree felt certain that she herself did
not have it. If only Cha-kwena would look at her as
Kosar-eh looked at Ta-maya! Just once would be enough to
last her for her entire lifetime.

*   *   *

Later, as the coals in the feast fire became glowing embers, sleep came to the little band. Ta-maya settled into Kosar-eh's embrace and closed her eyes. She felt satisfied to be his woman, to care for his children, and to busy herself with the everyday tasks of life. She exhaled dreamily. Now that the snows of winter had come to stay, she was even more content to pass the hours quietly beside her man. It would never have been so with Masau. Whereas Kosar-eh had found fulfillment in her, his sons, tiny daughter, and in the life that they led together, Masau had disdained the gentle, settled ways of her people. He had been driven by the ghosts of his savage past.

Thunder was growling in the snow clouds. Shivering, Ta-maya opened her eyes, feeling guilty because of her memories and stabbed, as she always was, with a spear of self-recrimination whenever she found herself content in Kosar-eh's arms. How could she love him so much? She had sworn to love Masau forever. How magnificent he had been! How he had adored her! He had sacrificed his life so that she might survive. Her heart ached as she thought of him alone, his spirit trapped forever within the mists and storms.

Again thunder rumbled. The sound seemed to be from the north. "Yes, my love, I hear you," she whispered. Again she opened her eyes. Was she hearing the voice of Masau calling her back to the land of his people? Yes! She felt certain that it was. "I hear you, my love. I will come to you. I will walk the wind with you forever. It is not fair for me to be happy in this life after you have died because of me."

Cha-kwena sat in the falling snow, on a boulder well back from the lakeshore. Not since discovering the body of Little Yellow Wolf had he sought the place where mammoth came to die. He could not say why he had decided to do so now, although something about Mah-ree's coming-of-age celebration had touched and disturbed him deeply. He had needed solitude to sort out his thoughts. Without even thinking about where he was headed, he had come here.

Now, alone beside the water in which the skeleton of Life Giver lay, he saw that the entire lake was frozen except for a few places where long, narrow rifts of open water marked where hot springs bubbled to the surface. As on the day that he had last been there, a single raven perched upon one of the mammoth's upraised tusks.

"Good day to you, Brother, Guardian of Animals and of the Sacred Stone!" said Raven. "Have you not left this valley yet?"

Cha-kwena made no reply; he knew that the words of mockery had come from his own head and not from the beak of any bird.

"He will not listen to you. Nor would he believe me were I to tell him that beyond the clouds and snow, the sun rises on better country and that he should go there now, before it is too late!"

Startled, Cha-kwena saw that a coyote had trotted out onto the ice and sat before him. "You are dead," the young man said. "I have seen your corpse." Disgusted, he took up a handful of snow, compacted it, and threw it at the figment.

Coyote took a hit on the snout, then shook away the snow. "That was not polite, Cha-kwena! Why hold a grudge against my kind because we attacked the great white mammoth? My brothers and I were only acting on the same instinct that has driven meat-eating animals since time beyond beginning. Mah-ree warned you that Grandfather of All had grown so old and weak that he was recognizable as prey; therefore the great one's death was not the fault of the animals whose very reason for living is to hunt and grow strong upon the weak."

Cha-kwena put his head into his hands. He would not let himself fall prey to visions. They were not real! Coyote was dead, and neither Little Yellow Wolf nor Raven could talk!

Cha-kwena rubbed his eyes. He thought of the dogs that had joined the coyotes on the hunt the day the great white mammoth had died. What would Mah-ree say if she knew that her precious Friend was among the ones that had savaged the totem before being killed that day?

Mah-ree . . . How lovely she looked tonight! How grown up! How truly beautiful. Had she guessed that he had longed to invite her to his fire, to ask her to be his woman? But he could not do that—not now, not ever.

Reflecting upon the joyous festivities within the cave, again he wondered how his people would react if they knew that their shaman had thrown away the sacred stone and killed their totem. He was not fit to lead them, not fit to take a woman; he was fit only to do the best he could and to hope that it would be good enough to keep those he loved well and strong and safe from danger.

Across the lake, a leaping cat screeched as though being disemboweled, although more likely it was in the act of disemboweling something else. Cha-kwena put his head onto his knees and closed his eyes. His spears were at his feet and his dagger was at his belt; but he made no move for his weapons. The lion-sized, dagger-toothed cat was not near enough to pose a threat. Cha-kwena wished that it were; he would like to be dead. The idea had an oddly calming effect on him. He relaxed and slipped off to sleep. . . .

In his dream he saw himself running wild across the land. He was Leaping Cat, big and brawny but slope hipped and slow footed. He became Coyote. Pursued by carnivores much larger than he, he ran and hid by assuming the forms of many animals. He leaped into the skin of a huge, fleet-footed stag, only to be brought down and devoured by predators that looked more like men—men with familiar faces—than like beasts. He recognized Shateh and Dakaneh. Next his spirit emerged through death. He was transfigured, an amalgamation of all the animals. Hoofed, clawed, fanged like Leaping Cat, with the head of Coyote and the antlers of Stag, Cha-kwena danced with Raven's clan and feasted on the bones of his totem.

He awoke with a start. He knew by the sun that it was noon. The wind was blowing steadily from the north, and the weather had grown dangerously cold. Through heavily falling snow, Cha-kwena caught the scent of animals on the wind. Looking around, he saw that the long-absent herd of mammoth was closing on him. He was terrified. Were they going to oblige his desire to quit the world? Even the calves were as big as bison, and the cows were huge, with enormous tusks and thick skin furred against the weather with long skeins of snow-encrusted hair. He recognized the freckled ears of the great cow and, too afraid to move, watched the herd as it continued to move closer. Then slowly, barely daring to breathe—and not at all in the manner of a man who wanted to die—he rose and positioned himself to use his spears.

The freckled cow huffed, shook her head, then turned away. The others of her kind followed her back through the tangled mammoth bones, past the nearly but not completely snow-covered mass of something big and bloody. When the herd had vanished into the distance, Cha-kwena ventured forward to look down upon all that remained of a crushed saber-toothed cat. The creature must have stalked him while he slept!

He stared with amazement at the remains. Had the mammoth protected him? It could not be! The idea was preposterous. And yet—

"Cha-kwena!"

The cry of a young woman caused him to whirl around. Mah-ree was poised on the flank of the hill that led down into the valley. His heart stopped. She could not find him there! She would recognize the bones of Life Giver within the lake and know that the totem was dead!

"Go back!" he shouted, and ran to intercept her. But it was too late. From where she stood, she could see it all.

Mah-ree moved forward in a daze of disbelief.

"It is not what you think," Cha-kwena said quickly, falling into step beside her. "The skeletons . . . the bones are very old. They—"

"It is the place of which the ancients told, the place where mammoth come to die." She paused, then moved forward to the shore and stared at the skeleton that lay within the ice.

"It is not what you think!" Cha-kwena repeated. "It is

not Grandfather of All, not Life Giver. The tusks look like
his, yes. But it is not he. Truly, Mah-ree, you must believe
me.''

With a shivering sigh of infinite remorse, Mah-ree
named him Liar. "Oh, Cha-kwena, he *did* need us! You said
that he did not, but he *did*. He was old and sick, and now he
is dead. The People have no totem . . . no hope . . . no
future! This place, this new land, it is a bad land. How could
you not have led us away from it?''

He was suddenly beside himself with his need to
justify his actions and assure her that everything would be
all right. Despite her heavy winter furs of twisted rabbit and
squirrel, she seemed small and vulnerable and in pain, like
a little injured animal that needed to be held and soothed
and stroked. He took her shoulders and drew her close.
Bereft, he did not know what to say, and so he spoke the
truth—all of it.

"You must not be afraid, Mah-ree," he said at last.
"The great white mammoth is dead, but it was only a
mammoth—no more or less than that. All these years we
have named it Life Giver and totem. But here we are, alive
and strong, and it is dead. There is no magic, Mah-ree.
There are no spirits protecting us or harming us. There is
just the wind and snow, and the sky above and earth below.
As surely as the sun rises out of the eastern mountains and
travels again to sleep in the west, we will do what the People
have always done since time beyond beginning—we will
walk into the face of the rising sun and find a new land, a
better land, and we *will* endure!''

The words were so well-spoken that Cha-kwena actually smiled at the sound of them before putting the girl away
from him, looking into her face, and then pulling her back
into an embrace and kissing her passionately. How warm
she was! How soft her mouth! He felt better than he had felt
in many a moon.

Mah-ree shoved him away with her mittened hands and
shrieked at him in rage, "I have not come alone into the
storm to be kissed! I have come to tell you that during the
night Ta-maya has run away. Kosar-eh has gone after her!
We have looked and looked, but there is no sign of them!

The snow has covered their tracks, and the weather grows worse! They must have been gone for hours. And now, after telling me that you have thrown away the sacred stone and killed the great white mammoth with your own hands, you ask me not to be afraid? Oh, Cha-kwena, how will we survive? And how could I ever have loved you?'' She turned and ran back toward the cave.

Stunned, Cha-kwena followed.

4

White . . . cold . . . an agony of yearning and burning lungs and aching muscles . . . Kosar-eh cursed the forces of Creation as he plummeted through a wall of exhaustion. How could Ta-maya have put so much distance between them? She must have left the cave in the shallows of the night, well ahead of the storm. But he, trapped within a full-blown blizzard, had lost all sign of her. Why had she left him? Even though he heard distant voices calling through the snow and wind, he would not turn back for home. Ta-maya was out there somewhere. His life was out there somewhere.

Kosar-eh drew his knife and went to work fashioning an impromptu shelter out of branches and snow. He settled in, protected from the wind, to wait out the worst of the storm.

Ta-maya stumbled on and on, oblivious to the cold and wind-driven snow. Strange spirits walked within her mind. She did not remember leaving her bed furs, donning her warmest winter clothes, lightly kissing Kosar-eh's brow, checking the baby, or smiling down at the boys and her mother and sisters before she left the cave and began her journey into darkness.

A soft, gentle snow had been falling then. Somehow it had lightened her steps during the night as she trekked back across the way in which she and her people had come into the wonderful valley. She was not alone. Whimper and Thump Tail had seen her passage through the woods and had followed. And *he* walked before her. Masau, Mystic Warrior, was guiding her through darkness and into dawn, through the storms and into night again, always toward the land of his people.

"I am coming, my love," she assured him.

His presence strengthened her, shielded her from exhaustion and the deadly effects of hunger and hypothermia. She was not certain how many times she sought shelter so that she might sleep, or how many times the sun had risen and set before she crested the pass through which her people had first entered the valley. All she knew was that the snowfall had finally lessened and the wind dropped considerably.

With the dogs still at her side, Ta-maya gazed down upon the desolate terrain. Her people had dwelled there in one poor camp after another until game and water had been exhausted, and they had been forced to move on. Far beyond lay the Mountains of Sand, the Red World, and, far miles across the sacred Blue Mesas, the Land of Grass. She sighed and closed her eyes. In that country she would give up her spirit to the clouds and dwell with Masau forever.

"You must go back, dogs," she said to Whimper and Thump Tail. "You have your own pack. You need not accompany me on this journey."

But the dogs, ragged pawed and slumping from hunger and fatigue, stayed with her. Ta-maya went on and on. After a while overwhelming exhaustion brought her to a dead halt. She weaved on her feet and sighed, realizing that Masau's homeland was still far away. Her union with her slain man would be accomplished long before she ever reached the Land of Grass.

She sank to her knees. She looked around at the

blowing snow and, although she had no idea where she was, thought that this would be a good place to die. The dogs nuzzled her. She paid no attention to their whining, nipping efforts to get her to her feet. She stared ahead and frowned within the extended, wind-buttressing baffle of her hooded robe. Her nostrils worked. She could smell smoke on the wind. And she could see a tall man holding a tasseled, feather-adorned spear as a staff silhouetted against the curve of the horizon.

The dogs were growling. Ta-maya cocked her head. The man was coming toward her, striding through the deep snow. He wore a bearskin robe, its hood thrown back; the wind was combing through his long hair. The dogs began to bark.

"No," she told them. "You must not warn him away. He comes for me. I must go to him."

But she could not move. Her limbs were numb, her body was heavy and irresponsive. Unwelcome tears of sadness stung beneath her lids, and she suffered an agonizing pang of longing—not for the phantom who was approaching her but for Kosar-eh. She turned her head and cast a quick look back toward the valley; but the pass loomed high at her back and was so far away. For one brief, bright moment, she imagined that she saw Kosar-eh standing on the heights, waving, desperately calling her name. Disappointment closely followed hope as she realized that the distortions of distance and weather were playing tricks on her. She was exhausted and alone with the wind and the dogs and the phantom who now called her name to take her to the world beyond this world. She slumped onto her side into the snow.

The barking of the dogs was frenzied now.

"Back! Get back! Get away!"

Ta-maya heard a man's voice—it was deep, commanding, familiar. The dogs yelped in pain, then, yipping, ran away. Suddenly all was unnaturally silent. Someone was bending over her, touching her shoulder, pulling back her hood. Ta-maya looked up to see the long, expressive mouth and eyes of one she knew and loved.

"Masau . . ." she whispered, and, as she slipped into

unconsciousness, sighed a truth that she did not know until now. "I do not want to die."

"Can it be?" The question bled out of Ban-ya as Shateh carried the unconscious woman into the traveling camp that he and his warriors shared with Dakan-eh and the People of the Red World.

"It is Ta-maya," he affirmed.

Ban-ya stood aside as Shateh entered his lodge. Young Warakan was at his heels like a pup frightened of being left behind. And Dakan-eh stormed in after them both.

"*I* will care for this woman!" said Bold Man. "She was promised to me long ago in the Red World!"

Shateh carefully lowered Ta-maya's limp form onto the sleeping furs that Wehakna had quickly rolled out. He stared down at the small form; her hood had fallen back. A low, ragged breath came from the chieftain as he said quietly, "I had forgotten what true beauty was."

Ban-ya found herself staring down at her old rival and girlhood companion. Even now, like this, exhausted and haggard, with her features blue and taut with cold, Ta-maya's beauty was undeniable. It was a perfect thing, a rare thing. Ban-ya's hands went to her own face. Men often called her beautiful, desirable; but next to Ta-maya she knew that she was less than the palest star shining on the horizon in the light of early morning, overwhelmed and insignificant in the greater light of the fully risen sun.

"I will take her to my lodge now," said Dakan-eh.

The chieftain was irked. "You cannot have every woman you see, Bold Man! This woman was the wife of my son. I do not know by what whim of the forces of Creation she has come to this camp, but I do know that by the laws of my people, she is now my daughter—or wife, whichever I choose. Either way, this lodge is her lodge. She will be cared for here."

Dakan-eh lost control. "This woman is the one woman of my heart! Twice she was seduced from me by the conniving magic of men who were shaman! Clearly the forces of Creation have heard my silent invocations and returned her to me!"

Shateh looked impassively at the man. "Had she wanted you, no man would have been able to take her from you."

"Not 'men'!" Dakan-eh erupted. "*Magic* men! First your son, then Cha-kwena!"

At the sound of the shaman's name, Ta-maya stirred and moaned softly.

Dakan-eh's eyes widened. Furious, he elbowed Shateh aside to kneel beside Ta-maya. He took hold of her furs. "Where are your people?" he demanded. "Is Cha-kwena still alive? If he is, I will kill him with my own hands and—"

His words were cut off as the chieftain grabbed him by his hair and pulled him back and away. Ashamed and infuriated, Dakan-eh staggered to his feet as Shateh took his place beside Ta-maya.

"Bring warm water," he commanded his women. Ban-ya hung back as the others obeyed. Tenderly he peeled off Ta-maya's moccasins and began to massage her frost-stiffened feet. "How far have you walked, little one?" he asked gently. "And what has set you to wandering alone into the winter storms?"

"I have come far," she whispered, "through the high pass and out of the valley over which white-headed eagles wing before the sun. I have come from a place of much game, where mammoth welcomed Life Giver to walk once more among his own kind." Delirious, Ta-maya reached up to touch the chieftain's face. "But you already know this, Masau, for I have felt your spirit at my side. I have heard you call to me, and so I have come, to be one with you, to walk the wind with you forever."

Shateh's face worked with pity. "Ah, little one who has always made my spirit smile, has it been so with you?"

Ban-ya exhaled in jealous loathing of her old friend as Ta-maya sighed, then slipped away into unconsciousness again.

"She is mine, Shateh!" Dakan-eh insisted through gritted teeth.

"No," Shateh countered evenly as he turned and eyed the younger man. "The girl is her own. It is clear that she still mourns for one she can never have. She will rest. Then, when she is well, she will guide us to her people and to the totem." He shook his head as he looked down at her beauty. "If the truth be told, I have wanted her since the day I first saw her walking at the side of my son. If she will have me, I will take her as my woman and thank the forces of Creation for such an exquisite gift." He paused, suddenly aware of Ban-ya standing sullenly in the shadows. His expression changed as he ordered her to come forward. "You have longed to be reunited with Bold Man of the Red World. Let it be so after you have given birth. I will give you back your son, and you will give me a son in return. I will not keep you against your will, Ban-ya. You have been a good woman to me even though I have not always treated you well. Now I say that you will be for Dakan-eh. Let there be no more words of hostility between us about this!"

"I do not want *her!*" exclaimed Bold Man. "Ban-ya has always been my second choice! Ta-maya was first! Is first! Will always be first with me!"

Ban-ya was shaking.

And it was obvious that Shateh was now finding himself hard-pressed to control his temper. "Go from this lodge, Bold Man Who Brings Rain. Take a party of men and mark Ta-maya's tracks. Tomorrow, if the storm spirits allow, we will follow her trail to the path she speaks of. Even now our enemies are closing the distance between us and them. It would be a good thing if we don't have to wait for the girl to lead us to her band. Or have you forgotten the reason why we have joined forces and traveled into this far and unfamiliar country?"

Dakan-eh glared murderously. "I have not forgotten," he seethed, then stormed from the lodge.

Humiliated, Ban-ya did not move.

Shateh looked up at her and asked with concern, "Why do you look so unhappy, Ban-ya? Have I not just given you what you have been trying to win from me for so long? Smile, woman! When this war is over and we are victorious, you will walk once more with your Piku-neh and Dakan-eh! Go now! Help the others to heat stones for the boiling bag and bring water with which to warm Ta-maya's limbs before the spirits of Cold do further damage to her flesh. She is your band sister. Have you no wish to help her?''

Disconsolate, Ban-ya moved to obey. She tried her best to ignore the sideward glances and smirks of Wehakna and Senohnim. From beneath half-lowered lids, she watched Shateh minister to Ta-maya with a concern and tenderness that nearly broke her heart. She was no longer Favored Woman of the chieftain. Once she had given birth, Shateh would give her away. But Dakan-eh did not want her. He had made that clear. They both longed for Ta-maya. She wished Ta-maya were dead. Tears welled within her eyes.

Ban-ya's mouth turned down as, with a vengeance, she began to throw stones into the fire. *Bold Man did not mean it,* she assured herself. *It was only in the passion of the moment that he spoke! And only because of her. But he does not want her! Not really! They would not be as good together as my Bold Man and I have been.* Suddenly she remembered Atonashkeh and knelt back from the work at hand. The corners of her lips twitched into a tight little smile.

''She is a beauty, that one,'' Senohnim was saying to Wehakna.

''She is another lizard eater!'' reminded the older woman with revulsion. Then she snapped at Ban-ya, ''Why are you just sitting there? Did you not hear Shateh tell you what to do?''

Ban-ya met Wehakna's glare with an expression of pure, guileless deference. ''Yes, Wehakna, I have heard. I am to help the sister of my band. And so I will.'' Smiling, she reached for a pair of bone pincers and began to prod and rearrange the coals. *Ta-maya has said that she longs to walk the wind forever with her lost Masau. I will help her to find him. Soon.*

Aware of eyes fixed upon her, Ban-ya looked up. Warakan was watching her. ''What are you looking at?'' she snapped.

''Nothing,'' the boy replied, and turned away.

Meanwhile, Dakan-eh took a contingent of loyal hunters from the Red World and obeyed Shateh's command.

Ta-maya's trail had been made easy to follow because the
dogs that the chieftain had put to flight had backtracked
over her footsteps. Dakan-eh, in a surly and vengeful mood,
followed eagerly. "I swear to the forces of Creation that
after this is over, Shateh will pay for the humiliation he has
heaped upon me this day! And Ta-maya *will* be mine—
whether or not she wants me!"

Standing nearby, young Hah-ri appeared uncomfortable; but the other hunters offered the low, dark laughter of
conspirators as they trotted beside their headman and
crested a high pass. They paused, overlooking a broad,
lake-filled valley. Clouds were lifting. The men caught their
breath in wonder, and Dakan-eh smiled.

"Do you know how long I have been searching for
this? Ah, we can forget the land of the ancestors. Better
hunting grounds lie ahead. Ta-maya has said that the totem
walks there with many mammoth. Now, at last, we will hunt
the meat that makes men strong!"

Hah-ri shook his head vehemently. He was agitated as
he said, "Cha-kwena is there. He has the sacred stone. His
powers are great. He will not let you hunt the meat of
animals that are totem to us."

Dakan-eh's lips curled back to reveal his teeth. "Cha-
kwena will have nothing to say about it. Soon he will be
dead, and the sacred stone will be mine. Then we will see
who is chieftain over all!"

From his hiding place amid tall boulders and weather
stunted pines, Kosar-eh could not see the large group of men
that had followed the tracks of the dogs to the top of the
pass. He held his breath and listened as Dakan-eh continued
to speak. Kosar-eh recognized their voices and from their
words knew that he must remain hidden or die. Having
already muzzled the dogs and thrown his traveling coat
over them to keep them still, he, too, remained motionless.
Men who had once named him Band Brother were enemies
now.

Appalled, Kosar-eh heard it all: Ta-maya was safe.
Praise the forces of Creation! But the many bands of the
Land of Grass had turned against Shateh and had allied

themselves with the People of the Watching Star. Kosar-eh was flabbergasted. How had those mammoth-hunting, woman-stealing, human-sacrificing tribesmen regained their strength? What prompted them to come across the land in search of both Dakan-eh and Shateh, who, in turn, were in pursuit of Cha-kwena? Why did they hold Shaman to blame for their dark turn of fortune? The young magic man could not possibly hold the power to make Shateh and Dakan-eh invincible against their enemies! Cha-kwena could barely assure his own fortune these days.

Dry-mouthed and barely able to breathe, Kosar-eh was torn by conflicting emotions. Now he wondered if he should make his presence known and assure his onetime band brothers that their accusations against Cha-kwena were untrue? He would never send the winds of darkness against those who had once named him Friend. But would the men believe it? Kosar-eh felt doubt. He also doubted that they would let him go his way after they discovered his presence. They would take him captive or kill him; but they would never allow him to return to the valley and alert Cha-kwena to the danger.

His hands flexing on his spear, a frustrated Kosar-eh heard Dakan-eh and the others turn back toward the encampment of Shateh. It was all Kosar-eh could do to restrain himself from rising and hurling his spear into Bold Man's back; but he knew that this would be impetuous and foolish. The other hunters would surely kill him, and it was imperative that he stay alive. Ta-maya was safe for now—the same could not be said for anyone else within Cha-kwena's band.

"Hay yah! The woman's tracks have led us to that which we seek!"

Ban-ya looked up from the special meat that she was arranging upon a bone platter; it was to be Ta-maya's first meal in Shateh's camp. Wehakna had cut cubes of fat, and Senohnim had pressed dried currants into the chunks in an effort to pique Ta-maya's appetite. After placing them on the platter, Senohnim had ordered Ban-ya to present them to the exhausted, storm-ravaged "sister of your lizard-eating people."

But now Dakan-eh's return to camp caused Ban-ya to set the platter aside. Excitement was rippling through the encampment. She rose, hurried out of the lodge, and caught her breath. Bold Man was not the only man to have returned. Teikan, breathless and stressed from his long trip to the encampment, was announcing that he and the lookouts whom Shateh had posted in the northern hills had seen a great gathering of armed people advancing toward them.

Shateh was glowering. "The People of the Watching Star?"

"Yes!" affirmed Teikan. "We got close enough to see that Sheela, arrayed as the Daughter of the Sun, walks before them! She wears a necklace made of a human hand and walks tall in the skins of two sacrifice victims! Nakantahkeh, Xiaheh, Ylanal, and all of the tribes walk at her heels."

"We will break camp," announced Shateh grimly. He eyed the land around him and put a reassuring hand on the top of Warakan's head. The boy, quaking, pressed close to the chieftain's thigh. "We cannot hope to stand and fight them here. We will go. We will seek the totem. Now!"

In a daze, Ban-ya responded to the call of Shateh's other women and daughters, who required her assistance in the taking down of the chieftain's lodge.

Wehakna cursed her as they worked. "We all know what Sheela will do to you if she lays hands on you!" said the older woman.

"Ah, if only we could leave you behind!" moaned Senohnim.

"And the son that I will bear to Shateh, would you leave him behind, too?" Ban-ya asked as nastily as she could, while hoping that Wehakna and Senohnim could not see that her hands were shaking.

Senohnim snorted in contempt. "I have given Shateh a son!"

And Oni added, "Everyone knows that what you carry

will be scaled and claw footed, a lizard boy from whom my
father will turn in shame!''

Ban-ya glared at the girl and reminded with equal
contempt, ''Better a 'lizard boy' than a puny whelp like
Senohnim's child, who is unfit to take the chieftain's
name!''

Wehakna growled and with a leer indicated Ta-maya.
''She is the one who will bear the son to take the name of
Shateh.'' She grinned malevolently. ''Lizard Woman will
care for her now as we move ahead of our enemies.
Ta-maya's feet are sick with frost spirits. She will have to be
dragged on a sledge. I give her into your keeping.''

Ban-ya had no choice but to obey. She made up the
sledge and, with a poke of her finger, roused Ta-maya.
''Come, old friend. We must go on.''

''Why are you here, Ban-ya? Where is Masau?''

''Mystic Warrior is a long time dead.''

''This is not his camp in the world beyond this
world?''

Ban-ya laughed harshly. ''This is the camp of Shateh.
You have come to him. You have told him the whereabouts
of Cha-kwena and your band. Now he will kill the totem.
Then he will be invincible, and you will be his woman. This
has made Dakan-eh very angry. You are trouble, Ta-maya.
Always you are trouble!''

Ta-maya's eyes widened as Ban-ya took her by the arm
and roughly hauled her to her feet, deliberately hurting her
as she forced her onto the travois. ''Why are you angry with
me, Ban-ya? I do not understand.''

''No, I suppose you do not. Soon there will be war and
death upon the land. Soon your boy shaman, your crippled
clown, and all who unwisely chose to side with Cha-kwena
when he stole the sacred stone will die. Soon Dakan-eh and
Shateh will be strong in the power of their totem. But
because of you, there will be no peace between them. But do
not be afraid, Ta-maya. Whatever happens, Ban-ya will take
care of you.''

5

A terrible silence fell upon the little band after Kosar-eh returned to the cave and shared his news.

Cha-kwena stared in mute incredulity. The dreams! The omens! The nightmares! They *had* been visions! He *was* a shaman, after all! But what kind of shaman? he wondered miserably. He had denied and subverted every power that the forces of Creation had ever bestowed upon him. He had led his people into a land of death. He had killed the totem, thrown away the sacred stone of his people, and turned allies into enemies. But what had he done to have brought Dakan-eh and Shateh to believe that he had cursed them, the People of the Red World, and those of the Land of Grass?

The answer came in an excruciating flare of memory as his gaze met Mah-ree's.

"Have you forgotten what the Ancestors have counseled? Speak aloud against no man, lest his helping spirits hear your words and turn them against you instead!"

His blood ran cold. It *had* been a curse; he had known it when he had uttered it. Now, just as Mah-ree had predicted, it had come back to haunt him. As she sat with her back against the wall of the cave and her knees pulled up to her chin, he did not know whether to scream at her, to look away, or to thank her for keeping the terrible secret of Life Giver's death.

"If the People of the Watching Star come here, they will kill and consume every mammoth in the valley," she said softly. "And they will consume us, too."

"We must flee!" cried Ha-xa, bold and commanding in her jaguar-skin cloak. "Come! We have no time to lose! We will gather up what we can and—"

"I will not leave Ta-maya," Kosar-eh said quietly.

Cha-kwena blinked, startled, as Ha-xa turned on the man. She spoke with a vehemence that did not quite hide her deep, underlying grief. "My daughter has chosen to run off from her people. Ta-maya is my firstborn, and I love her; but she is not my only child. I have my Tla-nee and the new woman, Mah-ree, to think of. You have your boys and the little one that Siwi-ni has given you! U-wa has Joh-nee to care for. We must take our own to safety, Kosar-eh. Ta-maya has decided with whom she would walk. She has placed her love for the dead above her concern for the living. She has determined her own fate, apart from us! You and Cha-kwena are the only men in this band! The forces of Creation have given you back the use of your arm. Now you must use that arm to save and protect your people. Come now! All of you! Why do you wait? We must hurry! Do not be afraid! Our shaman is with us, and the sacred stone of our ancestors is with him. Come, I say! We will walk strong in the power of our totem."

Mah-ree, not moving, watched the frantic preparations for the cave's abandonment. Now that it was indeed time to flee the valley, a strange, disconnected mood came over her. So much had happened since the day that Lion called them to the cave. There had been sadness and suffering in this land, but there had been joy and celebration, too. She looked around, reminiscing. In this place Kosar-eh had been given back the use of his arm. In this place Siwi-ni had given birth and died, and unbeknownst to the others, in a far place within this valley the sacred stone and the bones of the totem lay entombed forever within the ice of a frozen lake.

She shivered, suddenly cold and terrified. How would they survive without the talisman of the ancestors and the totem to keep them safe from danger? "I am afraid," she whispered.

Gah-ti came close. "I will walk at your side," he assured her. "I still have one arm, and I am strong enough to throw a spear with it. There are three men in this band now. You must not be afraid!''

Mah-ree was impressed by Gah-ti's bold declaration. He was brave; he was a man. She would never doubt that again. But now she was transfixed by the way Cha-kwena stood immobile at the lip of the cave and stared across the world. His face was set, his hand over his throat where the sacred stone would never lie again.

"We must go," he said bleakly.

"Where?" she asked, fighting down her bitterness, wondering why he did not warn the others that they had neither totem nor talisman to protect them. "Why? Winter is upon us! We do not know what lies beyond this valley. Lion is dead. He will not call to our enemies and show them the way to this cave as he once summoned us. They will come and search for us, but their looking will be in vain. They will go away, and we will still be here . . . in this place to which Life Giver has led us!''

"No," Kosar-eh disagreed. He looked at her out of eyes so sad that they seemed to be bleeding. "They will not go away. They will find what they seek. Our enemies know where we are. Ta-maya has told them.''

And so they took up their belongings and wended their way down from the cave and across the valley. They walked eastward in a softly falling snow until they reached the place where a turn to the left would take them over the low range of hills between them and the place where the mammoth came to die.

"Look!" exclaimed Gah-ti, pointing off excitedly. "Do you see that? A herd of mammoth stands at the crest of the hill. They show us the way to go!''

"Only Life Giver can do that!" reminded U-wa, then frowned. "Perhaps the totem is near. It has been so long since I have seen him! Grandfather of All should walk before us in this time of danger. Where is he, Cha-kwena?''

Cha-kwena's features tightened. "He is not here. Come, we must continue on.''

With North Wind at their back, they trekked through intensifying cold. Mah-ree fell into step beside Cha-kwena and whispered in a worried tone, "The mammoth will be killed. Shateh, Dakan-eh, and the People of the Watching Star will make war on one another, but it does not matter who is victorious. They are all mammoth hunters now."

"We cannot save the mammoth, Mah-ree."

"You don't know that!" Her voice was a mere croak.

He eyed her darkly. "I *do* know it. And so do you. Or have you forgotten that which you have seen lying dead in the lake beyond the hills? Go. Walk with the others. And keep the secret that you have shared with me. As long as you keep it, faith in the power of the totem will keep our people strong. My responsibility and yours, Medicine Girl, is to them, not to the mammoth."

"But you are Cha-kwena, Guardian and Brother of Animals!"

He did not want to be reminded of how far he had fallen. "I am Cha-kwena, Loser of Talisman and Killer of Totem! Leave me alone, Mah-ree. It is not a good thing for you to walk at my side."

Only with the onset of darkness did the weary travelers pause to rest. Snow had ceased to fall, but the cold was intense. Nevertheless, they made a fireless camp. No one complained; they would not have smoke or flames betray them to their enemies.

To Cha-kwena's annoyance, the dogs had followed them and now appeared out of the darkness to beg for scraps. Joh-nee and Tla-nee exclaimed with delight when they saw that two of Scar Nose's pups were with the others. The shaman frowned and would have driven them off, but Mah-ree glared at him in a way that warned him of her readiness to reveal his secret if he did not allow the dogs a place at least at the edge of their little camp. He nodded, too emotionally exhausted to care; what did it matter now? he thought. What did anything matter, except bringing his people out of this land of death?

"The dogs will be useful," said Ha-xa. "If they drag the sledges, we will be able to move much faster. And those pups must be as strong and lionhearted as their mother to have followed us all of this way."

Cha-kwena nodded. Ha-xa was right, of course. Without the dogs to assume extra weight, the burden of the pack frames had been excruciating. And the sledges that the People had been dragging proved such an impediment that Cha-kwena had considered abandoning most of their belongings before moving on at daybreak. His attitude toward the dogs changed, too, because the band no longer dwelled in a settled place. They were wanderers again, and only the Four Winds knew where the group was headed. It would be good for all concerned to share the burdens with the dogs.

Suddenly restless, Cha-kwena rose and sought high ground before pausing to look back across the way he had come. A few moments later Kosar-eh joined him. They stood in silence. Far away, fires were burning and drums were sounding.

"Our enemies are getting close," observed Kosar-eh. "And they do not seem to care if we know it." He eyed the clouded sky. "It may snow again before morning. If you continue on before dawn and luck is with you, snow will cover your trail. You and the others will be safe. But I must go back, Cha-kwena. I must bring Ta-maya out of the camp of our enemies!"

"Luck? When have I ever enjoyed that? Perhaps I should go back for Ta-maya, and you should lead the people on."

Kosar-eh frowned. "You are the shaman, Cha-kwena."

The young man's eyes narrowed. "Ah, yes, and what a shaman I am, too!" He turned his glance from Kosar-eh to stare across the night. He felt strangely empty, as though his skin were not skin at all but a casing of some kind. And inside that casing was nothing—no muscle, no bone, no blood, no substance. Now, suddenly, Vision poured into the casing of skin to fill his spirit with the blood of a shaman's dreams. . . .

"You have come far, Cha-kwena!"

He gasped. He saw his grandfather standing before him. Raven stood upon Hoyeh-tay's shoulder. Little Yellow Wolf was at his side. Owl was perched atop the old man's head, and Cha-kwena's medicine bag hung by its braided thong around the raptor's neck.

"Why do you stare, stupid boy?" asked Owl. "Someone had to take the talisman when one who had forgotten his calling to the shaman's path saw fit to throw the sacred stone away." The bird was as querulous as ever.

"Come, Cha-kwena!" invited Coyote. "You must not turn away from me again."

"Where do you want me to go? And why should I follow the dead?"

"Why do you hesitate?" asked Raven. "Are you afraid?"

"Of the unknown? Yes!" he cried.

"If you are to save our people, you must leave them," said Hoyeh-tay.

"Leave them?" Cha-kwena, not understanding, shook his head in despair. "Grandfather, help me to understand! Please give me the sacred stone!" He reached out for his medicine bag.

"No!" cried Owl. "You have thrown it away! It is not for you! Not yet. You must prove yourself worthy!"

In that moment Hoyeh-tay vanished into thin air. Owl screeched as he took flight and circled above. Coyote turned tail and ran toward the valley and the campfires of their enemies, while Raven cawed and flew off into the stars.

"I am *Shaman!*" Cha-kwena shouted in anger at Owl.

"Then go back along the path of lies that you have laid. Use the truth to erase the trail of blood and death. Remember all that you have learned, and do it before it is too late for you or Life Giver!"

"It is already too late! I have killed him!"

"Have you?"

"You know I have!" he moaned in despair.

"You must learn to seek light in darkness, Cha-kwena! You must learn to understand, to believe, and to follow!"

Breathless, Cha-kwena watched Owl rise higher and higher until, banking toward the east, the bird disappeared into the night. Bitterness touched him. If only he *could* follow! If only he *could* be away from the crushing responsibilities of the moment . . .

* * *

"Cha-kwena? What have you seen, Cha-kwena? To whom do you speak? And *whom* have you killed?"

Kosar-eh's worried voice brought Cha-kwena out of his vision. Blinking, feeling light-headed and weak-kneed, the young man looked long and hard at his friend, then stared back across the hills and toward the valley. His eyes burned as he focused upon the enemy's campfires. His heart pounded in cadence to the beat of their drums. A cold wind had risen out of the north and was sweeping away the clouds. Cha-kwena frowned. Kosar-eh had been wrong when he had predicted snow before morning. But if the scent and texture of this wind did not speak falsely, a great storm would come in two days' time.

Coyotes were howling in the valley. Or was it only the sound of the wind?

"Do you hear it, Shaman?" asked Kosar-eh, troubled. "Listen . . . I have never heard the like. It sounds as though coyotes are running back and forth between us and the enemy encampment. Yet, somehow, I think it is not coyotes at all but a trick of the wind."

A shiver went up Cha-kwena's spine. Understanding seared his mind. "Not coyotes. Dogs!"

Kosar-eh frowned. "The dogs are with our people in the camp, Cha-kwena."

"Yes! The dogs have followed! They have come over fresh snow and laid out a neat trail by which Dakan-eh, Shateh, and the People of the Watching Star will be able to follow us at first light."

Kosar-eh sucked in a breath of dismay.

Cha-kwena was so cold that he felt as though his body would crack. He looked up. Wherever visible among the clouds, the stars shone very bright. Into what black, light-bejeweled quadrant of the sky had Raven flown? Out of which of the Four Winds would Spirit Sucker come tomorrow when the little band was overtaken by swift and murderous warriors from the Land of Grass and the People of the Watching Star? Insight flared, and suddenly, out of the darkness, Cha-kwena saw the light of understanding. The dogs had instigated him into seeing the one and only action by which he might save his people's lives. He was heartened, appalled, and terrified as he realized what he must do.

"If I am to save our people, I must leave them."

"What are you saying, Cha-kwena?"

"You must listen to me, Kosar-eh," commanded the young shaman with a depth and strength to his voice that startled the older man and caused him to step back, awed and intimidated. It seemed even to Cha-kwena that he was speaking with the authority of the Four Winds. "You will do as I say without question. You will not leave this band to go in pursuit of Ta-maya! Ha-xa was right: You are no longer a one-armed clown whose only value to his people is to hearten them in times of adversity. The forces of Creation have returned the use of your arm and named you Kosar-eh, Lion Slayer, Man Who Spits in the Face of Enemies, Hunter and Provider for Many Sons. Now you must also be Guardian of the People."

"Not without Ta-maya at my side!"

"Perhaps someday she may be yours again—*perhaps*. But now you must rouse the women and children. They have rested long enough. Soon it will be dawn. Load up the pack frames, and harness the dogs to the sledges. Take my people fast and far into the face of the rising sun. Soon a great storm will come to cover your trail. By then our enemies will have what they seek and will no longer have any cause to hunt you."

Kosar-eh's eyes narrowed. "I will not let you give yourself up to Dakan-eh and Shateh! They will force you to lead them to Life Giver, then they will kill you and steal the sacred stone."

A calm had settled upon Cha-kwena. Now, as he recalled the words of Owl, Coyote, Raven, and Hoyeh-tay, he placed himself upon the path of lies that had brought tragedy to his people. Hoping that he would now begin to reverse misfortune, he dared to admit the truth to Kosar-eh. "I have killed Life Giver. To set his time-ravaged, wounded spirit free upon the wind, I have done this! The blood and flesh of our totem has entered my mouth. If what the ancestors have said is true, I will not be killed—I may even live forever! But you and our band will not if you do not do as I say and go immediately. I plan to lead our enemies on and on in pursuit of a totem that no longer exists—but never to the place where Grandfather of All lies dead lest they profane his bones. By the time those who have come against us discover my trick, the weather will have turned, and you and the band will be out of harm's way.''

Kosar-eh was shaken, yet he stood resolute. "And you?''

I will die, thought Cha-kwena. But lest Kosar-eh refuse to cooperate, he said coolly, lightly, "Am I not Shaman? Do you imagine that I will not find a way to be free of them, so that I may return to walk with you?''

"Then may the blood of Life Giver and the sacred stone of our ancestors keep you safe, Cha-kwena," Kosar-eh said fervently, grasping the young man's shoulders.

Cha-kwena's hand strayed upward to press the place at his chest where, beneath his tunic, the talisman had once lain warm and safe within his medicine bag. Now nothing was there—only an aching void beneath his palm and within his spirit. But in order to give heart to Kosar-eh and to speed him on his way, he replied bleakly, "Yes, the sacred stone . . . it will keep me safe!''

"May it be so!" said Kosar-eh as he drew Cha-kwena into a hard, ferocious embrace that had more "good-bye" than "good luck" to it.

Cha-kwena swallowed hard as he watched Kosar-eh turn and walk away. For a moment the shaman stood looking down at the little traveling camp. He gazed with love at the furry mound of Mah-ree as she bundled under her bed skins close to her mother and little sister. Feeling the aching sorrow of a lost love, wondering if he would ever again see any of those he loved, he turned and began to trot away into the wind.

6

In the encampment of the People of the Watching Star and their allies, Jhadel threw the sacred bones that foretold the weather, then examined them. "There will be a great storm. The People must go out at dawn, hunt whatever meat they can find, and prepare themselves for a long stay in this camp."

Enraged, Sheela whirled around where she was standing between Tsana and Nakantahkeh and glared down at where Jhadel knelt over the bones. "*We* are the storm, old man!"

"With the wind at our back, we will sweep across this land to feed upon the meat that other men have hunted," affirmed Tsana.

"They will run before us and die beneath the rain of our spears!" added Nakantahkeh.

"It will be so!" said Sheela, her eyes wild and her nostrils flaring with purpose.

Jhadel, shrewd and insightful, appraised her. Ever since Nakantahkeh had proved his worth by killing his daughter, he, Sheela, and Tsana had shared the same sleeping skins. Although there was jealousy between the two males, the alliance of three had nevertheless consistently overruled Jhadel. Today, again, although Jhadel spoke, he found himself without a voice. He shook his head. "Caution, daughter of Sheehanal, and wariness. These are the way to victory."

"For old men," she grated, and turned away.

"And for wolves and lions!" he snapped back.

She laughed harshly. "Only after they have lost their teeth and hunt alone, without the pack."

Jhadel jumped to his feet, head down, eyes blazing. "Before the attack the kind of prey you seek must be stalked, not baited. Your show of arrogance and power might cause our enemy to turn on us or run away! There should be no drums, no fires—"

"Be silent, Jhadel," she warned him. "I am not the girl who once cowered in fear of you. Behold! Daughter of the Sun has been reborn in me! And beware! I am more than weary of your old man's caution."

Shateh paced the peripheries of his encampment. The boy Warakan remained close at his heels. Ta-maya watched them from the lean-to that had been raised over her travois. She trembled and felt sick at heart as she looked across the encampment of sleeping warriors, women, children, and dogs. They were a force dedicated to the destruction of her band, and she had betrayed her loved ones to them. *How could I have done this?* she agonized. *How?*

"You must eat, Ta-maya," said Ban-ya, coming close to offer a platter of meat and fat.

Ta-maya remained lying on her side and waved the food away. "I cannot." She looked up at one who had been her friend in childhood and asked in earnest, "How can you walk with those who have turned against your people, Ban-ya?"

Ban-ya set the bone platter down beside Ta-maya. "I have not turned against my people, Ta-maya. Nor have you. You have done right by coming here. It is Cha-kwena who has turned away. He has cursed us all and must die. Don't you see this clearly now that you are away from his magic?"

"You cannot believe this!"

"I *know* it!" replied Ban-ya. "Now eat, Ta-maya. The women of Shateh have made this food for you, and if you do not eat it soon, it will be wasted."

"I will not eat. For what I have done, I want to die."

Ban-ya's voice held a nasty, hateful edge. "Neither Dakan-eh nor Shateh will let you die, Ta-maya. Shateh wants you. Dakan-eh wants you. Ask any man here who has looked at you, and he, too, will say that he wants you. Nothing has changed with you. Why pretend that you yearn for a corpse when you can have any man you desire—my man, her man, and hers and hers.'' She gestured broadly across the encampment. ''Why not look to your own man for a change? Are you Cha-kwena's woman now?''

''I am Kosar-eh's.''

Ban-ya guffawed, then quickly stifled her laughter lest she wake the camp. ''The crippled clown's? No wonder you have run away!'' She shook her head and chuckled. ''Eat now. Eat well. It is late. Our talk will disturb others.''

Ta-maya watched her walk away. Ban-ya had not changed. She was still the same hard-tongued, competitive, potentially malicious girl who had tried so hard to steal Dakan-eh's affection from her when they dwelled in the village by the Lake of Many Singing Birds. In the end, Ban-ya had become Bold Man's woman. Now she was the woman of a chieftain. Ta-maya could not understand her rancor, and she resented the way Ban-ya had laughed at the mention of Kosar-eh's name.

Without so much as a glance at the food, she sat up and watched Shateh moving back and forth at the far edge of the encampment. *How much he resembles Masau!* she thought, then sighed with infinite sadness. Masau was dead; she accepted that now. What a fool she had been! She remembered her mother's oft-repeated warnings to release Mystic Warrior's spirit to the world beyond this world before trouble came of her obsessive need to keep him alive in her mind. And she remembered her promise to Siwi-ni—a promise she had thoroughly broken. Instead of caring for Siwi-ni's man and children, she had consigned them to certain death.

Or had she? As her eyes remained fixed upon the chieftain, an idea came to her. Ban-ya had said that Shateh wanted her. She caught her breath, rose, and ignoring the pain in her cruelly frostbitten feet, began to hobble forward. If she were to offer herself to Shateh, perhaps she might be able to convince him to change his mind about attacking her band.

"Ta-maya . . ."

She paused, brought short by a familiar voice. Dakan-eh came from behind and turned her to face him. He kept his hands on her arms.

"The forces of Creation have brought you here," he said, and kissed her—passionately, possessively. Then he broke the kiss to look into her eyes and stroke her cheek with his finger. "I never doubted you were alive. I believed that someday we would be together. Now that you have come back to me, it will be so."

She knew that she should not be amazed by his arrogance, but she was. "Go away, Dakan-eh. I have been a fool to come among these people, but I have not been foolish enough to come back to you!"

"I am Bold Man Who Brings Rain! I am Brave Hunter Who Runs before the Whirling Wind to Save the People! How could you not want me?"

She turned her face as he bent to kiss her again. "Because you are also Man in Love with Himself!" she answered. "No woman can win your favor, Dakan-eh! You have always shone brightest in your own eyes, and your heart is so full of conceit that there is no room in it for anyone but you!"

He bristled. "Cha-kwena has poisoned you against me!"

"No, Dakan-eh. You have done that unaided, a long time ago. Have you not yet learned to stop blaming others for what you have brought upon yourself?"

"I *will* have you, Ta-maya!"

"No, Dakan-eh! You will not!" She shoved him so hard that he lost his balance and fell onto the platter that Ban-ya had left beside her travois. Then Ta-maya turned and limped away, leaving him to sit alone amid scattered pieces of meat and fat.

Wincing, she hobbled to the chieftain and paused respectfully before him. She lowered her head and eyes as he growled in annoyance at her presence.

"You must not walk, Ta-maya! Frost Spirits still live within your feet. If you walk on them, they can cause more than pain, they—"

"They can make your toes fall off!" Warakan piped. "Everyone knows that Frost Spirits make toes fall off, and fingers, and noses, and ears and the man bones of those hunters who go out late on a winter's night to—"

"Warakan!" Shateh, his eyes never leaving Ta-maya's face, silenced the boy firmly but gently. "Come, girl. I will carry you back to your place of sleep."

"You must not make war upon my band, Shateh," she said fervently, and drawing in a deep breath, she called upon all of her reserves of strength and courage. "I will be your woman. The man I have left behind will be my man no more. I will tell Kosar-eh that no matter what has been between us, Ta-maya is for Shateh, according to the way of our people since time beyond beginning, always and forever . . . if only you will not make war against my band."

The chieftain appraised her thoughtfully for a long moment, then shook his head. "There can be no peace between Shateh and a shaman who has cursed him, Ta-maya."

"Dakan-eh has spoken falsely against Cha-kwena!"

"Perhaps," conceded Shateh, lifting her easily into his arms. "But Cha-kwena and this man must be enemies, for it is in my heart to hunt the great white mammoth to take its power as my own. The People of the Watching Star are not alone in their quest to kill and consume the great one. I, Shateh, will do this, so that I will be strong and invincible against my enemies! So that I will be young again—the man I once was—for you, Ta-maya."

"No man may kill the totem, Shateh!"

"*I* will kill it. And when it is done, I will let this Kosar-eh and your people live . . . and you will be my woman."

As the Four Winds swept across the world, Kosar-eh stood staring at the fires of his enemies for one last moment before he turned to wake the band.

"Come! Everyone, we must go. Now!"

U-wa sat up and looked around. "Where is Cha-kwena?"

"He will not be coming with us. I will lead you now. Come, I say."

As he roused the band, he explained all that Cha-kwena had revealed to him. And as at last he led them ahead of the coming storm and into the rising light of dawn, the persuasion of every member of the band was needed to prevent Mah-ree from running away to be at Cha-kwena's side.

"You are Medicine Girl!" Ha-xa reminded the stricken young woman. "Since you were a little child you have been called to the healing ways. If Cha-kwena fails to follow us, you will be all that stands between us and Raven's clan! Remember the prophecy, Daughter! On the day that the great white mammoth dies, the People will also die!"

Little Joh-nee's chin began to quiver at the stern sound of Ha-xa's voice.

Gah-ti shook his bandaged head. "I have faced Lion alone. I will not be afraid to stand against Raven."

His brothers echoed him.

Mah-ree was still distraught. "How long will you be brave if Cha-kwena fails to keep our enemies at bay? And how can we allow him to do this alone?"

A worried U-wa drew Mah-ree into a consoling embrace as she spoke of her hopes. "We have all heard the words of Kosar-eh. Cha-kwena is strong in the power of our totem. He will not let the People die. He will confound our enemies, then he will find us. With the power of Life Giver working from within Shaman's body, he will find a way!"

Mah-ree fought free of Uwa's arms and stared in the direction from which the band had come. She dared not speak her thoughts aloud. If the People were still alive while the mammoth lay dead, she reasoned, then Cha-kwena had been correct about that part of the legend being false. And if that portion of the legend was false, so then was the belief that the one who killed it would gain immortality. A great weight of sadness settled in her heart.

"Come, Daughter!" Ha-xa called over her shoulder as Kosar-eh and the others trudged on, with the dogs pulling the heavily loaded sledges. "We must obey our shaman;

before the great storm comes we must put many long steps between ourselves and our enemies. Come, Mah-ree, you must set an example for the children! Look to Kosar-eh's example if you would strengthen your heart! Your responsibilities to your people far outweigh your love for any one member of the band.''

Mah-ree knew that her mother was right. Yet she continued to look back. Where was Cha-kwena now? she wondered. He had killed the great white mammoth but was no more invincible than Grandfather of All. Someday the shaman would die. Perhaps he would grow old; but that was not likely—he had thrown away the sacred stone of his ancestors and disdained the traditions and beliefs of his tribe. Because of him, the bones of his totem now lay in the frozen depths of a dying lake. No magic could help Cha-kwena now, and no mystic spirits would save him. He was alone in the wind, with the sky above and the earth below.

Yet, as surely as the sun was now rising over the far eastern ranges, no shaman could have been more wondrous or magnificent in Mah-ree's eyes than that one young man who cared so much about his people that he had dared alone to take on the might of their enemies.

Standing as tall as her meager height would allow, Mah-ree lifted her arms and spoke to the wind. She did not beg. She did not whimper. She commanded. "Take my words to Cha-kwena! Make him hear my voice! Tell him that with or without the power of our totem and the sacred stone, he *will* survive!''

Somehow, for the duration of her impassioned run of words, the wind obeyed. It took her voice upon its back as she cried, "Let there be magic! Let there be power in the Four Winds! Let the forces of Creation and the ghost of Great Ghost Spirit hear me and take these words to Cha-kwena: Be now what you have been born to be! Be Guardian and Brother of Animals . . . as clever as Coyote, as wise as Mammoth, as wary as Mouse, as watchful as Owl, as swift as Stag, as brave as Boar, as powerful as Bear, as insidious as Ant, as elusive as Bat, and as deadly as Rattler striking boldly in the full light of day! Hear me,

Cha-kwena! For if you fail to stand against our enemies and if there is no mystic world of spirits in which we may hope to live forever beyond this life, then how will I ever tell you that I was wrong on the day I ran from you? I love you, Cha-kwena! Always and forever! I love you!''

7

Without the band to slow him, carrying nothing but a single spear, Cha-kwena made good time. He loped like a young wolf. He took no time to eat or drink or rest. He had made peace with life and with what seemed to be the inevitability of his own death, but still he was afraid. Raven flew ahead of him now.

When he reached the periphery of the valley, the wind was blowing erratically, gusting around him from all four corners of the world. It was cold, so cold as it shoved him forward, then pushed him back. Cha-kwena found it difficult to control the urge to run away from the path that he had chosen; but when he called for courage, it came. He ran on and did not look back.

As he entered the valley, animals that had always been kindred to his spirit converged. They loped at his side or flew overhead: Coyote was with him, and Deer and Wolf, and Mouse and Rabbit, and Brother Bat and Hawk; Raven winged ahead of him, as Life Giver—the ghost of the great white mammoth—appeared to guide his footsteps toward the cave and home.

The young man was certain now that hunger and fatigue were conspiring to create illusions that would nourish his spirit as well as his tired body. When he spoke aloud to ask the animals if they were real, the sound of his voice sent the creatures—all except Raven—dispersing into thin air. The black bird whose presence was synonymous with death flew just ahead of Cha-kwena.

Disappointed and once again afraid, the shaman was nevertheless resolute. He ran on until the herd of mammoth appeared before him. They were real enough.

"Do you welcome me, or have you come to block my way? If you have come to warn me, I thank you, but I come knowingly into danger and must not be turned from my purpose. I cannot tell you if I will win at this 'game' to which I am committed; but if I lose, you will lose, too! My enemies are your enemies. You must go! Take your little ones and your elderly and follow my people into the rising sun. They will not hunt you. You and your kind will always be totem to them. As long as they survive, you will survive."

The mammoth swayed and huffed restlessly. The great freckled cow moved forward, extended her trunk, and nudged him backward. Taken off balance, he fell. The mammoth circled him. Expecting to be trampled, he scrambled to his feet and stabbed out with his spear. "I am not your enemy! Go! Go while you still can!"

But the cow did not go. She stood her ground and reached outward with her trunk. Brazening out the moment, Cha-kwena poked his spear at her, once, twice, just hard enough to draw a little blood and pain. Trumpeting with annoyance, she turned away. It was with an odd mix of gladness and regret that Cha-kwena watched the other mammoth follow her. He longed to go with them but knew that he could not. Hefting his spear, he continued toward the cave, where he would await the coming of his enemies.

Shateh brought his people to a halt at the entrance to the broad valley. Storm clouds lay to the north. Dakan-eh, wincing and rubbing his gut, leaned on his spear. Something he had eaten was troubling him. Trying to ignore his pain, he commanded Ta-maya to point out the whereabouts of her people.

"Never," she told him.

"Kosar-eh and the rest of your band will come to no harm," Shateh promised. "Nor will Cha-kwena if he stands aside and allows me to hunt what I will."

Ta-maya made no reply.

"Speak!" ordered Ban-ya, her mood black as she looked with a worried frown from Ta-maya to Dakan-eh.

Ta-maya set her eyes southward across the valley. Her expression revealed the endless depth of her sorrow. Then, suddenly, a hardness tightened her lovely features. "I will not betray my people to those who have sworn to hunt the great white mammoth. I will put my faith in the Four Winds and hope that my people have had the good sense to run before them."

Dakan-eh growled. "They will never be able to run far enough or fast enough, for wherever they go, Bold Man Who Brings Rain and Shateh will follow."

"Just as our enemies now follow us, Ta-maya," reminded Shateh. "We don't have much time for you to make up your mind. If we do not regain the power of our totem and end the curse of your shaman, we will all die or end our days as slaves."

She did not flinch. "I will not be the one to lead Raven to my people."

It was nearly dark by the time Cha-kwena reached the cave. Raven was waiting for him. The shaman shouted and waved the bird away, but it would not be driven off. It circled, then returned to alight on the top of a stunted tree that grew from the cliff face just beyond the cave's entrance. Cha-kwena glared at Raven. It glared back and cawed as though in mockery.

He turned his back upon the bird. He would have to face it and its clan soon enough when his enemies came. For the time being he knew that he must rest.

With a sigh, he looked around the empty shelter. Because his people were forced to abandon it so precipitately, many of their belongings had been left behind. There was food for the taking and even an old castaway blanket of rabbit fur to keep him warm. Shivering a little, he swung the blanket around his shoulders. Hungry, he pulled a smoked quail from a thong stringer from which not all of the birds had been taken.

Finding himself closest to where Kosar-eh had made his family circle, Cha-kwena settled down beside the blackened stones of the fire pit and debated raising a fire. Wood was stacked neatly close by, and next to that a neat pile of dried grass and cones for kindling. Cha-kwena decided against building a fire, for although one would cut the cold and dampness of the air, its light could prove a beacon to his enemies. He crossed his legs and tented the blanket over his head, effectively trapping the heat of his body within it as he ate the quail. The flesh was soft and tasted of the sage leaves and juniper boughs over which it had been smoked. He picked the bones clean, and after sucking them free of what little marrow lay within, he placed them in a stack to dry so that they could be used for burning at some later time.

A droll smile lifted the corners of Cha-kwena's mouth but did nothing to cheer him. The stacking of bones for burning was a lifelong habit; in the parched land of the Red World and on the many trails of his ancestors, firewood had often been hard to come by, so bones and dung had been collected and hoarded for future use as burnables. But now, sitting here in this lonely cave with his people trekking into the rising sun and enemies approaching from the north, Cha-kwena wondered if he in fact had a future.

His smile faded. He stared down at the little stack of bird bones. Were they a statement of optimism or of irony in the face of futility? He yawned. Only time would tell the answer to that question, and now he was too tired to ponder it further. He closed his eyes and, succumbing to exhaustion, dozed where he sat. . . .

He awoke and was startled to see that the fire pit had been roused to life. Flames burned high. His first instinct was to stomp them out, but he hesitated. The warmth was as delicious and welcome as the smoked quail had been. And Siwi-ni's ghost, nodding in maternal fashion, was sitting across the fire from him.

"What?" he exclaimed, and leaped to his feet. "How?"

"Sit down, Shaman!" Siwi-ni ordered, prodding the flames with a long stick. "I have not been waiting here alone in hope of bringing harm to you." The flames in the fire pit responded to the stirring by enfolding her stick and then leaping explosively high.

Cha-kwena instinctively stepped forward and tried to kick the fire out. But he was knocked onto his buttocks by some unseen force.

Siwi-ni's ghost chuckled at his expense. "It must burn. It must burn high and hot!"

"What are you doing here, Siwi-ni? Why are you not walking the wind with the spirits of the ancestors?"

"And how could I do that?" she asked peevishly. "How could I rest when I would always be looking back, waiting for enemies to come after my beloved ones? No, I will stay here until . . . it is finished."

"Your family will not come back to this place."

"True, but whether they live or die will be determined here."

Despite the flames in the fire pit and the warmth of his cloak and the rabbit-skin blanket, Cha-kwena felt cold. "You may not like the outcome, Mother of Many."

"We will see. We will both see," she told him, then the ghost of Siwi-ni and the prodding stick somehow became one, and as the flames in the fire pit guttered, the apparition was transformed into a blazing torch that flew across the pit and directly at Cha-kwena.

Without thinking, he defensively put up his hand, catching the torch. Miraculously, the flames did not burn him. He cast the brand down into the fire pit and was on his feet in an instant, stomping on the fire, attempting to extinguish its light before it was spotted by his enemies. He found it impossible to put out.

Voices came to him.

"The fire must burn, and the enemies must come."

"Nothing you can do will prevent that, silly boy."

He pivoted. The voices had come from the farthest recesses of the main room of the cave, beside the entrance to the inner cavern. Cha-kwena bent, raised the brand, and, squinting beyond the firelit circle and into the darkness, saw Hoyeh-tay, clad in the full ceremonial regalia of a shaman of the Red World. Owl, still wearing Cha-kwena's medicine bag, perched atop the old shaman's head. The bird was settled comfortably, like some stuffed adornment amid the high tufted grass of the shaman's bonnet.

"I have been waiting for you, Cha-kwena," said Hoyeh-tay.

"*We* have been waiting," the bird corrected indignantly. "Come, stupid boy. You must prepare for the coming of our enemies. You cannot meet them looking like *that* and hope to win!"

Cha-kwena looked down at himself. In the torchlight he could see nothing wrong with his appearance. "What do you mean?" he asked, but when he glanced up, Hoyeh-tay and the bird had turned their backs and were walking toward the labyrinthine interior of the cave.

"Come, Cha-kwena!" beckoned Hoyeh-tay.

"*If* you are Shaman!" Owl tossed back the words both as insult and challenge.

"I am what the two of you have made me!" he shouted angrily, then frowned as he looked around. "Where are Raven and Little Yellow Wolf?"

Old Hoyeh-tay chuckled softly. "Raven waits for what is to come!" As he vanished through solid stone, his voice reverberated outward from the sepulchral tunnels that veined the hollow of the hill. "And now you must walk in the way of Little Yellow Wolf! Follow me, Cha-kwena! It may not be finished for you yet."

"How can it *not* be finished for me? The great white mammoth is dead. I have killed the totem and thrown away the sacred stone. By these actions I have brought the wrath of the Four Winds down upon my people. When the enemies come I will greet them. With my life I will buy time for my people to escape."

"Perhaps. But now you must follow!"

With an exhalation of resignation, Cha-kwena obeyed. "Be this dream or Vision, I will follow. I have nothing better to do."

With light from the torch Cha-kwena followed Hoyeh-tay and Owl through total darkness and deep into the cave. The earth's interior was cold. Like invisible serpents, drafts prowled the labyrinth. They embraced him with icy arms and trespassed beneath his blanket and robe. He was shivering violently long before he reached the vaulted chamber in which he had spent so many days and nights painting the story of his people upon the wall. At last he rounded a bend and, holding the torch high, entered the cavern. There was no sign of the old man or of the raptor.

Cha-kwena called out. His voice echoed from a thousand unexplored corridors. Then, as he looked ahead, he caught his breath. There was a new picture on the wall! Cha-kwena stared, amazed to see pictographs that showed his little band walking into the rising sun.

He recognized Ha-xa by her jaguar-skin cloak, Gah-ti by his single arm, Kosar-eh by the baby in his arms and the sons who surrounded him, U-wa by the little girl who walked beside her, and Mah-ree because she was shown with one hand holding the tail of a mammoth . . . a tiny white mammoth calf, the last in a small herd that walked linked trunk to tail, with a great freckled mammoth cow leading the way.

Cha-kwena gasped as the meaning of the pictograph dawned on him. Was it possible? Had Grandfather of All passed his spirit on to one of the cows? Is this what the mammoth were trying to tell him before he warned them to leave the valley—that he had not killed his totem, after all . . . that Life Giver still lived, his spirit safe in their care, waiting to be reborn into the world?

Now, far beyond the cave, coyotes began to howl in protest to the rising beat of drums. Cha-kwena stiffened as he listened. His enemies were coming; they were close now, within the valley. Tomorrow they would find him. Tomorrow, when they demanded to be taken to the totem, he would lead them on and on until they at last realized that he had tricked them into straying far from the path that his people had taken. Then he would die.

In the tree outside the cave, Raven cawed as though in

confirmation of his thoughts. Cha-kwena heard the bird clearly.

But Coyote answered, "Nothing dies forever!"

At that moment the torch guttered and went out, leaving Cha-kwena in total darkness. Alone within the twisting tunnels of the hill he doubted if he could find his way out again. Frightened, he cried out to Hoyeh-tay and Owl, "Help me! If I am trapped within this hill, the enemies will never find me. Then how will I be able to save my people?"

There was no answer. Moments passed. He was aware of the pounding of his heart. "What is this, Grandfather? To what have you led me, Vision or death?"

"Stupid boy! Use your third eye! Or do you still doubt that you are truly Shaman?"

The wings of Owl brushed past his face. Cha-kwena jumped. The gentle, cajoling laughter of an old man echoed down the corridors, and then was gone. The young man stood motionless. A cold draft of air enfolded him and then seemed to draw him forward. Trusting, he followed. Instinct guided him. Or was it more than that? He doubted if he would ever know until, at last, he emerged into the main room of the cave to see that the fire continued to burn in the fire pit of Kosar-eh. Beside it, arrayed as though by human hands, lay the ceremonial attire of a shaman: a cape made of the body and head of a great horned owl and, most incredibly, a talisman strung upon a leather thong—the sacred stone of his ancestors.

8

The flickering light of the fire in the cave drew Shateh across the miles as surely as the magic draft of life-giving air had guided the young shaman out of the labyrinth. The chieftain would not allow his people to rest, for behind them, the drumbeat of the advancing People of the Watching Star rolled like thunder across the land.

Now, with the hills and firelight looming ahead, Dakan-eh went to one knee with a "whoof" of pain, then willed himself to rise.

"What is it, Bold Man Who Brings Rain?" asked Shateh.

Sweating, Dakan-eh replied through gritted teeth. "Cha-kwena!" He spoke the name as though it were a foul thing within his mouth and he had need to spit it out. "The closer we get to him, the greater my pain. When he is dead, my pain will stop. With my own hands I will make it stop! Come! Let us waste no time. We must go on."

Shateh nodded and gestured his people forward.

Dawn was coloring the horizon when the chieftain signaled a halt. He and his followers gathered at the base of a hill. Above them, a raven perched in the pine tree that sprouted from the rocks beside the entrance to what appeared to be a great cave. Shateh looked beyond the bird to see that Cha-kwena was waiting for them.

The chieftain frowned. The young man had changed since he had last seen him. His appearance was sobering: He stood boldly, limbs splayed, a spear in one hand, his head held high. Clearly Cha-kwena was no longer a callow youth but a man and a shaman to reckon with.

Shateh stood to his full height so that his bearing would equal that of the much younger man. He raised his spear arm and announced, "I, Shateh, chief and shaman of the People of the Land of Grass, have come to the far land beyond the edge of the world to seek the great mammoth totem and the shaman Cha-kwena."

"I, Cha-kwena, grandson of Hoyeh-tay and shaman of this far country, welcome Shateh and his people to the land beyond the Mountains of Sand."

"You must *not* welcome him, Cha-kwena! He comes to—" Ta-maya's warning was cut short as Teiken, standing beside her, slapped a hand over her mouth.

"No!" Shateh said, then commanded the warrior to release her. "Let my new woman speak. I do not come with lies upon my tongue. I have come into the land of Cha-kwena, but I seek no welcome from one who has sent the spirits of Raven and his clan to feed upon my people!"

Dakan-eh, snarling, leaning heavily on his spear, stepped forward to stand beside Shateh. Bold Man had mustered all of the dignity that a man in agony could manage. "Shateh does not come alone! I, Dakan-eh, Bold Man Who Brings Rain and Brave Hunter Who Chases the Whirling Wind, walks at his side despite the will of Cha-kwena! You could not keep me away, nor will you keep me from taking back my luck and sacred stone and—" Pain overcame him. Blood and bile oozed from his mouth as he collapsed into a paroxysm of hideous retching.

Pah-la, Bold Man's women, and a wide-eyed, grim-faced Ban-ya ran to his side as the man convulsed, gasping. His lips were white, his eyes rolled back.

"Aiee!" wailed Ghree.

Pah-la was beside herself. "What brings such pain? Ah, Cha-kwena, how can you inflict such hurt upon one who was once a band brother to you?"

"I have never wished pain upon Dakan-eh or any other man!" said the young shaman, and heedless of danger to himself, he came quickly down from the cave to stand among his enemies.

Shateh eyed his adversary. Cha-kwena had patterned his face with a paint made of grease and ashes, and he had attired himself in the full ceremonial regalia of a shaman of the Red World. Around his upper shoulders was a short, feathered cloak of owl skin, and the raptor's head was worn atop his own. Around his neck was a medicine bag, no doubt holding the sacred stone of his ancestors.

Pah-la was weeping piteously over her son and could barely make herself understood. "Please, Cha-kwena! Take away his pain! Do not let him die!"

Shateh saw the look of genuine confusion upon Cha-kwena's face. The women, except Ban-ya and Pah-la, moved away so that the shaman could kneel beside Dakan-eh, who was hemorrhaging from the mouth. These were, Shateh realized with a coldness in his gut, the exact same symptoms that Atonashkeh had shown in the last moments of his life.

"What have you eaten, Dakan-eh?" Ban-ya's voice sounded unnaturally high, panicky, as she smoothed his face. "What *have* you eaten?"

He tried to speak but instead vomited bloody bile as he reached up and clutched her wrist. He stared at her out of bulging, incredulous eyes. "What . . . have you done . . . to me?"

Ban-ya shook from the accusation and raged at Cha-kwena, "Take back your curse of pain and death! Take it back now, or in his name, I will kill you with my own hands!"

Cha-kwena was openly overwhelmed by Dakan-eh's condition. Bold Man, writhing, clutching piteously at his belly, suddenly lurched up and snatched the medicine bag, pulling it so hard that the thong snapped and drew blood from the back of Cha-kwena's neck.

"Now I will live! Now the pain will die!" cried Dakan-eh, shaking the talisman out of its pouch. "Now the forces of Creation are in the possession of the one man who is truly worthy to command them!"

"No man can possess or command the forces of Creation, Dakan-eh," said Cha-kwena. "They come to us as they will, as they choose and—"

"No!" Dakan-eh cried, mad with pain. "I will not hear it! On the stone I wish death to you and to all who have ever stood against my will! Die! Die now and take this pain from me!"

Cha-kwena looked over at Shateh. "He is like a wolf that has taken baited meat. I do not know what to do for him. You are also a shaman," he said, then added with utmost honesty, "perhaps your knowledge is greater than my own?"

Dakan-eh took Ban-ya's wrist again. She shrieked as, without warning, he twisted it so hard that everyone nearby heard the fragile bones crack.

"You," Bold Man rasped, "I saw you bring the meat to her . . . and I ate . . . without thinking . . . without remembering Atonashkeh. Ban-ya, what have you done?"

"Nothing! I have done nothing!" Cradling her broken wrist, she shrank back from him. "Wehakna and Senohnim fixed the meat for Ta-maya! I never touched it! I only served it, and at their command." She fell silent as a thought occurred. "And how could you have partaken of it, Dakan-eh, unless you went to her behind the chieftain's back?"

"You touched the meat. You put things into it. I saw you do it."

Ban-ya froze at Warakan's statement.

Everyone froze.

"What is this you say, boy?" Shateh's voice was as cold as the north wind.

Warakan seemed to be trying to make himself appear even smaller. "I . . . I saw her put things in the meat. And then I saw her bring it to the woman with frost spirits in her feet. But the woman would not eat. She sent Ban-ya away. Then she sat alone awhile. Bold Man came to her. He said that she would be his woman. He put his mouth on hers. She pushed him down, then went to talk with Shateh at the far side of camp. After she left, Bold Man took the meat and went away."

Shateh stood as though about to faint. It took him several moments to recover. No one spoke until the chieftain looked down at Ban-ya and said dangerously, "You have given baited meat to my son and to my new woman."

"No! Yes! But it was not my fault!" In a blind panic, Ban-ya pointed at Cha-kwena. "The dark spirits that Cha-kwena sent across the miles came to me, worked through me. Look up! Even now in the branches of the tree outside the cave Raven awaits for Cha-kwena's command!"

If Shateh had turned to stone, his stance and face could not have been more rigid. "Raven waits for Bold Man Who Brings Rain, Lizard Woman. Raven waits for Brave Hunter Who Chases the Whirling Wind. Raven waits for Liar Who Betrays Those Who Have Placed Their Trust in Him. And Raven waits for *you*, woman. Or perhaps he has been at your side all along?" He raised his spear.

Ban-ya cried out. "No, Shateh! I carry your child! Your son!"

"She lies . . ." The words came garbled from Dakan-eh's mouth. "She carries no child. She told me so on the day I allied myself to you . . . on the day she came to me in stealth to spread herself and tell me that she killed Atonashkeh."

"No . . ." mewled Ban-ya. "No, no, no, no . . ."

Dakan-eh's hand fastened in her hair. His body contorted into a horrible spasm of agony, but still he held her, deliberately hurting her. Despite his possession of the sacred stone, he could not but know he was dying. "You have killed me because I wanted her instead of you!" he accused Ban-ya, snarling though his agony. "I still want her, have always wanted her—never you!" Another paroxysm took him. Now he looked up at Shateh and sneered. "Old man, your magic is dead. Old men cannot make sons. Old men cannot keep their women from coming to me. And now Ban-ya will follow me to the world beyond this world, but I will not look back for her. I will wait for Ta-maya! I . . . will . . ."

In the last moments of his life he had not allowed himself to be less than what he had always claimed to be—Bold Man of the Red World, arrogant and proud to the end. Now his eyes widened, fixed, and suddenly dilated as his last ragged breath went sighing out of him.

Trembling, Ban-ya hung her head as Pah-la threw

herself across the body of her son. The many women of the Red World began to keen for Dakan-eh's spirit. And Shateh knelt and took the sacred stone from the hand of the dead man.

Cha-kwena watched and waited—although for what, he could not say. Kosar-eh had warned him that Shateh was his enemy and had come to kill him, to take the sacred stone, and to hunt the great white mammoth. But now, as Cha-kwena warily observed the chieftain, the sound of distant drumbeats came pounding across the land, and Shateh looked more like a weary, albeit still powerful, old man than a menacing marauder.

Listening intently to the portentous drums, the chieftain rose. He held the sacred stone in the curl of one great fist as he stood looking not to the north but to the east. "Have you sent your people there, Cha-kwena, into the face of the rising sun?"

"They are far from their enemies," Cha-kwena replied with bold evasiveness, wondering if the chieftain were guessing or drawing Vision from the talisman. If it was the latter, had he seen that Life Giver was dead?

"And the great white mammoth? Does Life Giver still walk before your band?"

Cha-kwena's heart lurched. Shateh did *not* know! The man claimed to be a shaman; but even with the sacred stone in his hand, he did not see that the great totem lay dead in a frozen lake beyond the curve of another range of hills.

Shateh fixed Cha-kwena purposefully. "The People of the Watching Star and their allies from the Land of Grass seek the great white mammoth and the sacred stone. If they find these things before Shateh finishes what he has come here to do, you and I and many of our people will die."

"And if you find them first, Shateh, the People of the Watching Star will die and *my* people with them!"

"And Life Giver will be slain!" informed Ta-maya, her eyes shining with tears that she had shed over the death of one she had once loved—over Dakan-eh, not the bold man but the brash, daring young child he had once been. "Shateh has sworn to kill Grandfather of All, Cha-kwena.

That is why he has come—to fulfill the legend, to take the power of our totem into himself by consuming its blood and flesh.''

"And you have led him to the hunt!" Cha-kwena accused angrily.

"No," contradicted Shateh quietly. "She has not. A fire in the night led me to this place. *Your* fire, Shaman, shining like a beacon from your cave. It drew me across the land. Ta-maya would not betray those she loves." He looked at her sadly, with endless regret, then opened his palm and appraised the sacred stone. "There is no power in this—not for me, not for Dakan-eh . . . only for Cha-kwena. Bold Man should not have taken the stone from around your neck. Perhaps you might have saved him." This said, the chieftain reached out, took Cha-kwena's free hand, and placed the talisman into the palm. After curling Cha-kwena's fingers around the sacred stone, he maintained his grip on the younger man's hand as he continued to speak in earnest. "Ta-maya has told you the truth. I *have* come to hunt and kill the great white mammoth. I am an old man and without his strength cannot prevail against my enemies any more than you and your band can stand victorious over them without me."

Ta-maya's eyes flashed rebelliously. "As long as Life Giver walks before us, we do not need you, Shateh! As long as we are strong in the power of our totem, our enemies cannot prevail!"

Shateh measured her words and, considering, looked closely at Cha-kwena. "Then why are you here? Why have you sent your band on without you? So that you could act as bait and lure their enemies away from their trail long enough to win them time to escape? If the totem walks before them, why would you do this, Shaman?"

Cha-kwena stood tall in the face of Shateh's insightful query. Perhaps the man was a shaman, after all. He debated giving the chieftain an honest answer. Not knowing what Shateh's reaction would be, the young man chose to remain silent.

The north wind was rising. It was very cold. Soon the storm would come. By now his band was far to the east. But had Kosar-eh had enough time to find a place in which to take refuge against the onslaught of the elements and to hide from the enemies' inevitable approach?

Shateh, still gripping Cha-kwena's hand, said, "Listen to the beat of war drums, Shaman. How long will your little band be safe from the People of the Watching Star? When the storm is over and the Warm Moon rises to drive away the winter cold, your enemies will search for them. And they will flee like rabbits before a pack of wolves and foxes. So will begin an endless hunt in which they and your totem will be the eternal prey . . . unless their shaman is wise enough to recognize the danger and realize that it is time for the great white mammoth to die. Let the totem's power be reborn in me! I can transform your people into predators who will not be afraid to turn and fight and drive the wolves away."

Cha-kwena tensed but again said nothing.

Shateh smiled with grim irony. "Dakan-eh accused you of sending the whirling wind across the miles to devastate him and my people. Dakan-eh said that your curse placed enmity between him and my tribe and brought death to all who passed within its shadow. For this reason I have sworn to kill you. But now I can see for myself that Dakan-eh spoke falsely. I have seen you set aside your spear and willingly place yourself into the hands of those who have come to take your life. You have placed yourself at risk so that you might try to heal one who had no wish for you but death. You are strong and sure and just in the power of your totem. You are not afraid of Raven and his clan. This, also, I have seen. So now I say that I would not name you Enemy, Cha-kwena."

"Any man who hunts the great white mammoth is his enemy and mine!" declared Ta-maya bravely.

There was a moment of silence before Cha-kwena responded to the chieftain, "If I lead Shateh to Life Giver, if I bring him face-to-face with his totem, will he then name me Friend and vow to honor my people as his own and to fight for and with them, *never* against them . . . always and forever?"

"No, Cha-kwena!" cried Ta-maya, bereft.

"This I vow!" the chieftain swore enthusiastically as he released Cha-kwena's hand.

Cha-kwena ignored Ta-maya's pitiful protest. He had committed himself to a dangerous ruse. Although the beautiful young woman now believed him to be a traitor to all that was sacred to their people, he made the sacrifice willingly. Taking Shateh to the bones of the great white mammoth might well be the last thing Cha-kwena ever did in this life, but soon the great storm would be upon the land, and with Shateh and the People of the Watching Star misled to the lake, Kosar-eh and the band would be safe.

Cha-kwena's hand tightened around the sacred stone. He retrieved the medicine bag and set the talisman safely inside. Within his mind a vision flared—of his people, of Mah-ree and the pups. *Be strong, New Woman.* He sent his love for her in silence upon the wind. *Remember me and know that all that I do on this day I do in gladness and without regret . . . for you!*

"We will go, then? To seek the totem?" asked Shateh.

"Yes. We will go," said Cha-kwena, and prepared to lead the People of the Land of Grass and Dakan-eh's followers from the Red World to the place where the mammoth gathered to die.

"Wait!" cried Pah-la. "Will no one mourn my poor bold son?"

"Ban-ya will mourn for Dakan-eh," replied Shateh coldly. "Pah-la, you will come with us away from our enemies. Ban-ya will remain behind to mourn for your son and to greet the People of the Watching Star!"

"They will kill me!" Ban-ya wailed.

"You have killed yourself, Lizard Woman!" Shateh told her. The chieftain ignored Ta-maya's softly spoken pleas for mercy on her onetime friend's behalf. He walked on and would not listen to the mourning howls of old Kahm-ree, either. "Do not look back, Grandmother," he said. He pointed at Ban-ya's bewildered little son. "Take that boy and care for him. You must live for the child. His mother is already dead."

They came in hushed and fearful silence into the valley where the mammoth came to die. The lake lay before them.

Snow was falling heavily as they paused at last on the shore in which Life Giver's great skeleton lay frozen. The shape and markings of the dead animal's extraordinary tusks were unmistakable. Han-da and the other lesser shamans of the Red World frantically shook their rattles and shouted to the spirit of Life Giver to rise again and return to the world of the living. Shateh, meanwhile, saw his last hope of youth and renewed power stripped away.

"You have lied to me, Cha-kwena." The chieftain's accusation was rife with threat.

"I have brought you to the totem," replied Cha-kwena, holding the older man's gaze. "And now I hold you to your vow—to honor my people and to fight for them as though they were your own."

The chieftain's eyes were slits in the wind; and in the darkness between the long, heavy lids there was a danger. "What sort of trick is this?"

Cha-kwena did not falter as he brazened on. "The strength of the great one is not gone. It is reborn." He looked deeply into Shateh's eyes. How much could he trust this man? If he told the chieftain of his vision on the cavern wall—about the white mammoth calf that would be born to the herd with which Life Giver once walked—might Shateh not be inspired to hunt the hapless creature and turn his spears against what might well be the last hope of the People? Cha-kwena could not be sure. And so he said, "The legend of the Ancient Ones has been fulfilled. I have slain the great white mammoth. His blood flows in me now. His flesh is my flesh. I am Cha-kwena, Shaman, Guardian and Brother of Animals, Keeper of the Sacred Stone, and immortal. Will Shateh name me Enemy while I am willing to name him Chief and Brother?"

There was dead silence as Cha-kwena's words went out upon the rising, bitter wind. The people stared at him, too stunned to speak until the strident beat of drums broke the unearthly quiet.

"Our enemies will soon follow us to this place," said Cha-kwena. "Shateh must take his people and go before the People of the Watching Star and their allies crest the hill and see the way in which you have gone and what awaits them here.''

The chieftain worked to gain control of his anger. ''Do not insult Shateh, chieftain and shaman and warrior of the Land of Grass. I stand and fight my enemies. Shateh will not run before them when Cha-kwena has the courage to stay!''

''You will not be alone!'' declared Teikan, stepping forward.

''This man will stand with Shateh!'' Lahontay proclaimed.

And now the warriors of the Land of Grass and the hunters of the Red World began to pound the butt ends of their spears into the snowy ground and shout that they were not afraid to fight.

''Are you immortal?'' Cha-kwena hurled the question at them. ''And you, Shateh, have you partaken of the blood and flesh of the totem? Will the Four Winds and the forces of Creation stand with you as they will stand with me? No! Remember your vow to stand with my people against their enemies! If you choose to stay, can you guarantee that Ta-maya's life and the lives of all who have followed you will not be forfeited to the greater force that will come to kill us here? Not again! You must leave this place while the snow will cover your tracks.''

Shateh looked unnerved. ''For what purpose will you stay, Cha-kwena?''

''To confound and mislead them. To be the bait that will draw the wolves away from those whom I would not see as prey.''

Shateh's eyes held no danger now. Instead they reflected respect and admiration. ''There is wisdom in what you say. But is there honor?''

''Shateh is chieftain. In the Red World it has been said by the Ancient Ones that a chieftain must value the lives of his people more than he values his own life . . . or his own honor.''

For a long time Shateh was silent, but he paced restlessly, thinking. He stopped abruptly and looked long and hard at Cha-kwena, then at Ta-maya. ''I will lead my people to safety in the east," he agreed, and would hear no further argument from anyone.

At the moment of the chieftain's departure, Cha-kwena said, "Hold," and held the sacred stone out to Shateh. "Take this. Its power will guide you as you go forth in my name. When you find Kosar-eh, tell him that I have placed it into the keeping of a worthy friend and shaman. Guard it well, Brother, and keep our people safe until I return to claim it."

Now the drums were silent. Now the moment of attack was at hand, and Ban-ya knew it. She crouched in the darkness of the cave, once the shelter of Cha-kwena's tiny band. A tunnel had brought her there as she fled the approach of the People of the Watching Star. Her flight did her no good; the forces of Creation had placed her and Sheela in the same cave.

Sheela offered no talk of waiting or of biding time or of resting or of taking food. Ban-ya watched in horror as her former slave paced near the entrance to the cave. A recently flayed skin was draped across the woman's back, and the head of a man sat impaled on the tip of her spear.

"They abandoned this shelter," Sheela seethed, her voice tight with anger. "But we will follow. They cannot escape us!"

"Dakan-eh's skin! Dakan-eh's head!" Ban-ya, quaking with horror, pressed her hand to her mouth lest she inadvertently speak aloud again. Peering from her hiding place, she saw and heard it all.

"We have come far!" Jhadel complained. "We must rest and eat. We must be at our best when we make war against them! There is no need to pursue them in such weather!"

"Old man, your weakness is more apparent every day," Sheela mocked him. "Stay here with the pregnant women and children, then. The warriors of the People of the Watching Star will go on."

Cha-kwena waited for them. The wind was gusting erratically, as restless as he was. He was not certain just

when he decided that the best place to greet his enemies
would be from the middle of the frozen lake. Spear in hand,
he walked carefully across the ice. It made unnerving
sounds as he passed over it, moving cautiously through long
banks of fog until he reached the skeleton of the great white
mammoth. Climbing high, he positioned himself atop the
skull of the totem.

The shaman's eyes squinted into the wind as he
scanned the mists. Not surprisingly, Raven and his clan
were gathering along the shore.

"You and your kind are always hungry," he said to
Raven.

"And you and your kind are so often eager to die,"
replied the bird.

Cha-kwena nodded. What Raven said was all too true.
As the shaman listened to the advancing drumbeat that
signaled the approach of the People of the Watching Star, he
rubbed a deep ache at the back of his neck. The raw, oozing
gash that Dakan-eh had made when snatching the sacred
stone from him seemed proof enough of his own mortality.
He held his bloodied fingers before his face and, with a sigh
of acquiescence, waited to die.

Leaning into the brutally cold wind, Sheela led the
People of the Watching Star down from the heights to the
shore of the lake. Jhadel followed reluctantly, dutifully.
Even before he saw the bones of mammoth strewn across
the land and the ravens clustering along the shore, instinct
told him that they would have need of a shaman and a healer
this day.

"Sheela, Tsana, wait! I do not like this place! See how
the hills run sharply downward all around? It is not a good
place to fight! There is no easy way of retreat."

Sheela scorned Jhadel. "The People of the Watching
Star do not retreat!"

"Those whom we follow have fled before us!" declared Tsana in disgust.

"There is no one here to fight," observed Nakantahkeh, revulsion curdling his usually steady voice. "There
are only bones and skulls of mammoth!"

"And something else, I think." Sheela's voice was as chilling as the fog that shrouded the lake. She pointed across the mists. "There . . . who stands there?" she called.

"Cha-kwena! Guardian of the totem! Come! Would you not like to kill the one who has slain what is sacred to you? You will never have his power now! It is mine! I am immortal!"

"We will soon see!" Sheela threatened.

"No!" warned Jhadel.

But Sheela, Tsana, and Nakantahkeh were unwilling to heed the advice of an old man. Shrieking and holding Dakan-eh's impaled head high with one hand and brandishing another spear with the other, the daughter of Sheehanal led the warriors of the Watching Star surging forward onto the icy lake. Sheela found the frozen surface to be precarious. Having trouble maintaining her balance, she paused only long enough to shake Dakan-eh's head from her spear and kick it out of the way. Then she ran on, kicking the head several more times before it rolled into a break in the ice and disappeared.

Jhadel, red faced, hung back on shore. He waved his arms and screamed for them to return. He saw clearly what they, in their excitement, had yet to see or feel. The weight of so many people moving at once across the ice was stressing the great, frozen plates that had formed over warm currents bubbling up from hot springs deep within the earth.

As Sheela led her warriors on, Tsana was the first to slip and go to his knees when the ice groaned and shifted. Jhadel saw other men felled by the jarring movement of an opening rift in the frozen surface. Still others, in sudden terror of being drowned, threw their weapons aside and were now turning back toward shore.

"Come! Join me!" cried Cha-kwena, fighting to maintain his stance. The pressure of the ice moving against the bones of the great white mammoth caused the skeleton to sway. "If I am going to die, let me not die alone! Do not run away!"

Jhadel stared, gape mouthed with incredulity at the courage and audacity of the figure that stood high above the ice atop the skull of the great mammoth. Never before had he imagined that a shaman other than one of his own tribe could hold him spellbound; but he was awestruck now.

Halfway between Jhadel and the shaman, Nakantahkeh was well out on the ice and somehow managing to hold on to his balance as he levered back and hurled a spear at Cha-kwena. Jhadel cursed as he saw the shaman duck the weapon; then the old man cheered when he saw Nakantahkeh prepare to hurl another. The second spear never left Nakantahkeh's hand; a third spear came singing over Jhadel's head to strike Nakantahkeh squarely in the back and propel him facedown onto the ice.

"What magic is this?" Jhadel cried, then turned to realize that it was no magic at all . . . or the greatest magic that he had ever seen.

A good-sized force of spear-wielding men and their dogs was swarming downward over the hills and—as Jhadel's eyes widened with disbelief—several mammoth came crashing through the trees behind him and from both sides of the narrow valley. In terror of losing his life, the old man threw himself flat into the snow and feigned death as the warriors and dogs and mammoth thundered past him.

Minutes later, after he was sure that death had passed him by, Jhadel looked up to see that on the lake, men who had not managed to get off the ice and take flight were being speared or driven back onto the ice by raging hunters. These newcomers stood ranked along the shore while furious mammoth began to make their way into the icy shallows to crush those men of the Watching Star who managed to reach shore unscathed. Jhadel began to weep. He watched as screaming men died beneath the pounding feet of mammoth or went down to certain death in the churning, icy deeps. Now only one warrior—the woman—remained alive upon the ice.

Sheela ran forward through the chaos and reached Cha-kwena just as the entire skeleton of the great white mammoth shifted hard to the left and submerged, taking them both down with it. Cha-kwena knew who she was, and although pure mindless killing madness shone in her eyes, his first instinct was to save her—until he felt a dagger slip upward beneath his tunic and graze his skin.

Because of the cold water, the pain was minimal; but he knew that the knife would go deep on the woman's next attempt. Grappling with Sheela, he realized that he must subdue her or be killed by her. She was strong, surprisingly muscular for a female, and taller than he. With enormous effort he managed to grip her across the throat and hold her under the water until he felt her relax. Then he was able to wrest the stone knife from her hand. He eased his hold and tried to bring them both to the surface. But suddenly, with powerful twists and kicks, she was at his face, gouging at his eyes, grabbing at his throat, trying to choke him. She left him no choice. He smashed her in the face with his fist as hard as he could, and as the blow struck, he knew that he had broken her neck. She went limp. He heard the life go out of her, bubbling to the surface. Somehow she still had a hold on him. Even in death her legs and arms were like vines all around him. He fought to be free of her and succeeded at last, but it was too late. His struggle had taken them too deep.

Icy water filled his lungs, and drowning, he gave himself up to Spirit Sucker. He had not expected the day to end with his still being alive in it; nevertheless, he would have liked to have thanked Shateh for trying, at least, to save him—even though Cha-kwena had duped the chieftain, and the chieftain had broken his word.

"Our enemies are no more," said Teikan, staring across the ice and fog. "Those who have managed to run away will be no threat to us now. Look, Shateh, the larger mammoth are going out to where the bones of the totem have gone down. It was why they came, I think—not for us but to protect the remains of one of their own against our kind."

Shateh was staring across the lake. The enemy dead were everywhere. But Cha-kwena and Sheela were nowhere to be seen. He shook his head as he watched the mammoth. His great fist remained curled around the sacred stone until its texture burned him.

"No! Cha-kwena cannot be dead!" The words that erupted from the chieftain were an invocation to and against the forces of Creation.

Warakan, standing close, said consolingly, "Shateh tried to help him. Shateh has fought a great battle. Those who have said that Shateh was weak and afraid have been proven wrong this day! Shateh has driven the enemies away. Shateh is a great chief and warrior, even if he did risk angering the spirits of the ancestors by breaking his vow to the shaman."

"I broke no vow!" Shateh retorted. "I told Cha-kwena that I would lead the people east to safety. I did not tell him that I or my warriors would stay with them while there was a battle to be fought! And what are you doing here, boy? Why are you not back with the women and children and old Lahontay?"

The boy stuck out his chest. "I am Warakan! Shateh has no son to stand beside him, so I have come to fight at his side! I was not afraid!"

Teikan, looking tired, said indulgently, "Shateh could not ask for a better son than this boy, who has no one to name Father."

The chieftain's features expanded into a look of amazement, but before he could speak, a great cracking sound was heard. Far out in the lake, the mammoth—shoulder high in water now—reached deep with questing trunks and tusks. Slowly, ponderously, their efforts raised the bones of one that had once walked before them. Pushing and heaving, they moved the ice and sent the skeleton forward into the shallows. Cha-kwena's body, draped face-down across the blunted tip of an enormous tusk, was lifted out of the lake and held aloft over the shore.

Shateh broke into a run. Like a youth he pumped his legs until, shouting the mammoth away, he plunged through the icy shallows, leaped up once, twice, and finally grasped the tusk. He swung himself up and in moments had the limp body of Cha-kwena on the ground. The sacred stone was immediately set around Cha-kwena's neck, and Shateh's large and able hands massaged the young shaman's chest and arms and limbs. There was no response. The chieftain tried again while the others looked on in breath-held silence. Still nothing. Cha-kwena's face was the color of ice at dusk, and his jaw was slack.

Shateh knelt back, bereft. "I can feel no spirit in him. But this Cha-kwena was a true shaman and, even in death, deserving of the sacred stone. No one but he is fit to wear it in this world or in the world beyond."

"Noooo!"

The anguished cry of a young woman had them all looking toward the eastern hills, across which Lahontay was now leading the women and children and a small band of strangers. The young woman ran ahead, sobbing Cha-kwena's name until she collapsed breathless beside him.

"Mah-ree! Wait!" one of the older women called.

"His spirit has gone to walk the wind forever," said Shateh quietly.

"No! I will not allow it! He will not go to that place of solitude where I can never hope to reach him! He will not! I will not let him! And I am not ready to follow him yet! I am too young! I have just become a woman!"

She took hold of Cha-kwena's shoulders and shook him so hard that his head lolled back, and water suddenly gushed out of his lungs. The young woman screamed, startled, and loosed her hold as others gathered by their shaman's side. He rolled to one side, choked, and lay gasping for air. He looked up with a half-dazed squint.

"Kosar-eh?" he croaked.

The man came forward. "Yes, my shaman?"

"I . . . sent you . . . away."

"I went away. To the east. But not far. Now I am back."

Standing behind Shateh now, the older woman, who, Shateh could see, looked much like young Mah-ree, looked down and nodded. "Medicine Girl ran away. She would not stay with us without Cha-kwena. We had to follow her. And now, behold, she has brought Shaman back from the world beyond this world!"

"No," said Shateh. "The totem has saved Cha-kwena and held him high on its great tusk. Even in death the great white mammoth has proved to be Life Giver, totem of the

People.'' His eyes narrowed as he saw the way that Ta-maya and Kosar-eh were looking at each other. ''Go to your man,'' he told her and, rising, indicated Warakan with a nod of his head. ''It seems I have a son who makes my spirit smile at last.''

That night Jhadel and the few survivors of the People of the Watching Star and their allies fled across the land. That night a fear-crazed Ban-ya huddled in the darkness of an abandoned cave and vowed that somehow she would survive the coming winter. That night North Wind blew away the storms, and at dawn, Mah-ree and Cha-kwena stood together and watched the mammoth moving off into the rising sun.

''We must guard them,'' whispered Mah-ree reverently.

''Yes,'' agreed Cha-kwena, and told her a great and wondrous secret. ''The great cow carries our totem.''

''Many moons will rise before that calf is born!''

''Many moons,'' Cha-kwena agreed. ''Who knows where she will wander between then and now?''

''It does not matter. Great Spirit is waiting to be reborn.''

''We must protect him.''

''We?'' he teased.

''Of course, Cha-kwena. I have told you. You will never be rid of me.''

''Nor do I wish to be.''

Her eyes went wide. ''Truly?''

''I am Cha-kwena, grandson of Hoyeh-tay, and Guardian of the Sacred Stone. Would I not speak truly, Mosquito? Wherever Life Giver goes, there *we* will follow. Into the rising sun, Cha-kwena and Mah-ree . . . always and forever.''

AUTHOR'S NOTE

Eleven thousand years ago the vast, two-mile-thick ice sheets of the Pleistocene were melting and retreating northward. Rivers swelled. Ocean levels rose. Continents were reshaped and laid bare. Between the Rockies and the mountains of the Pacific shore, enormous pluvial lakes filled the lowlands.

Gradually, however, the Age of Ice began to draw to a close. As the earth continued to warm, climate zones shifted radically. The huge inland lakes of the west began to evaporate and disappear even as the Great Lakes were being created. In this raw "new" world of the dying Pleistocene, animals, plants, and people adapted or died.

As in the previous five volumes of THE FIRST AMERICANS Series, the descriptions of the characters and lifeways within THUNDER IN THE SKY have been based on the most recent findings in the fields of archeology and paleoanthropology as well as upon the lore of Native American peoples.

Once again thanks must go to Dr. Richard Michael Gramly, Curator of Anthropology at New York's Buffalo Museum of Science and Clovis Project Director of the Richey Clovis Cache in Wenatchee, Washington, for going out of his way to share his expertise and insights, especially on zoonoses—diseases that are transmittable between animals and humans. His findings at the Richey Clovis Cache continue to shed new light on the ways of early man in the Americas and to challenge many old theories.

For those readers who may challenge my depiction of

453

well-established "cultures" at so early a date, I stand by "my guns." Ongoing research continues to reinforce my belief that the first Americans were a highly adaptive, creative, and spiritual people. The exquisite quality of workmanship displayed in the enormous stone chalcedony projectile points found at the Richey Clovis Cache in Wenatchee, Washington, confirms not only the skill of their maker but a pattern of established culture that lasted from five hundred to a thousand years as it spread from coast to coast from Alaska to Mexico and beyond. Although every textbook on the subject invariably continues to depict the first Americans as crudely dressed "spear chuckers" running about the world, it is my considered opinion that any group of human beings capable of raising to a uniform artform the extremely difficult task of stoneworking must also have been fully capable of sewing a straight seam in a hide, and of combing their hair.

Fragments of woven baskets found in Gypsum Cave not far from Las Vegas, Nevada, were made some 10,500 years ago when that desert landscape was still lake country. A Paleolithic Floridian was lovingly put to "rest" on a ledge at Warm Mineral Springs in Sarasota County some 10,300 years ago; beside his skeleton was a shell hook that had once formed the barbed end of a spear hurler. Approximately two hundred years later someone left a pair of fiber sandals in Fort Rock Cave, Oregon, at about the same time that the body of a toothworn old woman of some twenty-five years of age was placed into a southern California tar pit along with ritual grave goods that included a necklace of bone pendants, shell beads, a broken mano, the skull of a domestic dog, and bone *hairpins*.

Perhaps someday soon in some far canyon and as-yet-to-be discovered cavern, a painting not unlike Cha-kwena's will be discovered, and all that has been written herein will be seen to have been the truth.

Once again, special thanks are due to the team at Book Creations Inc., for editorial and research assistance, especially to George Engel, President, in appreciation of his good humor and encouragement, and to Philip Rich, Executive Editor, and Laurie Rosin, Senior Project Editor, for their patience; also thanks to Betty Szeberenyi, Librarian; Marjie Weber, copyeditor; and to Carol Carlson, Publicity, for all of her kind words along the way.

Thanks, too, to George W. Swanson, San Bernardino volunteer firefighter, for sharing information detailing his experience as an emergency medical aide with individuals who have been struck by lightning, or the force field thereof. And to Joan Lesley Hamilton. Joan, I never could have done it without you.

WILLIAM SARABANDE
Fawnskin, California